I0778428

A Fate Worse Than Fame

HEATHER O'BRIEN

A Fate Worse Than Fame

Copyright © 2025 Heather O'Brien

All rights reserved.

This is a work of fiction. All characters, names, incidents, organizations, and dialogue contained in this novel are either the product of the author's imagination or are used fictitiously. Similarities to real persons, living and dead, are unintended.

Chicago (That Toddlin' Town)
Words & Music by Fred Fisher (1922)
Public Domain

The Holy Bible, King James Version
Public Domain

Fourth edition 2025
(Previously published as *Embers From Ash and Ruin*)
[First edition 2010 | Second edition 2018 | Third edition 2023]

Published in Fernley, Nevada – USA by *Word Rites Media*

eBook ISBN: 978-1-962501-07-1
Paperback ISBN: 978-1-962501-06-4
Hardback ISBN: 978-1-962501-05-7

Library of Congress Control Number: 2025904165

Cover by Warren Designs

Praise for the Music is Murder saga

Step aside Roddy Doyle, there's a new voice in rock-n-roll fiction. *Lockhardt Sound* is a triumphant novel that weaves music into its language and the heartbreak of all your favorite songs into one book. Farin O'Connor leaps off the page, steals your heart, stomps on it, and somehow manages to return it to you better than it was when you gave it.

> *~ Jody Sperling, author the* Luke in Time Mysteries

[*Lockhardt Sound*] is a page-turning peek into the underbelly of the music business. Ms. O'Brien's take on the machinations behind the glitz and glamour of the music world is a stark reminder that all that glitters isn't gold, and that business isn't always business. Heather O'Brien is a prolific voice and an extraordinarily gifted storyteller.

> *~ Charlie Spickler, Writer, Director* Annie's World,
> Rescue! Brooklyn, *and* Bard of the Village

[The Music is Murder saga] is a modern-day masterpiece that is equal parts beauty and tragedy. Heather O'Brien doesn't only tell the story, she makes the reader feel like they are living the story.

> *~ Jacob Bunton, Emmy-winning composer,*
> *producer, songwriter and multi-instrumentalist*

Heather O'Brien's [*Lockhardt Sound*] is a rock'n'roll master class. This riveting ride of suspense, love, drama and heartbreak leads to surprises around the curve one never sees coming. Farin is headed for stardom and she's surrounded by a supporting cast of famous characters. But she is swimming with sharks. It's the shady, greedy, and sometimes mentoring world of the recording business. There are layers of motives, loves, family secrets, perversions, and assaults of the soul. O'Brien sends you a lifejacket while reading—you are buoyed by her incredible storytelling. Be prepared to be shocked, shaken...more so, you will be tremendously moved.

> *~ Ryan Rayston, author* The Quiet Sound of Disappearing,
> *and* Softly Goes the Water

The Music is Murder saga

Lockhardt Sound

A Fate Worse Than Fame

Ballad of Someday

Hit Makers

Feels Like the End

Betrayer's Lullaby

High Water or Hell

To learn more, visit: www.booksbyheather.com.

ACKNOWLEDGMENTS

For reasons known to those listed below, I would like to express my gratitude for your having endured, to varying degrees, the creation of this book. Thank you for your love, friendship, counsel, and unwavering support. It is in no small way a testament to you that this work was finished:

My family, Charlie, Skip O'Brien, Jana, Mike & Becky, Tracy, David B., Ryan, Rhona, Danielle, Jama, Cheri M., Sheila B., Joy, Kathy K., Lisa C., Elaine H., Bruce & Ruby, Alan & Barbara, Darryl, Cherie, Bob, P. Mike, P. Daniel, P. Dann, and P. Jake, and to Susan and Mary, for their hospitality during the Miami research leg of the series.

Continued gratitude to my Beta readers:

Erin Adams, Emily Conner, Rose Ferraro, Cherie Lawrence, Hugh Pitt, Christina Naughton, Ryan Rayston, and Kim Timperio.

This work would be incomplete without the help of those who selflessly gave their time, expertise, and technical assistance:

Dr. Emma Lew (Dade County Medical Examiner's office)
Trevore Fletcher (Criteria Recording Studios)
Sergeant Craig Leveen (Coral Gables Police Department)
Penny McCrea (the *Miami Herald*)
Doctors Phillips, Granovsky, Leff, and Krafcik (Sutter Medical Group)
Jacob Bunton (Lynam, Adler)
Faye McArthur (Dorothea Dix Hospital)
Sue Gray (Grays Café & Bar - Brenchley, Kent - England)
José G. López
Robert Cordray
Wayne Scoffield
John Holloway

Hear my prayer, O Lord, and let my cry come unto thee.
Hide not thy face from me in the day when I am in trouble;
incline thine ear unto me:
in the day when I call answer me speedily.

For my days are consumed like smoke,
and my bones are burned as an hearth.
My heart is smitten, and withered like grass;
so that I forget to eat my bread.

By reason of the voice of my groaning
my bones cleave to my skin.
I am like a pelican of the wilderness:
I am like an owl of the desert.

I watch, and am as a sparrow
alone upon the house top.
Mine enemies reproach me all the day;
and they that are mad against me are sworn against me.

For I have eaten ashes like bread,
and mingled my drink with weeping.
Because of thine indignation and thy wrath:
for thou hast lifted me up, and cast me down.

My days are like a shadow that declineth;
and I am withered like grass.

The Book of Psalms 102:1-11
The Holy Bible, King James Version

For Scarlette and Farin

CHAPTER 1

THE INSULATED WALLS OF CHRIS Grant's mansion did not absorb the squeal of brakes and tires screeching on pavement. They did not block out the rustling and abrupt "thud" that followed. From his second-floor vantage, the noises seemed to have originated from the street beyond the iron gate encompassing his property.

A moment later, quiet.

Chris lowered himself into his wife's hungry arms. He took her mouth with his, threading his fingers through her honey-brown hair. Her body arched to meet his, her lips ravenous as her fingers traced down the length of his back, her hands cupping and kneading his skin. "Oh baby. Mmm."

Weeks ago, they were strangers. Now, she was his bride. He had hoped she would make him forget.

Julie Swanson Grant represented a certain, if hollow, victory—and he had needed the win. For too long, he had come out on the losing side of a game he had never wanted to play. His prize? The most beautiful woman in the world, according to *Vogue Magazine*.

"You ready for me?"

She released an urgent, breathy, "Yes."

A battle raged inside him as he flipped Julie onto her stomach to take her from behind. He slid the tip of his tongue down the middle of her back, her ambrosial scent a foreign aroma filling his nostrils. Her pleasured moans threatened to scotch his internal fantasy, and his arousal. Julie should not be there, surrendering her sweat-soaked nakedness with eager hip thrusts. Another woman owned his thoughts. She haunted him without end.

Julie's lips parted as he entered her.

He moved as if on autopilot. Chris Grant—the grand master of seduction. An always-impressive performance. Yet, he felt nothing.

Revenge was not so sweet after all.

The sudden, repeated ring of the doorbell startled them both with its urgent, overlapping chime. Next came the thunderous pounding of fists on their door. Horrific shrieks followed. They shot up in bed and faced each other, open-mouthed.

Julie bolted to the window. Her hand shot up to cover her mouth. In a flash, she snatched her robe off the end of the bed and hurried down the hall. "It's Jordan. His car's in our bushes!"

Chris rose with a sigh, jerked on his jeans, then trudged to the window to see for himself. His younger brother's Jaguar rested lopsided atop the hedges inside the front gate.

Farin must have told Jordan about his visit two days earlier. How he had begged her to abandon her husband and run away with him.

He left the window and skinned on a T-shirt. Time to settle the score. If the alarming arrival signaled what he suspected, it would not end well. For either of them. They had come to blows before. In fact, Chris and Jordan had not exchanged a civil word in over a year.

He wondered how Julie would react when Jordan told her. Would it cost him his marriage, as it had already cost him the rest of his family? After Farin's most recent rejection, he had resigned himself to a life without her. She wanted it that way. Even if it killed him, he would honor her wishes.

Julie's cry reached him from the veranda. "Chris! Call an ambulance. *Hurry!*"

Chris snatched the cordless phone from his bedside, his heart leaping as he dashed down the hallway, dialing 911.

The call connected. Ringing tones commenced. He raced down the stairs, unsure what to tell the party who would pick up the other end. The last time he had called an ambulance, Farin had overdosed right here in his home. He had found her unconscious on his staircase, dead to the world.

"This is nine-one-one. What's your emergency?"

"I—uh." He rushed through the living room toward the front door.

"Hold please," the voice instructed.

Blinding sunlight streamed through the open door. Phone in one hand, the other shielding his eyes, he squinted out against the day. Julie's robed body crouched on the porch. Blood covered her hands and wrists. Aghast at the sight, it took a beat to recognize the crumpled heap at his wife's feet.

Farin moaned with every breath. Blood matted her hair, and covered most of her face. It crusted and flaked off her cheeks. Her arms and legs were awash in it. The lap of her expensive sundress was soaked.

She shuddered against the doorframe, a puddle of blood beneath her absorbing into his cement porch. Tears cut long, uneven swatches through the blood on her face. Her nose ran thinly.

Bile rose in Chris's throat. Myriad possibilities flooded his mind. Unpleasant, all.

Julie inspected Farin's body in fearful desperation. "I can't find where she's hurt!"

The operator returned to the line. "Sir, what's your emergency?"

"Chri-i-is." Farin panted between sobs. "Have to...Lockhardt...Bobby's house...J-Jordan's dea-a-a-d..."

Her words vanished into a slow, high-pitched, wailing moan.

"Send an ambulance!" he shouted into the telephone. "I don't know what's happened!"

"Sir, please stay on the line. We're sending units now."

Bobby's house? Jordan? Dead?!

"Take this bloody thing!" Chris thrust the phone at Julie. He did not run back upstairs for his wallet. Rather, he snatched his keys off the entry table and dashed out the front door.

Hastening past Jordan's car, he noticed the driver's side door had been left ajar, keys in the ignition. Into the newfound horror of the bright cloudless day, the warning chime pinged again and again. The Jaguar's interior no longer gleamed pristine white. From dash to floorboard, the hand-sewn leather was streaked with crimson and rust-colored blood.

Chris left yards of tread in his driveway as he peeled out and headed for Bobby Lockhardt's house. Heart thumping, he strained to recall the address. He had visited only once before, at Farin's request. Maybe he would remember once he made it to the general vicinity.

He had to.

The drive from Key Biscayne to Coral Gables took ten-to-twelve minutes in normal traffic. He fully intended to cut that trek in half.

He slammed his Porsche into fourth gear and sped under a red light, ignoring the blaring horns of other motorists as his frantic mind constructed a road map of Coral Gables. The image of Farin's blood-covered body rendered him incapable of clear thought.

The address flashed into his mind like a garish neon sign. He floored the gas pedal. Other cars whipped behind him as he worked the gears, passing them like stationary obstacles scattered in his path. Halfway there, he realized Julie would not know where to direct a second ambulance, let alone the cops. He slammed the car into fifth and fumbled for his cell phone.

He gripped the apparatus in his left hand, the gearshift in his right, and lifted his knees to the steering wheel. The Porsche reached eighty-five miles per hour as he punched the keypad with tremulous fingers.

The connection came through scratchy and tenuous. As before, the dispatcher asked, "What's the nature of the emergency, sir?"

"I don't bloody know! I think there's been an accident! Someone may have been seriously hurt."

Static reduced the dispatcher's response to indecipherable garbles. He shouted Bobby Lockhardt's address into the microphone, praying they heard him. "Get someone over there straightaway! Got it?" He stabbed the "end call" button, then threw the phone at the passenger side floorboard.

I'm coming, Jordan. Hang on.

He overshot the house doing one hundred miles per hour before the number plate affixed to the brick column registered in his mind. The Porsche screeched and protested as he stomped the brakes, dropped into third gear, and jerked it sideways. The vehicle spun in a complete one-eighty. The engine died as his foot slipped off the clutch. He popped the stick into second, turned the key, and floored it. The Carrera flung itself into Bobby's circular driveway like a bullet, raging to an abrupt halt mere feet from the front porch.

The expertly manicured grounds surrounding the Coral Gables estate exuded a surreal calm as he clambered out of his car. A breeze cooled the warm December afternoon. Birds chirped and warbled from their perches high atop telephone wires and Banyan trees. The neighborhood's serenity made a disturbing contrast to the vision of Farin cowering on his porch.

A visual sweep of the property for any other cars or people brought him to Bobby's heavily-lacquered, open front door. No sounds came from inside.

He lowered his eyes from the door to the front porch. The nauseating sensation of hurtling downward on a roller coaster overtook him. Bloody footprints blazed a smeared trail from the porch, down the steps, across the walkway, then vanished at the driveway a car-length ahead of his Porsche. Droplets of dried blood dotted either side of them.

Chris hurried through the door, then stopped short in the tiled entryway. Broken glass and household debris lay strewn and scattered around the open floorplan. Papers littered its floors. The living room sofa resembled a child's toy, effortlessly tossed upside down among the mess. Smashed photographs hung on the walls, frames tilted at odd slants, their glass covers shattered, jagged, and splintered.

Tomblike and inexplicable, the deafening silence disturbed him. He pushed through the rubble, overturned the capsized sofa, and plowed through the wreckage, trying to comprehend the bizarre surroundings. The stench of gunpowder and metal filled the air.

The wall farthest from the entryway caught his attention. An instant wave of nausea triggered his automatic reflex, causing his hand to shoot up and cover his mouth. Chunky, crimson spatter dotted the otherwise clean surface—dried blood and what instinct told him was body matter. It no longer ran down the minimally-textured wall. He choked back his nausea, his troubled eyes following the gruesome trail down to the mounds of debris cluttering the floor.

Finally, his vision landed upon the still frame lying atop a field of shattered glass in a pool of blood.

Chris hurdled over the mess to reach the misshapen form. *"Jordan!"*

He tried to convince himself he was wrong. It could not be Jordan. This body looked small, ashen. Fake. It lay like a carelessly discarded marionette, its arms and legs folded at odd, uncomfortable-looking angles around him.

Slowly, reality ambushed his denial. The parted lips. The slackened jaw. The dilated green eyes fixed vacantly upon the ceiling.

Blood caked in his blond hair, his face, and the small entry wound in his temple. His head sank into the pool of blood, bone, and matter beneath him.

"Jor—" Chris whimpered. He lifted his brother's head gently from the floor. A second wave of nausea hit him as his fingers identified the origin of the bloody pool he squatted in as a canyon in the back of Jordan's skull. He jerked his head aside as his body dry-heaved.

When the sensation passed, he rested Jordan's head back onto the blood-dampened shards of glass. "You'll be okay. You hear me? Hold on. I called the police. I called the ambulance. St-stay with me."

Tears welled in his eyes. He shook his head, pleading with his awareness to keep the unimaginable reality of the situation chained in the recesses of his mind. Jordan could not die. Not this way. Not when so much remained unsaid between them. Not before he had a chance to apologize. Not at the age of thirty-one. Not when things had finally begun to show some promise.

Moments stretched by in slow motion. Chris inched forward on his knees, the jagged glass slicing his jeans as he watched for some sign of life. With trembling fingers, he felt Jordan's wrist, then his neck. He lowered his ear to his chest and listened.

"C'mon-c'mon-c'mon," he whisper-pleaded.

Nothing.

He rocked back onto his knees and beheld the still form before him. Jordan's frame had never appeared so small.

In a final moment of acceptance, Chris hung his head, fused his brown eyes, and sobbed. His chest convulsed in spasmodic repetition. Unanswered questions vanished like smoke as reality's icy grip dragged him across the threshold separating fact and fiction.

Jordan lay before him. Dead.

He swiped away blinding tears, attempting to make sense of the situation at hand. Distantly, he heard sirens. Police cars and an ambulance would arrive any second. The authorities would want his statement. What could he possibly tell them?

Chris could not fathom why his younger brother lay dead at his feet, or why Farin shuddered on his porch, covered in what must be Jordan's blood—the same blood covering his own hands. He did not know Bobby Lockhardt's whereabouts. He did not know why Jordan and Farin had been at Bobby's house. He did not know why the place looked like a demolition crew had run through it.

"I'm sorry," his voice cracked.

A montage of childhood memories played in his head, as if their lives were a movie reel. Jordan as a toddler, following his older brothers around Chiltern Hills like a loyal puppy, always wanting to participate in neighborhood games with the bigger kids. Jordan always smiling, always calm, always kind. Jordan, Chris, and Ben making mischief in their small hometown of Bledlow. Their famous Saturday night carpet concerts. Swimming, sailing, traveling to Ibiza on holiday. Younger days. Happier times.

The memories dimmed until they dissolved altogether, the echo of a young Jordan's laughter fading into ether.

Chris looked again into Jordan's sightless eyes. They did not look real. Nothing about this scene appeared possible.

He touched Jordan's arm and said a clumsy prayer. His skin was still warm. With his thumb and index finger, he shut Jordan's open eyelids.

"Freeze, scumbag! Don't even fuckin' breathe!"

He whirled around, automatically raising his arms in the air.

The Coral Gables Police Officer who had shouted into the sad stillness of the house stood behind a loaded, cocked, and well-aimed semiautomatic pistol. Holding it with impressive steadiness, its owner leveled it directly at his face.

"He's my brother!" he spat through his tears.

As the words left his lips, Jordan's hand shot up and grabbed his wrist in a vice-like grip. He opened his lifeless eyes and hissed, "You're not my brother. You're a *thief*."

Chris bolted up with a start, his eyes darting of their own volition around his bedroom's interior. Terrifying images clung to him like cellophane packaging to skin. Beside him, Julie slumbered. The thin silk strap of her nightgown rested off her shoulder. He watched her as his breathing steadied. When he regained his sense of time and place, he noted the faint hint of dawn framing their bedroom curtains.

He had had this nightmare before. In it, he relived the events exactly as they had occurred. Right up until the cop shoved that cannon into his face. Only the end differed, leaving him unsettled and confused.

The police investigation had concluded that Jordan and Farin interrupted burglars at Bobby's house that day. One of the alleged thieves shot Jordan before fleeing. However tragic, the explanation made sense. What did not make sense was why, in the dream, his brother had grabbed him. Why Jordan had called *him* a thief.

Today in particular, the nightmare imprinted itself in his psyche. His heart hammered his chest.

He yanked back the covers and crept out of bed, realizing the futility of trying to fall back asleep atop sweat-soaked sheets.

Julie's hand shot out and fell on the warm, damp space beside her. "Everything all right?" she murmured through sleep-thickened lips.

"Go back to sleep."

She emitted a whining moan. Chris walked around the bed, leaned down, kissed her forehead, and righted the strap of her gown. She offered a groggy smile, then rolled over. Sleep reclaimed her before he stood upright.

He shuffled into the bathroom and shut the door. Absently, he washed his hands with soap and warm water, then shut off the hot and let the cold run. He rubbed cool water on the back of his neck, rinsing away the thin film of perspiration, then scooped up palmfuls to splash into his face.

A thief?

Staring into his brother's empty eyes that morning had changed Chris's perception of everything. He should have left Farin alone. Even though he still loved her to this day. But it was too late, now. For all of them. Too late to undo the past. Too late to apologize. Too late to change their fate.

He wished the burglars had shot him instead.

Chris cupped more water onto his face, then peered up at his dripping reflection. Unrealized pleas for an unrequited love taunted him. Farin's final refusal to start a new life together had undone him. She would have none of it. None of him. And she was right.

He yanked a hand towel off the hook beside the mirror and covered his face, wiping water droplets from his face and neck.

Julie would not wake for another couple of hours. He debated whether to call Ben. The idea that he would hesitate to contact his own brother on a day like today perfectly illustrated the divide between him and his family.

Chris flung the hand towel to the floor with a sharp flourish of his wrist and trudged downstairs to the kitchen.

He snatched the kettle off the stove, hooked its handle onto the faucet, then peered out the window while the vessel filled. Dense fog obscured his west-facing view.

When the kettle filled, he switched on a burner, covered the spiraled heating implement with the pot, and retrieved a teacup from a cabinet. He yawned and rubbed his eyes as he procured loose black tea and a strainer. The microwave's digital clock display read 6:17 AM. He calculated the three-hour time difference in his head. Ben would be up by now.

He lifted the receiver off the kitchen wall phone and dialed. His sleepy mind wondered if Ben ever had nightmares about their baby brother's death. If so, did Jordan call *him* names? Probably not.

Chris and Julie had relocated from Key Biscayne to Los Angeles a month after the funeral services. In two ill-fated moments, everything that mattered to him had vanished with no possible recovery. Miami offered him nothing but misery. Wherever he looked, he saw Farin's face. The survival of his marriage, and his sanity, demanded they leave.

To no one's surprise, Ben had disapproved of the move.

When the answering machine picked up, Chris replaced the receiver. Answering machines irritated him. Maybe Ben had decided to spend some time away. Or maybe he did not feel like talking today.

The sudden shrill of the teapot brought him back to present. Steam rose from his cup as he poured boiling water over the tea strainer.

Jordan's ghost was right to accuse him. He *was* a thief.

***

Chicago meant more than distance for Miles Macy. It meant a new, if overdue, start. He enjoyed having his family so close. Well, most of the time. He would enjoy them a lot more if his mother and sister would stop pushing him to settle down.

At times, his "Miami years" had felt more like a tour of duty in a war zone than the beginning of a successful journalism career. The *Post* had warned him to let up. His editor accused him of losing his objectivity. A year after Jordan Grant's murder, Miles agreed. The exhaustion accompanying his personal involvement with the Grants made the *Chronicle*'s offer irresistible.

He had paid his dues as a bottom-feeding journo for the Entertainment section of the *Post* for six excruciating years, having signed on fresh out of college. The *Chronicle* enticed him with better pay, his own weekly column, a prestigious title, and the chance to return to his hometown a success. He could put the bizarre goings-on in Miami behind him. Or try to.

As editor-in-charge, Miles had a degree of control over the content the *Chronicle* delivered to fans of the entertainment world. Months in, the AP and UPI had both carried his columns multiple times. He had witnessed firsthand the side of celebrity few people—even renowned reporters—ever glimpsed. His encounter with Chris Grant in a rundown bar years ago had changed his life.

Colleagues had idolized Miles at the time. He had had an "in" to the most controversial stories hitting pop music. Reliable exclusives of the Grants and their ill-fated escapades had earned him respect, and a wide berth. But the behind-the-scenes reality of the infamous family had sobered him. In the end, he had become obsessed.

Chicago had revitalized him. No regrets, save his one-time vow to never leave Florida's tropical paradise. When conversing with friends who still lived in the Sunshine State, he would chuckle when they asked how he could bear the frigid weather. "We've got the Art Institute, the Sears

Tower, *and* the Cubs. Besides, who can resist a city that turns its river green every March seventeenth?"

On days like today, however, he agreed with his Floridian pals. Blizzards made for a miserable commute into the office. Especially on one's day off. But when Miles woke up and realized he had left his laptop at work, he had no choice. Deadlines were deadlines.

Thursday's editorial needed something special—something befitting the occasion. The only problem was, he had yet to write a word of it.

As he peeled off his winter jacket and hung it on the chrome coat rack in his office, he considered the weather and decided to ride out the storm. He reconnected his laptop to its docking station, then let the machine boot up while he procured some coffee from the break room.

Something good. Something to rock the boat.

"Mr. Macy." A soft chortle came from behind him as he searched the shelves above the sink for sugar. "I never thought I'd see the day when you'd get your own coffee."

His secretary leaned, arms folded, against the door jamb. A pretty, petite brunette, she looked comical all bundled into her winterwear. He gave her a crooked grin. "Hey, Jeanne. Yeah. I'm sure it's not as good as yours, but I'll suffer through. If you like, I'll buzz you when I need a refill."

She pulled off her hat and shook out her pixied do. "Not a chance. I only stopped by to pick up the tickets I forgot to take home Friday. I'm on vacation the next two weeks, remember? Tell me you remember."

He sipped down his hot beverage as they strolled back to her desk. "You're really gonna leave me that long?"

"You'll survive." She opened her top drawer and retrieved the airplane tickets she had kept at the office for over a month as a surprise for her husband on their second anniversary. "Look at it this way. You've already learned how to pour your own coffee."

He indulged her with a smile of defeat, wished her a safe trip, then returned to his office. Seated at his desk, he stared at the computer's wallpaper. Where to start? The piece had to pack a punch. He wanted to ruffle feathers. If only he knew which fowl they belonged to.

Eight days ago, Miles had turned thirty years old. A sobering milestone. He needed to wrap up loose ends. This included answering some questions. Questions of unsolved murders. Questions surrounding dead pop stars.

Everything fit together. He knew it. Despite the judgments and ridicule of his peers, he intended to figure out how.

His fingers hovered in position above his keyboard, wiggling as he waited for inspiration. Then, inspiration hit. He tapped his intercom button. "You still there?"

Jeanne buzzed back. "I knew it. What's up? I'm on my way out."

"Do me a favor before you leave?"

She sighed good-naturedly. "Shoot."

"Call Stark."

A pause filled the line. "You've been warned about this."

"Not you too!"

"If you go, I go. And *I* don't want to go."

"No one's going anywhere."

Two years ago today—Friday the 13th, no less—Jordan Grant's existence had been snuffed out by a .38 caliber pistol fired at indeterminate range. The police had closed the case with a story so full of holes, his mother could have used it as a doily. Since then, one detective, two employers, and three supervisors had ordered him to drop it. "Or else." So, he had. For a while.

Jeanne buzzed him back. "You owe me one."

"Have I told you lately you're the greatest?" Miles teased, not completely insincere.

"I'm leaving," she said in that motherly tone of hers, though she was five years his junior. "If you need anything next week, ask Patti. I warned her—uh, told her—about you. I'm putting Stark through now. Don't get us canned."

He wished her a safe trip, then stabbed the blinking light on his telephone base.

"Well, if it isn't the Chi-Town Kid!" Charles Stark greeted. "How ya been?"

"Freezing to death! We're in the middle of a blizzard."

"I wouldn't know anything about that. I'm sweating like a pig. It's tourist season here."

"At least I can look forward to a white Christmas."

"It's all yours. So, what's up? You call to talk about the weather?"

"You know me. I'm just a guy after a story." He grabbed a pen and paper from his drawer, jotted down the date at the top, and prepared to take notes.

"A story, eh? This is homicide, not *Entertainment Tonight*."

"Even Hollywood sees a murder now and then."

"Fair enough. But Tinsel Town's not my jurisdiction."

"Yeah? How about something closer to home, then?"

Irritation replaced his casual tone. "What's on your mind, Macy?"

"Got any further information on the Grant case?"

"Grant case?" the detective echoed. "Which Grant case?"

"C'mon. Sooner or later, you gotta tell someone. Shouldn't it be me? For old times' sake?"

An exasperated breath filled the line. This, Miles considered a bad sign. The pen slipped from his hand. Charles Stark was a bulldozer of a man— and twice as immovable.

"I don't see why the whole mess still has your briefs in a bunch, buddy. It was a botched robbery. The accident was unrelated. Case closed. Unless you think the wife—"

"Farin dropping the hammer on her husband is about as likely as the Cubs winning the World Series," Miles snapped.

Stark gave a hearty chuckle. "And that coming from a fan! Well, there you have it. If it wasn't the brother, and it wasn't the widow, who knows? The pistol we found at the scene was a real piece of shit. I wouldn't have fired it, that's for sure. The shooter's lucky it didn't blow apart in his hands."

"If it was a robbery, why wasn't anything taken? Why shoot Jordan but let Farin get away? Why leave the gun? And why would she run to Chris Grant's house instead of the cops?"

"Listen, Macy. You're a bright guy. I know you wish you could've helped the lady, but it didn't work out now, did it? Do us both a favor and stop nosing around. We've wasted enough of Dade County's resources. If she were here, we could question her—maybe reevaluate the evidence. As it stands, the case is cold. So cold, it might as well be closed. And I'm not paid to open cases. I'm paid to close 'em. Time to give up the ghost, pal."

"If you're holding out on me, Stark, you know I can expose that little sideline you've got going on."

The detective's voice lowered. "Are you threatening a police detective?"

"I don't make threats."

"Neither do I. Now, as fun as it's been catching up, I gotta jet. But let me give you one more tip. Don't call me about the Grants again. If you're so hell-bent on getting more information, I'd recommend a séance."

CHAPTER 2

STARK DROPPED HEAVILY INTO HIS cracked vinyl chair, his potbelly clearing the decrepit desk by inches as he slammed down the receiver. He considered calling Lockhardt. But no. The son-of-a-bitch had warned him on more than one occasion to lose his number.

"What's wrong with you?"

"Nothing." He yanked open his top right desk drawer and rummaged through its contents, searching for an unused file folder. When he came up empty, he pushed it shut. As it closed, a passing glimpse of a dog-eared pamphlet left him defeated.

"I finished the report on the Coulby case." His partner tossed the stapled document across her desk onto his. "Look it over if you want. I'm taking an early lunch."

"Don't be late. We need to get statements on the rest of those witnesses from the Domino Park stabbing."

With a disgusted shake of her head, she snatched up her purse. *"¡Claro! Y yo soy tu traductora personal porque no tienes la capacidad para aprender español—en Miami! ¡Cabrón!"*

He humphed as she stomped out of the room, too frustrated to address whatever insubordinate insult she had hurled his way. Money was getting short. If he did not think of something soon, he could lose his future.

Excepting his partner, Stark's peers considered him a good-natured guy whose main ambition in life was to retire at fifty and spend the rest of his days in the Southwest. His desk drawers brimmed with books and pamphlets on Arizona cattle ranches.

Two years ago, he had deposited half the total cost of the ranch he picked out as good-faith money. Since then, he had scraped together the mortgage. Seasonal sharecroppers and occasional tenants helped. However, the remainder due seemed unobtainable.

Cattle ranches cost money. Yet despite eighteen years of loyal service and three commendations for valor, the Metro-Dade Police Department had given Detective Charles Stark little in the way of monetary compensation. When Macy's secretary had called earlier, he imagined

Arizona one mile closer. He envisioned a few payments he would not have to scrape together. Instead, he had found it necessary to hose down the astute reporter's fiery instincts again. Macy was good. Too good.

The memory of the Coral Gables Police Department depositing world-famous rock star Chris Grant in Metro's lap often came to mind, as that fateful day had begun to see his Southwest dream materialize. But ranch or no ranch, sometimes Stark wished he had never gotten involved.

Things at Metro had shifted for him, at the time. Sixteen years of dedicated service had finally earned him a detective's shield. He and his new partner, Alicia Alvarez, had worked only one other case together—a gang war turned massacre—and Stark predicted a war would soon break out between them as well.

Stark had paid his dues in the trenches. Alvarez? She had obtained her shield in three years. Apparently, his twenty-six-year-old Cuban cohort had a membership in AA—a twelve-step program officially known as Affirmative Action. A high-profile celebrity case would impact both their careers, one way or another.

It fell to Metro to investigate the over four hundred homicides in the Miami area each year. While an effective suburban force, Coral Gables PD had no homicide division. Thus, the Coral Gables cop had done little more than dial the telephone so Chris Grant could execute his one call before depositing him in the designated interrogation room, uncuffing him, and signing papers.

Stark had dispatched a rookie to procure a pair of flip-flops to cover Chris's bare feet, his bloodied shoes having been confiscated, tagged, and bagged as evidence.

"Well, well, well," Alvarez had taunted, eager as always to jump in. "What do we have here? You see this, Detective Stark? We got ourselves a regular Mick Jagger."

Stark pointed to the uncomfortable chair farthest from the door and motioned for Chris to take a seat. He did not respond to Alvarez's jab and knew she had not expected him to.

"So...you offed your brother, eh?" Alvarez had paced the long table, her cruel black eyes laser-focused on their suspect. With her heavy accent, she sounded more like one of the hoodlums they had busted in that gang war than a well-educated, newly-promoted police detective.

Chris rubbed angrily at his wrists. His eyes narrowed at Alvarez. "I didn't kill my brother. Why aren't you out there looking for who did?"

"What's the matter, Mr. Mick? Were those bracelets too tight? Did they hurt those million-dollar hands of yours?"

He sneered, inspected his bruised wrists, and spat under his breath, "Bloody bobbies."

"What did you call me?" Alvarez shot to his side and stuck her face in his. "Do you know how serious a murder rap is?"

Stark thanked the rookie who arrived with the flip-flops, then walked to Chris's other side. "Here. Put these on."

Chris wrinkled his nose. "I'm not putting those on my feet."

"We can't have you running around the station barefoot. It's regulation—health codes and all."

Alvarez snatched the rubber shoes from Stark and threw them to the floor at his feet. "Put on these *chancletas* or I'll call in an officer to put them on for you, with some ankle cuffs to accessorize. Trust me, Mr. Mick. You don't want me to dress you."

Stark watched Chris's expression of sheer hatred as he wiggled into the thin shoes. He sympathized. He often felt the same way. "Let's get down to business, shall we? We have some questions for you, Mr. Grant. First off, did you kill your brother today?"

Forty minutes of interrogation did not change their suspect's story. The department dispatched officers to his Key Biscayne home to round up both Farin Grant and Julie Swanson Grant. If this guy's story proved true, suspicion would soon shift from the brother to the wife.

Alvarez slammed her palms on the bare wooden table in front of Chris. She lowered herself in his direction. "You don't think I read the papers? Is that it? You think I don't know you been playing hide the sausage in your brother's delicatessen?"

The remark brought Chris out of his chair. He towered over her. "I've answered your questions for an hour. I'm not giving you bloody bobbies— yes, I said *bobbies*—anything else. I want my solicitor. *Now.*"

"Solicitor?" Alvarez guffawed, throwing her head back with sadistic glee. "*Solicitor? Madré Dios*, Mr. Mick! What you need a 'solicitor' here for if you got nothing to hide, eh? You better loosen that big mouth of yours or we're gonna put you in a nice little holding cell with some Cubanos who'd love to open you up."

Their eyes deadlocked. Stark grabbed Alvarez's arm and stomped toward the door. Chris needed to cool down. Alvarez probably needed a Midol or five. Stark needed to make a call.

As the door shut behind them, Alvarez jerked out of Stark's grasp and jutted her chin. "Don't *ever* touch me again, Detective. What's wrong with you? He's ready to spill. I know it."

To a degree, Stark envied his partner's passion. He had cared about his work once, had wanted to clean up Miami's filthy streets. But he knew now what Alvarez had yet to realize about the realities of law enforcement. It mattered nil who committed the crime or who became its victim. Chris Grant had money, and celebrity. Those were what ruled the courts and the cops. If she thought she could change this fact, she fooled only herself.

"You like him for it?" he had asked, plunging his thick hands into his pants pockets and rustling his keys.

"Yes," she said with a zealous grin. "Another hour and he'll be signing his autograph at the bottom of a confession."

"We can't hold him longer than twenty-four hours without charging him, Al. You know that as well as I do. He says he was with his wife. His story hasn't changed."

"Get her here," she had ordered, jabbing a slender index finger into Stark's crisp dress shirt. "And it's Detective Alvarez. Address me properly."

Stark disappeared long enough to make his call. Upon his return, he and Alvarez reentered the interrogation room. He hiked one leg up on a chair and leaned on his elbow. "Okay, look. We can wait for your attorney to get here and make a federal case out of this, but we haven't charged you...*yet*." He stooped down until his eyes were nearly even with his suspect's. Nothing intimidating. More like a friend or trusted associate. "We don't want to charge you if you didn't do it."

"I didn't!" Chris bellowed. "How many times do I have to tell you?"

"I know, I know." Stark nodded, the poster child for understanding. An act, of course, and not a very good one. But he had gotten the role of good cop by default. "There are a few things about your story that don't add up. Like the blood on your hands and clothes, see? Let's take it from the top one more time. You say you were home with your wife..."

A tap on the door some two hours later informing them the suspect's brother and attorney had arrived brought him relief. Not only was his story consistent, he had clearly had his fill of being bullied by a cocky female cop.

Alvarez had eyeballed Ben Grant and John Knowles as they entered the small interrogation room. "Looks like Mr. Mick here brought his big brother in to hold his hand. Sorry, big brother. You can't be in here."

After three hours of profitless interrogation, Stark cut Chris some slack and brought Ben inside. Maybe it would ease the tension. Maybe the guy would slip up or make a mistake if the tension died down. If not, at least it would piss off his partner.

With a total of five adults, three chairs, and a table, the interrogation room was cramped. Stark suggested they bring in more chairs, but Alvarez raised a hand in protest.

Chris addressed his brother through gritted teeth. "Get me out of here before I put this slag out of my misery."

With an agile sidestep, John Knowles wedged himself between his new client and an advancing Detective Alvarez. "Let's concentrate on how we can get my client out of here, shall we?"

"He's not going anywhere," Alvarez informed him. "We have questions your client needs to answer."

Chris nearly knocked Knowles over as he lunged for the detective. "I've answered your questions all afternoon! I didn't kill my brother! What more do you *want* from me?"

It had taken both Ben Grant and John Knowles to hold Chris back. Alvarez laughed from two feet away.

Stark edged toward the door, prepared to call for an armed officer. In his mind, he catalogued Alvarez's violations against their suspect. As the senior investigator, he could have—and probably should have—written her up. At the time, he had decided giving her a little leeway might be the smarter move. Someday, she might extend him the same professional courtesy.

"That's right, Mr. Mick." She reached behind her and grabbed her cuffs, as if pleased she might have occasion to use them. "Come for me. I got something for you."

Ben had shot Chris a warning look as Knowles addressed the detectives. "Are you charging my client, Detective? If not, I'm going to have to ask you to let him go. I suggest you direct further questions to me."

"How'd it feel to pull the trigger, Mr. Mick, huh?" Alvarez taunted. "Where'd you get the gun? You leave some prints on it? His little wifey help you plan it?"

Chris's face reddened with fury. "Don't *ever* talk about her!"

Knowles slammed his briefcase onto the battered wooden table and checked his watch. "It's currently four, Detective. Bully my client again and I'll file a harassment suit with Judge Cook before you clock out for the evening. We clear?"

Terrific, Stark had thought. Days earlier, Judge Cook had let a drug dealer found with over three kilos of nose-candy walk free because the arresting officer had put the wrong date on the warrant. The cops had arrested the perp at seven minutes *before*, not *after*, midnight. Professional courtesy be damned, Stark needed to affect some damage control. "Detective Alvarez, go get some coffee—*now*."

Knowles whipped his head at Chris and snapped, "Sit down and shut up or I'm off this case."

Alvarez turned on Stark with unmistakable rage. The vein on her neck throbbed like a steel drum. Perhaps considering the politics at work, she wisely closed her mouth to whatever retort she had planned.

As she stormed from the room, he added, "I take mine black. Two sugars."

She paused mid-stride and narrowed her eyes to angry slits. Stark gave an unrepentant smirk as she left. When only men occupied the room, he thumb-pointed at the door. "You'll pardon my partner's outburst, Mr. Knowles. I think it's that time of the month for her—if you know what I mean."

Ben Grant had hedged over to stand beside his brother. "What's going on here?"

Chris grabbed Ben's shirt. "Farin showed up on my front porch looking like someone had taken her skin off! There was blood everywhere, Ben. I went to Bobby's house and...Jordan's dead. I saw him. I was there."

"Why didn't you call me?" Ben accused through his clenched jaw.

"I *did* call you—three hours ago!" He shook Ben's lapels. "Where've you been?" He shook him harder, nearly punching him in the chest with each syllable as he exclaimed, "Jordan's *dead*, Ben! He's dead!"

Stark watched soberly as what must have been hours of frustration and worry finally hit Ben Grant. Chris pummeled his chest, raving in shock. Visibly overwhelmed with frustration and anger, Ben drew back his right fist, then brought it forward at great velocity into Chris's nose.

Nothing at that moment could have shocked Chris more. The blow carried him backwards. His legs encountered his evacuated chair. He tripped and ended up sprawled on the floor of the interrogation room, tangled in its wooden spindles. He kicked it away and hugged his knees to his chest. Wracking sobs shook his torso. Blood trickled from his nose and dripped onto his shirt.

Ben's brow creased as his sanity returned, bringing with it an instant sense of remorse. His shoulders sank. He stared down at Chris and extended a hand to help him up. "I'm sorry."

"Get away from me!" Chris spat, slapping him away.

Alvarez strolled back in with a single coffee containing mostly cream. She arched a curious eyebrow as she swallowed a sip. "We get our confession?"

"That's enough!" The abrupt shout from John Knowles startled the detectives, both edgy after a protracted interrogation session. "Either charge or release my client. Decide now."

Alvarez leaned against the wall, bending a knee to prop her heeled foot up against it. "We can hold him up to twenty-four hours without charging him, cowboy."

Knowles gestured and walked past her to the window just outside the interrogation room. The detectives followed.

With a swipe of his hand, the attorney split the blinds and inclined his head. Alvarez and Stark squinted at the blinding sunlight streaming into the room and peered outside for the first time in hours.

Alvarez's jaw dropped at the sight that greeted them. Beside her, Stark suppressed a grin.

News vans, cameras, reporters, satellite remote links, microphones, and a throng of lurkers surrounded the police station. It looked like a mob.

"Is this what you want for the next twenty-one hours, Detective Alvarez?" Knowles asked.

Their Metro-Dade colleagues had begun erecting a barricade to push the crowd back to the sidewalk. Stark feared they might need to break out the riot gear—a scenario he had not envisioned before making his earlier call to tip off the *Post*.

"Think how good you'll look on CNN when I file my harassment suit...and *win*. I can see it now." He ticked off points on his fingers. "Holding him without charging him on no evidence, violating his civil rights by continuing your interrogation after he requested counsel..."

Outwardly, Alvarez had appeared unshaken by the threat. Stark stared out the window. He saw Miles Macy milling around in the mob. He wondered how much dough he would get tipping off the *Post*'s most ambitious reporter. He caught his partner's eye, jerked his head to the side, and led her down the hall, out of earshot.

Alvarez's brown skin shaded red as she drew close, intermittently lifting herself up on the ball of one foot, fists clenched at her side. "I'll *never* get you a cup of coffee. I don't care if you're senior. Don't disrespect me in front of the perp. *Ever*."

He stared down at her, nonplussed. "Don't *you* shit on my investigation and give a lawyer grounds for a civil rights suit! What you did in there could cost us this entire investigation! Now wise up or I'll see you reading meters on South Beach for the rest of your career!" He bent toward her. "*Comprende?*"

Alvarez crossed her arms. "You need to retire, Stark. You're old and soft. This partnership's not working for either of us. I'm here to do the job. You want to make friends and eat donuts."

"If you have a problem with authority, we'll address it with the captain after we're done here. Right now, I'm cleaning up your mess. We can't charge him on what we've got. You'll have to accept that since I have more time on the force than the equivalent of a presidential term, I've got more experience. And believe me when I say I *don't* like him for it."

With an abrupt change of demeanor, she relaxed her stance. She swiped away a piece of lint from his shirt. "All right, partner. Let's charge him and do a skin test."

He rubbed the bridge of his nose. "We get him to agree to take the skin test first, then charge him if it comes up positive. If it's negative, he walks."

Alvarez shrugged and turned on her heel. "Your call, hero."

"Damn right it's my call!" Stark barked as he followed her back down the hallway.

Once everyone had reassembled in the interrogation room, Stark used his most reasonable tone. "Mr. Knowles, if your client will agree to a skin test, we'll agree to release him if the test comes back negative."

At the time, Metro employed three kinds of tests to determine whether traces of gunpowder or gunmetal residue existed on a suspect's skin. However, Fourth Amendment protections required they obtain either a warrant or consent to administer them. They explained the procedures in detail to Chris and his attorney.

The oldest and most reliable test was the swab method. The disadvantage, in this case, was time. Results could take days or weeks to come back from the lab.

A second method was the paraffin test. It was less reliable, since altered gunpowder contained no paraffin and therefore left no such trace. Many a savvy criminal these days used custom-loaded ammunition manufactured overseas and illegally imported to the States. Chris Grant hardly fit such a scenario.

The last test was a Trace Metal Detection Test. A chemical catalyst in aerosol form was sprayed over the suspected area—in this case, the skin of the hand. Under a black light, gunpowder and gunmetal residue would glow bright neon green or blue. This method promised reliable answers in a fair enough time frame.

If a suspect thoroughly washed his hands after firing a gun, he could defeat any of the available tests. But Coral Gables had arrested Chris with blood still on his hands.

Stark saw the wheels turning inside the lawyer's head. Knowles could force Metro to get the warrant. But if he did, the press would never let it go. As Stark predicted, he decided the deal sounded fair.

Knowles sucked his teeth, straightening his posture as if to assure all parties he had things under control. "I need a minute with my client."

Stark side-eyed Ben, who dipped his head towards Knowles and followed Stark out of the room. Stark motioned towards the coffee pot. "Can I get you a cup, Mr. Grant?"

Ben shook his head without looking at the detective.

Stark added, "I'm sorry for your loss."

Ben faced and stared at him, their eyes nearly level. His expression gutted Stark, leaving him inexplicably remorseful he had dared to say anything at all.

"Sod off," he said as the interrogation room door opened again.

Knowles peeked his head out and announced. "He'll do it."

Fifteen minutes later, Stark was leaning against the door jamb of the interrogation room with a good view of Ben Grant standing outside as the procedure transpired within. Knowles sat beside his client, looking harried.

The collection technician swabbed Chris Grant's hands for later lab analysis. Then, he sprayed the catalyst from his fingertips to his forearms. He brought out the black light wand and plugged the cord into an electrical outlet in the floor of the room. It flickered as the tech fiddled with the tubular bulb.

Outside the interrogation room, Julie Swanson Grant appeared near the booking desk, escorted by an officer. Stark had seen her on many magazine covers and recently on tabloids, superimposed into a shot beside her notorious playboy husband.

He scrutinized the image of the supermodel against the reality standing a few yards away. She looked older, disheveled, even plain in person. Jeans and a T-shirt. Hair pulled hastily into a messy ponytail. She stood with her arms crossed over her small-breasted chest, shifting her weight from one shapely leg to the other. When she spotted Ben standing outside the door to the interrogation room, she rushed over to him.

"Our home's a crime scene, Ben," she protested hotly. "There's police tape all across the veranda, the shrubbery, everywhere." She made a fist and gestured over her perfect shoulder with her thumb at the patrolman who brought her to the station. "Frankenstein here escorted me down for questioning. What are we all doing here?"

As Ben explained, Chris spotted his wife. He called out to her, "Where's Farin?"

Julie and Ben joined Stark, awaiting some conclusion to this bizarre chain of events. Arms still crossed, she craned her neck to peek into the room, pulling the corner of her lips to one side. "This is ridiculous. My husband was with me all day until Farin drove up into our hedges. She said Jordan was dead and over at Bobby Lockhardt's house. That's when Chris left, not before."

The technician managed to get the light to work. He waved it up, down, and around Chris Grant's hands and forearms. The results of the test made it overwhelmingly clear he had either scrubbed his hands and forearms like a surgeon as well as laundered his clothes, or he had not handled the pistol that killed his brother—or any other pistol, for that matter.

Alvarez shook her head in disbelief.

Again, Chris looked at his wife. *"Where's Farin?"*

A look of hurt and betrayal contorted Julie's perfect features as she met her husband's gaze. "I don't know, Chris."

Stark reclined into his chair and ponderously crossed his legs. Two years after the most notable case of his career, he remained stuck with a partner he could not stand, working in a city he detested, and worrying about a mortgage he could not afford.

Were he a betting man, he would wager he had not heard the last of Miles Macy. He wished he could give the reporter something—something to pad his bank account while avoiding Jameson Lockhardt's retribution. Dismissing the reporter out of hand had frustrated him. Their previous dealings had ended more pleasantly and more profitably.

Still, some things were better left buried. He cautioned himself to remember what was at stake. Some things he dared not discuss with anyone—least of all the media and *especially* Miles Macy. The eager reporter had gotten too close. Macy was too ambitious for his own good.

Truth told, the kid should be grateful he knew only what he did. Curiosity killed the cat and, in this scenario, it had practically killed the whole litter.

CHAPTER 3

IT NEVER SNOWED IN MIAMI. Not since 1977 anyway. And never at Christmas. Their flocked tree, beneath which colorful packages of red, green, and silver lay carefully displayed, stood as a paradoxical tribute to a day most often associated with roaring fires, heavy winter coats, and snowmen. But as long as children remained in the house, the Grant family would keep tradition—even if they donned shorts and tank tops as they sang "In the Bleak Mid-Winter."

The ringing telephone blasted the soundlessness of the studio as Ben carried a box of reel-to-reels in from the storage closet next to the engineering room. He opted not to pick up, forgetting his wife and sons had gone Christmas shopping. Soon, the ringing ceased.

Too many months had passed since Ben had organized his masters. Over the years, he had made good use of his studio, but since Jordan's death, Ben had lost much of his tireless dedication to songwriting.

He had penned his first hit song in the spring of 1969 at the age of sixteen. Since then, he had composed some of the most memorable pop tunes for the industry's leading acts. The '70s had been very good to him. During his twenty-five-year career, he had earned respect, many prestigious awards, and enough dosh to secure his family's future. The last ten, he had dedicated solely to Jordan's career.

The combination of Ben's songs and Jordan's voice had made both men legends in a highly competitive field. Until his death, Jordan had breathed life into Ben's work. Their bond had transcended family ties. An unexplainable sameness existed between them. Jordan's death had deeply affected him—personally and professionally.

Ben scratched his full, dark beard as he surveyed the contents of the first box. He had neglected to label much of its inventory, which irritated him. Years of completed and partial compositions filled dozens of reels. It would take weeks to sort the usable material from the rubbish. Next month, he would meet with a couple of struggling New York bands in need of original material. At Cheryl's urging, he had agreed to start writing again. Unlabeled, disorganized inventory illustrated his frustration. He felt ill-prepared for the upcoming trip.

He blew a coat of dust from the first container, opened and threaded the reel onto the player, then leaned back in his swiveled leather chair, grabbing a pen and his notebook before pressing "play." Methodically, he listened to the entire recording, jotting detailed notes on labels before swapping in another mystery reel from the box.

The morning passed slowly. Bits and pieces of incomplete melodies, humming, and vocal tracks, interspersed with nearly-completed works, brought back happier memories. He identified enough tracks to produce a previously unreleased album for Jordan's fans, a memorial they might enjoy—*if* LSI agreed to back the project.

Reel three contained a session he did not recall. On it, Chris played and sang a soulful, acoustic rendition of Paul McCartney's "Maybe I'm Amazed." A raw, impressive cover. Ben wondered whether he had intended to release it—whether he would ever record again. Despite their volatile relationship, he hoped so.

The fourth reel in the first stack contained a quick succession of reverb, the fumbling thump of a microphone, and echoed laughter through the studio speakers. The session transported him back years.

"Roll the tape, buddy," Jordan chortled happily. "It's late. I gotta get home. Farin will be here tomorrow. I wanna have this bloody thing finished."

Ben's voice had cut into the sound booth where Jordan stood poised to lay down a track, erupting with the giddy laughter typical of one of their all-night sessions. "We're rolling, ya prat. See the red light at the top of the door?"

"I think you're both pissed," Chris added, playing a quick riff on his guitar to keep his fingers nimble while waiting for his brothers' silliness to subside. "What did Cheryl put in that ginger ale, anyway?"

"Ben, come join us," Jordan beckoned from inside the booth. "It's been too long since the three of us had a go."

When the Grant brothers sang together, the sound was magic. Together, they produced a rare blend of harmonies too few modern-day groups could achieve—akin to older groups like the Everly Brothers, the Mamas & the Papas, Crosby Stills & Nash, and the Bee Gees. All harmonic geniuses. George Grant had always insisted the Grant brothers would have ranked up there with the best had they ever formed a group. For years, Jordan had unsuccessfully pestered his brothers to join him in making an album.

Ben closed his eyes as the music began. Their voices intersected and surrounded one another. The emotion of the piece overtook him.

"Thank you," he whispered aloud to no one, lost inside this moment preserved on tape—a moment shared with his family.

The studio door flew open, sending a startled Ben upright in his chair.

His youngest bounded breathlessly into the studio and stood beside him. "Mom brought home Chinese for lunch."

"That was a quick trip."

"It's almost noon, Dad." Kyle gave him a lopsided frown, then brightened. "You should see the cool stuff we found at the mall!"

Ben tousled his boy's straw-blond hair. Kyle looked like his mother, all kind eyes and delicate features. In a way, he resembled Jordan at thirteen. "I thought you went Christmas shopping. Sounds like you cheated, son. Hope you didn't pester your Mum too badly."

Kyle's small, parting lips revealed the trademark Grant smile, complete with perfect white teeth. He stifled a guilty laugh. "Derek was the one who mostly pestered. He tried to get her to go by that car dealership again. For a second, I thought she would!"

"We've a few months yet before anyone needs to worry about automobiles. Your brother needs to learn patience—and how to back up in a straight line. He only got his permit in September."

Kyle surveyed the room as the sounds emitting from the speakers pulled his attention. "Isn't that Uncle Jordan?"

Ben lowered his head, but forced a smile at his son as he rose from his chair. "I was going through some tapes here and came across it."

"Cool." Kyle grabbed his father's arm and tugged slightly. "C'mon, Dad. You gotta come in for lunch. Mom said. I gotta show you what we bought!"

He let his son lead him as far as the door. "Tell her I need to finish labeling this tape before I head in. Your dad's losing his organizational skills, I think. Will you help me after lunch? I could use another pair of ears."

"Sure." Kyle heard his mother's call from the back porch. "I gotta go. Don't take too long."

Ben watched his boy sprint away, then closed the door behind him. He switched off the tape and shut down the equipment, dreading the idea of leaving his studio refuge and facing the day.

He had tried, in his way, to inject temperance into the events surrounding the worst day of his life—before and after. Two years later, it still made no sense.

Days before Jordan's murder, he had found Farin on the sands of Biscayne Bay. Though always a fragile and frightened spirit, a distinct determination seemed to have replaced her fear that day. A lot of muddy water had passed beneath the shaky bridge of her and Jordan's marriage, but it was on the mend.

Then, Chris had arrived. Despite his better judgment, Ben had left them alone to talk. They assured him their affair had ended. He chose to believe them.

Forty-eight hours later, he received the call. That day resembled today in both time and circumstance. The boys had gone Christmas shopping with Cheryl, leaving him to work on Jordan's current project.

But unlike today, Ben had answered the phone. The news he received still left him reeling, as if the earth had dropped from beneath him.

"You need to call the Embassy."

Ben had met the demand with a disapproving snap. "I'm not your keeper. Whatever you've cocked up and gotten yourself into—"

"It's serious."

The gravity of Chris's tone alarmed him. Nothing, however, could have prepared him for the news.

"It's Jordan," Chris's voice cracked. "Ben...h-he's gone."

The words did not meet his ears easily. As they escaped Chris's lips, Ben's survival instinct kicked in. It surrounded him, causing every muscle in his body to go numb. He said, and felt, nothing.

"The police think I killed him."

Though arguably absurd, a funny sort of logic crept into the back of Ben's mind. "What are you talking ab—are you drunk? What have you done?"

He had no time to react. No time to let the news sink in. No time to ask questions. As the oldest, his first responsibility was to his brother. And so, he shouldered on.

He contacted the British Embassy in Washington, DC. Thirty minutes of shuffling between bureaucrats of different levels and functions found him on the line with a Consular in Miami. The gentleman acted in a less-than-urgent manner until he realized who Chris and Jordan Grant were, and thus Ben by association.

He put Ben on hold with the assurance he would return shortly. Fifteen minutes later, the man came back on the line. "We can have a representative at the police station in a couple of hours. Is there anyone you can call to meet him there?"

"I can call his wife."

"Will you be pursuing a transfer back to the UK?"

Perplexed, Ben replied, "What? My concern is getting him some legal representation."

Ben noted the rustle of papers and the Consular's hesitation. "Did you need us to get you a list of lawyers in the area, then?"

"I don't need a referral. I need to get my brother out of jail."

"Will you be registering with the prisoners' welfare charity?"

"I've no idea. Do we need to?"

The Consular put Ben on hold again. Each passing minute, Ben had to stop himself from grinding his teeth in frustration. Upon the Consular's return some twenty minutes later, he told Ben, "I'm sorry. There's little assistance we can offer. We can't get him released. We can't give legal advice. We're bound by certain diplomatic agreements—"

"So, you're telling me there's nothing you can do?"

The Consular assured him they would work in the background in any possible way. He also informed Ben that if Chris was found guilty of murder and sentenced to death, the Embassy would evaluate any valid request to support a clemency or pardon. "The situation is rather unfortunate."

"Right. Thank you for your help." Ben hung up in disgust. He had wasted an hour and a half and accomplished nothing. If the Embassy could not help, he would have to get a lawyer.

Despite recently severed ties with LSI, Ben figured Jameson Lockhardt would have an interest in Chris's predicament, particularly since the incident had happened at his son's house.

Ben called Jameson Lockhardt's office.

The phone rang once before Jameson's secretary answered. "Lockhardt Sound. This is Nancy. May I help you?"

"I need to speak with Jameson," he barked. "This is Ben Grant."

"I'm sorry. Mr. Lockhardt's away on business today. May I take a message and have him return the call?"

"It's an emergency. My brother's in trouble. It concerns both Jameson *and* Bobby. Is there a number where I can ring him?"

"He's not available by phone. What kind of trouble is it? Maybe someone else can assist you."

"He's at the police station being charged with murder."

Nancy gasped. "Jordan's been charged with murder?"

"No, Chris is being charged. With Jordan's murder."

"*What?*"

"In Bobby's house," Ben added.

Unlike with the Consulate, Ben was on hold for less than a minute. "Ross Alexander's going to call you." Nancy's voice trembled as she verified Ben's number. Before hanging up, she added, "I'm sorry, Ben."

When Ross called, the connection had sounded scratchy and full of static. "What can I do for you, Ben?"

Ross's calm tone had stymied him. Surely, Nancy had relayed the news. Ben repeated the information Chris had given him some two hours before. "Is there any way to get Chris out? He didn't murder Jordan."

"What was Chris doing at Bobby's?" Ross had asked coolly.

"Sorry?"

"Mirage's contract with LSI ended. We bear no legal obligation. Chris's presence at Bobby's house constitutes trespassing—"

"*Trespassing?* Jordan's been *murdered!*" Soberly, Ben realized this was the first time he had uttered this truth. Jordan was gone, and he would never see him again.

Ross continued. "Our deepest sympathies with respect to Jordan. It's an unfortunate situation. However, my representing Chris would be a conflict of interest. Even if it weren't, I practice corporate law. You'll need to seek independent counsel."

Ben ground his teeth, slamming the receiver into its cradle.

He struggled to remember the name of the attorney Jordan had retained some months ago. Had it been that long since Jordan had filed for divorce?

I should know the name. Know it. Know. Knowles—John Knowles!

"Coming soon, darling?" Cheryl asked, her soft Scottish burr soothing to his ears. "Food's getting cold."

Ben stood and scooted his chair in. "On my way."

He flipped off the studio lights and closed the door behind them, then draped his arm around her shoulder as they strolled to the house. "Was there a message on the machine? The phone rang earlier."

"No. No message."

"Probably Chris."

Try as he might, Ben still resented Chris for hurting Jordan the way he had. But it was more than that. On some level, Ben felt cheated. At least Chris had had the chance to say goodbye.

In the hours, days, weeks, and months following his murder, tragedy upon tragedy had shredded the soul of their family. The world had watched with gluttonous eyes as the chasm between he and Chris widened, a result of private—and not-so-private—arguments. The press grew fat with profit over speculation surrounding Jordan's death. Then, the news had gone from bad to worse. If their often-scandalous lives had etched a place in the hearts and minds of their fans, death drew them in with frenzied desperation.

News of Jordan's murder had ignited the airwaves. Fans around the globe set up vigils to their fallen pop star. They congregated at the scene of the crime amid mountains of flowers, cards, candles, and photographs. Lost and grieving for their musical hero, young girls held each other, mourned, prayed, and wept openly, unable to believe Jordan Grant was gone.

Television stations reported similar scenes. Fans gathered in front of their childhood home in England, the beach house in Malibu, the Key Biscayne home he shared with Farin, and Lockhardt Sound's New York offices. Radio stations dedicated hours to chronicling his life through his music, peppering archived interviews of Jordan among interviews from notable celebrities commenting on the tragedy.

"Such a talent," they declared. "He'll never be forgotten."

Reporters held nothing sacred in their lives. Not even Jordan's funeral. Paparazzi swarmed them like vultures, exposing a series of images of the grieving family at the funeral home, the grave site, the police station, the hospital. Tabloids ran stories bursting with casual slander. Fictitious accounts of Jordan, Farin, and Chris would linger for years.

Through the first anniversary of the tragic occasions, the media had bombarded them with interview requests. Anything to keep the legends alive. Pleas poured in from every medium, begging the family to speak openly about the bizarre series of events. Writers sought to pen official biographies. Unauthorized versions littered bookstores.

Accustomed to the trappings of fame, Jordan, Farin, and Chris had adapted to the constant attention. Ben's family had, until then, existed largely outside the prying lenses of the media. The deaths had submerged them into an enormous fishbowl. They could not run to the local grocery store without a constant barrage of paparazzi dogging their every move.

Ben eventually hired a security team to rid his home of curbside loiterers. For six months, he employed bodyguards to help avoid public confrontations while Cheryl went about her daily activities and the boys attended school.

The biggest blow came when Ben had to do the same for their parents in England. The press exempted no one in their family. Fifteen months later, George Grant succumbed to the grief and pressure when he died of a stroke.

Only recently had the firestorm burned down to a bed of dying embers. It sparked occasionally. Predictably, on certain days. Today, for example. Later, Ben would doubtless have to ring security to turn away some editor or producer who remembered the significance of this morbid anniversary.

Ben supposed he should feel touched. The world had immortalized those he and his family had lost. Indeed, a part of him was grateful. But more than anything, he wanted privacy.

Cheryl leaned her head against his chest. "It'll get better."

He gave her shoulder a loving squeeze as they went inside for lunch.

***

Miles rolled himself away from his desk and spun around to contemplate the view. From his twenty-second-floor vantage point, things should have looked clearer. But just as the continuing blizzard laid a blanket of winter white as far as the eye could see, Charles Stark's words lay shrouded beneath what Miles's hunches told him was a deliberate deception.

His hunches had never let him down.

He swiveled side-to-side, chewing his upper lip as he deconstructed their earlier conversation. Stark's casual dismissal of every question made Miles suspicious. The lack of concern when he had challenged Metro's decision to reclassify an ongoing investigation as a cold case after so little work felt...well, wrong. No usable fingerprints? Okay, reasonable enough if the robbery story was true. But no footprints? In a bloody crime scene? It must have been one savvy criminal, despite the botched burglary, accidental homicide, and letting the sole witness escape.

"Thought you were out today."

Miles turned to see his boss, Frank Harper. He waved him inside. "Me too. I'd originally come in to get my laptop."

"You get Thursday's column in?"

He gave Frank a slow, guilty shake of his head. "Not yet."

"Deadline's comin' up."

"I know."

"I'll leave you to it, then. Get it in and stay home tomorrow."

"Gladly."

Miles scooted back up to his desk and glided his middle finger along the laptop's touchpad to wake up his screen. A blank page greeted him. He hated blank pages.

If only he could access Metro's case files. Unfortunately, they had a policy against releasing data on unsolved violent crimes to the public. How convenient. Only more convenient was Miles's decision not to tell Frank Harper the subject of Thursday's column.

His preoccupation with the goings-on in Miami had come under fire before. It went deeper than his former relationship with Chris and Farin. It was as if his eyewitness account of the Grants' continued tragedy had obligated him to get to the bottom of it all.

In the Thursday, December 16th edition, Miles planned to present a commemorative op-ed spread to revisit those two-year-old events. Maybe revive some lingering questions. As he poised his fingers over the keyboard, he felt stymied again.

Think. What do we know?

He replayed the sequence of events following Jordan's murder in his mind, hoping to fill in holes Stark either could not, or would not. Had forensics not proven Chris's innocence, Miles might have gotten behind the idea of fratricide. Mirage's infamous lead guitarist's pursuit of his beautiful sister-in-law was well documented—most notably by Miles himself.

Coral Gables PD was located on Salzado Street, mere blocks from Bobby Lockhardt's home. Had a stranger murdered Jordan, why would Farin drive to Key Biscayne instead of the police?

Hoping the information would fatten his wallet, Stark had talked at first. The cop relayed a startling turn of events over the twenty-four hours following Jordan's death.

Once Chris's test came up negative, Metro's focus had shifted to Farin. A BOLO was issued. Airport, bus, and train terminals beefed up security. They searched each passenger, arriving or departing. Roadblocks sprang up along freeway exits. Every involved law enforcement agency received clear instructions. Farin Grant was a suspect in her husband's murder. She was to be apprehended and brought in for questioning.

What aren't you telling me, Detective?

According to Chris's statement, Farin claimed to have witnessed the murder. She had arrived at his home immersed in blood. Chris had driven to the Lockhardt home, leaving Farin with his wife. Julie stated Farin had sped away moments after Chris left. Police identified her blood, fingerprints, and hair at both Chris's house and the Coral Gables crime scene.

The next day, Jordan's vehicle was found at the Swan Hotel's immense parking lot in Disney World. Thanks to a timely tip from Stark, Miles had maneuvered into position to head up his own investigation before other news hounds could scoop him. That afternoon, Farin's dress was discovered at the inlet beach near Fort Pierce. It bore bloodstains they later confirmed as belonging to both Jordan and Farin.

Farin registered under her married name at the Swan Hotel the night of the murder. By the time police and reporters—including himself—arrived, she had vanished again. Had his keen powers of observation failed him, his investigation might have ended there.

Miles had spotted Ricardo Sanchez from the press camp near the front doors of the resort hotel early Saturday afternoon. The immigrant had stood apart from the crowd, his eyes darting between cameramen and police as he nervously rubbed his left upper arm. Disheveled and shifty, he looked like he had a story to hide. Miles slipped away unnoticed by his colleagues.

Ricardo Sanchez was a cab driver. He had picked Farin up outside the hotel around four thirty Friday afternoon. Due to the blonde wig she wore, he had not recognized her at first. But a few auburn tendrils loosened themselves from the disguise and, after seeing the news reports that evening, Ricardo recognized his earlier fare as the now-infamous Farin Grant. He told Miles he had driven her to a local bank at approximately four forty-five, then dropped her at Lightning Car Rentals near the Orlando Airport.

An hour after they met, Ricardo drove away with round-trip tickets to Las Vegas, three days' hotel accommodations, and four hundred dollars spending cash. Miles headed for the rental agency.

As it turned out, the manager of Lightning Car Rentals was not only easily bought, but also terrified at the possibility of being charged with aiding a known fugitive. Fortunately, Miles obtained exclusive access to both stories. Unfortunately, the trail had ended at the rental agency.

Miles called Stark Saturday afternoon to trade information. If Farin took a car instead of an alternate means of travel, she might still be in the area. In exchange for the cab driver's name, Stark confirmed Farin had withdrawn ten thousand dollars from the bank.

The deck seemed stacked against her, which confused Miles. He could not reconcile how Farin had mustered the requisite anger, hatred, or courage to shoot her husband—who she professed to love. His gut told him she ran not from the authorities, but from someone else. Who, he could not fathom.

When news of Farin's dress reached Miles early Saturday evening, he had headed for Fort Pierce, some two hours north of Miami and two hours southeast of Orlando. Based on the few details he had, he surmised she had stopped at the beach to wash away the blood and change into one of her traveling disguises. After fruitless hours spent questioning local residents, he checked into a local motel to rest for the evening before returning to Orlando.

Had he suspected that being away from his desk the following day might have changed the course of history, he would have gladly sacrificed the previous day's leads.

The next morning, he checked his voicemail before checking out. He was astonished to hear the message timestamped an hour before. Farin sounded as if her world had ended. Miles believed it had.

Her trembling voice moaned into the telephone. "I need your help, Miles. Please. It's F-Farin. Don't tell anyone y-you've heard from me. You need to set up a press conference for t-tomorrow. The funeral..." Her voice broke off into choked sobs. Miles felt an uncharacteristic catch in his own throat. "The funeral's set for noon. You know I d-don't trust you, Miles, but you're all I've got. Set the p-press conference up for two."

With that, the message had ended.

Miles traced the number to a phone booth in Key Biscayne. Knowing she had rented the car under the name Shae Wellingham, he easily located the hotel she had checked into the day before. On the drive back to Miami, Miles set up the press conference as requested.

He called the hotel, hoping to scoop the competition, but had to leave a message. Then, he dialed Chris Grant's number. Sources claimed Farin had not contacted Jordan's family after fleeing Chris's house. She had to have found out about the funeral arrangements somehow. Maybe Chris knew more than he had let on. Miles had to find out.

Beyond their first encounter at Stokey's bar in northern Miami, Chris had not opened up to him. Still, they had history. Miles knew how to ask the right questions—and which ones to leave unasked.

The minute he identified himself, Chris had barked, "What do you want, Macy? I'm on the other line."

"Have you heard from Farin?"

"Why are you calling my house?"

Miles heard the effects of alcohol or drugs in Chris's slurred voice. "I'll take that as a no."

"I'm hanging up now. No bloody comment. Leave us alone."

"Wait! I know where she is. She called me."

"No games, Macy. Not now."

"I'm serious! She asked me to set up a press conference for tomorrow after the funeral. What do you know about that?" The connection filled with static as he neared Miami. He had heard the local cellular towers had experienced a problem for the past couple of days.

"What press conference? Where is she?"

The connection worsened. Miles feared the line would drop. "I'll be back in Miami within the hour. Let's get together and talk."

"None of your schemes. The coroner's releasing Jordan's body soon. My family's in from London. Where's Farin? What aren't they telling us? What do you know?"

Macy shot more questions off, praying the connection would last. "Why were Farin and Jordan at Lockhardt's house? Why did she go to you instead of the cops? What did she say? Do you know what the press conference is for?"

"I'll leave your name with security at the cemetery tomorrow. After the service, we'll talk—you, me, and Farin. Now tell me where she is, you sodding parasite!"

An overpowering smile split his lips at the thought of an exclusive with both primary murder suspects. Against the scratchy connection, he shouted the name of the hotel, the room number, and the alias under which Farin had registered.

"I owe you a new suit, mate," Chris said before ending the call.

Monday morning, after several calls to Shae Wellingham went

unanswered, Miles headed for the hotel in hopes of catching Farin before she left for the funeral. He had done her the favor of setting up the press conference. Maybe she would give him a head-start on whatever story she intended to relay to the world.

To this day, the images from that trip across the Rickenbacker Causeway separating Miami from Key Biscayne had not dimmed in his memory.

The limousine. The crash. The explosion. Fire engulfing the inside, its orange and yellow tongues blazing out of shattered windows on the rear driver's side. Thick, choking blossoms of black and white smoke billowing out over the channel.

Every driver in the vicinity had swerved at the sound and sight of the blast. Following an initial cacophony of screeching brakes, the causeway became an impromptu parking lot. Several Good Samaritans exited their vehicles to assist anyone inside. Radiant heat prevented anyone from advancing within thirty feet of the burning vehicle or its incinerating occupants.

Traffic resumed across the causeway at a snail's pace once emergency vehicles arrived on the scene. Unable to turn back, Miles had continued southbound to the Sonesta, hoping his eyes had deceived him. Hoping Farin had not yet left her room. In the end, the desk clerk confirmed Shae Wellingham had indeed left the hotel in a black Mercedes limousine—the very limousine Miles had watched go up in flames.

An indescribable mix of nausea and shock had rested at the pit of Miles's stomach as he drove to Jordan's funeral to convey the shocking news.

Police, ambulance, and fire trucks funneled traffic down the left lane of the causeway, blocking the right. Rubberneckers slowed the procession. As Miles passed the smoldering wreckage, he stared, open-mouthed. Not one clear thought passed through his brain.

To say he felt close to Farin Grant was an overstatement. She had regarded him more like a thorn in her side than a friend or confidante. Admitting personal involvement with any story, particularly in his line of work, made him uncomfortable. Still, he felt the loss.

Sitting at his desk now, he tried to dislodge the memories. Stark's previous comment haunted him. "I know you wish you could've helped the lady, but it didn't work out now, did it?"

Miles swiveled away from his computer screen and back to the window. The *Chronicle* had thrown him a surprise party the afternoon of his birthday. Deflating balloons still littered his office. He had promised himself months ago to have this story wrapped up satisfactorily before he turned thirty. That day had come and gone without resolution.

How nice it would be if simply paying him to keep the story closed would satisfy his mind. Like Stark. Stark was paid to close cases—he had said so himself. The *Post* had tried to encourage closure as well, but they had never offered to pay him to do it.

Suddenly, Miles's eyes widened. A new thought, a thought so obvious he could not believe he had missed it, assaulted him.

Fact: Charles Stark was on the take. Money changed hands between the detective and anyone willing to buy his information. He knew. He should have known all along.

Happy birthday, you idiot.

As a belated present to himself, he determined he would find out who, besides the Metro-Dade Police Department, had paid Detective Charles Stark to close the Grant cases.

Satisfied and inspired, Miles began typing a piece he knew would solicit the perfect reaction for Thursday's column.

CHAPTER 4

ICKEY LOGAN'S OFFICE HAD CHANGED little. The dimly-lit yet pleasant room emitted an air of safety and confidentiality. The soft leather furniture, modern decor, and soothing, almost subliminally-low music piped into the room comforted Marci Lawrence's melancholy.

Dr. Logan looked older, heavier, grayer than he had some years ago, but his smile was the same. It spread warmly across what looked like false teeth.

Marci had never visited the psychologist as a patient, though she had accompanied Farin on visits during the five months he had counseled her. She was not self-conscious sitting on his couch. Rather, she longed to release the conflicting feelings pent up inside her.

"It's nice to see you again." Mickey shook her hand and took a seat opposite her. "How long has it been? I'm thinking...four years, at least."

"About six, actually," she said.

He thumbed through the file folder on his lap. She watched him browse the papers. It did not escape her notice that the label on the folder bore Farin O'Conner's name.

"Right." Mickey's eyes squinted behind his glasses. "Six years. I'm pleased you thought to come to me, Mrs. Lawrence. I admit, it took a moment to place your name."

"I'm married now," Marci told him. "It was my husband who suggested I see you. Well, someone. I didn't know who else to call. I've never done this sort of thing before."

Mickey smiled as if familiar with the comment. "I promise it'll be painless. It's not unusual for folks to seek counseling from time to time. You stated your reason for your visit had to do with..."

"Farin," Marci said, lowering her head. "Do you remember her?"

Mickey dipped his chin and shut his folder. He did remember Farin O'Conner. He remembered their sessions together, though he could not explain why. Throughout his career, he had worked with many patients suffering from chronic grief. On its face, her condition was unremarkable.

Perhaps her later celebrity status made her stand out in his memory. His most vivid recollection, however, was the day she announced she would not return. They had started seeing real progress. He told her he believed she had made the wrong decision, noting in her chart the choice to discontinue treatment came on the fifteenth anniversary of her father's death.

"It was two years ago today, Dr. Logan," Marci said. She slouched back into the leather couch and folded her arms. "I miss her. I know I should've moved on by now. I feel like I let her down."

"Why do you feel that way?" Mickey's face adopted a more clinical expression.

"We were always there for each other. Even as kids. Inseparable, you know? She was so screwed up. But you know that. Then, her career took off and she changed. I probably started missing her a long time before she died. I should've tried harder. Been a better friend when she needed me."

Mickey reached over from his chair to grab a pen and a fresh notepad from his desk, then scribbled some notes. "Do you feel you could have saved her?"

"No," Marci stated flatly, her eyes misting. "She was either working herself to death or running off, abandoning everyone who loved her. She started functioning less and less like a normal human being. No one could have saved Farin. We all tried."

Mickey scrutinized her face, her body language, her responses. "You feel your grief is prolonged?"

"I feel like there should be *more*." Marci retrieved a tissue from her purse. She dabbed the corners of her eyes. "It's not right. She was doing better. The affair was over. She and Jordan were planning a tour. They were talking about having children."

Mickey alternated between examining the folder before him and jotting down notes on his pad. "Forgive my failing memory. Didn't her husband die as well?"

"Three days before," Marci told him. She dropped her head onto her hands as the enormity of the circumstances found her. "I was in Miami for Jordan's funeral the day Farin died."

Mickey looked up from his notes. "I seem to remember being concerned she might harm herself. Was her death—?"

Marci softly shook her head. "It wasn't suicide."

The irony of it all hit her. Farin had spent her life grieving her father, who had also died by way of an automobile accident.

At the conclusion of their fifty-minute hour, Marci felt refreshed. Dr. Logan assured her it was not unreasonable to continue to miss someone who had shared their every deepest secret, thought, and memory.

The drive back from Santa Monica to Laurel Canyon took about an hour. As she drove, she thought about how much had changed in the last two years. She was married now, happy. Still, a void existed inside her. She had not understood it until talking to Farin's former therapist.

She and Elliot had celebrated their second anniversary last week. Their life was easy. Absent the prior years' turbulence. Elliot brought a completeness she had feared she might never find. She would have liked to have shared that with Farin. She loved Elliot. But Farin had been her confidant. Nothing—and no one—could replace that.

Her cell phone rang as she crossed Beverly Boulevard. She glanced at the screen before accepting the call. Her lips curled into a knowing smile as she answered. "Right on cue."

"Two years," came the effeminate voice on the other end.

"Two years," Marci echoed.

Marci and Dale Eastland had grown close since Farin's death. Few people knew her as they did. Few people understood her ups and downs, the bitter mood swings, the way her celebrity distorted her sense of self. After the move to Miami, Farin had detached herself not only from Los Angeles, but from her past. Marci suspected the move was also a buffer between her chronic depression and the smile Farin St. John's public image forced her to wear.

Refusing to turn the day of Farin's death into a morbid anniversary, she and Dale made a standing date to gather each January to celebrate her birthday. Dale made her favorite dishes. Marci brought wine. They shared memories, looked at photographs, and celebrated better days spent with their friend.

"How are we coping this year?" Dale asked. "You sound good."

"Better, I think. How about you?"

"You know me. Two days a year, I allow myself one tear. Then, I cook up a pot of chili, turn on one of her CDs, and—"

"I know the *and*," Marci interrupted with a bark of laughter, eschewing the intimate details of his love life. "How's David?"

Dale tittered at her embarrassment. "Driving everyone crazy. He's worried we won't be ready for the grand opening."

"It's coming up soon," Marci said. "Excited?"

"Honey, excited isn't the word. You and Elliot are still coming, right?"

"We can't wait," she assured him. "And you and I? We're still on for the week before?"

"Like I said, doll—twice a year, one tear. I'll see you in a month."

"We're gonna be okay. I'm glad you called."

The Lawrences lived a couple of miles from the Lookout Mountain Avenue home Joni Mitchell shared with Graham Nash when he wrote the song "Our House." Their place looked deceptively small from the vantage point of Laurel Canyon Boulevard's winding road, which passed in front of the stone fence encasing their half-acre property. Inside, friends and family found a tastefully decorated home befitting the lifestyle Elliot's fame dictated while appealing to his quiet nature.

Marci pulled into the garage at three o'clock, pleased to find her husband's Land Rover parked in its spot. He had worked at Universal Studios every day for the past six weeks. Marci missed having him around the house. She hoped his project would wrap up soon.

She entered through the garage door and tossed her keys onto the tiled kitchen counter, then perused the stack of mail Elliot had collected from the mailbox. Finding nothing interesting, she dropped the stack and headed into the living room. Elliot lounged on the sofa, mulling over the morning paper.

"You're home early." From behind the couch, she bent down to wrap her arms around his neck. "Can it mean you're almost finished?"

He mumbled as he leaned into her kiss and squeezed her arm with his free hand. His eyes were glued to the paper.

Marci snuggled into his neck and inhaled, losing herself in the familiar scent of his skin. She peeked over his shoulder and scanned the editorial page to see what had him so engrossed. "What has you so far away?"

Elliot's brows knitted in disbelief. An occasional disgusted grunt escaped him as he finished reading. At last, he folded the paper in four and handed it to his wife. "You'd think they'd let it go. Sorry, love. You might as well see it."

Marci frowned as she accepted the paper. "What is it?"

"Just read." He held out his hand, which she accepted, then guided her around the couch to sit beside him.

She leaned into Elliot's arms as she straightened the paper in front of her. The page contained editorials on the most recent LA water bond issue, various political hatchet jobs, and a critique of the movie Elliot had worked on some months back, which had recently premiered. She scanned this last, figuring the content had upset him, but the review was favorable. Finally, she came to an editorial picked up off the wire.

Giving Up the Ghost

-- Chicago, IL, Chicago Chronicle (AP), Thursday, December 16, 1993 by Miles Macy

A séance took place on the twenty-second floor of the *Chicago Chronicle* last night. No medium conducted the ceremony. The channel came through my computer terminal.

I communicated with the ghost of Farin Grant, who died tragically in a fatal car accident in Miami, Florida two years ago today.

I had many questions for Farin, the young singer who took the music world by storm five years ago on the Lockhardt Sound, Inc. label with such hit songs as *Woman/Child, Down Deep in Love,* and a string of back-to-back, chart-topping hits that catapulted her to stardom virtually overnight.

The redheaded beauty, wife of the also-departed and equally famous Jordan Grant, was on her way to her husband's funeral the day her limousine exploded and burned in a crash on the William Powell Bridge section of the Rickenbacker Causeway near Florida's Virginia Key. This reporter was present that day and saw Farin vanish in a thick cloud of smoke and an accompanying ball of fire. I stood on the bridge, unable to lend assistance to her or her driver, Charles Russell, who also perished in the blaze.

Farin's apparition seemed unwilling to speak to me at first. I had had the honor of interviewing the superstar many times during her career, but it was no secret she felt uncomfortable with the media hounds who buzzed around her like moths to her flame. Rumors plagued her celebrity regarding her personal life, including her affair with her brother-in-law, a miscarriage suffered after fleeing the States the day of her wedding, and her addiction to barbiturates. Still, I had a unique relationship with the pop princess. After some convincing, her spirit agreed to answer my questions.

Jordan Grant's murder three days before his wife's fatal accident has since been labeled a failed burglary-turned-homicide. The official story, in this reporter's opinion, holds no water. The Metro-Dade Police Department's investigative report, penned by veteran homicide detective Charles Stark, hypothesizes the couple stumbled upon a burglary in progress while visiting the home of Robert Jameson Lockhardt, Jr., son and heir to millionaire record mogul Jameson Lockhardt of Lockhardt Sound, Inc. The young Mr. Lockhardt was not in his Coral Gables home at the time but was, in fact, at an undisclosed location seeking medical treatment. Details of Mr. Lockhardt's condition were then, and remain now, unavailable.

It is speculated the couple met tragedy when they encountered an intruder or intruders unknown. Jordan Grant received a single, fatal bullet wound to the head. Hair, blood, and fabric samples belonging to both the Grants were found at the scene of the shooting. Farin Grant fled the scene after her husband's murder and drove to the home of Jordan's older brother, her own former lover, Chris Grant, who had recently married international supermodel Julie Swanson.

According to police records, Farin arrived on her brother-in-law's front porch covered almost unrecognizably in blood, both Jordan's and her own. When told about the murder, Chris Grant left the premises and raced to the scene of the crime, leaving Farin in the care of his new bride. While Julie Swanson Grant relayed what little information she had to the 911 dispatcher, Farin fled the scene and was never seen by friends or relatives again.

The day after the murder, Jordan Grant's vehicle turned up in a Walt Disney World Resort Hotel parking lot over two hundred miles from the murder scene, dried blood caked on the car's interior. Later that same day, Farin's sundress was found on a public beach nearly two and a half hours north of Miami. Despite having been partially rinsed of blood, forensics positively identified the garment. Blood belonging to both Farin and Jordan matched the samples collected at the scene of the crime.

At first, it looked as if Farin would become the primary suspect in her husband's murder. In the end, Metro-Dade PD instead ruled the murder a failed burglary attempt. Curiously, nothing was reported stolen from the Lockhardt property. The suspect or suspects have never been identified. In fact, other than Chris Grant, not one person of interest has been questioned.

My first question to Farin Grant was obvious. "If you had not died that day, you would have attended not only your husband's funeral but also a press conference, arranged by yours truly at your request. Why did you call that press conference?"

"I called the press conference to tell the world what really happened the day my husband died."

"And what did happen that day, Farin? Did you kill your husband?"

"I did not."

"If not you, then who? Can you describe the perpetrator to me?"

Suddenly, my computer screen swirled into the outline of a face that did not belong to Farin Grant. A male face. It came and went so quickly, however, I could make out no details.

"Why did you hide yourself from everyone after the murder? Why did you disappear?"

"I was afraid Jordan's killer would kill me, too."

"But why not go to the police?"

At that moment, a noise came through my speakers I could scarcely identify. It sounded like a cross between sarcastic laughter and a moan of utter despair. "I could trust no one."

"Will the killer ever be brought to justice?"

"Not in my lifetime, Miles, but maybe in yours."

"Did that person kill you, too, Farin?"

Farin answered only, "You were there."

With that, her phantom vanished, leaving me to wonder how many limousines spontaneously combust three days after the occupant witnesses the wrongful death of their spouse. Unfortunately, as was Farin's practice in life, her specter left without giving me the whole story.

What really happened that day at the Lockhardt home in Coral Gables? Who killed Jordan Grant and why? What could have happened that terrified Farin Grant to the point she could not trust the Metro-Dade Police Department for fear of her life? And what about her own mysterious and bizarre death?

Though Jordan and Farin Grant may be dead, this story is alive and kicking on the second anniversary of those tragedies. The next time I speak with Farin's ghost, I have no doubt my remaining questions will finally find their answers.

Salty tears trickled down Marci's face as she read. She remembered meeting Miles Macy the night she met Elliot, at an art show Mirage had played. Farin had often complained the reporter followed her all over Miami. It appeared he followed her still, even beyond the veil.

She wadded up the newspaper and tossed it across the room, then dissolved into her husband's arms.

"I suppose it's to be expected." Elliot rested his head against hers. Sometimes, he did not know what to say. Most of what he knew about Farin came from Chris. But he did know she and Marci had been like sisters.

She pressed her body closer.

"How did the session go?"

"Okay, I guess. I don't think I'm going back. He didn't say anything I didn't already know."

"What did he say that you already knew?"

"That I miss my best friend, and it's normal. He suggested getting a hobby or something to occupy my time since I'm no longer working."

Elliot stroked her thick, dark hair. "I finished the masters today. Post-production should be finished Monday."

"Wonderful." She nuzzled his neck as if it were a refuge.

"I'll have some time off, you know," he hinted pointedly.

"Can we do something? Maybe a trip?"

"What about a cruise?"

She brightened. "You mean it?"

He nodded. "Like a second honeymoon."

Minutes passed and neither spoke. Elliot continued to pet and stroke her, enjoying the feel of her skin and hair and filling himself with her scent. He had hoped to prepare, to find the right moment to bring it up, but knew the newspaper article might affect his wife's mood for days. He kissed her forehead, his lips lingering against her skin. Then, he dove in. "Why don't you stop taking your pills?"

Her body tensed beneath his embrace. When he tried a second kiss, he got a mouth full of hair.

She straightened beside him.

"It's time, Zoso. Don't you think?"

Anytime Elliot addressed her by her pet name, she knew he felt romantic. She stared at him, searching for clues as to why he might bring this topic up now. They had discussed children on and off for the last year, but agreed to wait for the right time. Did such a time even exist?

"Look," he continued, "I want kids. I want them with you. The doctor said you needed something to occupy your time. Can you think of anything better than a baby?"

She shook her head.

His normally stoic face broke into a smile as he peered down at her. "We have advantages neither of us dreamed of when we were children. I happen to know your parents are half toys in the attic for want of grandkids."

Marci imagined telling her parents their only child would be a mother soon. It made her smile, despite the heaviness of the day. The fantasy played out like a movie on a screen. Her mom jumping up and down, her dad cutting eyes at Elliot.

A single, coughing burst of laughter escaped her.

"That's what I thought." He waggled his eyebrows. "Besides, think of all the fun we'll have trying."

She leaned in and kissed him, then snuggled back into his chest. He surrounded her with his arms. She drew tiny circles against his chest and stomach with her index finger. "Yeah. Let's have a baby."

The idea suspended her sadness for some time before her thoughts drifted back to Farin. Marci had been excited at the prospect of becoming an aunt to Farin's child. Unfortunately, the excitement was short-lived.

A new sadness mounted within her. Farin would never see a child she and Elliot would have.

"Still thinking about...?"

She nodded.

Elliot cuddled her close. "What if you rang Chris?"

Her utter lack of movement told him all he needed to know. "I know you two don't get on well, Zoso, but perhaps it'll make you feel better. Even if you two don't agree on anything else, you know you both loved her."

"A topic we've debated since the night we met." She sat up to face him again. "I know he's your friend, but my opinion of him won't change. Ever."

"If I ring him, will you at least speak to him? Today's gotta be rough on him, too. Perhaps you'll both feel better."

Before she could refuse again, Elliot picked up the cordless phone beside him and dialed. A dozen thoughts rattled her mind. She had never trusted Chris. In the end, she had been right not to. He had played Farin's weaknesses like a game of Russian roulette. Marci had wished more than once that he had eaten that bullet instead of Jordan.

"Julie, hello." Elliot smiled and glanced briefly at Marci, then away into the emptiness of their living room. "Is Chris about?"

On the other end of the line, Julie Swanson Grant set her jaw. It came as no surprise to hear from the husband of Farin Grant's best friend. Not today. She cursed herself for interrupting her packing long enough to pick up. If only she had let the machine take a message.

"Hello, Elliot," she greeted, masking her disappointment as she stole a glimpse of herself in her full-length bedroom mirror. She raised a suspicious eyebrow, but painted a smile on her million-dollar face. "We haven't heard from you in ages. How are you?"

"Splendid, thanks. And you?"

Julie liked Elliot Lawrence. Elliot and Marci attended many of the same social functions as she and Chris, such as when Mirage received their lifetime achievement award at the Grammys last year. Julie was cordial not only with him, but with all the former Mirage members. Even Faith Peterson, who she despised. The band had meant everything to Chris. And though he might not admit it, she knew he missed his bandmates.

Today, Julie would have preferred to avoid their calls.

They chatted about the drizzly Southern California weather, plans to spend the holidays with relatives, and how they should get together for dinner sometime soon. When Elliot asked a second time to speak with Chris, Julie's jovial disposition audibly shifted. "I know what day it is, Elliot."

The pause on the line confirmed her hunch. "The last thing Chris needs is to relive this whole thing again. He saw the morning paper. We all did, I'm sure. Tell me you're calling about something that doesn't pertain to that woman."

"I didn't call to upset anyone. I know he's starting with Minor soon. I thought I'd chat him up a bit. Like you said, it's been a while."

Elliot heard the fumbling of the phone, then Julie's muffled voice call out to her husband. Her abrupt tone took him aback, though he understood it. It had to be torture to exist in a marriage knowing the one great love of Chris's life would never be she.

Another telephone extension picked up. Without so much as a goodbye, Julie hung up. When Chris greeted him, he sounded weary, bitter, and pensive. "What's up?"

They caught up on the safe subjects. Universal Studios had recently asked Elliot to write the scores to a couple of upcoming films. He would begin in the spring.

Chris contributed little to the conversation. Faith had called him a few days ago. She still lived with that intense painter/boyfriend of hers. Their enduring relationship surprised both men. Faith Peterson was the most difficult woman either of them had ever known.

"Perhaps she's found her calling," Elliot said, half-joking.

"As a nude model?" Chris asked without a hint of humor. "I've seen her naked, El. She doesn't look at all the way he paints her."

"You never told me you saw Faith naked."

"I thought we all had."

"Hmm. So, is she better or worse than this Henry bloke portrays her?"

Chris paused. "You didn't call to talk about Faith."

"What about the others? I haven't talked to them since last year."

"Me neither. Todd's still upset, I guess. Bloody mule."

Elliot made several abortive attempts to draw Chris out. The swaggering, hedonistic playboy of yesteryear no longer existed. Chris sounded ancient now, bitter. As if every forced breath he drew on this dark anniversary was an attempt to separate his emotions from the here and now.

"I'm meeting with Sam tomorrow," Chris said. "It'll be good to start recording again."

"That's brilliant, mate."

"It's time."

"And you've started writing your own material. Sam'll be thrilled."

"Yeah, well. I gave her a pretty hard time back when…"

When Chris's voice evaporated into nothing, Elliot knew the full weight of this day rested on his friend's shoulders.

Their last couple of years with LSI had been shaky ones. Without warning or explanation, Jameson Lockhardt had declined to renew their contract. Worse, he convinced the entire industry that working with them was *verboten.*

It had sent irreconcilable tremors through the band, with Faith and Chris at the epicenter. Everyone blamed everyone else for the breakup. Vicious accusations upended their bond—to their music, and to each other.

Faith's cocaine addiction had nearly killed her. Despite a stint in rehab, she relapsed twice before Mirage's contract expired.

Chris had left New York, effectively abandoning them. Rumor had it, Jameson's opposition to the move had sealed Mirage's fate. No one knew why.

In the end, it did not matter. Enough dirty water had passed beneath the crumbling bridge. Though other record companies eventually courted them, Mirage disbanded when their contract ended.

Since the breakup, Elliot had witnessed Chris's long line of defeats. Farin ended their affair. Jordan died. Farin followed. In the end, Chris withdrew into complete seclusion. No wonder Julie had concerns about his call.

"Listen. The real reason I rang you was to ask if you'd mind talking to Marci."

"Marci? What on Earth for?"

"She's having a rough go of it today. Perhaps if you two chat, it'll do you both good."

"Our talking never brought any good to either of us."

"Sometimes it helps when someone knows what you're going

through."

"*Going through*? What are you on about?"

Chris's sarcasm-saturated laughter filled the line, fooling neither of them. "C'mon, mate. Didn't you see the editorial?"

"What editorial?"

Had Elliot known that, at that moment, Chris had crossed the floor of his study to close and lock his office door, he might not have pressed the point. Had he seen the pain in his friend's eyes or the shredded newspaper that smoldered, no more than an urn of ashes in the middle of his desk, he might have apologized for calling, for suggesting he speak to Marci, for hoping they could, together, find some solace from the agonizing memories of this day.

Marci sat beside Elliot, her legs crossed and bouncing throughout their conversation. When Elliot attempted to hand her the phone, she shook her head and mouthed an emphatic, "No!"

He pushed the phone to her and whispered, "Yes!"

"*No!*"

He rested the phone against her ear. She heard her nemesis breathing on the other end of the line.

"Hello, Chris," she growled sullenly.

"Hello, Marci," came his ambivalent reply.

"Well?" she asked.

"Well indeed." A lengthy pause followed, testing and failing Chris's patience. "Is that it, then?"

"Elliot wanted me to talk to you. I don't want to anymore than you do."

"I see." With exaggerated enthusiasm, he asked, "So how are you, Marci? How've you been? Read any good trash lately? If memory serves, your nose stays buried in the tabloids."

"And if *my* memory serves, your nose has an affinity for bandages."

Elliot looked away, shaking his head.

"Your concern's touching. However, it seems my nose isn't the one out of joint today."

"No, I guess today doesn't mean anything to you at all."

"Another day of the year, I suppose. Of course, my birthday's about a week away. Did you call to wish me well?"

"No, Chris, I didn't call in the first place. If I had, it wouldn't be to wish you well. Maybe to wish you'd fall down a well."

"Always such a pleasure, Marci. Let's chat again soon, shall we? Oh, and Elliot tells me you two are planning to have a child. Best of luck getting knocked up."

"You sick son-of-a—" Marci's stomach churned as they played out their conversational tennis match. Nothing had changed. Chris had not changed. Not even Farin's death would change such a black-hearted weasel.

"Thank you, Marci. I've always held you in the highest regard as well."

She imagined the corners of Chris's mouth curling into a self-satisfied smile. He did so love his little mind tortures. "Don't you even care? Didn't you read the paper?"

"Of course I did," he answered matter-of-factly. "I'm sure Elliot's happy with the review. Perhaps Julie and I'll run to the theater next week and take in the film."

"You know what I mean. The column by that reporter? That Miles Macy?"

"Pure pulp. Can't say as I'm surprised you read it, though."

With a grunt of exasperation, she snapped, "Goodbye, Chris."

Before she could hang up, she heard him sing a melodious "Ta!" into the telephone.

She handed the handset back to her husband, her face contorted with pain and disgust. "He never cared about Farin. He used her, ruined her, and now he acts as if he barely remembers her."

With elaborate gentleness, Chris replaced the phone in its cradle. He peeled his fingers off it by force of will, then stared venomously at it, half-relieved and half-furious he had not flung the offending device across the room.

He glared at the ashes of the newspaper he had sent to a Viking funeral, willed his breathing to slow, then stared out his study window. Anger coursed through him in red-hot waves. His pulse throbbed in his ears. He wanted to break something.

A sharp pain along the flat side of his fist informed him he had slammed it with great force onto the desktop. A silver-framed photo of his wife leapt, then tumbled over on its face at the blow.

There came a rattle as the doorknob turned. A quick triplet of sharp knocks followed. He stalked across the study as Julie asked, "Why's the door locked?"

He yanked opened the door to find his wife balancing a tray with a hot tea service upon it. Without apology, he stepped aside. "Habit, I suppose."

She set the tea tray on the desk. Only then did he realize he had not righted her photograph. Too late, he realized she had seen it.

Without remark, she righted the frame and dressed it on his blotter. His features remained blank as she arched questioning eyebrows. He did not respond. "I'm leaving for Paris in a few hours, remember?"

Right. The modeling job in France. *France.* Of course. He bit back dark memories of the waiting room of *Pitié-Salpêtrière Hospital.*

He studied Julie's features, desperate to feel *something.* The stereotypical Midwestern girl. Tall. Slender. Her wholesome appearance made her beauty somehow ordinary. How much longer could she mask the tiny wrinkles around her eyes? How much longer did she think her career might last? Even under the most optimal circumstances, the camera made for a cruel judge. Soon, she would have to find new avenues for her career or risk more and more time at home. Perhaps he could assist her in finding some new endeavor. He owed it to her to at least try.

But not today. Today, he could do nothing for another living soul.

She stared at him, crestfallen. "You don't remember, do you? I've had this gig booked for weeks."

"Of course I remember." He snatched his keys off the desktop. "I just have a quick errand to run before I take you to the airport."

"Don't you want your tea?" she protested, pinching the bridge of her nose.

"No thanks."

She accepted the kiss on her cheek, then watched him dash from his office like a dog escaping a leash. Nothing he could have said would have masked the truth. Not only would he fail to return before she left for the airport, she knew the destination of this sudden, urgent errand.

He had yet to give up the ghost of Farin Grant.

CHAPTER 5

A WINTER RAIN LEFT THE Los Angeles streets wet and slick. Business commuters stayed in their offices during the brief but heavy noon hour storm, taking their lunches at desks, cubicles, or in company break rooms. When the shower ended, sunlight pierced the dark clouds. Bright rays beat down, creating mirrors out of rainwater pools, reflecting images of surrounding buildings, passing cars, and streetlights, and assaulting the eyes of those with light sensitivities.

Samantha Drake angled the vinyl slats of her office blinds upward so the early afternoon sun did not stream directly onto her glass and chrome desk.

On a scale of one to ten, the office rated a three in comfort and a twelve in style. Words like understated, impressive, sharp, and intimidating described both office and occupant. Never a pen out of position, never a stray file or misplaced folder.

Since starting with Minor 6th Records in the summer of '90, she had gone through seven assistants. Roughly one every six months. Former employees never claimed she treated them poorly. They simply could not maintain her perfectionism.

Colleagues revered her moxie, instinct, and business acumen. Her reputation as a kind, intensely firm employer had earned her a fair amount of respect. But only the unwise mistook that kindness for feminine weakness. Of all the heavy hitters at Minor 6th Records, Samantha Drake packed the most powerful punch. And why not? She had learned from the best.

She checked her gold link watch, then buzzed Deborah, the bright young girl with the gumption to stick it out beyond the usual six-month timeframe. "He should be here any minute. Show him right in."

"Yes, Ms. Drake."

Samantha wrapped her cold hands around the base of her oversized ceramic mug. She finished the last of her decaf, then rose from behind her desk and scanned the office for stray magazines or paperwork. For years, she had waited for this meeting. There could be no imperfections.

The well-stocked wet bar at the right end of the room thwarted an attempt to catch her full reflection in the mirrored panels covering its back wall. She wove, bent and bobbed her head between custom lighted shelves packed with exotic spirits and glasses of varying shapes and sizes, vying for a satisfactory glimpse. Her straight, jet-black hair perfectly framed her flawless face. Not a strand out of place. Smooth, even complexion. No need to powder her face or apply lip stain. Suit as crisp as when she put it on at five that morning.

A warbled ringtone announced a call on her private line. How clever of Deborah to customize the ringtone for her personal calls.

She crossed back to her desk and picked up, answering as if she did not know whose voice she would encounter on the other end. "This is Samantha. How can I help you?"

"Let's see. How could you possibly help me? What-say you and I meet at home tonight and give that question due consideration? Some people say I'm beyond help."

"Some people," she sniggered. "I wouldn't mention that to any of your patients. Your malpractice insurance rates could go through the roof."

"How's your day so far? Get soaked at lunch? Or did you skip it...again?"

"For the love of sushi, must you pay attention to all my bad habits?"

"Actually, I called to see if you'd had your big meeting yet. You seemed anxious about it last night. That's not like you."

Samantha Drake feared one thing in life: her love for Ethan Maxwell. He complemented everything in her world. Though their nearly fifteen-year age difference still made her cringe at times, she ignored societal biases regarding their romance as she did in matters of business. She regarded him as an equal. He respected her as a person, not an age. Moreover, her corporate position did not intimidate him. At forty-three, she had never dated a man who could withstand her heavy schedule and tough exterior. Their two-and-a-half-year love affair had suffered zero tension, monotony, or turmoil.

"I'm fine. If anything, excited. Apparently, this move of mine made the board very happy." She spun her chair around to peek through the Venetian blinds and found a decent reflection in the sunlight against her window. Using her thumb and index finger, she pushed a lone, rebellious strand of hair into place. "Still, there's history. I'd be lying if I said there wasn't a certain amount of personal satisfaction here."

"You can tell me all about it tonight over dinner. I'll make you a deal. You try to get home at a decent hour, and I won't let the Chief of Staff rope me into another double shift."

"You got it. See you around seven."

"I'll be waiting. I love you, Ms. Drake."

"I love you too, Dr. Maxwell."

It amazed her how he made her feel like a schoolgirl whenever they talked. Only more amazing was that she had finally found time for a personal life.

LSI had consumed seven years of her life—seven years without vacations, weekends, lunches, or sleep. Seven years without a life beyond the dungeon doors of its corporate offices. They had owned her outright. But not anymore. She had made her escape to the greener pastures of California.

But outside the safety of these walls, Samantha knew the dragon still lurked, roaring and incinerating everything in its path. The head of that dragon was Jameson Lockhardt.

Word had reached her shortly after her departure that Jameson intended to sabotage her new position as penance for her apparent betrayal. But the threat never materialized. Perhaps Minor 6th Records was too small to waste his resources. Or perhaps the controversies surrounding his most coveted acts laid waste his plans. Sam suspected the latter.

At the time of her exit, no record company in the world could touch LSI's worth. Jordan and Farin Grant were golden gods in a pagan industry of electric sex and synthesized sound. Mirage had laid the company's foundation from its inception. LSI had an impeachable track record. They could have continued indefinitely.

But something had happened. What, she did not know. And after today, it would no longer matter.

The phone buzzed. "He's on his way."

She pressed the intercom button. "Thanks, Deborah."

When the door opened, she stood, smoothed her skirt, and squared her shoulders as she rounded the corner of her desk, hand outstretched. "Welcome to Minor Sixth Records. It's good to see you."

"It's good to be here." Chris mirrored Samantha's smile, accepted her hand, and held it. "You look terrific, Sam. You haven't changed a bit."

"Now, be honest," she simpered. "You're supposed to say I look *better*. Has married life put you off your game or something?"

He indulged her with a chuckle. "It's difficult to improve on perfection. I'll give you this, though—you look better rested than the last time I saw you. What's it been? Four years?"

"Nearly, yes. It's amazing what a little sun and sanity can do for a person, isn't it?"

She drew him in for a quick embrace, then indicated the twin black leather sofas near the bar. "Can I get you a drink?"

"Better not." He jiggled his keys, then stuffed them in his pocket. He removed his bulky leather jacket and draped it along the back of the couch.

"Still driving that little white Porsche?"

"Porsche, yes. White, no. I got a new one after..." He cleared his throat and took a seat. "I bought a newer model after Julie and I moved here."

"Always the flashy one. How about a soft drink? Coffee? Or do you prefer tea? Goodness, Chris, it's been so long. Let's not be too formal, shall we?"

He agreed to a Perrier with lime, then settled back and crossed his legs. He surveyed the office's sterile yet stylish ornamentation. "Looks like there *is* life after LSI."

As she fixed their drinks, Chris noted the delicate beauty of her smile. It transformed her serious features. Samantha had rarely smiled in the years he had known her. She was a stunning woman. Until today, he had not noticed. She looked the same, but different as well. Still confident, but also relaxed and content.

"I was surprised you called. I'd just started thinking about a comeback. Something said it was time."

"It *is* time." She placed their drinks on the glass coffee table and sat on the sofa opposite him. "Are we sure there's no possibility the others will follow? Reuniting Mirage would—"

He lifted a shoulder with an awkward shake of his head. "We spoke a bit at the Grammys last year. Sometimes you can't go back."

She held his dark eyes. "I never sent my condolences over Jordan and I should have. I'm sorry."

His jaw tensed. Samantha pretended not to notice.

"Anyway, we'd like to get you in the studio right away." She leaned forward, extracted a sheet of paper from a thin manila folder atop the glass table dividing them, and slid it over. "Your agent got this last week. Since you were kind enough to meet me in person, I wanted to cover it with you as well. It's a proposed itinerary. We've scheduled a meeting with your publicist, planned some photo shoots—you know the drill. No reason to wait until the recording's done. Everyone knows you. This album will make Mirage fans *very* happy."

She clasped her hands together around a Monte Blanc pen, watching with satisfaction as he skimmed the document. He seemed to have gained a certain maturity since they had last seen each other. Then again, Chris had always handled his business, if not his personal life, in a professional manner.

"We haven't discussed material. Elliot wrote most of Mirage's songs. And...I-I know Ben wrote Jordan's. If neither of these are viable options, we'll start checking the vaults."

"Actually, I started writing my own material before the split. A bit of a departure from the stuff we were doing. More alternative than our traditional rock'n'roll. Pearl Jam-type stuff. Post-punk, sort of organic."

She listened intently, encouraged that they had started on the same page. Clearly, this new mature Chris had done his homework.

The '90s music scene had experienced a shift. In that respect, each decade was similar. Music was, and always had been, the linchpin of social and geopolitical change.

From '50s doo-wop and '60s-era protest and psychedelia, to the early '70s singer/songwriter craze and its later disco beat, music's transformative culture blew like a restless wind, a quenchless thirst for reinvention. The synthesizers, MIDIs, saxophones, and androgenous '80s vibe had run itself aground as people sobered from fear in the wake of the AIDS pandemic. Global awareness had increased, seeded by advances in technology and media worship.

A renaissance of social activism reminiscent of the American folk revival now permeated its core. Today's sound included deeper, acoustic resonance, a resurgence in messages of love and tolerance, and cries for equality. Hip-hop had become an indomitable force.

Performers had long-steered the ideological ship of human conscience. It thrilled Sam to see the tragedies of Chris's past had not caused him to miss the boat.

"I laid down some tracks at Ben's a few years back." He rested an arm along the back of the sofa. "They're not bad. Some are quite good, in fact."

"Sounds perfect." She mentally composed emails to colleagues. Chris Grant was back in business. And she had brought him here singlehandedly. "When can I hear them? Does Ben still have the masters?"

He looked up and away, as if trying to recall their whereabouts. Then, he dropped his head against the back of the sofa. "Forget it. They're with the old man."

Neither Samantha nor Chris uttered a sound.

She eased back into the sofa, repeatedly uncapping the Monte Blanc with a slide of her thumb, then pushing it closed again. Her gut warned her against a potential conflict with LSI. Then again, times had changed. *She* had changed.

Time to face the dragon once and for all.

She tossed the pen onto the table and clasped her hands together. "I say we get those tapes. Jameson has no right to hang onto them. The artist retains ownership, Chris. You know that."

He cocked his head. "You really think—?"

"Let me worry about the tapes."

"I can do at least one album without them."

"No problem either way. How's Julie these days?"

His lips tightened, but he wrangled them into a manufactured smile. "Excellent. She had a gig in France about a month ago, then stayed on to visit friends in Calais." He glanced at the silver wall clock at the end of the room. "She's stopping in Miami on the way back to spend some time with Ben and Cheryl."

Samantha scooted forward, folded her arms atop her stocking-sheathed knees, and adopted a look of intense contemplation. "I've been thinking about this for a while now. Your marriage is a good fit—for both of you. Maybe we can throw some extra work Julie's way as well, if she's available."

"How do you mean?"

"How would you feel about using her in a video or two? Maybe even the album cover?"

He grabbed his club soda from the table. Beads of condensation had pooled atop the coaster, causing it to cling to the bottom of the glass. He separated it and took a drink. "It's brilliant. I only wish I'd thought of it myself. I'm sure she'd love it."

"Perfect. I'll give Gloria a call."

Business concluded, Chris told Sam he had another appointment and should go. She thanked him again for meeting with her. He left smiling, which she considered a good sign.

When he left, she deposited herself back behind her desk. A smile stretched across her painted lips. *Chris Grant and Julie Swanson Grant in one day. What a coup!* She savored the success until she glanced down at her notepad and saw the word "tapes" underlined.

She envisioned calling Jameson and demanding their immediate release. Knowing the old man, he would tie her up in court as long as possible, only to declare the tapes had mysteriously vanished.

Probably best to take a less direct approach.

She picked up the phone and dialed Ross Alexander's private line from memory. When he answered, a distinct catch in her throat caught her unaware. She adopted her most professional tone. "Hello, Ross. It's Samantha Drake."

"Samantha! I haven't heard from you in ages."

"Now, Ross, I sent you and Josephine a card last Christmas."

"We received it, thank you. And I hope you got ours. It's good to hear your voice."

He sounded ancient over the phone, no longer the sharp, vibrant man she knew. It saddened her. She hesitated to tell him the reason for her call. It might cause friction between them, or between him and the old man.

She opted for small talk and asked about business. He sounded distracted, or as if something had broken his spirit. Too soon, a conversational lull forced her hand.

"Hadn't you better tell me why you called, Sam?"

She glanced at her watch. "It's late there, I know."

"I still have another meeting before I head home. So, what's up? I hear congratulations are in order. I'm glad Chris found a home."

"He just left, actually. That's why I called. I hate to ask for favors when I've nothing to trade but..."

An uncomfortable pause filled the line. "I'll make sure nothing happens to the tapes."

She clutched her chest. "You will? Oh, Ross, thank you."

"I'll do it as soon as we hang up. But I have to be honest—I doubt Jameson will release them. Not to Minor. Especially not to you. No offense."

"None taken. But as his lawyer, you know he can't keep them."

"I'll do what I can. Sometimes he listens to reason, if you can believe it."

A sharp bark of laughter escaped her lips. "Not for a minute."

His mischievous laughter eased the tension. Though Sam might not describe them as friends, their relationship was anything but adversarial. More like war buddies—and she adored his wife, Josephine.

She studied the back of her left hand and realized he had aged almost half a decade...and so had she. "I appreciate anything you can do. I don't expect miracles."

"Good. I think I used my last miracle some time ago."

"Speaking of which, what happened to Jameson's plan to ruin my career here?"

"Um..." Ross stammered, then assumed a nasal, professorial tone, mocking Bobby Lockhardt's boardroom manner. "I believe that plan was overcome by other events that greatly overshadowed it in importance, thus forcing a reevaluation of certain priorities."

Samantha emitted a guilty chuckle. "You nailed him."

"Years of practice," he demurred.

"But seriously, why did Jameson give you my job after all those years? Was it something I did? Something I didn't do?"

When he answered, all humor had left his voice. "I'm still in that role. It wasn't you."

"No!"

"You should have expected no one could replace you, Sam."

She frowned. "That's sweet, Ross, but it makes no sense. Isn't it a little...oh, I don't know...*beneath* you?"

"I'm the only one he trusts."

A burning sensation filled her stomach at the cryptic remark. A sensation she had not felt in years.

"I should go. As I said, I have another meeting. I'll do what I can about the tapes."

Before he replaced the handset in its cradle, he heard her say, "Thanks again, Ross. Give Josephine my best, and take care."

Ross called storage. He instructed a clerk to find and deliver the tapes to his office. As he gathered his things for his meeting, it struck him how small his world had become. Professional obligations had run off the few friends he once had. He could not recall the last time he had attended church. His entire world had shrunk to include only his wife and this forsaken company.

His hips protested as he rose from his desk. Things like standing got harder to do each year. Constant stress did not promote graceful aging. Each night, he spent more time in the bathroom and less in bed with his wife.

When he caught his reflection in a mirror, the shock of silver framing his thinning pate startled him. Thick brindled hair should be there above a wrinkle-free forehead.

Getting older is the pits.

He ambled into Jameson's office with a reluctant step. Each day, the same practiced courage as he entered this lair of lies. Each conversation, swearing his blind allegiance to the man who stood before him, a beacon of wealth and opulence at the bridge of this ship of fools. Each day for the last twenty-one years, Ross had surrendered a piece of his soul.

Jameson did not stand as Ross entered. He grunted and gestured at the uncomfortable 18th-century sofa set against the far wall. Surreptitiously, Ross studied his employer, his longtime friend, his colleague, and noted how old he looked—how old they *both* looked.

Fine, perfectly-groomed white hair had replaced Jameson's once-bushy blond mop. His timeworn face bore wrinkles, mostly across his brow and at the corners of his eyes. He possessed understandably few laugh lines. Heavy jowls tugged his puffy lower lids down near the crest of his cheeks. They melted into his fleshy second chin, disappearing beneath the collar of a heavily-starched dress shirt.

His eyes, however, had not changed in decades. Observant and cunning, those cerulean blues still conveyed a reptilian lack of mercy.

Ross knew that mercilessness all too well.

"You're late." Jameson set aside the *Financial Times* and removed his reading glasses. "What kept you?"

"Samantha Drake called."

Jameson huffed. "What about?"

Ross decided it best to open the meeting on a less contentious note. Better to table the request for the tapes until Jameson's thoughts struggled with higher priorities. "Shall we clear our agenda first?"

Jameson flourished his wrist in agreement.

Ross clicked his pen, poised it over a fresh notebook, and watched Jameson's formidable six-foot frame rise from his desk.

"I haven't mentioned my retirement plans to Bobby yet. There's too much at stake. Too much left to do."

"When the time's right, you'll know."

"Megan Price's sales are still steady, but even I can't expect her to bring us back to black. We need a broader stable of artists. I won't leave my son a failing company."

He scribbled some notes.

"He'll sink or swim on his own merits, of course. What he does with LSI after I'm gone is up to him. But what I leave him reflects on me. I don't want my biography penned as abandoning a bankrupt enterprise. I can't— I *won't*—leave until we're on top again."

Ross maintained a neutral expression.

LSI currently had no acts in the Top 100—and had not for months. Save legacy sales of Mirage, Jordan Grant, and Farin St. John albums, sales had tanked. Megan Price was an anomaly. Country and Western had never buttered their bread.

As bad as Lockhardt Sound's fiscal situation looked, the reality was worse. This quarter threatened to reveal a deficit situation for the first time in their history. Accountants had exhausted all the ways to dress numbers. Unless they experienced a revival of new artists, records, tours, and sales, the company would have to surrender unclaimed stock. Two of the Big Six were saber-rattling over a potential merger. Pundits gave weight to rumors of a bailout.

"Grass roots." Lockhardt balled up and shook his fist as he stood and began his telltale pacing. "We need to get back to grass roots."

Ross set his notepad and pen aside. "Could you be more specific?"

Jameson faced him, steel in his eyes and the set of his mouth. "*I* built LSI alone. *I* discovered Mirage alone. Epstein had his precious Beatles. Grant had Zeppelin. Stigwood had his Bee Gees. And I had Mirage. Every top act we've ever produced, I discovered and nurtured myself."

Ross set his jaw and looked down, plucking a piece of lint from the leg of his trousers. Jameson's rewritten version of history was funny, in an irritating sort of way.

"And that's exactly what I need to do now. I know talent and I know this industry. I know what the public wants and I know what sells. I've been in this bloody office a long time, and time is one thing I'm short on. I've set a deadline. I'll meet it."

A flash of disbelief carpeted Ross's features. "It's been twenty years since you 'built LSI alone' and 'discovered' Mirage. Things have changed."

"Why do you always doubt me?" Jameson's voice echoed through his office walls. He came to an abrupt halt before the large corner window with its impressive view of the New York skyline. "Never once in the time I've known you have you taken my word at face value. I've never—*ever!*—

been wrong."

Ross bristled at the near-accuracy of his words, careful not to mention recent examples disproving his claims. He knew Jameson viewed him as a well-compensated Doubting Thomas. How convenient, his selective memory. But at least the old man's proposed strategy would keep him out of the office.

How he welcomed Jameson's retirement. He looked forward to the long hot shower he would take the morning after Jameson's final day. Sometimes, he feared the decades of blood and destruction would never wash away.

He repositioned himself on the uncomfortable sofa that had, for some years now, retained the outline of his posterior. "I'm playing devil's advocate. That's what you pay me for."

Jameson returned to his desk. He held up his right hand. "I've already made arrangements to start scouting some new acts. I'd intended to head south for some time anyway. This will give me a good excuse."

Ross raised an eyebrow.

"I know, I know. Anyway, about your conversation with Samantha Drake. What does she want?"

He cleared his throat and retrieved his pen and notepad. "Chris sent some tapes up before Mirage's contract expired."

"Samantha wants the tapes."

"Yes."

"Done. What else?"

Ross stared open-mouthed at his boss. "You'll release them, then? No fight? No courts?"

"Was I unclear?" Jameson snarled. He leaned in and pressed his intercom button. "Stacy?"

"Yes, sir?"

"Mr. Alexander has a task for you. Make sure it's handled before you leave this evening."

"Yes, sir."

Ross rose from his seat, consulted his watch and, with a curt nod, left the office.

Moments after his enormous door closed, Jameson's telephone rang. Simultaneously, his fax machine began to buzz and whir. The noise startled him, as he had left Stacy instructions not to disturb him. Then, he realized the call had come in through his direct line.

He stabbed the speakerphone button. "Lockhardt. Who's this?"

"It's Stark."

"I told you never to call me here, Detective."

"Check your fax machine."

Jameson stalked to the machine and snatched the paper out of the collection tray, then returned to his desk and settled into his tufted leather chair. As he read, his eyes darkened.

"You get it?" asked Stark.

Jameson growled into the phone. "Indeed."

"I warned you that reporter wouldn't give up."

"And it appears he has quite an active imagination. But this article's a month old."

Stark's voice drifted to Jameson's ears, penetrating a cloud of wrath. "You'd said not to call so I kept my mouth shut. But I thought you should know. That's gotta be worth something, right?"

Jameson sneered, revealing upper canines a fraction longer than his otherwise perfectly even teeth. "Don't worry, Detective. I won't forget your efforts on my behalf. Rest assured they'll be rewarded commensurate with their worth."

"Care to mention a hard number so I can budget?"

"I'd rather surprise you. Good day, Detective."

Jameson severed the connection. His left hand clutched the facsimile of a recent editorial authored by one Miles Macy of the *Chicago Chronicle*. He made a fist until his skin stretched every wrinkle on his hand taut and smooth. With no wasted movement, he held his hand over the top of his shredder and then opened it, allowing the paper to fall to its destruction.

Slowly, his pulse and breathing normalized. He buzzed Stacy again. "I'm going out for about an hour and won't be available."

He snatched his gloves and jacket, inserted his magnetic key into his private elevator, and descended to the first floor. Popping the crease of his jacket collar, he stepped out and strode through the lobby, out onto the blustery New York street. Outside the building, a beggar solicited spare change. Jameson made a mental note to have him removed upon his return.

He pulled the folds of his gabardine trench coat closer and walked apace to the tiny delicatessen across the street on the opposite corner. When he stepped inside, he beelined to the rear, ignoring the establishment's patrons as he stalked past the counter.

Positioning himself in a tiny alcove between the men's and ladies' room, he withdrew his handkerchief. A beat-up, graffiti-covered payphone hung on the wall beside a vending machine. Without removing his wool-lined black leather gloves, he unhooked the sticky receiver with his handkerchief and wiped it down before bringing it to his ear. He gripped the right middle finger of his glove with his teeth to remove it, then dug into his pocket to retrieve his change, which he stacked on top of the payphone. He inserted over ten dollars in quarters before dialing. Seconds later, the call connected. It rang once before ominous silence told him someone had answered.

"It's me," Jameson said.

"It's been a while."

The voice on the other end of the line did not sound human. Its tones and inflections were the product of a sophisticated voice scrambler.

"I have another job for you."

"I've got a contract at the moment."

"I'm in a bit of a hurry."

"I'll be in touch soon."

The individual on the other end of the line hung up.

CHAPTER 6

JULIE SWANSON GRANT HATED FLYING. It terrified her, which made her feel vulnerable. And she hated feeling vulnerable. She sat strapped into a first-class leather seat, which also—*and thank you very much for this*—acted as a floatation device in the unlikely event of a "water landing." Her fate rested solely on the skill, sobriety, and attention span of a man whose favorite activity probably involved flirting with the flight attendant every time she brought him a fresh cup of coffee.

Her knuckles whitened as her fingers clawed the seat at each tiny sound. Somewhere over Virginia, her sinuses had finally cleared. Her ears no longer popped or ached, but she knew, in the unlikely event of an uneventful landing, she had all that to look forward to again once she headed home.

Her seatmate during the international leg of her trip had recognized her the second she boarded. He hosted some imbecilic radio show in New York, a Howard Stern wannabe. The man claimed to have been in Paris taping farcical reports of the Tour de France. Interesting, considering the Tour did not take place in January.

The jerk had spent the first two hours of the flight trying to convince her to appear on and disrobe during his show. At that point, she had obtained a different seat. When she glanced back minutes later, he had fallen asleep.

Sleep. How she wished she could sleep on an in-flight aircraft. Some people had no problem. They nodded off as the fixed wing caught the jet stream and reached a ground speed in excess of the speed of sound, at a cruising altitude several miles above the planet. They dreamed happy little dreams and, whenever they happened to wake, sure enough, a perky flight attendant stood ready with a complimentary rum and coke. How nice for them.

Julie had never, ever slept on an airplane.

She had taken her first flight at the age of six. A DC-10 flying from Denver to Portland on a trip to visit her grandparents. During that flight, the stewardess—for not only could you call them that back then, you were actually *supposed* to—offered to show her the cockpit. Her parents had insisted she go, promising she would get some wings like a real plane captain to wear on her new dress.

When she had entered the cockpit, the pilot turned around in his seat, smiled, and handed her a plastic toy plane. Beside him, his copilot snored, head tilted back upon his seat, face toward the roof of the cabin. Julie had watched in horror as the plane's steering gears turned left, then right, all by themselves. Aghast, she slapped the toy out of the pilot's hand, screamed, and raced back toward her parents. As she dashed down the aisle, the DC-10 had encountered turbulence, sending her headlong onto the floor.

Turbulence. Turbulence was one of those fancy words airlines used to avoid saying, "This is something that could kill us but we'll never admit it." Kind of like "water landing." She had not seen any pontoons on this plane and doubted it could actually land on water, though she did agree with the flight attendant's assessment that such an occurrence was unlikely. Crashing into the ocean seemed much more likely.

She signaled for another gin and tonic. The steady infusion of alcohol during her flight back from France had barely taken the edge off. Her adrenaline had battled its effects with the aircraft's occasional dipping and swaying. On the flight back from Switzerland with Chris the day before their wedding, he had plied her with gallons of liquor, probably hoping to avoid her breaking the bones in his hand. She had squeezed his fingers like a vice each time the aircraft buzzed, hummed, flew too fast, flew too slow, flew too high, flew too low, zigged, zagged, jigged, jagged, jolted, or jumped.

Closing her eyes, she pretended she was not a seatbelted prisoner in the belly of something far too heavy to fly forty thousand feet in the air, she thought of her husband. Since Mirage had disbanded, Chris had done almost nothing with his life. The first six months, he had moped, even after the move to LA. She would return home from gigs to find him staring at the walls. He had only inconsistently shaved or bathed and almost never stepped outside. Mostly, he lay around and drank.

Then, he started pulling himself together. He put his sleep schedule back in order, started going to the gym twice a week, and ate better. He stopped drinking every day. Over the last year, he had acted almost normal and had displayed more affection. Now, he had finally gone back to work.

Samantha Drake had become one of her favorite people.

Between flights, Julie had picked up a message from him. He told her Samantha suggested using her for some aspect of his album—a video or maybe even the cover. The prospects gave her hope. If successful with a video, maybe she could parlay the exposure into acting roles. The album cover would put her face in front of more people than the last *Sports Illustrated* swimsuit spread and present her in a different light to an expanded audience.

The stewardess, flight attendant, air bitch—whatever they wanted to be called—brought her a fresh drink.

"How long before we land?" She flinched as the plane hit an air pocket.

"We're ahead of schedule, so we should arrive in Miami in about forty-five minutes."

She downed her drink, then unstrapped to go to the ladies' room. She maneuvered herself into the tiny metal cell, closed and latched the door behind her, and checked her appearance. The wavy metal mirror made her look like a fun-house reject but she compensated.

Most of the world would argue she looked half a decade younger than her thirty-two years, but the lens did not lie. In terms of modeling careers, she was ancient. The Monroe Agency had negotiated her biggest deal only three years ago, at what was normally the tail end of a model's ride.

She frowned at her distorted reflection, searching for wrinkles around her eyes, overly large pores, or skin discoloration. Without her looks, she might as well be a housewife back in North Platte, Nebraska, washing dishes and raising kids. Like her mother. The thought chilled her.

The Paris shoot had not gone well. The creative director had complained about her body and her age. She could not sing. Someone had once joked that as an actor, she was one heck of a model. Even worse than her fear of flying was the fear her career would end abruptly—and soon.

She vowed to stretch it out as long as she could.

When Julie returned to her seat, she flagged down the flight attendant for another drink.

The woman's perky smile wavered as her eyes scrutinized Julie. "We'll be landing soon, Mrs. Grant. After this last, I'm afraid our drink service will stop."

Her mouth twisted into an arrogant sneer as she raised an eyebrow. "Then bring me two."

Landings were almost as bad as take-offs. Had she the luxury, she would travel to her appointments by ship, train, or automobile. Friendly reminders that flying was not only the safest way to travel but also the fastest made her want to scream. Still, in her career, time mattered.

Julie missed Cheryl. As a former beauty queen and pageant winner from an early age, they understood each other. This pit stop in Miami would give them a chance to catch up. It would also help her avoid LA. During their last conversation, Chris had not sounded like he missed her. She needed to talk to someone about her life, her career, and the future of her marriage—such as it was. Cheryl would understand.

When she arrived at Miami International Airport, her driver collected her luggage from Baggage Claim while she signed autographs. No water landing for flight 2146. No reason to use her seat cushion as a flotation device. She even returned her seat back and tray table to its full and upright position when a muffled voice made the request over the plane's intercom. Once again, Julie had avoided becoming a statistic.

The drive to Key Biscayne calmed her frayed nerves. For the next two weeks, she would enjoy Ben and Cheryl's hospitality and soak up as much sun as Florida's January climate allowed. No planes, no flash bulbs, and no rushing out of bed to get to hair and makeup.

Julie shuddered as the limousine passed their former Harbor Drive home. It looked like an ominous, vacant shell, though they paid handsomely for its upkeep and security. Chris still owned the forsaken property, though she had urged him to sell. It probably did not matter either way. Farin Grant was dead. Chris was hers. End of subject.

Cheryl greeted Julie's limousine at the front drive, arms outstretched and welcoming. As the driver unloaded Julie's bags, the women locked in a warm embrace.

"You're here!" Cheryl chirped happily. "How was your flight?"

Julie grunted. "Let's just say the color in my knuckles should return by dinner. Where are my nephews? I come bearing belated Christmas presents."

"I told them not to bombard you right away. The room's all ready. You go freshen up."

"Perfect. If I'm not downstairs in an hour, I've passed out."

A hot shower eased the tension in Julie's weary body and countered the residual fuzziness in her head. She toweled her hair dry, slipped on a sleeveless Giorgio Armani, then headed back downstairs.

Cheryl bustled about the kitchen, skewering marinated chicken, green and red peppers, cherry tomatoes, mushrooms, and onions for the grill.

Julie snagged a tomato and popped it in her mouth. "Need any help?"

"I'm grand." Cheryl pointed a skewer at an empty chair. "Have some wine. Relax. You must be exhausted. Each time we make that flight, we're pure done in. Christmas before last, we struggled to keep our eyes open for days after we got home. When did you last sleep?"

Julie poured a glass of Chardonnay and sat at the kitchen table. "About twenty-two hours ago. I'm at the stage where I'm so tired, I can't sleep."

Cheryl shook her head in sympathetic solidarity and continued prepping dinner. Julie watched in silence. She had last seen Chris's family that same Christmas. They had rendezvoused in Bledlow for the holidays. It was the last time the men saw their father alive. "Where's that husband of yours, anyway? I thought he'd be here to greet me."

"I sent him to fire up the grill. How did the shoot go?"

"I'm glad it's over."

Julie relayed the details while Cheryl finished the kabobs. Cheryl grunted in astonishment or disgust at all the appropriate times. When the salad was ready to toss, she toweled off her hands, poured herself some wine, and joined her at the table. "Sounds worse than Barbados."

"And here I thought that would be the disaster all others had to measure up to. I'm exhausted."

Glass aloft, Cheryl waxed into her Scottish dialect to toast her friend. *"Here's tae us. Wha's like us? Damn few, and they're a'deid. Slange var."*

Julie touched her glass to Cheryl's and took a hefty gulp, then leaned back and closed her eyes.

Cheryl studied Julie's artfully made-up features, detecting the subtle bags beneath her chocolate eyes. She noted subtle wrinkles at the corners of her mouth. More confirmation she had made the right career choice. Had she continued down Julie's current path, she would have suffered similar strain. Motherhood had its own challenges, but its rewards out-measured any money or fame. "When did you say you last slept?"

"I got about three hours before I left for the airport yesterday." Julie refilled her glass, finishing off the bottle.

She patted her sister-in-law's forearm. "Sleep in tomorrow. Day after, we'll have a spa day."

Julie groaned with anticipation. "That's what I'm talkin' about. Mind if I call Chris? I don't want him to worry."

"Of course!" She retrieved the cordless phone and handed it over. "Should I step out?"

Julie wiggled her fingers at Cheryl to stay, then brought the phone to her ear. A moment later, she said, "I got the machine."

Cheryl glanced at the wall clock and subtracted three hours.

"It's me. I'm at Ben and Cheryl's. The flight was fine, but I'm beat. Call me when you get this message. Love you." She pressed the end call button, handed back the receiver, and sipped her wine. "I'm starving. The chicken smells fantastic."

"It's the marinade. I'll jot down the recipe."

Ben strode in from the porch and greeted Julie with a warm smile. "How's my favorite sister-in-law?"

She rose to accept a one-armed hug. "I'm this close to eating those kabobs raw."

"It shouldn't be much longer. I had to clean the grill."

Cheryl touched her husband's arm. "Fancy some wine, darling?"

Ben pressed his lips together in consideration. "That'd be lovely."

"Marvelous. Open us another bottle and pour yourself a glass, won't you?"

Chuckling at the easy trap he had fallen into, he procured a bottle from the rack and grabbed the corkscrew off the counter.

Julie placed her empty wineglass on the table. "I talked to Chris a few days ago."

Ben offered a disinterested, "Oh?" The cork freed itself from the neck of the bottle with a soft pop. "He get his nose fixed yet?"

Cheryl glared a warning at him, which he ignored.

Julie snorted. "He was just trying to get a rise out of you."

Ben topped off Julie and Cheryl's drinks, poured himself a glass, then set the bottle on the table. "I'll pay for it if he decides to." He picked up the heaping tray of kabobs with his right hand and carried his wine with his left as he elbowed his way out the French doors. "Tell the boys dinner'll be ready in a few minutes."

Cheryl gently squeezed Julie's forearm. "Pay him no mind."

Julie lifted a slender shoulder. "It's fine. Sometimes, I feel like punching Chris myself."

"When he saw Chris at the funeral with that enormous bandage and black eyes, he felt terrible. While at Mum and Dad's, I think he still pictured Chris all bandaged."

"He provoked Ben the entire time. His nose healed fine. You wouldn't even notice if you didn't know it had been broken. Chris likes to be an ass."

Cheryl stood and untied her apron. "I'll call the boys and have them bring out the salad. Let's move outside, shall we? It's a lovely evening."

Hurricane Harbor lay not a hundred yards beyond the Olympic pool at the end of the large cement patio. Gentle waves sloshed against their boat dock in steady, calming susurruses. An evening breeze whispered about them with humid, salty breath. The setting sun transformed the bay into a blanket of sparkling saffron crystals. Julie imagined what LA might look like right now with its congested valleys and murky sky. She savored her tropical getaway as she filled her lungs to capacity.

The boys arrived, carrying plates and a heaping salad bowl. Derek and Kyle had shot up in the past year. Fifteen now, Derek had grown a good four inches taller and had started filling out. He favored his father in build and looks, save the blue eyes and a fading splash of freckles across his nose. He had greeted Julie on her way upstairs to settle in and enthusiastically pointed out two or three wispy hairs that had sprouted on his chin.

Kyle's more delicate features mirrored his mother's. His willowy thirteen-year-old frame was more grace than athleticism. He had kind green eyes and wore a near-constant grin, as if perpetually the recipient of some inside joke. Julie noted his cracking voice. Where Derek now directed his energies into girls, his band, and an obsession with obtaining his driver's license, Kyle remained focused on boating, scale models, computers, and astronomy.

They thanked Julie for their gifts and asked about Paris as Ben tossed and served the salad. Julie chatted with them about the Louvre, the Eiffel Tower, the Seine, the Arch de Triumph, Notre Dame, and other notable landmarks. She wolfed down her food, barely chewing as everyone chatted over dinner. Ben had grilled the kabobs to perfection.

The telephone rang, sending Derek upright with a cry of, "I'll get it!"

Cheryl cut eyes at her husband. "Right on time."

Ben called at his son's retreating back, "Tell Summer you can't talk long. We have company. And if another call comes in, answer it."

"*Okay*, Dad!"

Cheryl leaned toward Julie, the back of her hand at her lips. "Derek has a girlfriend."

Julie rinsed down a mouthful of chicken with a gulp of wine and grinned. "Oh?"

"She is not!" Derek barked before pulling the sliding glass door shut behind him.

"Summer Reece," Cheryl continued. "She's a cheerleader."

"Oh *my*!"

"He's quite smitten, I'm afraid. And he's been driving us mad with his learning permit. He can't wait to drive her to the movies, I think."

"Do you like her?"

Ben interjected, "Oh, yes. She's a sweet girl."

Cheryl nodded. "She is. Her family lives here in the village. We know them from church. She's a pretty lass, too."

Julie raised her chin at Kyle. "How about you, Casanova? Romancing anyone?"

Kyle scrunched his nose and made a face. "No way!"

The adults laughed and Ben mussed his youngest boy's hair. "Son, start taking these dishes into the kitchen and tell your brother to get off the phone and help."

Kyle stacked up several plates and scampered toward the house.

Julie watched him disappear inside. "Your boys are so handsome. And so well-behaved."

Cheryl and Ben beamed the way parents do. "Have you and Chris talked about kids yet?"

She adjusted herself in her seat, rattling her head. "Maybe in a few years."

Ben scooted back his chair, laced his fingers behind his head, and stretched out his long legs. He stared past the pool and out over the darkening Bay. "One thing I can say about Chris. He loves our boys. And he always doted on..." His eyes darted to the bare bolts rusting at the end of his pool where his diving board had been. "He always doted on Chase."

Julie dabbed the corners of her mouth with her napkin. "I never met him."

In the ensuing silence, Derek and Kyle returned for the last of the dishes.

"He was a good lad, like his father," Ben said. "Excuse me. I'll be right back." He rose and went inside, leaving the women alone.

Cheryl softened at her husband's retreating form. They listened to the waves slapping the dock. "Chris still blames himself about wee Chase."

Julie finished her wine. She fixed her jaw and stared off into the middle distance. "Yeah, well, my husband lives with a lot of ghosts."

When Ben reemerged, he topped off everyone's glasses with a fresh bottle before sitting down. "I sent the boys up."

Julie took a mouthful, rolling the wine on her tongue, unsure what to say.

He swirled the contents of his glass. "So, how's he really doing? I read he signed with Minor."

"Chris is Chris. You know."

Cheryl frowned at her. "What's the matter, pet?"

A rebellious tear stole down Julie's cheek, which she promptly—and angrily—swiped away. "The same thing that's always the matter. The same thing that's been the matter since before I married him."

Not again. Ben leaned back in his chair and crossed his ankles under the table.

"Like I said, Chris lives with a lot of ghosts. One in particular. And we all know her name. She crowds me out of my own house. And she's got plenty of help. The day I left for Paris, Elliot called Chris. I'm sure Marci was behind it. It was the day that stupid story was in the papers. The second anniversary of the ghost's death and all. A *séance* nonetheless!"

Cheryl scooted her chair closer and rested her hand on Julie's shoulder.

She sniffed, then shook her head. Her sadness transformed into stark, cold anger. "He left right after the phone call. I haven't seen him since. He didn't come back to take me to the airport. Not that I expected him to."

Cheryl clutched her chest, her fine manicured nails splayed in disbelief.

Ben dared to interject. "Marci and Chris have known each other a while. Maybe he needed someone to talk to."

Cheryl whipped her head around. "Did he talk to *you*?"

He lowered his head and returned his attention to his wineglass.

Julie continued, bolder now. "He didn't go to Elliot's—certainly not to see Marci. There's no love lost there. Besides, I know *exactly* where he went."

"You...you don't think he's having an affair?" Cheryl asked.

"I know he isn't. At least not with a living, breathing woman."

Slack-jawed, Ben leaned forward, refilled his glass, and took a hefty gulp.

Julie looked past her in-laws, her gazed fixed and far away. "If Marci hadn't interfered when they buried her..."

He shifted uncomfortably in his seat, trying to maintain his usually calm demeanor. His wife and sister-in-law outnumbered him. Neither had a good word for Farin—even in death. But Marci did not deserve Julie's criticism. "Farin's burial arrangements were Jameson Lockhardt's idea, Jules."

"Well, whoever it was." Julie waved a dismissive hand in the air. She finished her wine, then snatched the bottle from the table. It sloshed with an inelegant glug into her glass as she filled it to the brim.

Ben and Cheryl exchanged concerned looks.

Cheryl stood. "Perhaps it's time for bed."

The closest thing either of them could come to labeling the next noise to escape Julie's twisted mouth was a snarl.

"I'm not tired yet." She took another drink, then stared bitterly at the cement patio.

"Okay." Brows arched, Cheryl eased back into her seat.

Ben had never seen Julie in such a state. It suited what he had long suspected was her more aggressive nature, but he found it unattractive. He strained to ignore her offhanded insults. He and Cheryl had worked through their similar disagreements. He accepted Cheryl's judgment of Farin as she accepted his defense of her.

When Julie's rant became impossible to ignore, he blurted out, "Nothing made sense at the time."

Cheryl shot her husband a side-eye.

He soldiered on, heedless of the private discussion he and his wife would doubtless have alone, upstairs. Of the fact that Julie had been there at the time, witnessing all that transpired. "We'd spent three days making Jordan's funeral arrangements. Dealing with the police. Trying to find answers. Avoiding the press. And as we left the cemetery, we learned of Farin's accident—from a *reporter*. So, there we were, faced with another funeral. Farin had no one. No one except Marci and us. We were her family."

Cheryl glanced down and examined her nails.

"And just so we're clear, Marci's family, too. So, when Lockhardt stepped up and offered to help, I was relieved. He did what we couldn't. It's the one decent thing the man ever did for this family."

Julie rolled her eyes. She set her wineglass on the table. "But isn't one burial enough, Ben? Even for *her*?"

He clenched his jaw, reminding himself Julie was family, too. "Farin would've wanted to be near Jordan and her father."

She flounced back into her chair. Bitter images of Jordan's funeral flooded her hazy mind. Fans crowding the cemetery gates. News crews.

Police ensuring unimpeded traffic flow. Security guards maintaining their privacy. And Chris beside her, bandaged and bruised, one eye swollen shut. He had spent the entire service glancing over his shoulder, waiting for *her*.

"And now, the ghost remains close enough for Chris to pine away forever." She tossed her head back to finish her glass, then frowned at the empty bottle.

Ben's tone flattened. "Take heart, Jules. There was hardly enough of her left to bury anywhere."

Julie scoffed. "You know what's laughable, right? After all this time, she's still the focus of every conversation this family has. Look at us! Look at *me*! And I'm the one who brought her up!"

He stood and adjusted the waistband of his jeans. "I have work to finish. I'll be up in a bit."

Cheryl extended her cheek to his lips. She watched him retreat to the studio, staring in his direction long after he disappeared.

Julie buried her spinning head in her hands. "I'm sorry."

"I don't know what to say, Jules. It's no secret I lost respect for Farin when she came between Jorie and Chris. But you know how much Ben loved her. I agree. If this family could have one conversation without bringing up these dreadful memories, we'd be a sight better for it."

Julie stared at Cheryl through a bleary, drunken haze. Daggers stabbed her heart with each reminder of the affair. Her jealousy defied reason. She had not even known Chris at the time. However, this fact brought her no comfort.

"I wouldn't have wished her dead," Cheryl continued. "No one should suffer such a tragic death. But I'm done in with the constant defense of her memory. We need to put it behind us once and for all. And you need to talk to Chris about it."

Julie looked at her, deadpan. Cheryl might as well have suggested she take up hang gliding.

"I'm serious." Cheryl stood and beckoned her into the house, hoping to convince her to sleep off the two bottles of wine she had consumed in the span of three hours. "It's time. You're a mess. From what you tell me, Chris is still a mess. So, talk to him. He's your husband, not hers. Save your marriage. Exorcise your ghost."

In the studio, Ben sat pensively behind his console. Not only did he have no work to finish, he was ahead of schedule. He had finished mixing his latest compositions yesterday. They were not due in New York until the end of the week. Moreover, he had finished labeling his archives.

Normally, the studio's empty stillness provided a perfect environment for composing. Tonight, it stifled him until he felt he might choke.

Ben regretted the distance between himself and his only living sibling. The chasm widened with every rare encounter. All the bad blood, the blame, the sorrow. How had they arrived at this dismal place? And why had he perpetuated that tension?

Until not so long ago, he had considered himself "the fair one." The one who remained neutral despite personal feelings. The one whose birthright included certain obligations to his brothers and their parents. Now, he existed beside them in a vast, dark maze, with no compass to guide them back into the light.

Ben had forgiven Chris's imperfections. Affair or no affair, he had lost a brother and sister-in-law, too. How ironic that Ben held at bay the only other person in his family who did not condemn Farin. To be sure, Chris had changed since their deaths. But not all changes were for the worse— even if his sullen animus had ruined their final holiday with their father.

The time had come to resolve years of resentment. Someone had to do it. Mulish Chris would never make the first move. It was not his style. But it was exactly Ben's style.

As for Julie, Ben did not regret his harsh words. Farin had not been such a bad kid. Lost? Yes. Frightened? Sure. Confused? Certainly. But she was not the ice that split the stone. Moreover, she had been Jordan's wife.

He pulled open his shallow console drawer, retrieved his address book, and leafed through its pages until he found the Lawrences' number.

It rang twice before Marci answered. When Ben identified himself, she greeted him warmly.

"I'm not calling at a bad time, am I?"

"Of course not! Elliot and I love hearing from you. How are Cheryl and the boys?"

"We're well. Derek's organized a band with some kids from school, and he's discovered cars and girls."

Marci gasped. "He's driving?"

"Learner's permit. Cheryl hasn't driven herself to the store in six months."

"I can't imagine how much they've grown. How's my favorite mariner?"

The memory made him smile. "Other than sounding like a frog, he's about the same. Sometimes it seems Cheryl's got the pre-empty-nest blues. Other times, it seems she'd like to pack up the lot and ship them off to college. How are you and Elliot getting on?"

"Good. I've been thinking about calling Cheryl for a while now, but then I get busy and forget. Elliot and I are starting a family."

"You're pregnant? Congratulations!"

"Not yet. But we're officially trying."

"I see. You'll have to keep us updated. Cheryl will be thrilled. She hasn't shopped for baby clothes in years."

Marci chortled into the line.

An awkwardness enveloped him from nowhere. He hated resurrecting the past. Would they ever do anything else?

"Go ahead," Marci prompted, as if she knew his next words before he did.

He exhaled into the receiver, his breath thick with remorse. "I, uh...I was wondering. Have you seen Chris?"

Abrupt silence replaced their lighthearted banter.

"No, I haven't."

If he closed his eyes, he could almost envision the bitter scowl on her face. "I didn't call to upset you. Julie arrived today and said something at dinner that made me curious. She said Elliot called Chris a few weeks ago and she hasn't seen him since."

"Are we worried?"

"Nothing like that. Julie's been out of the country on a shoot. I was just wondering if by chance he'd visited you and Elliot that night. I imagine you were pretty upset. We all were. That article in the paper..."

"It didn't help, for sure. Why won't they let her go?"

He paused. "What about you? How are you holding up?"

"Most days, I'm good. I have a nice life. Nice home. I love my husband. It's all so pretty and perfect. You know that life. You have it, too. But sometimes, I wonder. Why couldn't Farin ever settle into hers with Jordan?"

He stared at the soundproof paneling covering the far wall of the studio. "I know what you mean."

"You're the only one who gets it. I did talk to Chris that day. He was cold. Like he doesn't remember. Like he doesn't care."

"He cares."

Marci snorted. "I used to think so. I thought he felt something—not love, but something. After chasing her so long, you'd think it'd show. But there was nothing. *Nothing.* What a waste."

More than ever, Ben regretted bringing it up.

"He used her like he used all his other women, I suppose. But Farin was different. She was special. And she loved Jordan so much."

He listened as she unleashed her frustrations. It seemed to be the night for it. "I wish I could end this nightmare for all of us."

Marci sniffed, then cleared her throat. "Sorry. I'm venting. I usually only do this in Santa Barbara. I'm sure even Farin's tired of it by now. She never did agree with my opinion of Chris."

"Still visiting, then?"

"As often as I can. My parents still live there. I visit pretty regularly. I talk to Farin. The groundskeepers probably think I'm crazy."

"It's healthy, you know. Letting the grief out."

"The shrink I visited a few weeks ago said the same thing. Sorry you got caught in the undertow."

The conversation lingered a while, then Ben told Marci he needed to go. He promised to call again soon and wished her well. "One more thing," he added. "Next time you visit, give her my love."

"I'm driving up tomorrow," Marci whispered. "I'll tell her."

CHAPTER 7

THE SANTA BARBARA SKY DRAPED threateningly over the cemetery's tombstones and monuments. A fitful breeze blew in from the Pacific shore, tugging at the cypress and spruce like an impatient, attention-seeking toddler. Ominous thunderheads clustered near the frightened earth, gathering their resolve, silently announcing they would weep rivers before the noon hour.

An intermittent, howling moan rose like mist from a gravestone or statue. The hateful gust battered the marble and granite, as if the wind itself gave voice to those who could no longer speak. Bouquets of flowers in various stages of decay lay scattered about the tombs. Loving tributes to fallen loved ones. Weakened by the twisting gale, they sacrificed their petals to the air, tumbling from its force to skid the grounds amongst the lost souls.

Near the back of the property stood an upright, granite monument arched into three sections. Normally, such a headstone could hide in anonymity among similar constructions, unremarkable in every way. Below the overlarge inscription proclaiming the family name "O'Conner," its center portion bore the name Kelley David. Into the left arch was etched the name Bethany Ann. The name heralded by the living rock on its right side, daughter to this unlikely pair, had become a tourist attraction bare hours after the artisan had inscribed it. The name read Farin Shae.

No fans congregated in the cemetery today, taking snapshots, straddling the gravestone like a wooden fence, lighting candles, or defacing the marker by declaring their undying devotion to the resting pop princess in garish spray paint—spray paint the groundskeepers regularly, huffily, and expertly removed. Today, in the face of an imminent squall, the garden of stones lay undisturbed.

In the murky false twilight before the coming storm, a ghostly, solitary shadow fell across that carefully-tended name. Its long hair twisted and danced to a mournful tune played by the spiteful breeze, the form as still as the granite upon which it fell. Then, like mercury rising in glass, liquid, careful movements brought the shadow's owner closer.

A pair of hands reached out and, with incongruous gentleness, lay a bouquet of lemon petal jonquils atop the monument. The flowers almost immediately surrendered to the will of the tormented wind, but strong fingers caressed its blossoms, tenderly holding them in place. The left hand, bearing a thick, expensive wedding band, held the offering in place. The right stroked the name with trembling fingers. A grievous sigh burst from parched lips, then lost itself in the capricious bluster.

He had not bothered to shave this morning before making his northward pilgrimage from LA. His fine clothing hung disheveled and wrinkled upon his frame. The double-breasted Gucci trench coat wrapped around his body flapped in the breeze about his calves. Heavy with darkened bags, his brown eyes squinted against the wind and fatigue. His complexion was sallow. His lips trembled occasionally, the inconstant gates holding back a flood of emotion.

"Happy birthday—well, a day early." The futility of his words clamped down on him even as his teeth bit into the inside of his cheek.

The answer to every unasked question he ever had lay beneath him in the cold earth. The whole of everything he had loved. Guilt and regret mocked him like possessed spirits chanting dissonant lullabies. Her memory haunted him without mercy.

Still-frame photos from his nightmare flashed before his mind's eye in panoramic Technicolor. The thief who had seduced his brother's true love. Every tribulation his family had faced since that time had his fingerprints on it. He alone had charted the course of their destruction.

He had tried everything to banish the image of Jordan's body on Bobby Lockhardt's living room floor. Bargaining with God. Relocation. Sleep deprivation. Booze. Grass. Pills. Nothing worked. Worse, he could not will himself to stop loving the woman whose name was carved into his heart deeper, and more permanently, than it was carved into the stone before him.

"I'm lost, you know. I never should have touched you in the first place, and all I want is to touch you one more time."

His ability to navigate his marriage, his family, and his career involved keeping up the lie that his dalliance with Farin had been just that. Nothing more. But if denying his feelings while she lived proved difficult, maintaining the lie after her death was exhausting.

And yet, Farin had only ever pushed him away. No matter how he tried. No matter what he did. No amount of sacrifice had moved her.

"You never loved me, Farin. You never even said you liked me very much."

As if the words spilling out catalyzed some inner volcano, Chris felt the fault lines of his soul tear and give beneath their weight.

The call from Miles Macy two days after his brother's murder tormented him to this very day. Macy had exchanged Farin's whereabouts for an exclusive interview. Chris had eagerly agreed. However, for reasons he would never understand, he did not try to see her. Lost for words, he had hovered outside her hotel room, then left a bouquet of jonquils at her door.

The following day, he had stood over his brother's grave, opposite Ben and Cheryl and his nephews. Opposite his parents. Opposite the newlywed Marci and Elliot. An island of sorrow, despite his wife and the male members of Mirage flanking him, he did not see the casket encasing his brother's remains. Rather, he saw the image of a blood-soaked corpse.

Julie had stood bravely beside him, no more than a distant distraction to him. His battered face throbbed with each heartbeat. Every few seconds, he had peered through swollen eyelids at the guarded gates, awaiting the arrival of the reporter and Farin. Neither had attended the internment.

Mid-ceremony, a limousine had arrived. Chris had reeled with overwhelming disappointment when not Farin, but Jameson, emerged. The old man strode up and stood beside Chris, donning a ridiculous-looking fedora that dipped below his left temple.

Then, as the grief-stricken mourners had egressed to their waiting vehicles, a silver Nissan 300ZX had raced into the parking lot, its tires screeching as its driver fishtailed to an abrupt stop. Macy had darted from the car. Panting with shock, he had relayed the news of Farin's death.

"We never said goodbye."

Days after they laid Jordan to rest, half of Farin's ashes were buried with him in Miami. Jameson had arranged to have the second half interred beside her parents in Santa Barbara. The same group of sorrowed souls stood over the freshly-laid sod of Jordan's grave to pay their respects, this time to his temporarily-widowed bride.

Amidst a sea of red and white roses, a single bouquet of yellow jonquils rested defiantly. His world had crumbled. To this day, it remained in ruins.

"I miss you. I just...I *miss* you."

When his legs could no longer support him, Chris collapsed atop the grave. Heaving sobs wracked his body. He maneuvered himself to lie face down above the ground where Farin would have lain had her remains not incinerated in fire. His nails dug into the moist ground, making agonized fists as the past twenty-five months hit him so hard, he thought he might lose his mind.

"Why can't I let you go?" he bellowed, defying the startled, horrified glares of an older couple passing by a few yards away, carrying a mixed bouquet of wildflowers to lay at a friend or relative's headstone.

Continuing this silent vigil would not change a thing, he told himself. If he did not start putting his career and marriage first, he would lose everything—every lifeline that kept him afloat in the sea of pain he found himself drifting in with no shore in sight.

Slowly, with grim determination, Chris stopped his tears and lifted his head. His face contorted in an eerie absence of the grief that had moments before burst from his being like a breached dam. Through bleary eyes, he stared at the symbols carved into the granite before him.

He had not openly mourned for Chase, or for Jordan. But he had mourned Farin every miserable second since her death. Now, instead of embarrassment at his open sadness, a light vacuum replaced the heavy emptiness within. He rubbed away the tears with the back of a dirty hand, then stood and shook his head, discarding the images crushing his tired mind as a dog shakes off water. A new sensation washed over him.

Farin had led him on. The first time they had made love, she had practically ripped her own clothes off, offering herself to him, sacrificing her body on his altar of passion. Only later came the recriminations, the harsh words, the distant disgusted glares, the pushing away.

She had known the depth of his feelings. He had told her. He had shown her time and again. Who had found her and stayed with her when she miscarried in France? Not Jordan, and not anyone else. Far from sending him away, she had run to him when Jordan kicked her out. Had he turned his back on her? Never once. He had invested everything he had to see her through. Who had rushed her to the emergency room when she overdosed on booze and Valium? *He* had.

As powerfully as his sadness had overtaken him, this new feeling rushed in to fill the void of his banished grief. His face grew hot. His jaw locked so tightly, his teeth ground together on emptiness and bitter spit. Hot bile rose in the back of his throat. His pulse raged through him as his fists clenched the sod he had ripped from the grave to mushy pulp.

"I do hate you, you know!" he hissed at the headstone through grit teeth. He opened his fists, allowing the ruined earth to fall at his feet. "I did everything for you! Everything! Always the little girl fantasy. Always the damsel in distress. Until you needed what Jordan couldn't give you. *Then* you'd have me around! Well, congratulations! You were the death of me! I died that day right along with you—like I died every time you left me. I hope you burn in Hell!"

"If anyone should be in Hell, Chris, it's you!" Marci exclaimed from barely a yard behind him. "Go home to your wife! You can't hurt Farin anymore!"

He spun around so quickly, he nearly tripped on his own feet. His coat flapped about him like a gown. Hot anger shot from his eyes. He snarled an angry, near-automatic, "Oh, what are you doing here?"

"*Me*? I could ask you the same thing, you weasel!"

A gust of wind skidded the bouquet of jonquils to the edge of the gravestone. Chris caught it before it fell. Gently, he relocated them to the base of the marker.

Marci's eyes narrowed at the gesture. When she parked her car, she had seen a black Porsche nearby but had thought nothing of it. Then, as she made her way closer, she had recognized the telltale bouquet atop the marker. Had she not heard his tone as she approached the site, she might have believed he had come to pay his respects. For a moment, she had hoped Ben was right.

"You never knew Kelley or Beth, and I know for certain you never cared about Farin. So why are you here?"

He stood immobile before the only living creature whose presence shook him to his core. Whenever he saw Marci, he saw Farin. Their similarity of spirit unnerved him.

"You made up your mind before you even met me," he muttered, turning back to the marker.

"What are you talking about?"

"I wasn't talking to you," he snapped as he studied the grave.

Marci twisted her face into a patronizing sneer. "Are you drunk? Is that it? You get bombed and bring your stupid yellow flowers—which she *always* hated, by the way—to taunt her when she can't get away from you anymore? You couldn't make her stay in life, so you stalk her in death?"

He spun around again, glaring at her. She matched him indignantly, planting her feet at the edge of the grave. Chris stood atop the plot between Marci and the marker.

"Why don't you go climb back into that overpriced Volkswagen of yours and leave us alone? You have no business here."

As their eyes deadlocked in their usual contest of wills, he realized she was right. He finally understood what he had to do. Everything inside him wanted to crawl into the ground and give up. But no. The time had come to release Farin from the dark caverns of his troubled soul.

He faced the stone marker and swallowed hard, tears brimming his eyes. All the sadness, all the anger, all the things left unsaid, and all the things that would never come to pass settled upon him as he resolved himself. He released them, accepted them, and in his deepest being, released her.

Regaining his composure, he knuckled away the hot tears and reset his thoughts. He would not let Marci best him as she had so many times in the past. "I was just leaving. I didn't expect to see you here." He strode purposefully towards his car, barking back over his shoulder, "You don't usually visit on Thursdays."

Marci's brows wrinkled as he trod past her. "Wait."

A heavy gust of wind caught Chris as he stopped in place. Immediately, she regretted her outburst. She figured—hoped—he would pretend he had not heard her. But he turned around. His hair whipped and curled in the breeze. Sad eyes appeared solemn, even glassy. She told herself it was the wind. The weasel did not cry. But in that moment, he looked oddly vulnerable.

She fought the urge to comfort what she suspected might be an outward display of remorse. His words had astonished her at the implication he knew when she did or did not visit the cemetery. To her knowledge, he had never stepped foot in this place.

"What do you want?" he growled, bundling himself into the folds of his dark, woolen coat.

Marci scowled, then softened. "I just need to know if you actually cared. The thing that was so hard for Farin all those years was the belief you really loved her. She didn't want to hurt either of you."

She stepped gingerly over Farin's grave and closer to Chris. He jutted his chin at her approach.

"You and Jordan were polar opposites. How is it she loved you both? She never said it out loud. Heaven knows I wouldn't have approved, but I knew. *Please* say you felt something for her. I need to know she wasn't just another one of your toys."

The honesty of her words was a wrecking ball in the pit of his stomach. Perhaps Marci was not the only one with questions. She said Farin had loved him. Her words moved him.

Almost.

He filled his lungs, then exhaled slowly as he once again gathered his resolve. Too much had been said and done between Chris and Marci to start anew. Even though she had married one of his best friends, their only real bond—if they had one at all—had been Farin. But Farin was gone. No way would he succumb to Marci's sentiment now. It did not matter anymore. Nothing mattered anymore.

He plunged his hands into his jacket pockets and clinched his jaw, determined to extinguish the flame and bury Farin O'Conner's memory once and for all. He regarded Marci with a wry grin across his parched lips. "Let's not pretend we have anything to say to each other. The only thing I feel for your friend here is—"

"What?" She inched closer and squared her footing, holding Chris's eyes with her own. "Those were some pretty strong words you were throwing out when I showed up. Why would you condemn her so? What could Farin have possibly done to you?"

He stooped a shoulder her way, as if to impart some deep secret. "She was a fine piece of ass." He winked, satisfied as her aspect turned decidedly horrified. "It's quite boring without her."

Marci slapped his cheek full force, then buried her face in her hands, weeping with anger, disgust, and grief.

Outwardly, no hint of emotion crossed his features. Chris remained composed despite the ballooning feeling in his throat and the stinging in his cheek. Inwardly, he knew he deserved far worse.

"Take heart, Marci. Farin may be gone, but she left you her temper."

He trudged to his vehicle without looking back. The high-pitched whine of the overpowered engine cut through the intermittent wind and, in a streak of black, he followed the winding cemetery road down the hill and disappeared through its stately gates.

Marci chastised herself as the screech of his tires receded. She had been a fool to think, even momentarily, he would ever change. The sting in her palm gave her great satisfaction. She had wanted to slap the smirk off that arrogant face for years.

She unwrapped the bouquet of white roses she had procured from the florist near her parent's house and arranged the perfect buds along the base of the gravestone. She would never forgive Chris for coming here to desecrate Farin's memory by hurling hateful words at her gravestone.

Without ceremony, she picked up the bouquet of jonquils, walked them to a nearby trash receptacle, and tossed them in. She recalled the first time Chris had sent the same type of flowers to their Glendale apartment. The first in a long line of wasted floral arrangements. She and Farin had deposited them into the garbage disposal, grating the buds into pulp with the assistance of a wooden spoon.

The memory lightened Marci's mood, though she made a mental note to stop by the cemetery office on her way out and ask them to please clear any such future floral arrangements from Farin O'Conner's grave immediately.

***

Death and Dismemberment Mark LSI Downfall
-- Chicago, IL, Chicago Chronicle (AP), Tuesday, March 1, 1994 by Miles Macy

Lockhardt Sound, Inc. published its fourth quarter results last week and the outlook is bleak. For the first time in the recording giant's history, LSI reported a loss. In this case, a significant loss. Bobby Lockhardt, Vice President, Public Relations for the company and only child of LSI president Jameson Lockhardt remarked, "Though we show a loss this quarter, it does not reflect a trend. This is a wacky business, always in transition. LSI was bound to come up in the red sooner or later. In our case, it just happened later. We've already put solid plans in place to recover by next quarter."

When asked specific questions about those plans or whether rumors of a bailout held any validity, Bobby Lockhardt declined to comment. Support for the company among industry pundits remains lukewarm. Sales have not improved since the aforementioned "solid plans" were announced.

In this reporter's opinion, this could mark the beginning of a trend that may well signal the beginning of the end for Lockhardt Sound. Two years ago, Lockhardt's company dominated the industry and the charts with such groups as the legendary Mirage and solo artists such as Megan Price, Jordan Grant, and Farin Grant. Today, Megan Price is all that remains of that legacy, though she has yet to recreate the record-breaking sales of her debut album.

Jordan Grant and wife Farin, both tragically killed within days of each other, are no longer here to bail the company out. They will never record or tour again. And what about Mirage? Their contract expired with LSI less than a month before Jordan Grant died and, for reasons unknown, the company opted not to renew. Resultant strife amongst the band members prevented them from signing as a group with another label.

Where are they now?

Former bassist and primary songwriter Elliot Lawrence lives in Los Angeles with his wife of two years. He composes musical scores for several notable Hollywood studios and states he has outgrown the rock'n'roll scene.

Faith Peterson, the outrageously-dressed and highly-outspoken former keyboardist, still resides in New York and has apparently beaten her addictions of some years ago. She announced last month she is working with top designers to produce her own clothing line. This line is greatly anticipated by the Greenwich Village crowd.

Drummer Lance Turner moved back to his native England. He is currently hitting the skins for a local band in London. Sometimes-girlfriend Ivy Spencer continues to insist Lance is the father of her year-old son. Rumor has it a paternity suit has been filed.

Former lead singer Todd Dalton resides in his private estate in County Kent and has announced no plans to come out of retirement. The reclusive Mr. Dalton also adamantly refuses all interview requests.

Perhaps most notably, Mirage's former lead guitarist and notorious playboy, Chris Grant, brother to the late Jordan Grant, now lives in Los Angeles with his wife, international supermodel Julie Swanson Grant. He recently signed a lucrative contract with Minor 6th Records to produce a solo album.

The aftermath of the deaths of Jordan Grant and wife Farin Grant, coupled with the dismemberment of Mirage—the staples that kept LSI at the top of the industry for over two decades—have dealt what may turn out to be a *coup de grâce* to the recording company. Unless Lockhardt Sound, Inc. can pull another miracle like Mirage out of their empty pockets, the company may become vulnerable to a hostile takeover. Time will tell whether LSI has any magic left.

***

Jameson Lockhardt met his old friend on the editorial page of the *New York Times*. His friend welcomed him. Embraced him. Made Jameson's eyes see the world in a sharper, if redder, perspective.

That friend, who had stood by him and with him through a lifetime of struggle, a failed marriage, and his son's medical problems, now told him to buck up and meet every challenge head-on, as he had all along. The time had come to reevaluate his present priorities and step up the calendar.

His old friend went by the name Anger.

Anger hovered beside him at the bank that morning while Jameson checked on his various accounts and loans. Anger reminded him to obtain a roll of quarters, which he promptly unrolled and let fall loose into his right trouser pocket. Anger ensured he did not forget to grab Tuesday's issue of the *New York Times* as he retreated to his waiting limousine. Anger declined the offer of coffee or a donut when they stopped to execute the next errand of the day.

The dirty delicatessen smelled of fresh bread, processed meat, and cheap coffee. The little cowbell affixed to the top of the door announced his entrance. Neither customers nor employees glanced up at his arrival, despite the fact he repeatedly slapped the tightly-rolled copy of the *Times* against his thigh, causing the pocketful of change to jingle unmelodically.

Jameson stalked to the alcove between the restrooms. With undisguised distaste, he wiped the payphone with his monogrammed silk handkerchief. He inserted the quarters, which lightened his pocket considerably, then dialed the international number from memory.

The usual clicks and whines commenced as the call rerouted around the globe. Finally, it connected. It rang twice before the receiver on the other end unhooked.

"I'm growing impatient."

"The problem will be gone within twenty-four hours."

"Good!" Jameson snarled.

He slammed the handset back down, then walked Anger back out into the New York street.

CHAPTER 8

T HE KILLER ENJOYED HIS CHOSEN vocation. It required skill, a keen eye, cat-like reflexes, good judgment, and great timing. Plus, it was never boring.

Having evaluated the situation, he decided this could not be a simple, if undetectable, car bomb. It could not even be a faked suicide or bathroom mishap. This target would be armed and on edge. The devil was in the details.

He had arranged for Detective Charles Stark to receive a call from his best informant around four o'clock that afternoon. Through other than legal channels, he had learned that Manuel Ortiz routinely tipped Stark off on the inner-city gang wars, racking up a pile of solved cases for the detective over the years. From there, things had fallen into place.

As it turned out, "Manny" was an agreeable, if nervous, accomplice when properly incentivized. A taste of bombita and an IRWIN C-clamp locked uncomfortably around the family jewels soon had him eager to assist.

From a battered payphone off 5th Avenue in Overtown, a semi-automatic leveled at his forehead, Manny made the call. As was his stated custom, he refused to tell Stark anything over the telephone. He insisted they meet at the Port of Miami docks at ten, and that he bring twice the usual payoff.

Even four feet from the receiver, the killer heard the detective's response.

"*Twice*? Who the hell do you think I am? David fucking Rockefeller?"

Manny's wide eyes darted sideways to the killer. When he cocked the pistol, Manny stuttered into the phone. "N-n-no, chico. This is the *shit*, I'm telling you. You, uh, you know that John Doe lieutenant you was lookin' fo'? That motherfucker who done shot that hoochie Missy May over in Liberty last month?"

"You know where he's at?"

"I might, I might."

"I don't pay twice for *might*, Manny. In fact, *might* don't pay shit."

"You want this, dawg. We got some new playas out here. Shit's escalatin'! We're talkin' white shoe droppin' from the *sky*, you feel me? Think you'd know about Little Bo if not for me?"

"You're confusing me with narcotics, Manny. I deal in bodies, not powder. Remember?"

The killer pushed the cold steel barrel harder against Manny's temple. Manny winced and shut his right eye. "Stark, man, hear me out. I-I got something bigger than Missy May, yo."

"What?"

"Nuh-uh. No way. We already talked too much shit on this phone. I gotta dip, man. These motherfuckers get hella salty seein' me chillin' too long. If I don't shoot out, you'll be investigatin' *my* case, you feel me? Catch you tonight. Bring the cheddar. You don't like what I got to say, we be renegotiatin'. Peace."

Manny hooked the handset onto the payphone base with a trembling hand. With sharp eyes, the killer spied the rundown neighborhood before lowering his weapon and pulling Manny out of the booth with his free hand. Now, to finalize their preparations.

At ten o'clock on the dot, Stark arrived on the pier but did not see his CI anywhere. He performed a cursory search of the grounds, then went to the utility shed at the end of the dock and tried the door. When it opened, he stepped into the darkness.

Manny stood against the far wall opposite him, shirtless, hands behind his back. One could have written an epic based purely on the informant's Central American mythologically-themed tattoos. The man's dark eyes stared at Stark in unabashed terror. By the time Stark noticed the transparent packing tape covering Manny's mouth, the bullet had already pierced his chest.

The killer temporarily holstered the smoking automatic, drew Stark's service revolver, fired two rounds into the informant's chest, then wiped it down and put it in the dead cop's hand. He then removed the tape from the kid's hands and mouth. Isopropyl alcohol applied with gauze cleaned off the adhesive from the kid's still-warm skin. The cleaned automatic soon found itself planted in the kid's hand. It fired one last round into the wall near the door.

He double-checked the evidence, assured all the angles aligned, and left half the cash the cop had brought for the deal. The other half he packed into his duffle, trading it out for the three kilos of uncut cocaine he planted on the kid.

Time to go.

***

The only thing Detective Alicia Alvarez hated more than Charles Stark was the idea of breaking in a new partner. In fact, she hated it so much, she had considered taking the captain up on his offer to transfer to Vice. But no. At twenty-eight, many of her colleagues—particularly the men— already decried her relatively short experience in law enforcement. She knew the deal. She represented a statistic. If she had a couple of bastard kids, she might be a lieutenant by now.

She had grown up in the slums of Miami proper. The last of seven children and the only daughter to Ruiz and Evangelina Alvarez, she had learned to take—and give—the hard hits. She had long since come to grips with her looks. Stop-traffic gorgeous. Whatever. But her bite was worse than her bark. She made sure of it.

People envied what they considered her advantages, but they did not understand. She had earned everything they thought they had given her.

As for Stark's fate, she was indifferent. Like many of their colleagues, he had been on the take for years. Her refusal to participate in such backhanded police work had isolated her. Some insisted she felt superior. Others feared she might narc. She made no secret that those who supplemented their incomes with what amounted to blood money sickened her, but kept what she knew to herself. And while she did not buy the scenario of a drug bust gone wrong, she figured Stark had spent plenty of time earning his fate.

His widow had yet to stop by and collect her husband's belongings. They sat in a white Bankers Box on the floor beside his emptied desk, which faced Alvarez's. Alicia routinely tripped over it amidst her comings and goings.

Today, she had passed on a lunch date with her aunt in favor of awaiting new hire Detective William Bridgeman. Not two days after Stark's death, her captain had hand-picked him to fill the vacated position.

Alvarez knew nothing about this Detective Bridgeman, but did not relish their upcoming introduction. Territorial? Perhaps. In any case, she intended to lay down the rules. If the veteran detective knew what was good for him, he would stay out of her way. She would not let him treat her like some rookie fresh out of the academy. Those days were over.

She reclined, cross-legged, at her beat-up desk, absently rolling a blue felt tip pen across her desk pad calendar with her left middle finger. Every few minutes, she glanced up at the wall clock. When Stark's former line rang, it did not shock her. His telephone had rung steadily over the past few days.

Uncrossing her legs, she straightened in her chair and snatched up her own receiver on the second ring. She stabbed the button for Stark's extension and announced with a sharp, harried growl, "Homicide."

"Detective Stark, please," came the male voice from the other line.

"Who's this?"

"Miles Macy with the *Chicago Chronicle*. Is he available?"

Her LCD read a Chicago number with the letters CHICAGO CHRON beneath it. Probably harmless.

"What can I do for you, Mr. Miles Macy with the *Chicago Chronicle*?" Her accent stepped hard on the "Ch" in "Chicago," making it sound like "Chick-AH-go." Despite years of speaking fluent English, she sometimes sounded like Ricky Ricardo on an *I Love Lucy* rerun.

"I can call back if he's out on a case or at lunch or something," the reporter offered.

"Detective Stark doesn't take lunch anymore, Mr. Miles Macy," she said pointedly. "I guess you could say he's out. Permanently. You're a reporter, eh? Don't you read the papers? Keep up with the news? Stark got shot last month. He's dead. Now, I'll ask you once more, *gringo*. What can I do for you?"

There came a pause. "Nice attitude, Detective. Why so hostile?"

She sighed with marked exaggeration, rolling her eyes. "Did I hurt your feelings, Mr. Miles Macy with the *Chicago Chronicle*? Tell me. What would a Second City reporter want with our notorious, and very deceased, Detective Stark all the way down here in sunny Miami?"

On the other end of the line, Miles Macy sat incredulous in his office, staring out his window at the bright but chilly midday as the female detective verbally frisked him. Stark had mentioned his partner a few times. Never in a flattering manner. Now, he understood why.

The shock of hearing his Miami police informant had taken a bullet made the hair on the back of his neck spike. "There was a motor vehicle accident yesterday on Miami Beach. It involved a member of the music band, the Core. There was a fatality. A pedestrian. I was wondering if charges have been filed against the driver yet. Will it be treated as vehicular homicide?"

"You a celebrity stalker, Mr. Miles Macy?"

"Look, Detective. You need the media. We need the cops. Right? It's nothing new to either of us. Now, if I can get a little information, we can both happily end this conversation."

Out of the corner of her eye, Alvarez spotted her captain. He strolled toward her, laughing as he conversed with the stranger he was escorting to Stark's desk.

The stranger carried himself with an air of friendly confidence as they approached, a Duchenne smile parting his lips to reveal straight, white teeth. In his arms he carried a lidless cardboard box containing, she suspected, a few personal belongings.

She glowered at the pair. It looked like her new partner had arrived.

Her first clear thought was that he needed a tan.

The holstered weapon at his side looked suspiciously like an old Colt 1911 .45, non-issue piece. That would have to go in favor of a .38, a .40, or a 9-millimeter standard issue. The single-breasted wool suit, though it hung well on his frame, would melt this guy like ice cream in about half an hour outside. He would lose the beard, too, if he was smart. That stuff might fly in the Motor City, but here in Miami, this guy was looking forward to a new wardrobe, a lot of sunscreen, and a shave.

"You still there?" came Miles Macy's exasperated query.

"Of course I'm still here!" Alvarez snapped into the receiver. She watched Detective Bridgeman set his box down on Stark's desk. He gave their captain a firm handshake. When the captain turned and looked at her expectantly, she lifted her index finger, then pointed to the phone. "This man you asked about. Yes, he's been charged. Talk to Detective Freeman at extension 2554. It's his case. Is that it?"

"Uh, one more thing, Detective. About Stark. What went down?"

"Detective Stark's death has been ruled a failed drug deal, Mr. Miles Macy," she said, an angry glint in her eyes as she decided how best to introduce herself to her new partner. Before slamming down the receiver, she looked at Captain Ward, then Detective Bridgeman. She pitched her voice so both men could hear. "That's right. A dirty cop. We don't take kindly to dirty cops around here."

The line disconnected with an abrupt *BANG*, leaving Miles with an eerie feeling. He knew Stark. A bad cop? Yes. On the take? Most definitely. A drug dealer? No way.

Though perhaps off base, instinct prompted him to make one more call to Miami. This time to Sandra, a one-time lover and current AT&T employee. He requested all the phone records made to and from Detective Charles Stark in the last six months.

***

"Honestly, Ross, is it even worth it? We're leaving three months late and only get one month for vacation. Isn't the point to get out of Greenwood Lake and avoid New York winters? It's already May!"

The Alexanders had purchased their Palm Springs winter home twenty years ago, and had since considered it one of their better investments. They looked forward to their annual sojourn to California, which provided a two-month escape from icy weather.

The small town of Greenwood Lake nestled off the highway northwest of New York City. The daily commute to and from Manhattan was often grueling, but was worth the sacrifice. Josephine had never cared for city life. The Alexanders had agreed early on that if they ever adopted, country living was a more conducive environment for raising children. Alas, it never happened.

Ross commiserated with his bride as he loaded their luggage into the trunk. "It's my fault. I didn't expect him to make the announcement so soon. And now—"

"—and now you're back to working nights, weekends, and holidays. Will it ever end?"

If he had anything to say about it, yes. Tying up a quarter century's worth of loose ends was no mean feat, but he was determined to see it through.

Josephine checked her face in her compact, then clicked it shut and tossed it into her purse before climbing in the passenger's seat. "You remembered the tickets, right?"

He patted his suit jacket. "Right here."

She nestled into her seat, her gloved hands clutching the handbag on her lap. "And no discussing business. You promised. Having only a month is bad enough. But not being able to celebrate our fortieth anniversary in California? You owe me."

He started the engine. "I do. And yes, no business talk for the next month."

This did not, however, prevent Ross from thinking about it.

Driving to the airport, he pondered the absurdity of Jameson's decision to act as a one-man A&R department, going out on the road to scout new acts. At baggage check, he changed his mind, reminding himself Jameson rarely failed when he set his mind to something. While Josephine catnapped on the plane, he contemplated LSI's potential fate should Bobby take the reins in a mere nineteen months. By the time they arrived at their Southern California oasis, he was confident he could keep his vow—and his head hurt.

Josephine spent the first week making their spacious wrap-around home livable. Each year, she performed the same ritual. She selected and purchased new linens. She paid in advance for the pool man, the grocer, the maid, laundry service, and carpet cleaners. Their year-round landscaper procured flowers from the garden to brighten up the interior. By the time she finished, every room swam in California hibiscus, amaryllis, and fire lilies.

Their master bedroom had an exquisite view of the pool located squarely in the center of the courtyard. Josephine loved her morning swim. Ross loved watching her glide through the pristine water like a swan on a crystal blue lake. He loved the way she moved, the way she laughed, the way she wore her hair. Every smile, every breath Josephine breathed, reignited his love and adoration. He rarely referred to her as his "wife." For forty years, one month, and twenty-one days now, he had called Josephine his bride.

As Ross packed a black leather gym bag with a shaving kit and a change of clothes, he heard her dripping footsteps approach their bedroom's sliding glass door. She stepped inside and headed for the master bath, humming and toweling her hair. Her relaxed smile caught his attention as she disappeared to engage the shower.

Fit and healthy as any forty-year-old woman, she appeared younger than her fifty-nine years. She took care of herself physically, emotionally, and spiritually. A natural beauty, Ross reveled in the envious looks he received from colleagues when they attended various functions, though it annoyed him when strangers periodically referred to him as her father.

She returned wearing a white terry robe and kissed him good morning. Glancing at his bag, she said, "We just got here. Are we leaving already?"

"I have an appointment in Los Angeles at one."

The light in her eyes dimmed. "Appointment?"

"Mm-hmm."

"In LA?"

He nodded, clearing his throat.

Her smile faded, then disappeared altogether. She recognized the somber expression she had hoped he had left in New York. He did not have to say another word. She knew.

The one problem the Alexanders had experienced since exchanging their vows was Ross's relationship with Jameson Lockhardt. The midnight meetings and secret dealings of two years ago had nearly forced her hand.

She had not left him then, but she had packed a bag—not unlike the one Ross packed this very moment. It remained hidden away in the hall closet, awaiting the moment she could take no more. Of course, this fact would come as a complete surprise to her husband.

Fortunately, around the time Farin and Jordan passed—may God rest their souls—a sort of peace settled upon Jameson and slowly filtered down through the ranks of LSI. It had happened just in time to save their marriage.

Now, without comment, Josephine watched Ross stuff silk boxers and a pair of slacks into his bag. His shaky hands did not escape her notice. She exercised patience until he looked up, then folded her arms and waited for an explanation.

"I'm meeting Samantha Drake. Chris Grant made some tapes before Mirage left LSI. She wants them."

"Samantha!" Her smile and lilting laughter shooed away the tension in his shoulders. She sat on the edge of the bed and removed his slacks from the bag, refolded them to minimize wrinkles, then replaced them. "I haven't seen her in ages. Shall I accompany you?"

"No! I...I-I mean, it's just some loose ends I have to tie up. It shouldn't take long. I'm packing a bag just in case."

Behind his bride's hazel eyes lay more questions than he felt comfortable answering—especially with the raised left eyebrow. He hated the situation in which he found himself. He hated it more with every passing day. "Really, darling, you'd be bored stiff."

"Oh, I don't know." She untied her robe, twirling one end of the sash playfully in her hand as the folds parted to either side. "It's been a while since I had the chance to do some real shopping. Can't you hear the echoes through the valley, Ross? Rodeo Drive is calling me."

It took him no time to give in. Whatever fear had stowed away in his bag, it did not belong in California. Samantha posed no threat. The only threat posed to him sat thousands of miles from their Old Las Palmas neighborhood. Even then, Jameson knew of his meeting and had voiced no opposition.

With a lecherous grin, he moved to his wife, slipped his arms inside her robe, and pulled her perfect body close. "You win, as usual."

***

Samantha arrived at O'Hearnes Pub almost an hour early. Unfamiliar with Redondo Beach, she wanted to give herself ample time to find the hole-in-the-wall Ross had suggested. Mostly, she wanted to avoid overshooting the location and winding up in Long Beach. Years as a resident of the greater Los Angeles area had not improved her navigational prowess, a fact Ethan Maxwell often teased her about.

She took the 405 South and wove through the heavy flow of traffic, then exited onto Artesia and headed west towards Aviation Boulevard. Once on Aviation, she spotted the 7-Eleven and signaled. The little pub nestled unobtrusively after the convenience store. She pulled into the parking lot and breathed a sigh of relief. Without the instructions Ross had emailed her last night, she would have never found the place.

A paint-oxidized Toyota Starlet and an old Jeep Scrambler were the only other cars in the compact parking lot. Neither looked like something Ross would drive. She checked her appearance in the vanity mirror, applied her red lipstick, pressed her lips together, then flipped the visor shut. Stepping out of her BMW, she scanned her surroundings just to be safe. Not exactly her type of neighborhood.

"Don't be such a snob, Sam," she admonished herself aloud. She retrieved her purse and briefcase, shut the door, activated the alarm, and stepped into O'Hearnes via the side entrance.

Thick, stale smoke assaulted her as the door closed behind her. She coughed and waved her hand in front of her, as if such an act would chase away the carcinogens and gift her with fresh air. To the left of the hazy room stood a long black bar. To the right, a worn regulation-size pool table. A pool stick rack separated the men's and women's restrooms. Tacked beside the rack was an enormous poster of Julie Swanson—bikini-clad and prenuptial—holding a bottle of imported premium beer. A multicolored jukebox crouched against the far wall.

Despite the near-empty parking lot, patrons peppered the establishment. Some sat at the bar, keeping to themselves as they nursed drinks and produced more smoke. Others hunkered among a series of six booths against the far wall. Samantha wondered if Ross had pulled some elaborate joke on her.

She approached one of the black vinyl barstools, leaned her briefcase against its chrome base, and placed her handbag on the counter. Her slim-cut pencil skirt impeded her ability to ease onto the stool, so she backed into it and lifted herself up with the heels of her hands.

She heard a snigger, then, "You just know a man decided the appropriate height for the average bar, am I right?"

A surreptitious side-glance identified the voice as the bartender.

"Most times, I don't have that problem. Even on the odd occasion I wear a skirt like yours, I've got a few inches on you. More in stilettos."

The female bartender stood nearly six feet tall, with impressively long blonde hair. She glided over to Samantha, a slow sway to her hips as she dried a beer glass with a damp rag. When she spoke, the cigarette between her lips bobbed up and down. "What can I do ya for?"

Samantha smoothed her skirt, then reached for her bag. "A Rob Roy, thanks."

Why Ross had refused to meet at her office, she did not know. If his intent was to avoid suspicion, she could have suggested any number of alternatives. Two business executives in a place like this would stick out like the summer sun during Barrow, Alaska's winter solstice. Fleetingly, she wondered if Jameson was playing his old games.

The possibility did not faze her. She kept a careful watch on industry standings. LSI was losing its foothold. When Ross called the night before to announce his sudden visit and asked to see her as soon as possible, she had sensed an air of urgency in his voice—an urgency only those people close to Jameson could possibly understand. Maybe he needed a job.

The bartender slid a small square napkin in front of her, then placed her drink on top. "Here you go. One Rob Roy. Should I start a tab?"

"I'd appreciate it. I'm meeting someone."

"You got it."

Samantha sipped her drink and tried to get comfortable. The place was a far cry from Spago's. She crossed her legs, squared her shoulders, and jutted her chin to the leering advances of the gentleman three stools down.

"Oh, good. You're early, too." Ross approached her from behind. Without so much as a proper greeting, he waved her toward a booth and muttered his order to the bartender. He looked over his shoulder at Sam. "Did you order lunch?"

"This place serves food?" She collected her bag and briefcase, tossed them into their booth, then embraced him before slipping into her seat.

"I'll pass."

Ross's flicker of a troubled smile reminded Samantha how long it had been since they had seen each other. Although always in impressive shape, he looked frazzled, beaten down, and—sadly enough—as if he had finally surrendered. It disturbed her to think, had she stayed with LSI, she might look the same in twenty-five years. She had not returned to New York, even to visit, since joining Minor 6th.

They chitchatted through two rounds of drinks, discussing their respective home lives, their families, the hot tickets on the A/C charts, and the enormous changes in the industry.

"I wish you'd brought Josephine with you. I'd love to see her."

Ross's eyes bulged at the suggestion. He did not reply. He did not need to.

Knowing how protective Ross was with his wife, Sam wondered again if this meeting might be some sort of trap. Then, as quickly as it seized her, that familiar foreboding released its grip.

It was nothing, she told herself. An unfortunate side effect of working for LSI was its effect on its employees' nervous systems—an agitated state from which she herself had suffered long after leaving.

Poor Ross. After such a long tenure, he might never recover.

He toasted his straight scotch to her second Rob Roy. "You've done well for yourself. You always were meant for greatness. I'm proud of you, Sam."

She smoothed straight the dampened cocktail napkin with her thumb and index finger before replacing her glass. "You were always kind to me. If it hadn't been for you, I can't say I'd have stayed as long as I did. I guess I left without thanking you. That was wrong of me. I hope you understand."

He waved off the gratitude. "Honestly, I feel terrible about the way things ended. I never set out to jockey myself into my current position. It's good you moved on when you did. You could have never gone so far at LSI. The old so-and-so has a firm grip, you know?"

Her eyes settled on the large bulge protruding from Ross's pinstriped suit jacket, which lay neatly folded atop their table. She suspected its contents had resulted in today's overdue meeting.

He appeared uneasy as he took longer sips of his drink, glancing around the bar every few seconds. Perspiration dotted his forehead.

Sam reached across the table and touched his forearm. "Are you okay?"

He procured a monogrammed handkerchief from his trouser pocket and dabbed his brow. "It's the heat. We're usually down here so much earlier in the year. Josephine's reminded me a dozen times. She'd sure give me a big 'told you so' if she could see me now, huh?"

Samantha's presence unnerved him more than he had anticipated. At one time, he had thought of her as a sort of surrogate daughter, though he had never told her. Professional protocol had hindered any true friendship, but he and Josephine had always wished they could have gotten to know her better. She was the only person who could understand his impossible position. He worried that, if he did not pull himself together soon, years of hidden truths would come crashing down around him like an unforeseen rockslide.

"You really should try the pastrami. I, uh...I try to come in here at least once when I'm out this way." He visually swept the room, inspecting the small crowd of blue-collar types who had stopped in for a liquid lunch. With a nervous chuckle, he added, "It's one of the few places I go without our friend knowing my exact location. If I were paranoid, I'd swear he has me followed."

Samantha's lips parted. She followed his line of sight. "Jameson knows you're here, right? You said he agreed to give me the tapes—"

"Of course." Ross waved her off again, stuffed his handkerchief back in his pocket, then reached over to retrieve the bulky packet. He handed it to her with a steadied hand. "I'm sorry this took so long getting to you. I hope it hasn't slowed things down for Chris."

She accepted the envelope, but examined its contents hesitantly, as if half-expecting to find it booby-trapped. "I'm afraid he had to start without them. I didn't want him out of the public eye any longer than necessary. These'll have to wait for his next project."

"How's he doing? I've heard plenty of buzz. Everyone's anticipating the new record. Is he well?"

She set the package aside. "Is he well? Are you sure you're all right? You never liked Chris."

"I never said I didn't like him."

"You didn't have to. Everyone knew."

He encircled the lowball glass with both hands, sliding his thumbs along its rim. "It's complicated."

"What isn't?"

He snorted absently and jiggled his glass. "So, is he? Well, I mean."

"Most of the time. You know Chris. He has this brooding dark side—always one for the dramatics. Like he's driven by more than just melodies and lyrics. But you should hear some of his stuff. He's no Dylan, but you'd have never pegged him as such a poet."

The bartender delivered Ross's sandwich. He nodded his gratitude, then spread a stiff paper napkin across his lap. "I suppose it makes sense, losing Jordan and all." He glanced down at his meal. It looked suddenly unappetizing. "And of course, there was Farin." With a scrunch of his face, he pushed his plate away. He drained his scotch, then held the empty glass aloft until the bartender lifted her chin in acknowledgement.

Samantha leaned in, head low. "What was the deal there? I always wanted to ask."

Ross tucked his chin. "Have you asked Chris?"

"I'm asking you. Anyway, I always had a feeling Jameson's little angel wasn't all she was cracked up to be. I figure there had to be an affair. But with which one—or was it both?"

"Nothing like that, I assure you. Not with Jameson, anyway." He evaded her inquisitive stare, frowned at his sandwich, then picked up and offered her half. "You really should try the pastrami. Aren't you hungry?"

She made a face and rattled her head. "I'll pass."

Truth speared his insides like a spitted pig. He dared not. It could cost him his life—or something simpler, like prison. Neither option was appealing. He dropped the sandwich on its plate, retrieved his handkerchief, and dabbed at his forehead.

In a single movement, Samantha slid out of the booth and crouched beside him. "What is it, Ross? You look like you just saw a ghost."

He studied her concerned expression. If anyone would understand, she would. If anyone could be trusted, she could. Years of lies and cover-ups assaulted him, as if never before that moment had he felt his own conscience. His psyche shredded. All at once, he was desperate for a confessor.

"I wish I could tell you, Sam. I wish I could tell someone. But I can't. It's my life I'm gambling with."

Her eyes widened with concern. "This is serious."

He cupped her upper arm to support her as she stood, then motioned her back to her seat, twisting his neck back and forth as he pulled at the knot of his tie.

Samantha surveyed the smoky room. "It's Jameson, isn't it? Are we in danger here?"

He slid out of the booth, finished his scotch, then reached into his back pocket for his wallet. "I should go. I have to pick up Josephine in front of Gucci's by four."

She checked her watch. "It's not even two thirty. Please sit down. If this is as bad as I suspect, you need to tell someone. And if it's about something illegal involving the old man, you'd do better to talk and save yourself."

The room closed in on him. The scotch had warmed his stomach and numbed his face. His racing heart pounded in his ears. The life-sized poster of Julie Swanson tacked to the back wall smiled at him. As if someone had hit the bar's volume button, voices sounded louder—the laughter, the flirting, the tall tales. He resigned himself to the knowledge he should not drive. Grudgingly, he sat back down and laid his hands flat on the table, palms down.

In all the years they had worked together, Samantha had not betrayed the smallest of confidences. He calculated the risk-to-reward ratio of unburdening his soul against potential consequences. Dates, times, places, and faces hurtled through his mind. Even if he decided to, where should he start? How much should he say?

"If I—"

Eyes wide and worried, she urged him to continue.

The only question that mattered was simple: did he trust her? A large part of him knew he could. An even larger part knew he had no choice. "There's no unringing this bell, Sam."

"What is it, Ross? You're scaring me."

With that, he knew he would tell her everything.

CHAPTER 9

J OSEPHINE ALEXANDER DID NOT TAKE kindly to the announcement
that Jameson Lockhardt had demanded a conference call halfway
through their vacation. They had already delayed, then reduced, their
trip by weeks. Ross had promised no business dealings.

She stalked after him from the bedroom to the den as he prepared to
call in for the meeting. "Why not tell him no? He has no right to do this.
This is supposed to be our sanctuary *away* from that man."

Ross rummaged through his files. As he extracted the few folders he
had smuggled into his luggage, his shoulders slumped with guilt.

Josephine's eyes enlarged, then slit, as she confronted him in open-
mouthed betrayal. "You brought *files*?"

"In less than two years, it'll all be over. We can spend entire winters
here. We can move here permanently if you like. I'll be retired. LSI will be
no more than a distant memory." He checked his watch. T-minus five
minutes. "It could be worse. He could've insisted I fly back to attend the
meeting in person."

She planted herself in the doorway, arms crossed, still wearing her
cream-colored satin negligee. "If he'd done that, it'd be worse than you can
imagine."

Ross took in his wife's beauty. Her lips pouted tightly in a disapproving
frown, her brows low above her gray eyes and luscious lashes.
Breathtaking, even in anger.

"What could be so important that it can't wait until we get back? Can
you at least tell me that much?"

He settled behind his desk, threading his fingers atop the folders he
had laid carefully before him. "He's concerned LSI will be bankrupt before
he steps down. We've massaged numbers and spun for the shareholders
for some time now."

With a downward tilt to the corners of her mouth, she shook her head
and turned to leave. "I refuse to believe it's as bad as all that. In any case,
please don't be long. You promised we'd go into town and see a matinee."

He watched her disappear down the hallway, then picked up the receiver and dialed the office. Ever since his lunch with Sam, he had found himself unburdened and slightly paranoid. Might this urgent, mandatory meeting have anything to do with his visit to Redondo Beach a couple of weeks ago?

Only eighteen months left to worry about Lockhardt Sound. Soon, he would announce his own retirement plans and get out as cleanly as possible.

"Lockhardt Sound. This is Stacy. May I help you?"

"Good morning, Nancy. Jameson's expecting my call. Is he ready?"

"Hello, Mr. Alexander," Stacy Goldman chirped happily. In her most considerate tone, she reminded him—as she often did—that her name was Stacy. Nancy Chambers had left Jameson's employ some time ago.

"Forgive me, Stacy," he flustered.

"It's no problem, sir. Transferring now."

Almost immediately, a fumbled bustling filled the line. Someone had placed him on speakerphone. "Jameson," he greeted awkwardly. "Who all's there?"

"Morning, Ross. Dad wanted me to sit in. How are things out on the Left Coast?"

His jaw tightened, then relaxed. "Fine, Bobby. How are you?"

"I'm good, thanks. Sorry to have you call in on your vacation."

"Not a problem," he lied, rising from his desk to shut his den door. He nearly dropped the handset as the cord stretched the distance. "I hope this won't take too long, though. I confess, I have plans today."

"We have a full agenda," Jameson barked over the line. "Let's get to it, shall we? We'll make it as brief as possible. I know how busy you are relaxing. First order of business: I may put off my retirement for another year."

Ross dropped his head onto his hand and kneaded his forehead, dreading the speech he would have to give his bride.

"LSI must be totally solvent again before I step down. The good news is, you'll have longer to get my affairs in order. You'll need to work closely with Bobby during this transition period. I want him fully briefed."

"Got it." He scribbled some notes on the legal pad he had extracted from his top left-hand drawer. He wondered how much thought Jameson had given to handing over the company to his son. Though seemingly recovered, might Bobby once again ditch the anti-psychotic medication maintaining him? Placing a man in his condition at the head of a multimillion-dollar corporation presented incalculable risk. "I'd recommend you hold off announcing any plans to push back the date. It could result in unintended consequences. Creditors may lose confidence."

"And it would make for bad press, Dad. We can pull it all together in less than two years. Right, Ross? We can do it."

He adjusted himself in his seat. "With your father on the road and you following my lead, I foresee a smooth transition."

Silence followed. "Very well. We'll give it another year and see what happens. Next order of business. How was your meeting with Ms. Drake? Did you give her the tapes as you'd planned?"

His stomach churned. "She was quite pleased. She sends her regards."

Jameson huffed doubtfully.

Bobby piped in. "*Sam*? Ross, you saw Sam? I haven't talked to her since before she left! How is she?"

"She seems well. You know, Jameson, I heard about Megan. Is she okay? She's down in LA now, isn't she? Any idea why she canceled those last three dates in Europe?"

"She's exhausted, I suppose. She's been on tour for nearly two years now. I spoke with her manager this morning before you called. She's on the mend and intends to get back into the studio in a month or so."

He scanned the contents of one of the manila files before him. "You know her contract's up in a few months, right? We should start negotiations."

"Good catch. We can't lose her, especially now. Which brings me to our next order of business. I want to get out on the road as soon as possible. I've had my feelers out and have put together a tentative schedule. Even with the potential extension of my retirement date, I can't wait any longer."

Ross hesitated to broach an unpleasant topic. Maybe Bobby's presence would mitigate a heated reaction. "Have we identified what capital you'll use to fund this expedition of yours? I've gone over our financials..."

"I have, actually. We'll talk details when you return. Time to unload some excess baggage, I think."

"I'm going with you on your trip, Dad," Bobby cut in.

"We'll discuss it later," Jameson said. "I told you, son. I need you here. As LSI's spokesman, I count on you to keep a positive spin on things."

Ross detected disappointment or frustration as Bobby pressed. "I can't keep up this glass half-full line. Who do we think we're kidding? Lately, all

I've told the press is a whole lot of nothing. We know it. *They* know it. You started LSI with a little elbow grease and a lot of determination. I intend to maintain your legacy. We need things to go as scheduled, including your retirement. I can't sit around at my desk like a school kid, with Ross my teacher—no offense, Ross."

"None taken," he assured.

"I can learn a whole lot more out there with you than I can from behind these four walls."

Jameson cleared his throat. "As I said, we'll discuss it later."

Ross felt almost sorry for Bobby. So naïve, so wet behind the ears. How could Jameson turn this boy of thirty-seven into a full-fledged president in eighteen years, let alone eighteen months?

The conference call ended shortly after the trio finished planning their next move. As he hung up, Ross wondered how much LSI would suffer under the side effects of the medication Bobby injected into his system every day. Would his memory ever return? Might he someday remember shooting Jordan Grant through the temple while his wife watched, helpless to change the tragic course her own life took as a result of that moment?

Something told him no matter how Bobby tried, he would not spend one day as President and CEO of Lockhardt Sound, Inc.

***

The off-season approached. Any day now, the tropics would welcome the first of their annual summer storms. Natives had not yet seen clouds on the horizon, but they could smell the changes on the wind. Temperatures rose. Days grew longer. Hotels booked fewer rooms. Many hospitality employees readied themselves to venture by boat to America where they hoped to find work for the next six months. And so it went every year, from June through November.

St. John locals complained of a drought. They welcomed summer rain. But neither Chris nor Julie noticed a water shortage. The sun caressed the lush, green foliage as they basked in its perfect climate. The humid air was warm but not stifling. A lovely island paradise, the idyllic backdrop for the debut video from *Aftermath*—the vehicle that would usher solo artist Chris Grant back onto the top of the charts.

Minor 6th eagerly anticipated the release. They had initiated a publicity campaign before Chris finished recording. Samantha had made good on her decision to use Julie on the CD jacket as well as the video. She had even hand-picked the video location. For the first time, Chris and Julie, man and wife, would work together.

Photographers, security, and a film crew booked every room at the most luxurious hotel on the island and secured a private beach for the shoot. Hype surrounding the project had reached a near-frenzy. Fans waited impatiently for the video's release.

They had chosen "Obsession" as *Aftermath*'s debut single, a haunting, intense ballad about a man who yearns for the one woman he can never make his own. Chris had written the song the day before he met Julie at a chateau in Geneva, Switzerland in May of '91.

Though few people would miss the song's true meaning, he did not care. He had constructed *Aftermath* as a sort of catharsis—a cleansing of the soul. He melded material that suited not only his past and present, but his future as well. The song represented a low point from which he could jump into a healthier, happier state.

He had steadily recovered since his final visit to Santa Barbara. He had stopped sending flowers to Farin's grave. Constant reminders that once flooded his existence had ebbed away. Even Samantha's choice of location did not unsettle him. St. John was just an island. If anything, Chris found it fitting. So what if an island bearing Farin's former last name served as the backdrop for the video of a song he had written for and about her? Coincidence? Who cared? With Julie beside him, it no longer mattered.

They checked into their villa Tuesday afternoon, building in a day of relaxation before Thursday's filming. The crew had arrived the Sunday before to prepare various shots. Security had cleared the area of onlookers and fans who might try to sneak on set. Everything checked out fine. Knowing Julie would need a day to recover from the flight over, Chris made arrangements to spend Wednesday sequestered in their room.

"How are you feeling?" he asked after her shower that evening. "Better?"

"Much." She removed the towel from her head and fluffed her straight hair with her fingers.

"I'm ordering room service. Think you'll be able to get anything down?"

"I'm still a little tipsy, but I'm starving."

He took her hand and led her onto their patio, where he had prepared the table. A glass of champagne from the bottle the hotel had left chilling in their suite awaited her. He handed her the flute.

With a coy smile, she toasted his glass. "I'm glad we're here together."

"There's nowhere I'd rather be." He sipped the bubbly libation, then drew her to him, threading his fingers through her damp hair. "You look beautiful."

She giggled. "I have no makeup on and I'm wrapped up in a cotton towel. I won't be beautiful until tomorrow."

He kissed her tenderly. "You're always beautiful. Besides, I like the wet look."

Julie sensed Chris's romantic intentions as he held her. Whatever had gotten into him in the last few months, she harbored no complaints. It was as if some mysterious switch had gone off in his head. From the time she had returned from Florida, Chris had behaved like an entirely different man. Attentive, loving, playful.

At first, his metamorphosis had left her wavering between suspicious doubt and cautious optimism. Had he experienced some epiphany while she worked in France and later visited his family? She had returned to LA prepared to confront his behavior as Cheryl had suggested—to exorcise her ghost. But no need. Had aliens abducted her husband and sent a replacement, or had Chris turned a corner? Either scenario worked for her.

"Did we ever find out about the weather?" she asked as they cuddled on the patio. "I'd hate to be rained out."

"Bother the weather." He caressed her back. "Let us be rained out. We'll stay here together and ride out the storm."

She released a deep breath. "And what would we do for days on end if we were stuck here in a storm?"

Chris kissed Julie with all the passion he had lacked throughout the majority of their married life. "Shall we go inside?"

She searched his eyes. Raw honesty replaced the carnal neediness that had permeated their early marriage. When she studied him, she not only saw the real Chris Grant, she saw herself for the first time—*ever*. A distinct calm had settled upon him like a fire blanket extinguishing a flame. They had truly become one person, as if they both understood what that meant.

She settled into his chest. "Let's wait a bit. The sky's perfect. I want to enjoy being here with you, in the quiet of this place. Just for a moment. I'll live on it forever."

The moment melted into a timeless void. They talked, laughed, and discussed their dreams for the future. Julie shared her deepest fear: that she would grow old, ugly, and unable to continue her current path. She confessed to a mounting insecurity. If she lost her career, she could not imagine going on.

"A modeling career isn't a forever vocation, love. That's just the way of it."

She pressed into him and stared beyond the patio at the fronds of a palm tree swaying in the early evening breeze. "What would you do if you couldn't play anymore? If you lost your arms or your fingers and you couldn't play?"

He stroked her bare arms and shoulders. "I'd come home to you. You're where I belong. And you belong to me, too."

"You wouldn't miss it? Playing? Recording? Being on the road?"

He nuzzled his cheek into her damp hair. "I understand what you're saying—about regret, and loss, and all that rubbish. At this point, I'm just grateful I can feel anything at all. You're my second chance."

"I wish it were that easy for me."

"Maybe it'll get easier in time. I haven't been there for you like I should. I intend to change that."

She closed her eyes. Though she had never believed in an all-powerful life-giving force to whom she could pray, she found herself inexplicably thanking the Great Whoever for her husband's transformation.

"Maybe we can share a dream together," he suggested. "It would be fun trying, at least."

"What dream is that?"

"I'd like to start a family."

Her eyes darted from the lazy palm to the bottom corner of the patio. "I..."

"I've wanted kids since Ben and Cheryl had Derek. Funny, huh? Me?"

Every muscle in her body tensed. Her gut reaction? Outright refusal. She would not become a mother. Not now, not ever. Mothers were old women who had given up their lives and their bodies for screaming, needy brats. Children were a non-negotiation. "Being pregnant would change my body—"

"I realize it might complicate our present lives, but I'd like to discuss it more seriously at some point. Even if we decide to adopt."

When she could find no words, she nodded against his chest.

He tucked his chin and gazed down at her. "Yeah?"

She swallowed hard, angled her face upward, and manufactured a smile that would convince Aristotle the earth was flat. "Of course. I want you to be happy."

He beamed at the concession, outsmiling her with the purest and most beautiful expression she had witnessed from another living being. So much so, she almost changed her mind.

They cuddled and kissed long after talk of careers and children faded to black. In time, they moved the conversation indoors. He removed his T-shirt, dampened and creased by her towel, then disrobed her and peeled off his jeans. They made love with the lights on, Chris reassuring her as he moved over and inside her that she would always be beautiful in his eyes.

Later, they lay in the afterglow, staring at one another in sated tranquility. She traced the lines and features of his face with her eyes, noting the subtle imperfection where Ben had broken his nose.

The corners of his lips rose as she changed positions to let him spoon her.

"Why are you smiling?"

His arms tightened around her waist. "Because I'm happy."

She covered his arms with hers and squeezed, unable to recall him ever having uttered those three words. Believing he had to mean it.

"But there's one thing we need to discuss."

"What?"

"I forgot to call room service."

Julie fiddled with her hair while Chris called for and managed their order. When it arrived, she listened as he instructed the attendant to arrange the meal on the patio. His easy banter flattered her, for she knew their interlude had left him satisfied.

They stayed in their villa the rest of the night and the entire next day. For Julie, their working vacation eclipsed their initial meeting in Switzerland so long ago. Before, he had looked disheveled and plagued by the gut-wrenching pain of Farin and Jordan's reunion. Now, he was free. Free of all that haunted him. Though she had initially resented the idea of releasing "Obsession," she no longer cared. By some miracle, that obsession had ended. The ghost was gone. From now on, Chris belonged solely to her.

***

Lockhardt Sound Drops Standards

-- Chicago, IL, Chicago Chronicle (AP), Tuesday, July 12, 1994 by Miles Macy

Lockhardt Sound, Inc. announced the sale of its Miami-based recording studio, Standards, to Hit Works yesterday afternoon. No public figure was announced, although the deal is rumored to have been between forty and sixty million dollars. This sale occurs only two weeks after LSI heavy hitter

Megan Price fell ill and returned to Los Angeles, resulting in the cancellation of the last three dates of her worldwide concert tour, which kicked off nearly two years ago.

Hit Works beat out industry giant Earshot Entertainment for the acquisition. In a press release, a public relations officer announced they were, "…pleased with the timing, the price, and the purchase."

LSI acquired Standards Recording Studios, a South Florida icon for over twenty years, when the company first appeared on the music scene some decades ago. Standards furthered such careers as Farin St. John, Jordan Grant, and an impressive list of who's who in the recording industry.

Attempting to dispel rumors that the sale was yet another step on Lockhardt Sound's long but certain trek to bankruptcy, LSI's Vice President of Public Relations, Bobby Lockhardt, insisted, "This sale is just good business. We've outgrown the need to own and maintain the studio. We've retained ownership of several studios here in New York and LA. This sale just removes a lot of unnecessary overhead."

Asked how the sale would impact those people no longer employed by LSI, Mr. Lockhardt had this to say: "The terms of the sale ensure these individuals will remain employed at compensatory wages. There should be no impact at all."

When asked the impetus for the sale, Mr. Lockhardt said, "LSI is in a state of rapid growth internally at the moment. We're reorganizing our business in an effort to centralize operations in order to keep up with this growth. We foresee a period of high sales in response to this effort beginning mid- to late-fourth quarter."

Though this may be true, industry pundits are unconvinced. In response to the release of assets, Lockhardt Sound stock has dwindled, falling nearly three points while Hit Works spiked more than five. Earshot Entertainment remained unchanged. With the exception of Jordan Grant, Mirage, and Farin Grant albums in December, LSI sales units have fallen steadily since the fourth quarter. Profits have suffered.

One industry pundit speculates this sale amounted to a delay tactic, a bluff in an effort to gain ready capital. Such capital could be used to court successful acts into signing with LSI in an attempt to revive their former position and stave off further vulnerabilities. Other theories claim the capital will go towards paying off interest and loans in order to improve the third quarter results when they are published.

What no one will say—*on the record*—is that Lockhardt Sound spins more propaganda than records these days. The sale of their Miami-based studio does little to remedy their ailing financial situation. Their claimed "reorganization" has yet to materialize and, in this reporter's opinion, may not have happened at all. With the studio gone and their only living money-maker too ill to perform, it will be interesting to see how LSI further covers its assets.

CHAPTER 10

L ANCE TURNER DROPPED HIS KEYS on the table nearest the door and skinned out of his sweat-soaked T-shirt, wiping his face and neck before tossing it to the floor and heading to the bathroom. He kicked his grass-stained tennis shoes in separate directions, then paused long enough to strip off his socks, which he also discarded randomly before shedding his shorts and boxers and letting them fall on the linoleum floor.

He engaged the shower, then trudged back to the living room to check his machine while the water heated up. Its blinking red display announced twelve messages awaited him.

With a mischievous smirk, he asked aloud, "What are you up to now?" He doubled back to the bathroom, figuring it was better to shower first and tackle the machine after he had rid himself of his own stench.

This daily ritual rarely varied. Up by noon, rugby from two to four, home for a shower by five, then band practice from nine to midnight—longer if he had a gig. He played locally now, which suited him fine. As Mirage's drummer, he had globe-hopped too many times to count. He found the predictability of his current schedule comical at times. No one would have believed he would grow up. Not friends, not family, and certainly not his former bandmates.

Lance had never been accused of being out of control, per se—particularly compared to Faith. He had never conjured up her brand of devilment. His was more a lack of responsibility. During his tenure with Mirage, someone else managed his schedule, answered his fan mail, laundered his clothes, and ordered his meals. He had never even bought a flat. He had been the wild card of the bunch. No one knew what might happen to him if the band fell apart.

The public had typecast them all—Womanizer Chris Grant, Pretty Boy Todd Dalton, Ostentatious Faith Peterson, and Enigmatic Elliot Lawrence. Rumors exploded after Mirage's demise, speculating at what fate might befall them. No one could have guessed what Lance Turner might do once Jameson cut the umbilical cord, forcing them to exist on their own.

The shower beat down on him hot and soothing. He had played harder than usual today. Lately, he had pushed himself physically. On some level, turning forty bothered him. Perhaps he felt he needed to prove something, although he could not fathom what that might be. Or perhaps the physical activities he enjoyed grew more taxing as the years passed. A part of him wished he could turn back time. He hated the idea he had passed his prime. He did not feel old by any means.

"Predictable," Lance said out loud as he washed. "If we were still together, I'd be the *predictable* one!" The irony tickled him. On Mirage's last tour, he nearly missed a gig in Barcelona because he had taken off to catch day two of France's 24 Hours of Le Mans.

His townhouse was close enough to London to access reality and remote enough to avoid it. He still kept late hours, but no longer destroyed his body with drink and recreational drugs. His local band was good enough to stay employed, yet not so good they found themselves on every radio station in the free world. Mirage royalties would support him more than comfortably for the rest of his blissful life. He had his rugby for exercise. It was as close to settling down as he had ever hoped to become.

Now, the only wild card in his life was Ivy, but even her insane randomness had become predictable. The few reporters who periodically pestered him often said negative things about her. She minded far more than he did. From where he sat, she was not so much "loud" as she was passionate. She did not want to control him; she just wanted to know where she stood. Someday, he might even tell her.

Lance rarely dried himself after a shower. Rather, he wrapped a towel around his waist and let himself dry naturally. The coolness of the air against the droplets of water sliding down his body invigorated him. It drove Ivy crazy, of course. She despised walking about the townhouse barefooted, only to encounter areas of damp carpet. For the first six months of their relationship, Lance had showered twice a day just to watch her reaction.

He exited the bathroom and headed out to confront his messages. "Okay. Let's see the damage for today." He queued up the machine, then pressed play.

The first message started off nice enough. "It's me. I need to know when you'll come 'round for me. Ring me when you get in."

"Not bad, sweetheart," he mumbled. "Must be a good day."

The next five messages grew increasingly impatient. "Where are you? I bet you're there and just not picking up. Not nice, Lance. *Lance?*"

Messages six through nine were little more than screaming obscenities, the last of which threatened him bodily harm should he not call the moment he walked in. "I promise if you don't pick up this bloody phone, I'll come over there and remove some quite necessary parts of your body! Try kicking *those* balls around with those wankers you call mates. I'm serious! Ring me!"

He chuckled. "There you are."

Two hang-ups accounted for messages ten and eleven. He figured she had lost her voice by then. Just as well. Perhaps she would avoid getting herself kicked out of the club tonight.

The last message took him by utter surprise.

"Hello, Lance. It's Samantha Drake. I was hoping to catch you but I guess you're out. I hope you'll call me back. If we miss each other because of the time difference, let me know when would be a good time to catch you. Thanks. Oh—why don't I leave you my home number as well? Here it is..."

He replayed the message twice to get the number, then let the machine clear his tape. He sat down on his couch and stared hard at the numbers. What could Sam possibly want? It seemed like a million years since he had heard from her. For a full five minutes, he debated whether or not to return the call.

At last year's Grammy Awards, he had chatted with the others about their post-Mirage lives. He had heard plenty of gossip but knew better than to believe it. It made him happy to know that, overall, everyone had landed on their feet. Elliot had his composing. Minor 6th had just contacted Chris about doing a solo record. Faith was shagging a painter in New York.

Only Todd kept himself apart from the group. How anyone managed to coerce him into showing up to accept the award in the first place, Lance could not guess. To the producers', and the fans', disappointment, Todd had refused all requests that they perform during the show.

Years after the fact, the agony of losing the band still stung its former lead singer. Their brief interaction was strained. He acted uncomfortable in their presence. Every so often, he cut hateful glares at Chris. In fact, he did not speak one word to Chris the entire night.

When it came time to accept their Lifetime Achievement Award, Todd made sure Lance, Elliot, and Faith stood between him and Chris. Historically the co-sex-symbols of the group, they looked like a pair of beautiful, awkward bookends.

Lance loved them all getting together again. Faith had even brought up the idea of a reunion. But the notion was short-lived. Elliot claimed his current commitments would last at least a couple of years. Todd had no interest in anything that would require him and Chris to be in the same room. And for Chris, something seemed off.

Leaving the auditorium later that evening, Lance had watched Chris hand his new and very prestigious award over to a fan who had managed to slip past security. In a thousand lifetimes, Lance would never forget the look on Chris's face when he thrust the statue at her. As if the honor meant nothing to him. As if nothing did. He had walked off and disappeared into his limousine before the young girl could collect herself.

Hindsight had given Lance peace. Sure, he was as surprised as anyone else when the old man sacked them. He had lashed out in anger at first, blaming everyone but himself. He accused Elliot of trying to distance himself. Such immeasurable talent, and so much more to do with it than stay with an aging rock'n'roll band. Faith did not help matters, he had insisted, what with her getting all cocked up on cocaine and what-not.

But ultimately, the blame fell on Chris. Everyone knew his entanglement with Jordan's girl had ended them. It made no sense that something so personal could put Jameson off his boat, but everyone accepted it as fact.

Now, none of it mattered. They were family. Families had the occasional row. For his part, he wished them well and loved every bloody one of them.

"Hello?" came a groggy male voice.

"Um…hmm." Lance stammered. "This is…uh…Lance Turner. Sam—er, Ms. Drake—left me a message to ring her. Is she about?"

"Do you know what time it is?"

Lance glanced at his wall clock and swore under his breath. "Sorry, mate. I'm crap with figuring time between us and you yanks."

The man groaned in protest. "Hang on."

Whoever had answered covered the receiver. Lance could not make out the muffled conversation. At least no one raised their voices. A few seconds later, Samantha picked up a second extension. He heard the other hang up.

Her voice sounded sleepy but alert. "Thanks for calling me back. How are you?"

"Sorry about the timing. I got your message and wanted to ring you straightaway. I was surprised to hear from you."

"I understand. I didn't know if you'd return my call."

He inhaled and started to speak, then paused to consider his words. "You should've said something before you left New York. I deserved that much. There, I've said it."

"I'm sorry. It was complicated. It would take hours to explain and I'd bet neither of us have that kind of time right now. But you're okay? You sound good."

"Of course. It's not like you left me brokenhearted or anything. We had a good go. I just thought it would've been decent of you to at least...Forget it. I just wanted to finish where we left it before we move on."

"You're right," Samantha said, her voice soft and low. "I owed you more than that. And more than anything, we were friends. I hope we can stay friends. Years too late but, there it is."

He sat down on the carpet beside the phone table, the damp towel loosening at the waist. "Still trying to claw your way to the top?"

"Not anymore. I'm here."

He could tell by the sound of her voice she was smiling. The corners of his mouth drew upward in automatic synchronization. "That's brilliant. I think I'd heard something about Minor, but wasn't sure. I don't keep up on things so much now."

No living soul knew about the affair Samantha Drake had had with Lance Turner. No one at LSI, and no one in Mirage. They had agreed they both had too much to lose if word got out. Mostly, the relationship was casual. She remained doggedly focused on furthering her career. He spent most his time in the studio or on the road. Neither had sought a long-term commitment. They saw each other when mutually convenient.

Toward the end, however, Lance's feelings for her had deepened. He never mentioned it, but she was wiser than she would ever know for leaving when she did. Despite his admonition, leaving before giving him a chance to protest was best for them both.

"Listen, I can't talk long. I have an early meeting and need to get back to bed, so I'll get right to the point. I want to talk to you and the others about reuniting."

His stomach flipped once, then again. "Serious?"

"Absolutely."

"All of us?"

Sam sputtered a sleepy laugh. "Of course, all of you. I realize there's a lot to be worked out, but if you're willing to discuss it, I think it could be huge."

The idea played out in his mind. "You know, Sam, Faith brought this up last year and nobody wanted to do it."

"She did?"

"Yeah."

"I see."

"Faith and I thought it might be a good idea, but Elliot's real busy. And Todd, well..."

Samantha said nothing.

"Have you talked to anyone else?"

"You were my first call."

"What about Chris? What does he think?"

"I didn't want to get his hopes up before talking to the rest of you. He's doing well. I didn't want anything distracting him. I need him sharp for the upcoming release. You know how it is."

"Sure." Twenty years of memories assaulted him—recording, touring, press conferences, photo shoots, sneaking into and out of hotels around the world, Sam sleeping in his arms. For a moment, he romanticized his career. Only the good bits, of course. Before their call, he had proclaimed himself the predictable one. Now, he was torn. "How's he doing with the whole Jordan thing? Last time I saw him, he was a wreck."

Samantha cleared her throat. "He's, um...fine."

"Nowhere to go but up from that situation, was there?"

Her voice quieted. "I guess not."

"He ever tell you what happened? I hope for his sake they find whoever did it. Bloody maniacs in this world. And then to lose Farin? Poor bloke."

There came a loud pounding at his door. He knew instantly who stood on the other side—even before her mouth started going. For a few moments, Sam's voice had transported him back to his former life. Now, the spell was broken. He lived again in Tunbridge Wells—a would-be has-been with no complaints.

He stood, cradled the phone on his shoulder, and cinched the damp towel around his waist. "Can you hold on a sec? Someone's at the door."

"Actually, I need to get going. But listen—I'll call you back soon about the reunion. I'm not giving up yet."

No sooner had Lance returned the receiver to its base than Ivy Spencer burst inside. She scanned the townhouse with a suspicious sneer, checking every room as if expecting to find someone lurking in a closet or under the bed. Finding no one, she stomped back into the living room.

She crossed her arms and scowled. "All right. What's going on? And don't tell me nothing, because we both know you're a lying bloody dog."

The sight of Ivy made him smile. She looked striking when angry. "Hello, love. I just got your messages. Ready to leave for the club?"

She backed away in disgust when he moved in to kiss her cheek. "I'm not going anywhere with you! Not now, and not ever!"

He advanced, arms outstretched. "Oh sweetheart, don't be that way."

"No!" She slapped his hands away. "Why didn't you ring me when you got home?"

"I smelled awful. I needed a shower."

"I need money," she snapped flatly, pouting with the change of subject. "For the baby."

He exaggerated an eye-roll protest, but one corner of his mouth lifted with unchecked mischief. "What now? I just gave you money last week! What about the father? Can't he help out?"

When not in the middle of a raging fit, Ivy had gorgeous brown eyes. Big, warm, expressive brown eyes. But when she was mad, they transformed into cold, black slits. Most people avoided her when her eyes narrowed. Lance, however, was not most people.

"Don't bloody do this," she warned, cheeks red with fury.

"What? You'd think the bloke would want to help take care of his son."

"He's *your* son! You *know* he is!"

He shrugged, then ambled to his bedroom to dress for the evening.

She followed closely. "Don't walk away from me, you wanker!"

"Look," he said, slipping on his jeans. "I'll give you all the money you want, right? Is that all you want from me? Money? Fine! I couldn't care less about money. But Ivy, you need to be honest. Colin's not mine, biologically speaking. Why do we have to do this? Just tell me the truth and I'll give you all the money he'll ever need. His father can bugger off."

The tears came next. "You don't love me. You don't give a toss about me or Colin. You're ashamed of us. Admit it!"

He skinned on a shirt, then wrapped his arms around her. "No crying, sweetheart. It'll be all right."

Ivy lived with her parents in a council flat in Chatham, a less affluent neighborhood than his. She drew little in terms of wages and relied on her parents to make up the rest. Though he never encouraged such thoughts, he knew her assigned social class embarrassed her. He had suffered similar humiliation prior to Mirage's success. Britain's social structure was brutal. As it stood, he envied Ivy's family's closeness. Except his brother, he had no real familial connections—especially a father.

While Ivy often acted like a raving lunatic, there were things about her others did not see. In fairness, Lance rarely saw them either. Still, he could make her feel more comfortable if he tried. He could reassure her instead of behaving as if he tolerated her because her tantrums amused him. And even if they did amuse him, it was not the only reason he kept her around.

They met eighteen months ago on the cross-channel ferry, the Pride of Dover, in the duty-free shop. He was buying champagne and cheese for a date. She was buying a pack of cigarettes and cheap beer. The moment he saw her, he fell in love. Why, he still did not know. Visually, she was not the most attractive woman he had ever seen. She stood all of five foot two, with an average if stocky build and short, spiked blonde hair. Her large teeth looked crammed into her elfin mouth. Overall, a nearly cartoonish appearance. But she was utterly vibrant. Spirited. He loved her the moment she casually turned to him and demanded the difference in the money she needed to make her purchase.

As for Colin, Lance could not be his father—no matter how hard Ivy insisted. The timelines did not fit. He and his bandmates had played a short tour in Germany at the time she got pregnant. Though he did not understand her reasons for insisting otherwise, he knew it had nothing to do with his former fame or money. She only used money as an excuse to fight when they had nothing else to quarrel about.

"Let's make up and be happy," he urged, kissing her damp cheeks.

She shook her head, frowned, and stuck her lips out. "I don't want to go out now."

"Of course you do. That's why you keep me around, isn't it? To pamper you and treat you like a queen and parade you around the clubs?" He felt her smile against his chest.

"You hardly treat me like a queen."

"But I do. I really do."

"I need money for the sitter." She sniffed.

"A sitter? What about your mum and dad?"

"They're on holiday. Left this afternoon. They'll be gone for a week."

"So, it's just you and the baby?"

Ivy nodded sadly.

"I see." He held her closer. "That's what this is about, then. Well, why don't we go pay the sitter, go out for the evening, and tomorrow, I'll bring you and Colin here to stay with me for the week? Will that make it better?"

She looked up at him. The sparkle in her eyes told him she wanted to agree, but she possessed more pride than any person he had ever known.

"Come on, now."

"He's your son, Lance."

"Let's just go. We'll sort this another day. But not now, love. It's nearly six o'clock. I'll be late for practice if we don't leave for dinner straightaway."

In the end, she gave in. But as they left, she swore that, one day soon, she would prove Colin was his son. "I'll have one of those paternity tests. *Then* you'll be sorry for the way you treat me."

He grabbed his keys off the table and nudged her out the door. "Let's drop this now so I can tell you about the call from America. Don't you want to hear about it?"

Ivy stepped out into the hallway, then waited while Lance closed the door and secured the lock. "What about it?"

"Minor Sixth Records wants to sign Mirage back up. Have another go."

"You can't," she blurted out without a thought. "I won't let you."

He chuckled as they walked to his car. He wondered what type of engagement ring he would buy her. Whatever he picked out, she would certainly make him exchange it.

***

The first single from *Aftermath* was released at the end of May, with the completed work following in early September. Chris had progressed quickly in the studio, aided considerably by some of the best session musicians in the business.

Throughout the summer, eager fans of the former Mirage member locked up radio station phone lines with requests for the single. Overnight, Chris Grant once again became the talk of the industry. To his relief, the chief topics discussed by the papers did not include pot shots at his past. Within a week of its release, "Obsession" skyrocketed to number one and remained there well beyond *Aftermath*'s September 2nd release date. Record stores the world over sold out their inventory as fast as it arrived.

Six days following *Aftermath*'s release, the "Obsession" video won one of two MTV Video Music Awards for which it had been nominated. Another three nominations came in for the Billboard Music Video Awards that November, where it swept.

In his acceptance speech, Chris credited Julie with "Obsession's" success. Everything about the shoot had worked. She had shone like never before, emitting an airy freeness to her seductive overtones that perfectly translated to screen. During the filming, he had been awestruck by her skill and beauty. How happy he was to have her, and how lucky he was to realize it before it was too late.

Their relationship's newfound solidarity spilled into their professional life. At last, they fully belonged to one another. Though he hated to admit it, Farin's rejection had done them both a favor. He and Julie were similar creatures. They made an impressive team. Unlike darker times in his past, the Chris of today would have resisted the urge to stray. Moreover, he could finally make love to his wife without seeing the face of another woman.

The *Aftermath* publicity campaign extended through the holidays. Fans and critics received its second and third releases with enthusiasm. And Minor 6th Records rang in the New Year celebrating their most profitable year to date.

Chris had not only reinvented his career; he had made over his entire life. Promoters pressed for a summer tour of the states and hinted at the inevitability of a worldwide commitment. Minor called for a new album. While his team worked to balance what promised to be a hectic schedule over the near future, Samantha called him in for a meeting shortly after the first of the year.

When he strolled into her office that January morning, she noted a distinct bounce to his step. His winning smile was as genuine as it was out of character. Though pleased with the accolades received for *Aftermath*, and the prestige that came to her personally and professionally as a result of that success, she was distracted.

Her forced smile failed to warm the coldness of the space as she handed him a mug of boiling water, a spoon, and a teabag, then sat down opposite him on one of the leather sofas. "Where's Julie? You two are inseparable these days."

"She's a bit run down, actually." He tore open the packaging, submerged the teabag into the water with the spoon, and then set it to steep atop the glass table separating them. "I suspect life on the road's finally taking its toll."

"I know a good doctor," Samantha offered, only half-joking.

"No worries. Just a stomach virus or some such. She's fine. We're fine.

I trust you and Ethan are well?"

She smiled despite her distraction and extended her hand for inspection. On her left ring finger, she displayed a three-carat diamond engagement ring. "Like my Christmas present?"

He leaned forward to examine the large rock, whistling his approval. "Congratulations! When's the big day?"

"We haven't set a date yet." She sank back and examined the ring with sorrowed eyes, then let her hand fall to her side. "It's your fault, you know. If you were less successful, I could take some time off."

He lifted and touched his mug to hers. Finding the liquid too hot, he returned it to the table, then sat back and crossed his legs. They chatted about the status of his summer tour. "But I wanna get back into the studio as soon as possible. This momentum won't last forever. Did you ever get those tapes from Jameson?"

She wrapped her hands around her mug, sipped its contents, then held it to her. Averting his eyes, she answered in a faraway voice, "I have them. Once your tour dates are finalized, we'll discuss a new album. But bring Julie. Minor has a little memento for her to thank her for her contribution to your success. Nothing much, just a token, really."

Chris narrowed inquisitive eyes. "You okay, Sam?"

She did not answer. For months, her meeting with Ross had haunted her like a forsaken companion. Had she known the horrors her former compatriot would confess that day, she would have passed on the tapes, the meeting—all of it. Instead, she had become an inimical accomplice in Jameson Lockhardt's sick and deadly game.

"What's wrong? And don't say it's nothing. Did the old man threaten you? Did he bugger up the tapes? What?"

She stood and smoothed her skirt, avoiding Chris's confronting stare as she crossed the room and split the blinds with her hand to view the cloudy sky. Being alone with him was discomfiting. She had counted on Julie accompanying her husband to this meeting.

With a shoulder roll, she strengthened her resolve and adopted her executive face. "The tapes are fine. I've had them for months now. We can use them on your next album."

The words echoed in her mind, accusing her. ...*months now.*

Chris was happy, she told herself. Julie was happy. *She* was happy. Ethan had proposed. Maybe they would have children. Or maybe it was too late. She might be too old. She was too old. Too old, in any case, to dig up the past. What had taken place had nothing to do with her.

As she struggled to conjure a plausible excuse to evict Chris from her office, she cursed Jameson Lockhardt. In her mind, his evil, icy grip squeezed her throat. Chris would go insane. His career would suffer, as would hers—and that would be the least of their worries.

The feel of his hand on her upper arm startled her. "What's going on, Sam? You look like you've seen a ghost."

She studied his features, then shrugged him off and crossed back to the sofa on shaky, stocking-sheathed feet.

Her conversation with Lance had triggered the pendulum of guilt slicing through her conscience. Their affair had marked the end of a negative spiral in her life, though she harbored no regrets. He had helped her in ways she could not label. But after speaking with him, she had reexamined the life she created. The results were unfavorable.

Evading a moral responsibility for even one moment, let alone weeks and months on end, sickened her. Farin Grant was a human being. Those who loved her deserved to know the truth about her death.

She pointed to the sofa opposite her. "I need to know what happened."

He eyed her quizzically.

"With Jordan."

"Why?"

She ignored the question. "And Farin."

He tucked his chin. "What's going on, Sam?"

She pushed her palms together as if in prayer, momentarily fusing her eyes. "I never knew the details, but you and Farin were obviously involved on a deeper level than Jordan suspected. And what about Jameson? We both saw how Farin's presence affected him. I need to know why. Did she confide in you?"

He listened intently at first, then rattled away agonizing memories of Farin's bloodstained clothes, her tear-streaked face staring up at him in shock and terror. "What does it matter now?"

He stormed from his seat, snatched his mug, and dumped it in the sink. She leaned forward and rested her elbows atop her knees, lacing her fingers.

Chris gripped the edge of the wet bar. "I don't know what it was. Farin unnerved him. My brothers and I saw it the day they met. I don't think Farin noticed. She would've told me while she was living...with me."

Samantha urged him on. *"Tell* me."

"Three years ago..." Again, he saw her in his mind's eye, huddled and trembling on his doorstep, covered in blood. "Why are you bringing this up now, Sam? I've moved on."

She sprung from her seat and went to him. Jaw clenched, he looked away. "I know you don't want to relive this, but I need to know the entire story. *Please.*"

"Why?"

She pursed her lips, staring at him with pleading eyes.

"Does this have something to do with my tapes? How could it?"

She led him back to sit beside her, resting a hand on his shoulder. "Tell me."

He relayed what he knew of Jameson's dealings with Farin, including the fact that Mirage's demise was punishment for Chris not heeding Jameson's demand to leave Farin alone.

The more he spoke, the easier it came. He left little out. It no longer mattered. In fact, it relieved him to say it out loud.

As he continued, he shared pertinent details of their brief life together and his lingering guilt over Melody's death and, later, Farin's suicide attempt. At last, he told her about the day Farin arrived on his front porch announcing Jordan's murder.

His nostrils flared in defiance of the buried feelings clawing their way to the surface. "I couldn't understand what she was saying. Just that Jordan was shot. At Bobby's house. That he was dead." He lowered his head to his hands as the images of Farin's body and Jordan's melted into one. "She was drenched in my brother's blood."

Samantha stared at him, rapt and aghast. Her eyes welled as she clasped his shoulder. She hated having to ask, even as she pressed him to continue. She had to know. All of it.

"I went to Bobby's."

"Did Farin go with you or—?"

He stiffened, embarrassed on some level that he had poured out his pain. Too late. The dam lay in ruins. "Julie said Farin left right after I did. Then, she disappeared. I never saw her again. When I got to Bobby's, Jordan was dead."

Samantha covered her gaping mouth. "I knew you'd been questioned but I had no idea you found him there! Oh, Chris. It must have been horrible."

"The police took me in for questioning. If you kept up with the news at the time, you probably know the rest."

She nibbled absently on a finally manicured thumbnail as she rose to pace the floor. "And then Farin called a press conference?"

"You have a good memory."

The compliment prompted a fresh pang of guilt to accost her middle. "Anyone know why?"

"Not that I know of. Sam, can we please—"

"What happened to her body? Her...remains?"

"*What?*"

"Just..." She stopped and gave a frustrated shake of her closed fists, then massaged her temple.

Chris repositioned himself in his seat. "Jameson and Ross went to the coroner's office. There wasn't much left of her to identify. She'd been sitting practically on top of the gas tank when the car exploded. It...apparently, it nearly incinerated her. The heat even melted her wedding ring. They needed dental records to identify her."

She jerked her hand from her forehead. It froze in mid-air. "No family?"

He bobbed his shoulders. "We were the only family she had. Ben talked to Jameson. I was...I couldn't...Anyway, Jameson offered and I guess we just agreed. By the time we'd pulled it together enough for another funeral, he'd arranged everything. He even had her remains placed in two urns so she could be with her parents and with Jordan."

Sam sat back down. She stared past him. "No one questioned him? Not even you?"

"Honestly? I thought he did the right thing for once."

Incredulous, she brought her hand to her chin, delicate fingers curling over her mouth, tapping her upper lip. The details swirled in her mind. "I'll never know how he does it," she mumbled under her breath.

"Does what?"

"The sleazy son of a—"

"What are you on about? Where did this come from? Why now?"

She recalled Ross's disposition at O'Hearnes that day. So frightened. He had sworn her to secrecy. But this confidence she could not keep at peril to her soul. "I met with Ross...a while ago."

Chris bobbed his head, frustrated. "Right. He gave you the tapes. And...?"

"He thinks Jameson's having him followed."

He blew air through his lips, then shot her a wry grin.

Her expression assured him she was not kidding.

"Why? And what does it have to do with Farin?"

Samantha wondered if Chris would forgive her for not telling him sooner. How the truth would impact them all. One thing was certain: nothing would ever be the same again.

"Because Ross knows what happened."

"What are you talking about?"

She looked up at him. "There's something I have to tell you."

CHAPTER 11

"Jᴀɴᴜᴀʀʏ ɪɴ Nᴇᴡ Yᴏʀᴋ ɪs my undoing. The light's wrong. Too fucking cold," muttered Henri—*just* Henri, *no last name, "and the 'H' is silent"*—as he lit another cigarette. His dark clothes had accumulated an impressive collection of paint stains over the years as he went through his red phase and then his blue phase. Lately, he focused on blacks and flesh tones, specifically the black leather and flesh belonging to Faith Peterson.

Faith still found his French accent charming, but she was in no mood for charm. She grunted in disgust. "Cold? I'll give you cold. I've been standing here all afternoon! I'm freezing my tits off."

"They're nice tits. Now hold still." He set down his bunny brush, seized a signing brush, then ran it through a glob of flesh-tone pigment before applying the color to the 4' x 6' canvas propped upon the easel separating them.

"I'm getting stiff! How much longer?"

For a solid hour, she had balanced on her left foot. Her right thigh muscles ached from her having held her foot behind and level with her head which, by Henri's instruction, tilted upward. Her striking green eyes fixed on the far corner of the ceiling twenty feet away. She stretched out her other arm, graceful and level with her shoulder. Though nude, she looked like a ballerina—something no one would ever label the unbridled New York native. If he did not finish soon, she would cramp up.

Henri studied his work, heedless of her complaints. He brushed the canvas with loving strokes, the agility of his large, stout fingers remarkable as he glided and shaped the oils on his most recent masterpiece with delicate precision. "Be still."

"Hurry, Henri. I want to go home."

He peeked up from behind his easel. "We are home."

"Then I want to go over there." She flounced like a pouting child, gesturing twenty-five feet across the warehouse floor to their makeshift living room.

"*Fine!*"

A sudden crash of art paraphernalia told her she had crossed the line.

He cast his signing brush into a jar of turpentine and overturned the table that held his impressive supply of paints, brushes, jars, pencils, charcoal, pastels, linseed oil, and watercolors. The paint splattered onto the floor—the cerulean blue, Prussian green, ruby red, beige, and black mixing with a generous amount of linseed oil—causing the paints to bleed into one another atop the dried reds and blues that had previously found themselves toppled over in one or another of Henri's artistic tirades. "I can't work like this. It's ruined. Fuck it! Get dressed."

With a self-satisfied simper, Faith lowered her leg, then bent over to work out the kinks in her thigh muscles and the small of her back. She stood upright on both feet for the first time in over an hour, stretching her arms high above her head. Slipping into her robe, she said, "There's a party in the Village tonight."

Henri hunkered upon his stool, sucking his cigarette. "Leg cramps, hunger pangs, stray eyelashes, bathroom breaks, itches. It's always something."

That Faith could sit still for no more than an hour, sometimes two, annoyed him to no end. Still, he had amassed a dedicated following since she had started modeling for him. Most of his loyal admirers bought his work for the sole purpose of displaying a nude painting of the former rocker on the wall of their home or business. This did not bother him. No matter how frustrating, he appreciated Faith's beauty and overt sexuality.

Bypassing the paint puddle, she slinked to his side and kissed his cheek. His nostrils emitted a thick cloud of smoke. She fanned away the pungent haze, then moved in to rub his back. She scrutinized the canvas, squinting to fully appreciate the subtle nuances. "Whaddya say? Wanna go?"

He scoffed. "Parties. People. What a farce."

Faith scrunched her mouth to one side but said nothing. She knew better than to argue with Henri when he fell into one of his artistic moods. Rarely did she remind him that she had abandoned her Brownstone to live in the rotting upstairs of an otherwise abandoned warehouse for nearly the same rent. On some level, it amused her.

Its wide-open space left her agoraphobic, at first. Then, she resented the lack of privacy the overhead glass and flimsy bamboo room dividers afforded them. But once she had settled in, she decided she liked living with her tragic, brooding painter.

"Stay home and mope if you want. I'm going."

"Leave me now." He exhaled more smoke as he angrily stamped out the last cigarette of his second pack of the day.

They had cohabitated for far too long for her to laugh outwardly at his eccentricities. In many ways, she admired the devotion to his chosen vocation, even though it brought him little financial success. She supplemented his meager income without complaint. She believed in him completely.

She crossed the warehouse floor into the kitchen area. "Hungry? I'm hungry."

He grunted, shifted in his seat, then passed his left hand over the center of the canvas without making physical contact. His stare remained fixed. "I hunger for perfection. Therefore, I starve."

Faith opened the cupboard doors and mulled over its options. "We're all out of perfection, but we've got tuna."

She opened a family-sized can, drained the oil, grabbed a fork, poured a tall iced tea, and then sat on the couch. Between forkfuls of tuna straight from the can, she leafed through the latest edition of *The New Yorker*.

A painful knot formed in her right thigh. She middle-knuckled the cramp for some minutes while Henri stared unblinkingly at his canvas. "I'll never get it right, you know."

Ah, self-pity. Everyone's favorite. "Get what right?" When she dug her knuckle deeper into her calf, the pain made her wince.

"You know what I mean."

"Awww. Does my widdul Picasso have a pwobwum wif his gweat big paint bwush?"

"You don't understand."

She twisted around in her seat, swirling her fork his way as she spoke. "I bet if you showed me your great big paint brush I could help. I like your paint brush. I bet I like it more than all those chicks who buy your porno paintings of me."

His eyes scanned his work, immersed and intent. "They think they see you there. I can't even see you there. I know what I want to do but my hands...they betray me."

Pitching her voice in conciliatory surrender, she asked, "Want me to pose again?"

Henri did not answer right away—he never did. He stared at the canvas as if awaiting direction. Suddenly, he righted his table and began arranging his supplies in haste. "Yes! Hurry! I think I have it now!"

She stifled a mischievous grin, making no attempt to move from where she sprawled on the couch. "Say you'll come to the party."

"What? Yeah-yeah. Sure. Hurry up, now."

"Promise?"

"Yeah, yeah. I promise! *Dépêchez-vous!*"

She strolled back over to stand in front of him. Four steps in, the telephone rang. Henri's freshly lit cigarette bounced up and down between his lips. "Oh, fuck me, not now!"

"Take it easy. I'll get rid of them." Not wanting Henri to lose the moment or—more importantly—lose her date for the party in the Village later that evening, she picked up and barked into the receiver, "Yeah, who's this?"

A warm chuckle from the other end identified the caller long seconds before she heard his British voice. "You haven't changed a bit, have you, dove?"

"Elliot!"

"Yes, yes. 'Tis I. How are things, my lovey?"

"Fantastic! How the hell are you?"

A hail of paints and brushes crashed to the floor behind her.

"Am I interrupting?"

"Nah. Something fell over."

Henri looked up at the ceiling. "Fate! You conspire to thwart me!"

Faith covered the receiver and watched her lover stomp off to the converted cargo job of an elevator, an ancient relic of post-World War II New York. "How've you been?"

"We're fine, dove. We think of you often but today in particular." Elliot could not quite keep the cat-that-hears-the-can-opener sound out of his voice.

She scrunched her forehead. "Why's that?"

Chuckling in earnest, Elliot said, "My beautiful wife has informed me that congratulations are in order. Apparently, you're engaged. What did you do, lovey? Get him pregnant?"

"And from which reputable journalistic publication did she glean this obviously credible information?"

She heard the rustle of his paper.

Elliot chortled, then cleared his throat. "'Faith Peterson's newest addiction,' it says, 'is an unknown artist who paints nothing but nudes of the former Mirage member. He reportedly proposed to the famous ivory-tickler-turned-fashion-designer on a recent trip to Las Vegas. So overwhelmed was the redheaded diva by the proposal, sources say the couple tried to marry that very night. State laws regarding sobriety during the ceremony were all that prevented it, but we are happy to report Faith Peterson is definitely engaged. Pictured here, Melvin Theodore Leberwitz, who legally changed his name to Henri three years ago—'"

"*Leberwitz*? What the...*Melvin*?"

"So it says here," he confirmed, cracking the paper authoritatively. He cleared his throat again and continued. "'—changed his name to Henri three years ago, donned his most festive attire for the attempted nuptials.' And it goes on from there. You get the gist."

"*Theodore*?"

"You should see the photo, Faith. They have his head sitting atop some bloke wearing an Elvis Presley suit—sequins and all. I must say, though, I suspected it wasn't really you the moment I noticed a conspicuous absence of leather and no part of your stomach showing in the ensemble. You're in a dress, if you can imagine."

"It's white, isn't it?"

"And *pink*!" Elliot added, clearly delighted.

Faith suppressed a shudder. "Well, then any fool would know it isn't me. Am I gonna have to call my lawyers?"

Henri trudged back into the main loft from the elevator area, muttering, "Fucking thing never works. Everything's broken. I can get nothing done."

On the other end, Elliot grinned. "Might be a good idea."

Henri picked up the extension in what Faith referred to as the bedroom of their open, three thousand square foot loft and shouted emphatically, "This is too much! I must *work*!"

Faith replied dryly, "I'm on the phone, Melvin."

After a few seconds of silent confusion, Henri muttered, "Sorry," and hung up.

Elliot guffawed. When his sides started to ache, he handed the telephone to his wife. "Hi, Faith. It's Marci. Elliot's laughing."

"Hey, Marci. Weird shit, huh?"

"I didn't think it was true. That's why I had Elliot call."

Faith rubbed her eyelids. Henri rummaged in the kitchen for coffee filters. "No. We're still just living in sin. Besides, I hate Vegas."

"That's what Elliot said. So, how are you?"

"Still sober—that's usually the question people want answered first, ya know? Anyway, business is taking off. I'm looking at a show this fall."

"You'll have to send me a catalog. Oh, and hey, did Minor Sixth Records call you? They called Elliot."

"Yeah, Sam called. But it'll never happen. I know I suggested it at first, but I'm having a blast with the fashion thing. The boys and I had some fun times, but I'm too old for that life. The Grammys were cool, but whatever. Music's changed too much since we started out. It's all computerized and digital. You don't even have to have talent anymore. Too much glitz," she laughed at the irony of her own words. "Even for me. Better to leave the band scene to the younger kids coming up. Some of them aren't too bad, I guess, except for all that rap shit."

"I get it. Anyway, Elliot's back, so I'll let you go. Nice talking with you. Hang on."

After a brief shuffle on the line, Elliot's voice filled the void. "Anyway, dove, thought you should know about the headlines."

"I hope I can return the favor someday."

"I heard Marci ask you about Sam."

"Yeah," Faith's voice softened. "What did you tell her?"

"It was more personal than business, really. It was great catching up."

"I think she called everybody. Chris seemed pretty happy about his solo stuff the last time I talked to him. Come to think of it, I don't think I've talked to him for about a year. You talk to him, El?"

"We stay in touch. He and Julie seem happy. The album's still hot."

She sighed. "I worry about him, but I feel creepy calling now that he's married."

"Rubbish. Julie's a brick. I'm sure they'd love to hear from you."

She gave a doubtful snort. "Whatever."

"Anyway, you're right. Sam called all of us. She's behind it, not him."

Faith lifted a hip to half-sit on the stool owned by the artist formerly known as Melvin. Mirage's rise and fall played in her memory. Being with the boys at the Grammys had sparked temporary nostalgia, but had extinguished.

Bitterness no longer plagued her. They had lived a dream for two decades. But she had woken up. While grateful to have maintained their camaraderie through many battles over ego, money, and popularity, Faith could not deny the heavy tax levied upon her by that lifestyle.

"It'd be a kick to play together again, but I'm too busy. Besides, when I hear our songs on the radio, I can't remember playing half the shit. It was great at the time, but I don't miss waking up in the mornings wondering where I am."

"I understand. And I'm lined up for two scores with Universal and a gig right behind that for Sony."

"Big projects?"

"Mmm...fairly, yes."

Their conversation unsettled her, though she dared not acknowledge why. For longer than most modern marriages last, they had crawled all over each other's lives, seeing each other through heartbreaks and triumphs. Few secrets existed between them. Now, they exchanged birthday and holiday cards. The "have-tos" had evaporated like mist. Their oneness had scattered like ash.

"So, what's the master plan, El? You trying to score every movie Hollywood makes this year?"

"I'm no posh New York fashion designer, but I get by."

"Better be careful or you'll wind up with an Oscar. How would that look next to all the Grammys? I mean, I think they'd clash."

"You know, the bloody things sat in a box in the garage for months. Marci found them and made me put them up on the mantle."

"I keep mine in the bathroom. They remind me of little commodes."

Elliot laughed. "Don't ever change. My world would be so boring."

"I better let you go. Thanks for calling. And for the heads up."

"Not a problem. If you're out this way, drop in."

"I will. And...if you talk to Chris, have him call me, okay?"

"Surely. You know we love you."

"Love you too. Tell Marci I said bye."

"Will do." As Elliot replaced the receiver, he glanced at Marci and smiled. She had positioned herself at the kitchen counter with her tabloids spread strategically before her. "Hungry?"

She nodded without taking her eyes off the page. "Starving."

He grabbed sandwich fixings, a jar of pickle spears, and a fresh pitcher of sun tea from the fridge. "I'm using the last of the sourdough."

"I'll put it on the list," she muttered, engrossed in her reading.

He assembled their lunch like a pro, smearing the perfect mustard-to-mayo ratio, then adding sprouts, iceberg lettuce, and two thin slices of tomato. A little cheddar cheese, a generous helping of roast beef, and *voila*.

He handed it across the kitchen island. "For you."

She kissed the air, set the plate beside her open magazine, and accepted a glass of tea without looking up.

A squealing screech brought him out from behind the counter before he finalized his second masterpiece. He craned his head to peer out the kitchen window but could not see past the Italian Cypress framing their curved driveway. "Did you hear that?"

Marci held up a finger, her attention focused on a *Globe* article about the OJ Simpson murder trial that had started last Thursday. Her untouched sandwich and some chips languished beside her. When she reached a stopping point, she looked up. "Were those tires?"

"I hope no one took the corner too fast."

"We don't usually hear much from the road, do we?"

Elliot shrugged, wiped his hands on a dish towel, then went to the front of the house. No sooner had Marci stood to follow him than the doorbell rang in several overlapping chimes, followed by urgent fist-pounding. He hurried to answer. Marci hovered in the hall, curious.

Without checking the peephole, he opened the enormous oak door.

"What the—?" Elliot greeted, aghast.

Chris steadied himself against the doorframe with one hand, bent forward, panting for breath. "I need to...I need to see her."

The last and only time Chris had visited their home, he had called ahead for assurance that Marci was away. Julie had gone to Jamaica for a shoot, so Elliot had invited him over for a beer.

"We just talked to Faith. She wants you to call her. What's up?"

"I need to see Marci." Chris gulped for breath, though he did not appear winded. His dark features contorted as if in shock. He pushed off the side of the house and started inside.

Elliot raised his hands, blocking his entrance. "Whoa, whoa. Slow down, mate. Maybe that's not such a good idea."

Chris rested his hands on his hips, dropped his head, and shook it absently. "I can't," he whisper-panted his disbelief. "It's not..."

"What are you on about? Is everything okay?"

Chris swallowed hard and let his hands fall to his sides. He looked straight through Elliot. "Is she here?"

"Marci told me about the cemetery last year," Elliot warned. "Now, you're my mate, and nothing will ever change that, but Marci's my wife. I won't have you turning up and upsetting her. Don't make me choose between you two. Whatever it is you've come to say, say it to me."

"Bugger that," Chris spat. He raked shaky fingers through his hair.

Elliot noticed his hands—in fact, his whole body—trembled. His face was pale and sallow.

"I'm not here to fight with her—or you."

"What, then?" He planted his arm high against the doorframe.

"Marci!" Chris shouted from outside the front door. "Please! I need to—" His voice broke, then wavered. "I need to...I need to tell you."

"Tell me what?" Marci's icy voice reached them from the back of the foyer where she stood, arms crossed, a look of undiluted hatred fixed across her face.

Chris raised one hand as if to ward off an invisible blow. "I've never had much to say to you before. The only link between us was..."

"Are you drunk? Did you come to my house drunk?"

Elliot faced his wife. With a wordless glance, he pleaded Chris's case. They did not need a scene on their front porch.

Marci huffed, then turned and stomped toward the living room. Arms still crossed, she plopped heavily onto the sofa. Elliot nestled protectively at her side.

Chris sat down atop their large, square oak coffee table. His breathing slowed as he flattened his lips and stared intently at her, then Elliot, then back again.

Something in his expression chilled her. She grabbed a throw pillow and clutched it tightly in her lap.

"We've never had much to say to each other," he began again, resting his elbows on his thighs. He leaned forward. "The only link between us was Farin. And she's why I'm here."

The couple emitted a synchronistic sigh of exhaustion. Elliot slank back into the couch.

Marci squinted, jaw set, and gave the throw pillow an angry squeeze. "We said all there was to say at the cemetery."

"Yes, the cemetery." Chris's face contorted in agony. His words pushed forward through a barricade of denial, his spirit hovering far away, separated from the numbness of his body. He was about to change the course of Marci's life, just as Samantha had changed his bare hours before. "That's just it. I don't know who's buried in that grave, but it's not Farin."

After one full beat of silence, the corners of Elliot's mouth twisted in distaste. "You're bloody mad!"

"You *are* drunk," Marci accused.

Chris shot his friend a look both grave and serious. He leaned in closer. "Not a drop, but I certainly could've used one a couple of hours ago."

"This isn't amusing, mate."

Marci's voice reached Chris's ears, barely audible. "What are you saying?"

"She's alive," he said.

The couple gasped in unison.

"*What*?" Her exclamation lingered in the eerie stillness of the room. All color drained from her perfect features even as the blue of her eyes deepened. She remained fixed on Chris's staid expression. Her body grew heavy and cold.

"Zoso?" Elliot squeezed her hand.

"It's not possible." As she voiced her doubt at the absurdity of Chris's proclamation, something inside her believed him. "How? What happened? Where is she?"

Chris had asked many similar questions when he learned the horrifying truth, but Samantha could answer few of them.

Jameson had warned him to stay away. Chris had gambled and lost not only everything he wagered, but he had used Farin, Elliot, Faith, Todd, and Lance to up the ante. And then there was Jordan. Chris had betrayed his brother in every possible way.

Facing his friend, he choked out a feeble apology. "I-I'm sorry, mate."

Elliot frowned in disbelief. "It's been three years! If Farin's alive, where on Earth is she? How did you find out?"

Too little information in too little time. Too many unanswered questions. Too many decisions to make. Chris scarcely knew where to start. He muttered only one word: "Lockhardt."

***

Julie flitted about the patio in her Victoria's Secret negligee. Dahrvey cosmetics, Chanel perfume, Brigitte Bardot updo. She dressed the table to ensure a picture-perfect appointment of plates, cloth napkins, egg salad, fruit salad, and oversized glasses for her homemade lime and mint-infused sparkling water.

Should she include a flower bouquet? No, probably too much. She opted for a single long stem red rose positioned just so.

Once confident over the casual elegance of her arrangements, she sat and waited peacefully, patiently. She surveyed the open space for imperfections. Not bad for January. Mild temperatures made the pristine pool water almost impossible to resist. And while not in the bloom of spring, ornamental trees and potted plants infused life and color into the bricked surface.

She flexed her hands to inspect her manicured nails. Immaculate. The red could not have matched her ensemble better had she worn her nightie and its matching feather boa high-heeled slipper sandals into the salon. Hopefully, Chris would return soon.

For months, she had savored the memory of their St. John video shoot. The publicity and accolades she had received had increased her value and demand—an impressive shot in the arm at this stage of the game. The only thing that eclipsed the warm days of sun and camera were the nights she and Chris spent making love.

He had come alive before her eyes, unlike anything she had experienced in prior years. When not in the shot, she had lingered on set with the crew and watched him, mesmerized by his passion and intensity. Truly in his element. On point during the day, and all the more so at night.

Since then, she had resented the demands on her time. She did not want to take extended trips away from home. Thanks to some fancy schedule shuffling by the Monroe Agency, she had managed to sync up most their schedule. Gloria Monroe had artfully declined three gigs and successfully negotiated the relocation of four others. As a result, Julie had stayed on track with the *Aftermath* publicity tour for all but five weeks of the last seven months.

Unfortunately, they had spent their anniversary apart, with Chris in Chicago and her in New York. He had sent her three dozen roses as a consolation with a note promising they would celebrate later. A week before Christmas, he returned and instructed her to pack. She figured they would fly back to England for yet another uncomfortable holiday with his family.

When their international flight landed, she found herself—more than a little tipsy—in Adelaide, Australia. He had arranged a trip to Thorngrove Manor, the very place they had spent their honeymoon. As was the case on their first visit, neither of them saw anything but the inside of their hotel room for a full week.

Julie smiled, calculated, added, and guessed. She glanced at the Tiffany wristwatch he had given her last week and wondered fleetingly what kept him. He had promised his meeting with Samantha would not go beyond noon. Maybe traffic held him up.

Today...oh today. It would redefine their future. She exhaled against the tiny flutters of excitement centered in her middle and savored the anticipation. A near-constant smile lingered at the corners of her artfully pigmented lips. She had choreographed their afternoon like a Broadway production. He would tell her all about his meeting with Samantha over a leisurely lunch. Then, she would take him upstairs to celebrate.

Cheryl's advice had hit the bulls-eye. At the age of thirty-three, after three and a half years of marriage, Julie found herself hopelessly, with schoolgirl total commitment, in love with her husband.

When she recognized the familiar rumble of Chris's Porsche pulling into the driveway, she stood, cast off her silk robe to reveal her perfect body, then rushed into the den and engaged the CD player. Bach's "Air on the G String" filled the room and drifted through speakers in the house and grounds.

By the time he found her on the patio, she stood posed at her chair. She held a single red rose in her hand, skimming its flowered petals seductively across her cleavage as she cooed, "Good afternoon, darling. I prepared lunch. And...I also made a bite to eat. I hope you're...hungry."

Chris shuddered at the sight that greeted him. Julie. The red teddy. Red. Blood red. His conscious mind told him his striking wife stood before him, half-naked and inviting. He should be aroused. He should be smiling—nay, purring—at her attempted seduction. Instead, he found himself blinded in a crimson fog. He forced a weak smile as she glided to his side and planted a sensuous kiss on his lips. His body stiffened at the contact.

She pulled back and faced him. Her forehead wrinkled at the subtle rejection.

He searched her eyes. In his mind, he apologized for what he was about to do. Distantly, he noted the melodious strains of Bach. He thought he smelled egg salad.

Her head and shoulders quivered. Nostrils flared, she inhaled and forced the sides of her mouth upward, then turned to pour his drink. "I'm sure you've had a long morning. Did you and Sam have a productive meeting? I can't wait to tell you about my day! First, I..."

He listened as she relayed the events of her busy morning, unsure how to explain. His morning had been anything but happy—and her day would soon take a turn as well.

Julie fussed over their lunch fixings as she tittered, set their plates down, and took her seat. When he remained standing, she glanced up at him with wounded eyes. "Aren't you going to sit down?"

He lowered himself into the cushioned patio chair opposite her.

The familiar, faraway look he had worn like a death mask for all but the last few months of their life together leveled her. The balloon she had ridden all morning deflated.

You're going to ruin everything.

She had done all she could to banish the ghost haunting the Grant mansion. Apparently, the exorcism her sister-in-law recommended had failed. Well, too bad. The game had not yet ended. She had one card left. An ace up her sleeve.

She suppressed her wrath, willing her racing heartbeat to slow. With a raised brow and a practiced smile, she jutted her chin and asked emotionlessly, "Have you been visiting the cemetery again?"

He shook his head.

"Then what aren't you telling me?"

"I saw Samantha today." He stared down at the lunch he knew he would not touch. As he explained, he watched a look of horror transform his wife's million-dollar face.

He weighed his words as he informed Julie that Farin lived, that Jameson had hidden her away, that he did not know why or how it had happened, and that he did not know where the old man had her. It was the second time he had told the story, and it made no more sense than when Sam had broken the news to him.

Julie sat, stunned. Behind her blank expression, her thoughts raged. It could not be. Slowly, reality bored its way from her ears to her brain, skated along the ice in her veins, then settled like worms of molten lead in the pit of her stomach. Farin Grant. The ghost. The bitch.

"You're going after her," she stated before Chris uttered another syllable. As numbness overtook her senses, she watched her husband rise from his seat. Her clear, unseeing eyes fixed themselves on his vacated chair. "Aren't you going to eat first?"

He crouched beside her, unsure what he could do or say to make things easier. The only comfort he found, if he could find any at all, was in the knowledge that Julie understood. She knew what he had to do and she knew why. "I know you're hurt," he whispered. He kissed her velvet cheek. "I have to do this—for Jordan."

Julie remained frozen in place while Chris hurried upstairs to pack an overnight bag and shaving kit "just in case." She let him kiss her goodbye. Moments later, she heard the roar of the engine, then the chirp of tires as he headed off into the day. She stood long enough to slip back into her silk robe, then retook her seat and stared at her untouched egg sandwich.

In a sudden flash, she sat up and swept her arm furiously across the table, sending plates, glasses, silverware, and crystal serving bowls flying across the patio. The noise of shattering glass startled her. She turned and surveyed the mess. Had her public stolen a glimpse behind her mask and beheld her uncorked rage, the image would have replaced the memory of every spread she had done in her career.

She inhaled sharply. The lines in her face fell away, replaced with tight control. She eased back into her seat and again regarded the chair opposite her.

"I saw the doctor today," she spat ruefully at the unoccupied space. "We're having a baby."

Without ceremony, she punctuated her sentence by kicking the empty chair, sending it skidding and tumbling toward the pool.

CHAPTER 12

MEGAN **P**RICE **B**REAKS **L**OCKHARDT **S**OUND **Barrier**
-- Chicago, IL, Chicago Chronicle (AP), Tuesday, January 17, 1995 by Miles Macy

Lockhardt Sound, Inc. lost its premiere recording artist to Minor 6th Records yesterday. Country and Western headliner and fan favorite Megan Price abandoned LSI's sinking ship, signing a lucrative five album contract with Minor 6th Records, following in the footsteps of yet another former LSI artist, Chris Grant. In a press release, Vice President Samantha Drake said, "Minor Sixth is thrilled to sign Megan. We believe we can handle her needs a little better than LSI at this point in her career. It's good timing for us and for Megan. We're looking forward to her next album, and Minor is behind her one hundred percent."

Megan Price was unavailable for comment, but a spokesperson for the singer said, "We aren't denying that some of these negotiations took place while Megan was here last year, but those negotiations were in no way connected with Megan cancelling her final tour dates."

Bobby Lockhardt, Vice President of Public Relations and only son of LSI president, Jameson Lockhardt, had this to say: "Everyone here at LSI is happy with the move. It looks like a good fit for Megan. We're extremely proud of her accomplishments. As you know, LSI has never traditionally been a Country and Western label. The time LSI and Megan shared will always be important to us. We wish her much success."

Responding to Mr. Lockhardt's remarks, Megan added through her spokesperson, "Megan had conflicting emotions regarding the move from LSI. Although she continues to have warm feelings for Lockhardt Sound, the change simply made sense."

Megan Price first appeared in the spotlight with a number one album and several public appearances with her one-time boyfriend, Jordan Grant. When asked how Megan felt about being on the same label as the brother of her late boyfriend, Miss Price had no comment.

Rumor has it the move came about because LSI could not offer Miss Price nearly as lucrative a deal as Minor 6th. This happened only six months after LSI sold off their Florida-based recording studio to Hit Works in an attempt to raise liquid capital. The question is, now that Megan Price is no longer the Minnie Pearl in LSI's straw hat, what will become of the former recording leviathan? Despite insistence by LSI executives over the last year that they are lining up some blockbuster albums, none of those records have materialized in the marketplace.

For the last two years, Megan Price has been the only living artist in the LSI stable generating revenue for the company. Furthermore, after Miss Price became ill last year and had to cancel her last three concerts, LSI's budget constraints prompted their withdrawal of sponsorship support, forcing promoters to cut short the remainder of her schedule. Megan should face no such issues with Minor 6th. It is clear to this reporter Megan Price made a sound decision.

***

Ross Alexander wandered his empty Palm Springs home, half-reveling in the quiet and half-missing his bride. As had become custom, Josephine had arranged to spend the first night of their vacation playing bridge with a circle of friends she had become acquainted with during their yearly vacations. This gave Ross a much-needed pause between the life he left in New York and the two months of freedom he so enjoyed.

The rain storm they encountered upon their arrival had stopped hours ago. The humid post-storm petrichor of the glistening grounds wafted into the house through the cracked windows along with a light breeze.

He checked his watch. Josephine would probably stay out a few more hours. Perhaps a little television to numb his scattered thoughts. Nothing dramatic, nothing deep, just a bit of light humor to cleanse the film of New York filth from his mind.

Remote in hand, he nestled into his recliner, then clicked through several channels before settling on a *Green Acres* marathon. A guilty pleasure. As an afterthought, he considered fixing himself a scotch—the only component absent from his serene evening. Well, a good scotch and his bride. But she would return soon. Let the vacation begin.

As episode number 74, "Jealousy, English Style," ended, Ross took advantage of the commercial break to use the restroom and fix himself a Dewars on the rocks. The freezer and refrigerator were mostly empty. The first thing on Josephine's agenda for tomorrow would likely be a trip to the market.

At the age of sixty-eight, Ross enjoyed the predictability of his personal existence. Jameson's retirement, and his own, were less than a year away. Sometimes the anticipation overwhelmed him. Soon, he would sever the ties that bound him to Jameson Lockhardt.

As he returned to the soft canned laughter emitted from the television, he swore he would dismiss all business-related thoughts for the whole of their vacation. Not once had he kept this annual pledge, to himself or his bride. Maybe this year, his last, would be different.

The telephone rang at a quarter past eight. He muted the television before picking up the cordless extension from the end table beside him. Josephine was probably checking in to break the news that her bridge game had evolved into something interesting and she would run later than expected.

With a chuckle, he pushed the "call" button on the handset and whispered lovingly, "You're right on cue. I'm fine. Yes. Nick at Night's running a *Green Acres* marathon, so I'm in good company. You have a wonderful time." He paused to listen to his bride speak. "Yes, we can go to the market tomorrow. I love you. Drive safely. The roads may still be a bit slick."

Ross lay the handset on the table and reclined fully in his chair. He took a long, slow sip of Dewars and pressed the volume button on the remote. The phone rang again. Smiling, he muted the television once more and grabbed the handset, wondering what piece of information his bride had neglected to give him. "You know," he answered as if their previous conversation had not yet ended, "Arnold the pig's going to Hollywood to become a star. I'm missing the best part."

"Pig? What?"

The voice took him aback. He felt oddly invaded, and a little embarrassed. "I, uh, thought you were Josephine. Hello, Bobby. What can I do for you?"

A good-natured, if forced, chuckle came over the line. "I realize it's late, Ross. Sorry to call like this. I have news."

He consulted his watch, annoyed that LSI had already interrupted his trip. "Actually, it's not late at all. Not here, anyway. Is everything all right?"

Bobby's tone grew somber. "It's Dad. He asked me to call and let you know he's delayed his trip south by a few days. You knew he was planning to scout that band in Raleigh before having me join him out on the road."

"I assume Childs has taken a turn for the worse."

"He died this afternoon."

Ross paused. "I see."

The news of Lionel Childs's stroke days before had hit Jameson hard. Though the physician had eleven years on him, the loss would cause a level of panic few would witness. It hammered another nail into Lockhardt Sound's coffin. It brought Jameson face-to-face with his own mortality. But more than anything else, it ended two decades of practiced discretion.

Bobby would doubtless come to the forefront of his father's mind. The boy's treatment necessitated the immediate recruitment of a replacement.

While the Haldol prescription would not expire or deplete overnight, the drug was a highly controlled substance—one that meant the difference between sanity and madness in Bobby's case.

"We'd just visited him in the hospital Saturday. Dad was on the plane when he got the news. He seems upset, but doesn't want to talk about it. You know how he is."

"Indeed, I do."

Unanswered questions skidded like stones across the pool of Ross's thoughts. Had Childs ever cursed the day he sold out to LSI? Had he experienced remorse for the crimes he committed against those Jameson sent his way? Did his conscience bother him when Farin O'Conner became addicted to the tranquilizers that nearly cost her life? Did he feel any regret over Farin's ultimate fate? Even at the end?

Guilt fed Ross's curiosity, even though he had not personally prescribed medications or made arrangements. He wondered whether Childs had repented before he died, or if he now burned in eternal Hell. In fact, he wondered if he would someday share that ultimate fate.

Perhaps he would never be free of Lockhardt Sound. Childs had merely died first. One by one, they would all die. Part of him feared he would spend eternity with Lionel, Jameson, and the other faceless souls who had perpetuated the lies, a citadel built on a foundation of rotting, decaying flesh that called itself LSI.

"Is there anything I can do for your father, Bobby? Has he thought about the funeral?"

"Louise is handling the arrangements. I figured that'd make you happy. You've had so much on your plate with the whole retirement thing. Dad told me to tell you he'll understand if you don't make the funeral. He wanted me to make sure you know he's rescheduled Raleigh for Friday. He'd have called you himself but he's flying home right now. The funeral should be in a couple of days."

"How are you holding up?" Inside, Ross rebuked himself. The fewer questions he asked, the sooner he could get off the phone and procure another Dewars, which he had drained within moments of hearing the news of the physician's passing. Decades of confinement resulting from phones attached to cords subconsciously anchored him to his seat.

A bubbly, exhaled breath filled the line. "It was a shock, but not really, you know? I mean, the doc was eighty. He wasn't gonna live forever, right?"

"Of course."

"But that's not your real question, is it? You're talking about my meds."

Ross castigated himself for opening Pandora's Box. He had told no one that he believed Childs had cheated Bobby. How could any physician prescribe antipsychotic medication without consulting a qualified specialist? Was Ross the only one who had ever second-guessed the diagnosis?

He looked down into and jiggled his glass, regarding the lonely, melting ice cubes.

"I know Dad's gonna worry. He'll think I'm gonna blow off my meds like I did before. Well, that's not gonna happen. *Ever.* I've never told my father this. I've never told anyone besides the doc but I might as well tell you now. My little trip to La-La Land scared the hell out of me. I can't even remember it. One minute I'm at a party with Farin, the next I'm in some psych ward. There are entire weeks I can't place."

Bobby sounded as clear and sane as Ross had ever heard him, but he pictured the subtle facial tic that had hallmarked itself as the one viewable piece of evidence of the drug's side effects. "Son, you don't have to—"

"No, let me finish. Jordan died at my house. That really shook me up. And what's worse, I can't even remember what planet I was on at the time. If I hadn't gone off my meds, maybe I would've been home that day. Maybe Jordan would be alive. And Farin...if Jordan hadn't died, maybe she'd still be alive, too. Now, I've shed about as many unmanly tears over that whole situation as I can. I can't explain why, or how, but I feel responsible. So trust me when I tell you I'll never put myself—or anyone I love—in danger again."

Ross swallowed hard. His throat felt dry. He needed another drink. "I believe you. And I know how hard you've worked to overcome the challenges in your life. Your father knows, too. If he didn't think you were capable of running LSI, he'd have just made arrangements to sell it off. You know that, right?"

A burst of cynical laughter bored into Ross's ears. "No, he'd have never sold. He'd have just decided to live forever. You and I would both go to our graves and my father would curse our weak, pathetic souls for giving up so easily."

He hung his head, chuckling softly in agreement.

"He's given LSI a real kick-start lately. We finally have some hope, what with the acts coming up now. The media can say anything they want about my dad, especially that—what's his name? Macy? Yeah, Macy. Miles

Macy. Macy and all the rest of them can say what they want, but you and I know. My father's a *genius.*"

Ross sucked at the melted ice cubes in his glass, hoping for a taste of something other than water.

"LSI's on the comeback trail, and it's all his doing. I can only hope to accomplish half of what he has. Anyway, it's nearly midnight here. I'm gonna let you go. Just wanted to give you the news about the doc. May God rest his soul and all. Dad will be in touch after the funeral. Give my love to Josephine, and for Pete's sake, enjoy your vacation. I'll be fine. You'll be fine. Dad'll be fine. LSI will be fine. Good night, Ross."

Bobby had a way of making light of serious situations, yet Ross could not deny his pride as they signed off. The boy was everything in the world Jameson loved. Almost every move the old man had made related to his son. Though no one could know the depth of devotion his father held for him, Ross had to hand it to him. He fought hard for his sanity.

In moments like this, Ross agreed with Jameson. Telling Bobby the truth about that fateful morning in Coral Gables would only bring unnecessary pain to an already troubled soul. In many ways, the shooting felt like another accident. Besides, no court in the land would have convicted Bobby Lockhardt of murder. The steps Jameson had taken to ensure his son had an alibi for the time of Jordan's death gave him a chance to get well again—with Childs's help, of course. Bobby did not have a mean or manipulative bone in his sane body. If he knew the truth, it would destroy him.

As for LSI, Bobby was right. A new wave of talent had washed onto the industry's shores. Ross clung to the hope those musical beacons would steer them back into the black. LSI had extended its credit and creditors to the brink. Even studio time had cut into the fast-depleting resources. Hopefully, they would not need to liquidate other assets.

He sank into his recliner and shut his eyes to clear his mind. His thoughts roamed to the one as yet untouchable asset that would keep LSI afloat amid the stormy sea, if necessity dictated: Double Maguffin. Jameson had spent years building the dummy company for a rainy day, but only Ross knew the details of its invisible operations and the power that lay within its carefully constructed lines. Not even Jameson could match Ross's talent for hiding things in plain sight.

A quick succession of knocks echoed from the hallway. He knitted his brows and glanced at his watch, unable to guess who might come by so late on his first day in Palm Springs. Probably a neighbor welcoming him back to town. No matter. He was in his pajamas. No need to further disrupt his yearly rite of passage between chaos and solitude. He would exchange greetings after the market tomorrow. Maybe invite everyone for afternoon cocktails. Josephine would love to entertain. Tonight—what was left of it— was his time.

Another series of knocks brought him out of his chair. He crossed the long, tiled foyer, wondering if perhaps Josephine had left her house keys at her friend's place.

"I thought you said you'd be late." He unlocked and opened the front door.

He barely made out the tall figure standing on his front steps before pain slammed his eyelids shut. A powerful fist connected with his jaw. His eyes reopened in time to watch the ceiling whip past his spotty field of vision. He felt the force of the blow peripherally as his arms windmilled in the unhelpful air. His body hurled itself backward until his full length slammed jarringly onto the tiles.

"Where is she?"

It took Ross several seconds to register what had happened. He propped himself up on his right elbow and rubbed at his throbbing face with his free hand. He tasted blood from where his lower lip split against his teeth.

When his mind finally focused, he saw Chris Grant towering over him. His dark eyes had narrowed to threatening slits above clenched teeth and flared nostrils. His fists balled, positioned to strike a second blow.

It occurred to him he might neutralize the situation if he displayed some measure of fear. Maybe Chris had lost his mind. Instead, he took the blow in stride in defiance of his throbbing jaw. Twenty years ago, he could have taken him. At least the fall had not broken his hip.

He did not blame Sam, though he wished she had warned him. Once he had unburdened his soul, it had been a matter of time. If anything, he wondered what had taken so long. One thing was certain, though: after tonight, his days were numbered.

"Get up!" Chris stepped forward, drawing back his hind foot, poised to kick.

A woman appeared from behind, positioned herself beside Chris, and grabbed his arm. "This won't get us anywhere. What are you thinking?"

Whimsically, Ross noted the brunette was not Julie Swanson Grant.

He wondered where he had picked her up and how long it had been going on. It surprised and disappointed him on some level. Though Chris had once graced the front page of every tabloid with conquests, paternity suits, and all manner of unseemly allegations, Ross had heard the rocker was a reformed man.

He rolled over, lifted himself up on all fours, then made his way to his feet, stumbling twice before steadying himself against the wall.

"Where is she?" Chris demanded again, his voice only slightly less lethal.

"You don't understand," he mumbled thickly through injured lips. He rubbed his jaw with one hand, waved the couple inside with the other, and then moved past them to shut the front door. "I'm a dead man if this gets out. You know Jameson almost as well as I do. You were his protégé."

He eyeballed the couple, then motioned them into the living room. With trembling hands, he picked up the remote and killed the television. The ensuing silence took on an eerie quality. He wished once more he had refilled his glass. "Can I get anyone a drink? I'm sure we could all use one about now."

Chris pressed uncomfortably close. "This isn't a social call. I *know*. I know everything. Now, tell me where he has her or I'll break your bloody neck!"

Ross fixed his aging green eyes on Chris and studied him at length. The woman hovered between the foyer and living room, arms crossed. He lifted his throbbing chin her way. "I don't believe I know your friend."

"Marci Lawrence. Farin's best friend," Chris grumbled hotly. "One of the many people you and the old man destroyed when you invented your little story."

Ross squinted her way. A vague recollection flashed in his mind. The funeral, he decided. He must remember her from the funeral. One of them, at least. "My bride will be home soon, Chris. Let's be civil. Josephine knows nothing about this."

"Then tell us where he has her. If you're concerned about your wife finding out, start talking."

"When did Sam tell you?"

"This morning."

Ross flattened his lips, frowned, and nodded in surrender. Fleetingly, he congratulated himself for not divulging more damning information to his former colleague.

"Where *is* she?"

"I take it you haven't called the police."

"Not yet."

"Smart man."

Marci stood anchored between rooms. "Is it true, Mr. Alexander? Is she still alive?" Her voice quavered.

Ross looked at and past her, then pointed toward the kitchen. "I'm going to get some ice—and a drink. I'll be back in a moment. We can figure this mess out. Have a seat."

Marci's legs nearly failed her before collapsing onto the sofa. Chris stood, chin jutted forward in defiance.

"Sit down," she urged with a stern whisper.

He shook his head. "I don't trust him."

"Well, you can't beat it out of him."

"I will if I have to."

Her muscles had tensed the moment Chris relayed the news and had yet to relax. The last few hours had strung together in a blurry montage of disbelief. This morning, she and Elliot had stayed in bed late, cuddling and discussing his current project, how disappointed they both were she was not yet pregnant, making love, reading the paper, calling Faith. Elliot had made lunch. Then, Chris had appeared with news she could scarcely comprehend. Farin. Alive.

From there to Palm Springs, things got sketchy. Chris had left temporarily to pack an overnight bag but told them he would return as soon as possible. Elliot had packed her a bag as well while she sat at the edge of their bed, too shocked and numb to move. Upon Chris's return, he had insisted Elliot drive them to a car dealership. For some reason, he had wanted her to buy a car. A used car—older model. Chris and Elliot parked across the street at a gas station while she transacted the deal.

Before they took off, Elliot had loaded their bags in the vehicle, kissed her goodbye, and made her promise she would call him from the road. Now, hours later, she and Chris crouched in Ross Alexander's home like gate crashers at a black-tie event. His answers would determine their next move.

She wondered where Jameson Lockhardt had kept Farin all these years. Was she safe? Healthy? Unharmed? When no one came for her, had it broken her heart? Marci hated to admit it, but some of the animosity she had harbored for Chris Grant evaporated the moment his fist connected with Ross Alexander's jaw.

She peered over her shoulder but could not get a clear line of sight on their host's location. "What if he's lying? What if he's in there right now, calling Lockhardt? He could kill her. What have we done?"

Chris's sightless eyes darted about the room as he weighed her words. "He wasn't kidding about Jameson. The old man would kill Ross if he knew he'd told Sam the truth. Ross is scared to death right now. That's why he'll tell us what we want to know."

She stuffed her trembling hands beneath her thighs and studied her longtime nemesis. The raw emotion he had displayed at the graveyard so long ago, and then again at her place earlier today, had vanished. In its place, she witnessed conviction and an uncanny stillness. No ties. No entanglements. He possessed the grim determination of a man on a mission, as if he had signed on to fight a proxy war. Not for Farin, but for a friend. A close friend. A brother.

Ross returned with an ice pack, a decanter of scotch, and two glasses. He poured them each a drink, then sat down on the edge of his recliner and held the ice pack against his swelling cheek. As he beheld his unwelcome guests, he collected his thoughts. Not exactly the relaxing evening he had anticipated. How would he explain his injury to his bride? "I can't help you get her back," he announced in his most rational tone.

"But...she's still alive?" Marci repeated before Chris could respond. Tears welled in her eyes.

Ross held her stare. The pain on her pretty face read like a diary entry. The fearful hope reflected in her eyes acted on him like a mirror. It demanded he view himself without excuse.

Despite intimate knowledge of Jameson's dark dealings, he had never before this day hated the man. In fact, he had spent much of his career assisting him. But tonight, the agony he had helped create played itself out on his living room carpet. He now knew, without question, he hated his only friend. Moreover, he hated himself. "Yes, Mrs. Lawrence, the last time I saw her, she was alive."

Chris plopped down beside Marci. "Where does he have her?"

Ross dropped the ice pack and both his hands onto his lap. He hung his head. "Dorothea Dix has her, so to speak."

Chris's forehead creased. "Who's Dorothea Dix? And what has she done with Farin?"

Years of practiced loyalty urged him to relay a story—*any* story—that would throw his unwelcomed guests off the trail. Every part of him wanted to lie. Then again, a lie would only delay the inevitable. His options were few. He could die now, at Chris's hands, or later, under circumstances that would never in a million years lead back to LSI.

His features melted into expressionless resignation. "Dorothea Dix is a mental institution in Raleigh, North Carolina. The oldest in the state. Bobby's spent time there, too. Childs took her there after the accident."

Marci shuddered. "Then she *was* in the accident. But how could she have survived? The police told everyone she...she burned to death."

"That was someone else."

The hair on Chris's neck stood on end.

"Farin was taken shortly after she left her hotel, before the explosion. Jameson found out where she was staying and arranged to take her before she could make it to Jordan's funeral."

"But why?"

Ross shook his head.

Chris stood, his demanding voice echoing Marci's query. "*Why?*"

He grabbed his glass, gulped its contents, poured himself a refill, and sank into his chair.

"She'd called a press conference," Chris said.

"That, she did."

"It had to have had something to do with the old man."

Ross fumbled with the ice pack, repositioning it against his aching jaw.

Chris stepped toward him. "Tell me!"

Calmly, Ross gestured for Chris to move aside, then reclined his chair.

"She was his favorite. He canned Mirage over her."

Ross scoffed. "The dissolution of your contract had little to do with her."

Chris paced the floor. Occasionally, he mumbled under his breath as he struggled to connect the pieces. Ross finished his drink, poured yet another, then raised his eyebrows along with the decanter at Marci. She shook her head and scooted back into the sofa.

"She disappeared after Jordan's murder. None of us had any idea where she...How did he find her?"

"From you." Ross glared at the back of his head with flinty eyes.

Chris spun around. "*What?*"

"Well, you and that reporter."

"What reporter?"

"That reporter from the *Miami Post*."

"Macy?"

Marci faced Chris, aghast. "*You* told him?"

Chris blanched as the implications beset him. "You're lying."

Ross shrugged. "Afraid not."

"Macy may have told him, but *never* me."

The effects of the alcohol handed him a decent buzz. The jaw pain had dulled a bit, as had his inhibitions. Maybe a few choice revelations would hasten their departure. Maybe the right details would prevent them from asking the more obvious questions. He brought his glass to his lips and took another drink. "Do you remember talking to Jameson on the phone the day before Jordan's funeral?"

Chris raised his hands to his hips. He looked down and left. "I spoke with him briefly, yes. But I didn't know where she was. He asked me if I'd heard from her, and I told him—"

"You told him you hadn't. Then, another call came in. It was the reporter."

Lips parted, he muttered an incredulous, "How do you know that?"

"You never ended the call with Jameson. Somehow, the lines connected. I don't know the details. I'm a lawyer, not a phone technician. All I know is, when Macy struck a bargain with you regarding an exclusive in return for Farin's whereabouts, you agreed. And Jameson heard everything."

Chris collapsed onto the sofa, dropping his head in his hands.

Tears spilled down Marci's cheeks. She stared at him in disbelief. "You handed her over to Jameson Lockhardt wrapped in a bow."

His fingers threaded his hair until they curled in frustration, making angry fists. "What about the ashes?"

Marci peered at Ross.

He adjusted himself in his chair. "You got what you came here for, so..."

"If Farin was taken from the hotel, then who did we bury?"

"I really wouldn't know," he lied, avoiding eye contact. "We didn't have much time to plan. Jameson paid someone to tamper with the car, and then replaced Farin with someone else before the accident. It was surprisingly simple."

Marci slid forward, arms folded atop her knees. "But Farin's face was known worldwide. The coroner would've known if the body wasn't hers."

The increased warmth in his belly infused him with a certain amount of courage. He sloshed more of the decanter into his glass, vowing it would be his last. "There isn't much money won't buy."

She scrunched her face into a disgusted frown. "He paid off the medical examiner's office?"

"He didn't have to. They see hundreds of bodies a year. The remains were almost completely incinerated. Falsified dental records and several dozen witnesses—including that reporter friend of yours," he said, pointing at Chris, "—ensured a misidentified corpse."

Chris looked up at last. His angry, bloodshot eyes bore into Ross's. "And then what?"

Ross crossed his ankles. "She was a bit banged up from being manhandled, but otherwise unharmed. A physician acquaintance of Jameson's kept her unconscious during the funeral, then flew her directly to Raleigh."

Marci's hand shot up to cover her mouth as she gasped, "The funeral?"

"She was there?" Chris sucked in his cheeks.

Despite his increasing alcohol fog, Ross knew they had waded into dangerous water. "As I said, you have what you came for. I told you where she is. I'll assume you're going after her. Be careful. Jameson's not a gracious loser."

Chris ignored the warning. "Farin was at the top of her career. The money she made for him was astounding. Word on the street is the old man's going to lose his precious company, and soon. There has to be more to the story."

Ross sat his glass on the end table beside him, then slid his hand along the inside of the chair to retrieve the ice pack, which had slipped out of his hand. Time had come to show his guests the door. Josephine would be home soon. He wanted to catch another episode of *Green Acres* before bed. Maybe brew a small pot of coffee. As he struggled with the lever for the leg rest, he noted the throbbing in his jaw had returned.

Chris rose, stalked over to Ross, and pulled him free of the apparatus. "What is it?" he pressed. "What's so important he would want to hurt Farin and risk losing LSI?"

"I...I can't say for sure."

"You're lying," Chris snarled, his grip tight around Ross's upper arm.

"Take your friend here and go."

"Spill it or we wait for your wife. Right, Marci?"

Marci stood, arms akimbo, and gave a curt nod.

Ross yanked free, nearly losing his footing. "The press conference."

"What about it?"

"Farin called it because she had some information about…" He dared not venture further off course. The fury in Chris's eyes told him he may have reached a threshold. "She'd discovered some of Jameson's secrets."

For several minutes, Ross performed a tap dance that would have shamed Gregory Hines. Giving Farin Grant a fighting chance at life more than satisfied his guilt over the happenings of the last several years. To relay the entire truth—the truth about Bobby, about the shooting, about Jordan's murder—was impossible. He had done more than his fair share. They had what they needed to make their next move. If they succeeded in their quest, Farin would likely give them the rest.

In the end, Chris backed off, caught Marci's attention, and jerked his head toward the door. He tarried in the foyer, calling back, "It's not over, Ross. The next time we see each other, you'd better be prepared to tell me everything. As it is, we can't afford to waste any more time standing around and listening to you mumble. If you know what's good for you, you won't alert the old man."

"We both know he'll find out eventually." Ross tasted bile in the back of his throat. As he watched Chris and Marci disappear into the night, he wondered how many more nights he had left to spend with his beautiful bride.

He checked his watch, then staggered back to his recliner and searched for the remote. In the stillness of the room, solitude overcame him. He hoped Josephine would return soon.

CHAPTER 13

J AMESON LOCKHARDT SAT AT THE end of the last pew in St. Michael's Cathedral. Periodically, he glanced over his left shoulder, wondering what kept his son. Down the center aisle in front of the pulpit sat the coffin of Dr. Lionel Childs. Inside the open casket, Lionel looked unlike the man he had known so many years. His still, reposed state melted the man's face into his chin. Makeup covered his features, masking the drained color of his skin—the pallor of death.

For reasons Jameson could not fathom, Louise Hayes had chosen a crisp white suit for her father's send-off. It fit his tall, robust body to perfection. It also made him look like an ice cream vendor. Fitting, considering the Good Doctor/Good Humor Man now lay as cold as ice and had dispensed goodies for decades.

Jameson recalled an old film, *The Island of Doctor Moreau*, where Burt Lancaster wore only spotlessly clean white linen suits. While the nearest dry-cleaning establishment was likely several thousand miles away from the island, Moreau appeared immaculate in every scene. When Jameson first saw his longtime associate clad in such preposterous apparel, he had fought an overwhelming urge to laugh.

Childs would have never chosen white. Nothing pure for the man who had spent his entire medical career selling his advantages to the highest bidder. Jameson had to wonder how much Louise knew about her father's questionable practice. In their decades of dealings, Lionel had said little about his family. Did Louise know the truth? Was that the reason she had chosen such an absurd get-up? Might she think a white suit would fool God? That it would grant Lionel entrance to the Pearly Gates?

Jameson chortled at the idea despite himself. He covered his mouth, coughing into his fist in an attempt to mask the humor of the situation. Where was Bobby, anyway?

God. Jameson Lockhardt defied God and all He stood for. He rejected the belief that any Supreme Being had a hand in, much less the ultimate authority over, the lives of every living soul. No. People made their own decisions. They either wielded their own power or became victims of someone else's. And when death came, it came. Nothing existed beyond death. He likewise did not believe in ghosts, angels, purgatory, confession, repentance, Heaven, or Hell.

From time to time, Jameson had boasted to his associates that if a god did in fact exist, he would be it. Did he not possess the power and influence to manipulate, control, and maneuver hundreds of lives? Where was God while he made life- and career-changing decisions for those who found themselves in his sphere? Where was God the day his son killed Jordan Grant? Or when Farin Grant vanished, reportedly dead to the world?

Even here, in this supposedly sacred space, the notion a god existed who could make him atone for his so-called sins brought a cynical sneer to his lips. He buried his self-satisfaction over his rebellion behind a closed fist. Several past conversations—including one he had with Lionel shortly before his death—assured him the physician shared his atheism.

As the priest took his place at the pulpit and began the funeral mass, Bobby slid into the heavily-lacquered pew beside his father. He placed his damp trench coat beside him, then leafed through the program he had received in the vestibule, perusing its contents as he leaned in to whisper to his father. "Sorry I'm late. Car trouble. New York winters, huh?"

Jameson acknowledged him with a single nod. A somber expression etched into his ruddy features, he feigned interest in the priest's opening words. His mind harkened back to the day he first saw Farin at Jordan's house. Like today, that day had begun with a funeral.

The path their lives had followed from that meeting had taken many turns, good and bad. Mirage's success, as well as that of Jordan's and Farin's individually, had secured what he believed would be an untouchable dynasty of power. Had Chris not forced his hand with his unrelenting pursuit, things would have doubtless ended differently—for them all.

As with most of his decisions, Jameson entertained zero remorse over disassembling Mirage. In a rare expression of paternal concern, he had attempted to fill the void Farin felt over losing her father. To watch over and protect her from further harm—specifically, the emotional damage he knew Chris could inflict with his predilection for female conquests. He had tried to provide a life that would eclipse the loss of her youth. No living soul knew the depth to which he empathized with that loss. Chris should have heeded his warning. Instead, he had paid the price—they all had.

What a waste.

While LSI had initially profited from the scandals and tragedies surrounding its biggest stars, the sensationalism of the big-ticket story soon fizzled out, save for a certain reporter who refused to let the story—and the Grants—die. Only in hindsight did he realize losing his top acts might cost him his life's triumph. For months, he had watched LSI's inevitable downward spiral.

The time had come to do what he did best. If any chance remained that Lockhardt Sound would be resurrected, it lay to him. Especially now with Samantha Drake—the most talented A&R head he had ever known—gone and, as yet, unreplaced.

"It's snowing," Bobby whispered as the service concluded. "Do we have to attend the burial? Not to sound heartless or anything, but I've got a ton of work back at the office."

Jameson inclined his head and whispered back, "Before you leave, say something nice to Louise."

Bobby's cheeks flushed, as they always did when put in personal situations with beautiful women. "We only met that one time, Dad. I was like, seventeen. She probably doesn't even remember me."

"I'm not suggesting a date, son. She's married. But you owe it to Childs, do you not, to spare a kind word for his only daughter? After all he did for you?"

Heads bowed, mourners offered a collective "amen" to the final prayer, ending the funeral service. The assemblage stood and organized into a single line to file past the open coffin for a final farewell to Lionel Childs.

Jameson spotted Louise standing at the left front pew. He caught her eye, lifting his chin and brows. With a sad smile, she handed her toddler to her husband, then signaled with her index finger she would make her way back to him. Jameson nudged Bobby's arm before side-stepping into the aisle.

Bobby asked sheepishly, "Louise doesn't know about my..."

"I doubt it."

"You said Childs gave you the names of some doctors who might pick up his practice. Should I make an appointment with one or all of them to discuss...you know?"

He shook his head as he eyeballed the crowd. "I met with each of them personally the day after Lionel passed."

From halfway down the aisle, Louise raised a delicate hand, wiggling her fingertips. Jameson nodded.

Bobby crossed his arms. "Shouldn't I have gone with you?"

"What for? Once I make a decision, I'll arrange an introduction."

"But I'm the patient."

"The replacement is for *all* LSI, Bobby, not just you."

"You retire in ten months. Shouldn't I be involved in some of these decisions?"

Jameson huffed.

When their son began to fuss, Louise doubled back to her husband. She glanced over her shoulder as she wove through those heading outside and again lifted her index finger. "Sorry," she mouthed. "One minute."

Jameson nodded graciously even as he clenched his jaw, inhaling through his nose. Childs's death had required he make some tough decisions. Decisions that wrestled his attention away from business matters. He disliked distractions—almost as much as he disliked children.

With shaky hands, Lionel had written the names of possible successors as he lay on his deathbed. Jameson had neglected to apprise Bobby of the subsequent meetings as he had yet to decide if he would include the situation with Farin in their discussions. In the end, he had opted to leave her out of it.

Jameson had kept Farin in confinement, in every sense of the word, for one reason. In time, that reason had proven...misguided. Now, there was no reason to prolong her life. He no longer fostered guilt over the death of her father. No longer felt compelled to step in as a would-be surrogate to a grieving orphan. Those whose lives had been affected by that tragedy had passed on, save Farin and the participants.

Nonetheless, remorse lingered over the rape. Jameson knew himself to be a hard man, but he had never advocated sexual assault. It disappointed him that his son still had so much to learn about the refined application of force.

From the back of the church, Jameson watched the pantomime of Louise and her husband quarreling as their son wriggled free and pushed through mourners, headed for the open casket. The husband snatched the toddler up and walked back to finish their conversation. Undaunted, the boy leaned away from his father with outstretched arms and screamed for his mother. Moments later, father and son disappeared through a side door.

Louise paused, stared at the people filing past the coffin, and dropped her head in her hands. When her shoulders shook from sobbing, an elderly couple stepped forward to comfort her.

Bobby stepped forward. Jameson shot his arm out to stop him.

"Shouldn't we go to her?" Bobby asked.

Jameson stared ahead, unmoved. "We're fine back here."

As the train of mourners waned, two suited men appeared from a room opposite the one Louise's husband and son had used to exit the sanctuary. They flanked the open casket and stood, hands folded before them, until the last person filed past, then glanced at Louise. She nodded mournfully, then grabbed a tissue from a box the church had placed in the pew.

The men lowered the casket lid as Louise wept. Jameson watched solemnly as his ice cream vendor associate of many years disappeared. Inexplicably, he harkened back to the man who had been like a son to him: Jordan Grant.

Most people believed Chris had captured the majority of Jameson's favor during their long association. On many levels, it was true. Chris had amused him. Jameson had enjoyed the young rebel's unabashed zeal for the rock star dream. He admired the boy's unapologetic manipulations and exploits. More than anything, he reveled in the knowledge Mirage had brought him the three things that mattered most: money, power, and freedom. Never once had he regretted the sacrifice it had required of him and his son. For years, Chris had played his part as if he had known why.

Jordan was another story. Innocent. Earnest. The antithesis of his older brother. He had learned the rules of the game, followed the demands on his career to the letter, and still managed to keep his feet on the ground amid the tempest of stardom. It had fascinated Jameson. Jordan had earned his respect. A rare phenomenon indeed, and one Jameson had confessed to no one. Jordan was everything Jameson had hoped Bobby might one-day become. Alas, that would never happen. Ironic, perhaps, that Bobby had singlehandedly quashed Jordan's ability to grow in his father's esteem.

Sometimes, Jameson worried he had gone soft. Had Jordan's death renewed his pity for Farin? Had he allowed her to linger all this time in order to pay some cosmic debt? If so, he had to kill her. He would not blunt his razor-keen judgment on the whetstone of sentiment.

He would head for Raleigh first thing, see her again, and make his decision. The one-time expense of ending her life would far outweigh the expense—and risk—of paying a new, unvetted physician to perpetuate it indefinitely.

Louise reached them at last, her stunning features obscured by sorrow and fatigue. She nodded at Bobby and extended her hand to Jameson. When he accepted, she drew closer, kissing his cheek. "I'm sorry, Mr. Lockhardt. As you can see, it's been a difficult day."

When she released him, Jameson plunged both hands into his jacket pockets. "Not at all. How are you holding up?"

She glanced down, blowing out her tension-laced grief. "Okay, I think. Organizing everything was more stressful than I thought. I can't remember my mother's funeral taking so much out of me." Before she could elaborate, the sound of her son's cries from behind her captured her attention. She turned to find her husband bounding up the aisle in pursuit of the little runaway.

Bobby smiled and moved into the aisle. Arms wide, he crouched down on one knee, positioning himself to intercept. With a contented giggle, the toddler slammed into and wrapped his arms around his mother's stockinged calves. Louise sighed again, frustrated, then hefted him into her arms.

"Sorry," her husband said, joining her. "I tried."

"It's all right." Louise snuggled the boy. She kissed the top of his head, positioning herself central to the small group. "Mr. Lockhardt, I don't believe you've met my husband, Nolan. Nolan, this is Jameson Lockhardt and his son, Bobby. Dad worked for them for...well, for as long as I can remember. How long has it been?"

"Longer than your father or I would have liked to admit." He shook Nolan's hand.

Bobby stood to shake Nolan's hand as well, then made comical faces at the boy. Louise mouthed a grateful, "Thank you." Bobby winked, then looked at the boy cross-eyed, blowing bubbles through his lips.

"Terrible twos," Nolan quipped, running his flattened hand along his waistband to fresh-tuck his dress shirt. "This one keeps us on our toes."

Bobby wiggled his fingers toward the boy's side, prompting the youngster to squeal with delight. "What's your name?"

Louise drew her head back to address the boy. "Can you tell Mr. Lockhardt your name?"

Eyes twinkling, he gave Bobby a wide smile, revealing a full set of primary teeth, before jerking his head away to bury it in the crook of his mother's neck.

Nolan mussed the boy's sandy brown hair. "He's a bit on the shy side."

A doubtful sputter burst from Louise's lips as she transferred him from one side to another and began hip-bouncing him. "Not often. Anyway, this is Oliver."

Bobby wove his head left to right, trying to catch the boy's eye as he played peek-a-boo in his mother's arms. "Hello, Oliver."

Jameson clasped his keys inside his pocket and squeezed. "I know you need to get over to the cemetery. I'd wanted to see you before Bobby and I took off. Unfortunately, we have a meeting we were unable to reschedule."

Louise's forehead creased with disappointment. "I'm sorry to hear that. It would've meant so much to Dad. Any chance you can make it to the memorial later on? I decided to have it at his place to make it easier on everyone."

He explained the meeting would keep them for some time and that he had to get home to pack for his upcoming trip. Before she could mount further protest, Oliver wiggled out of her arms and beelined toward the pulpit. Nolan sprinted after him, leaving a frazzled Louise to say their goodbyes.

"I understand," she said. "I'm sorry we didn't have a chance to catch up. And Bobby, gosh, it's been—"

"A long time."

"Ages!"

He shook her hand. "You have a lovely family."

"Thank you. I'm pleased you both came."

"We wouldn't have missed it."

Jameson cut in, "Please let me know if you need anything. You have my number." He accepted an awkward embrace, then insisted they take off.

As they made their way through the vestibule, he heard her call to her husband, "Nolan! He's headed for the Holy Water!"

They descended the steps of the cathedral in silence. Bobby twirled his coat around his shoulder and slid his arms into the sleeves. He stalked after his father to a waiting limousine, his feet crunching gravel and a light dusting of snow. Jameson barely noticed. The idea of Lionel Childs receiving a Catholic funeral dressed like the Pope on holiday amused him.

"I'm going to Raleigh with you," Bobby insisted as the driver stepped out and opened his father's door. "I'm getting out on the road with you like you promised."

Jameson held up a hand and shook his head. "Not this trip. It won't be very interesting, I assure you."

He jammed his fists into his pockets. "You can't keep putting me off forever."

"Where did you park?" Jameson scanned the parking lot for Bobby's silver Cadillac. "Do you want to ride back with me and have the driver retrieve your car later? We could grab a bite to eat on the way back to the office."

Bobby's shoulders sagged. "Sounds great. But I'm not letting this go. I've worked my ass off to make sure things'll be okay for the next week or so. I'm going with you."

"You said you had so much work at the office you couldn't attend the burial."

"And you told Louise we were late for a meeting that would keep us all afternoon."

Jameson studied him through squinted eyes.

Bobby nodded knowingly. "That's right. I learned from the best."

Indeed, Bobby had become quite the businessman. Savvy. Self-confident. A man who would make an average father beam with pride. Then again, Jameson was no average father.

"We can discuss it over lunch."

Bobby crawled inside after his father. He adjusted himself in his seat. "Talk all you want. I'm already packed."

The driver pulled out of the church parking lot and headed for the city. Soon, the men settled into their typical cocoons of silence. Jameson wondered at times what went through his son's head. Did he dwell on business matters when in quiet reflection? Did he dream? Plan?

For the most part, Jameson indulged himself little self-analysis. Such restraint had served him well over the decades. He preferred to look at his existence in terms of strategy—well, strategy and instinct. Where it concerned Bobby, instinct told him Farin had played an integral role in building the boy's self-confidence. Thankfully, he had never learned who or what Farin represented in his life. Previous unpleasantries and the terror of subsequent events remained locked in Bobby's outer conscience—right where they belonged.

Overall, he had no regrets. Well, perhaps one. Perhaps, in the one moment out of a billion when he allowed himself to buy into the more human aspects of life, he regretted one thing. Once Bobby was gone, their legacy would evaporate like mist on a lake. If Jameson had one regret, it was that he would never have a grandchild. During rare moments of whimsy, he wondered if he should spend more quality time with his only son.

He patted Bobby's knee. "All right. Come to Raleigh. But be warned: it's no picnic out there. You'll watch and learn...and keep your mouth shut."

Bobby brightened. "Yeah?"

"Why not? You've worked hard these last few years. It'll be good to stretch your legs a bit. But you'll need to meet me down there. I have to wrap up a loose end."

Bobby frowned, curious. "What loose end?"

"Just something I promised Lionel I'd take care of. Nothing for you to worry about."

***

Miles returned from lunch to find Jeanne Vacher blocking his office entrance. She bore the brunt of her svelte figure on her left foot while expectantly tapping her right. Arms folded, one eyebrow arched upward, her lower jaw protruded beneath pinched lips. She clutched an unsealed *Chronicle* envelope in her hand. And she had that look on her face.

Instinct told him he would owe her one hell of an apology, though he knew not why.

"I can explain." He raised his hands and shoulders. Just the right amount of remorse in his tone. Just the right measure of contrition. Add a dusting of charm.

Whatever the issue, it worked. Jeanne stepped aside. She bowed slightly, flourishing an arm to grant him entrance. When he walked inside, she followed, shutting the door behind them.

Her pure blue orbs flickered with equal parts fear and anger as she backed him across the office, stabbing the envelope into his chest. "Why didn't you tell me?"

"What did I do?" He bumped into his desk, then slid around it to take his seat. "We can talk this thing out. We always do."

Leaning down, she planted her hands atop the desk. "I told you. I *need* this job!"

"What are you talking about?"

"This!" She flung the envelope at him, then collapsed with a huff into the chair facing his desk. "It came for you about twenty minutes ago."

Confused, he eyed her, then picked up the envelope and removed its contents. When he unfolded the memo and read, he could not suppress his delight.

"I knew it!" Jeanne spat.

"It's not as bad as it looks. Promise."

"What are you *thinking*, Miles? I can't believe they approved the request!"

He smiled as he reread the form. "They've been bugging me to take some vacation for a while now. Why wouldn't they approve it?"

"But...to Miami?"

He waggled his eyebrows at her, folded and replaced the approval form, then stretched sideways to slide the envelope into the side slot of his laptop case.

"You'll get in trouble in Miami."

He propped his feet atop his desk to cross his ankles, his fingers laced behind his head. "I'm wounded. You've wounded me."

"Why can't you let it go? What do you think you're gonna find?"

The smile ran away from his face. "Answers, Jeanne. I need answers."

She snorted. "You're gonna get us both fired. If you're gone, I'm gone. You know that."

"No one's going anywhere. You'll see."

They sat in silence. Miles could think of no polite way to ask her to leave. Pulling rank seemed unfair, given the circumstances. Even if he did have a deadline.

She had confided in him some weeks ago that her marriage had veered onto a rocky path. They had attended counseling, but things did not look promising. It was no time to find herself on the unemployment line.

With a disapproving shake of her head, Jeanne stood at last to return to her cubicle. "Door open or shut?"

"Open. And if you need to talk, you know..."

She headed out. A moment later, she returned, plopping a manila envelope onto his desk. "Here. I forgot. This came for you, too. Postmarked from Miami. Yippee."

He glanced down, wide-eyed. "Thanks. And hey—Jeanne?"

She turned back, a blank expression sheathing her face.

"I need you to close that door after all. Sorry."

She sucked in her lips, shutting the door behind her without another word. Miles watched her trudge back to her desk, sit down, and lower her head onto her closed fist. He searched through the clutter on his desk, jotted down a quick note, then turned his attention to the task at hand.

The nearly-flat, oversized envelope filled him with hope. Sure, it had taken a long time to procure, but if his hunches were right, it was well worth the wait. Maybe it was a sign that he had received the package and his vacation approval on the same day.

Despite his initial doubt, Sandra had pulled through for him. He made a mental note to call and thank her for the assistance. She had taken quite a chance getting him the information.

A tinge of guilt pricked his conscience as he searched for his letter opener. He knew the score. His former lover had obliged him this indiscretion hoping a spark of intimacy might once again ignite between them. Their five-month relationship had not ended badly, but it had ended. She had wanted more out of their coupling than he. Simple. Cliché. Yet true. Though he wished her well and promised they would remain friends, he had heard from mutual acquaintances how hurt she had been the day she woke up to find a note instead of his body beside her.

Slicing through the envelope's creased seal, it dawned on him that it was lighter than he had anticipated. Unevenly distributed. He tossed aside the letter opener, then plunged his hand inside with all the enthusiasm of a young child with a box of Cracker Jacks, groping for the prize at the bottom.

He frowned when he made contact with something other than expected. Something...soft. Slowly, he extracted the black G-string.

First, she had made him wait nearly a year before fulfilling his request. Then, she had used the information like a dangling carrot before an unmotivated mule. He peeked inside the envelope. Empty except a personalized memo card with Sandra's handwriting: *Call me.*

He had to give her credit. She had style.

Miles examined the undergarment at length. Silk, hemmed with lace edging. Size medium. Guessing what closer scrutiny would reveal, he glanced through his office's glass wall to ensure he had not attracted any unwanted attention, then lifted the garment to his nose. He sniffed, then smiled. Yes, just as he suspected. Sandra would do anything to get a rise out of him. With a good-natured chuckle, he noted she had accomplished her mission. He consulted his Rolodex, then rang the Miami number.

Before she could purr her greeting, he whispered, "Now why did you do that?"

A sinful giggle filled the line. "You got my package?"

"I'd know that scent anywhere. Now tell me, why did you send your panties to Chicago?"

"What's the matter? Don't appreciate a little mischief? Don't worry. I've got what you want. Did you think I wouldn't...come through?"

He leaned back in his seat, crossed his legs, and twirled the contents of the envelope on his right index finger. "You're a bad girl, Sandra. What am I gonna do with you?"

"Come to Miami and we'll figure something out."

He glanced at his laptop case, then down at the rise in his pants. "I need those records. Either you'll help me or..."

"The records are here, Miles. Right here. You remember the way, yes?" With that, the line disconnected.

He chewed at the inside of his cheek as he returned the telephone to its cradle. It would be a busy afternoon. He needed to finish next week's column, get a flight, book a hotel, and arrange for a car. He would leave for Miami Saturday.

Originally, he had planned to go straight from the airport to the police station. Perhaps entice Detective Alvarez into having lunch. He had thought he would have everything he needed by then to help nail Jameson Lockhardt to the wall. Now, it appeared he would have to make a little detour first. But if Sandra expected him to wash her unmentionables before returning them, she had another think coming.

He glanced down at the note he had written earlier, then buzzed Jeanne.

"What do you need?" she asked somberly.

"I need you to have dinner with me."

She swiveled around to stare at him through the glass. "Why?"

"Why? C'mon, Jeanne. I'm a guy. I'm not good with the whys."

She tilted her head and waited.

"Okay, okay." He leaned onto his elbows, fixing his eyes upon her. "I wanna buy you dinner. It's the least I could do after not telling you about Miami."

The corner of her mouth edged upward. "Is that all?"

"Be ready at seven. And let your husband know I'll have you home at a decent hour."

CHAPTER 14

ANOTHER TRIP TO MIAMI. ANOTHER flight from hell. Another eight nauseating, fear-infused hours on an airplane warding off the advances of her fellow first-class flyers. To make matters worse, her condition prevented her from crawling inside a few gin and tonics for a modicum of comfort. The flight attendants offered, but she dutifully declined. The next seven or so months would be the longest in her life. In the privacy of her mind, she generated a litany of curses so powerful they could have fueled the Boeing 747 cocooning her to Florida.

Before leaving for the airport that morning, Julie had jammed five periodicals and two books into a carry-on. The first, *What to Expect When You're Expecting*, she had picked up the day she found out she was pregnant. Maybe in an attempt to adjust her attitude, show Chris she could change her mind about having kids. She had yet to crack the spine.

The other, *Hollywood Husbands*, was a guilty favorite. It came out in 1986, the same year she had left North Platte for Los Angeles. In fact, the spunky, Bruce Springsteen-idolizing model Jade Johnson had inspired her to take her shot. She kept her dog-eared copy of the novel with her while on assignment and must have read it a dozen times in the last nine years.

Halfway to LAX, she realized she had left the bag upstairs. Irritated at the oversight and anxious over her impending trip, she had forgotten to stop at an airport newsstand to purchase a passable substitute to occupy her mind for the multi-hour flight.

The meager choices offered up from the seat-back pocket ahead of her left much to be desired. She browsed the *SkyMall* catalog at length, then thumbed through the airline's current issue of *Hemispheres* magazine. The featured destination for their ongoing series, "Three Perfect Days," was Chennai, India. Inwardly, she scoffed. She had once spent *two* days in Chennai on a photoshoot. It had been anything but perfect.

Desperate for something to distract her, she picked up the tri-folded safety card. Mostly pictures depicting what to do in case the jet plummeted to the ground in a ball of fire. Inside her head, the swearing grew louder and more sincere.

And the plane had not even pulled away from the gate.

It did not escape her notice that she had caught the attention of the suited businessman seated beside her. He had the window seat, yet apparently found looking over her shoulder as she leafed through the inflight journals more interesting. She considered politely suggesting he grab his own complimentary copies. But that might encourage unwelcome communica—

"James. The name's James. Not Jimmy. I hate when people call me Jimmy. My mom used to call me Jimmy. Couldn't stand it."

She assumed he had directed the comment at her, but did not respond. For both their sake. Under non-pregnant circumstances, she and Tanqueray dealt decisively with men who could not take a hint.

"I know you," he persisted, nudging closer, a smug half-smile revealing straight but coffee-stained teeth. His breath confirmed he had imbibed a cup or two that morning. Conversely, she caught a whiff of his Acqua di Gio. At least he had not bathed in it.

James-not-Jimmy backed off. He casually stretched his blockish frame, monopolizing their shared space. "I get it. You're one of *those* types. No worries, princess. I'm no threat. No need to look down your pretty nose at me." He harrumphed, then turned his head to peer out the window.

With a hearty exhale through glossy lips, she returned the borrowed magazine to its seat-back pocket, folded her arms, and shut her eyes. She had not given one thought as to how she would break the news of Farin's resurrection to Ben and Cheryl. What could she possibly say?

The bitch is back. Chris left to find her. No, I don't know where. No, I haven't talked to him in a couple days. I just figured this was the best place to be until I hear more. Oh, and also, I'm having his baby. Perfect timing, huh?

Man, she needed a drink.

When the flight attendant began her pre-flight safety demonstration, Julie held her breath. Hobbled without a way to counter her anxiety, she made a mental note to call Gloria after she returned to LA. Until she had this baby, she would not take another flight.

"Nervous flyer, eh?" James-not-Jimmy snickered.

She ignored the remark and tried to focus on something else. Anything else. But every image that came to mind involved Farin Grant's tragic fairy tale and her husband reprising his prior role of Prince Charming. Damn it, anyway.

The plane pulled away from the gate and headed for the runway. Her pulse pounded in her head like a 120 beats-per-minute backbeat. She swallowed hard as the ear-splitting whistle and the whine of engines increased. When the back wheels lifted off the ground, she shot her hand out to grab the small armrest to her left. Instead, she squeezed James-not-Jimmy's hand.

Without missing a step, he turned and smiled. "Now that's more like it. What-say I order you a drink? You look like you could use one. Lemme guess—you're a bourbon girl, right?"

She recoiled, sneered, and angled her body away. Glancing around the first-class cabin, she noted the flight was completely full. Just her luck. No chance of changing seats. No alcohol. No idea where her husband was. And no way to take the edge off.

By the time her heels hit the airport carpet at Miami International, her nerves were raw. She snatched up her handbag and sprinted from the death tube as quickly as she could push her way through the line of irritated, if polite, fellow passengers. A flight attendant scrunched up her face in disapproval. The last thing she heard was James-not-Jimmy call from behind her, "Typical celebrity—think they own the whole damn world!"

Calm returned in record time. Once again, she had avoided certain death from a thirty-thousand-foot fall. The idea of repeating this nightmare on the way back did not appeal to her. Best not to think about it. More pressing problems lay ahead.

Jumpy and mentally exhausted, she nonetheless surprised herself when she popped into the women's room to primp before heading for baggage claim. Somehow, she appeared as poised and graceful as if about to head down the runway for Yves Saint Laurent. Fresh, sharp—and sober to boot! She refreshed her lip gloss, brushed and fluffed her hair, then proceeded through the terminal on rubber legs. For the thousandth time that day, she wished she could have a drink.

Several alert fans spotted her as she descended the escalator. They rushed her and begged for autographs, to which she graciously consented. She wore her runway smile like a bobby pin. A cold, mechanical, carefully placed artifice that made her appear natural in every aspect. Now more than ever, she needed the public on her side. Maybe she should have spared James-not-Jimmy a few kind words after all.

She beamed, charmed her fans, and posed for snapshots as the more chivalrous among them fought each other to help her with her luggage. Before long, she spotted Ben and Cheryl coming toward her. Their warm smiles nearly wiped her own from her face.

Nearly.

They knew nothing. Nothing about the pregnancy. Nothing about her husband sprinting off on a quest to resurrect the ghost who had haunted their days and nights since the moment they met.

She maintained a happy, if practiced, façade as Ben disappeared to load her luggage into his Land Rover.

Cheryl locked her arm in Julie's. They marched past gawking bystanders as they left the terminal. "We were so excited when you rang us and said you were coming! Perfect timing. I need a girls' night."

"Sounds great! But we'll have to raincheck it until tomorrow. The flight was hell."

"I bet, you poor dear. But you'll be happy to know I managed to track down an entire case of the ninety-two White Burgundy. That should set you right. How long can you stay?"

On the drive to Key Biscayne, Julie listened to anecdotes about her nephews. She giggled appropriately at the tale of Cheryl wandering onto the patio one night two weeks ago, only to discover Derek and Summer Reece in the middle of what looked like a serious kiss.

Cheryl craned her neck around and back to face Julie, who sat behind her. "I don't know who was more embarrassed—Summer or Derek. Poor dears."

"You were a sight more embarrassed than either one of them, love." Ben chuckled. He pulled into the driveway, extracted Julie's bags, and placed them in the foyer, then doubled back to park the car. Cheryl and Julie grabbed her smaller bag and headed upstairs, leaving the rest for Ben to deal with later.

"You sounded pretty serious on the phone, Jules."

"It seems every time I visit, I'm in some state or another, doesn't it?"

"We love your visits. You know that."

You won't love this one.

Ben brought up the remainder of her luggage. "Anything else I can help with before I head out back?"

Cheryl pecked his cheek. "We've got it from here. But mind the time. The boys'll be home soon. We'll be ready for dinner by six."

With a wink and a nod, he left them alone.

Ben and Cheryl's intimate interactions triggered a rush of emotions inside her. Rage and jealousy topped the list. For a moment, she regretted her decision to come. No part of her wanted to watch Ben Grant's reaction to the news that his favored sister-in-law lived. But what choice had Chris left her? Someone needed to tell his family what had transpired, and judging from the light banter from the airport back to the house, Chris had not called his brother with the news.

Then again, maybe this personalized touch would win her sympathy points from Cheryl.

"I did laundry this morning while we waited to go to the airport. You unpack while I grab your towels."

She pointed at a stack of folded linen atop the tallboy. "Aren't those the towels?"

Cheryl threw her arms up. "Aye, that's right! I brought them up already. Sorry. My mind's failing. Must be old age."

"Old age?" She smiled despite herself. "You're like three years older than me."

Cheryl collected the linens, then headed for the guest bath. She gave Julie's arm a gentle squeeze as she passed.

Julie dragged her luggage on top of the bed to unpack. For the first time ever, she envied her sister-in-law. Cheryl never worried about aging. Or losing her figure. Having Derek and Kyle had carved a thin set of stretch marks into her ever-so-slight belly pooch, but she did not seem to mind. In fact, she wore them with pride. Never even covered them when she donned a bikini, which she still looked great in. Her marriage and family contented her. Julie wished she felt like that.

The thought of stretch marks undid her. She vowed to ask her obstetrician what she could do to prevent them. She had heard somewhere about a lotion made with aloe, vitamin E, lanolin, and avian collagen that gave the skin temporary elasticity. If that did not do the trick, she would opt for dermabrasion or microsurgery after the birth. Whatever it took. Likewise, she refused to breastfeed. The loathsome ritual made her shudder. Never would she surrender her body to the demands of motherhood. This child would *not* steal her beauty.

"You okay, Jules?"

Julie studied her hands. They lay idle atop her suitcase. Slender and taut. Pretty. No unseemly lines or wrinkles. Her manufactured smile had fallen away.

She turned to Cheryl, expressionless, and plopped down on the foot of the bed. "Am I okay? Am I okay." She pondered the question as she patted the comforter. "I have something to tell you. You and Ben. The reason I flew out. You need to know. Something terrible—I mean, something…I still can't believe it myself."

Cheryl sat beside Julie. She rested a comforting arm around her shoulders. "Is it Chris? I thought everything was fine. You two've been so happy lately."

She shook her head. "It's nothing like that. Not yet, anyway. We've been happy. Happier than I imagined we ever could be." In a rare moment of transparency, she dropped all pretense of poise and dignity and surrendered to the heaviness she had felt since the day Chris told her. Her eyes shut against an impending flood of tears.

No. She would not go that far. She would not cry. They would never make her cry.

Drawing strength from some inner well, she squared her shoulders. "I'll start with something easy to believe. I'm pregnant. I found out a few days ago."

The tension obscuring Cheryl's delicate features evaporated. Her lips parted, then curled at the corners as her downward-turned brows arched upward. She squeezed Julie's shoulders. "You had me worried something was wrong. Well, of course you're emotional. Oh, Jules! As happy as you and Chris have been lately, it's only fitting—"

"Wait—"

"When are you due?"

"Around Sept—"

"You *must* stay long enough for us to go shopping!"

"Cheryl—"

"Ooo, those wee onesies! What theme are you thinking for the nursery?"

"I haven't really—"

"Why didn't Chris ring us earlier?"

"Because he doesn't—"

She sprang from the bed. "Let's go tell Ben!"

"*No!*" Julie tugged Cheryl's arm until she sat back down. Her next words stuck in her throat. "There's more."

Cheryl folded her hands in her lap. "What is it?"

She relayed the facts as Chris had explained them before leaving their home three days ago. Cheryl remained silent the entire time.

When Julie finished, Cheryl sat stone-faced beside her, eyes flitting sightlessly about the room, lips mumbling unspoken words. "She's...*alive?*"

Julie nodded.

"We're sure?"

"This isn't something Sam would've made up."

For long moments, they sat in silence.

Cheryl felt numb. Too stunned to speak. She should be happy, or at least thankful Farin's life had been spared. Maybe concerned. Sympathetic over what could have possibly happened to the poor girl. She should rush out and tell her husband the "good news," just as she had tried to do about the baby before Julie stopped her. But her knee-jerk reactions were nausea and disbelief.

Heaven help her. How could this be true?

It had taken her family years to mend. Three long, painful years. Chris and Julie had finally begun making a life with each other—expecting a baby, no less. Her own life had calmed. The boys had made peace with losing their uncle and his wife. Ben had not mentioned Farin's name in weeks. What now? How could she explain this to their sons?

Guilt pricked her conscience. If she were honest, she would admit the news disappointed her. How cold had she become that she would prefer Farin dead?

She turned glassy eyes to her sister-in-law. "Where is she? Where's she been? How did this happen? Forgive me, Jules. I don't understand."

Julie clutched fistfuls of comforter in her hands. "Chris didn't say...and I didn't ask."

"What? I can't imagine he'd leave knowing you're—"

"I didn't tell him."

She gasped. "You let him leave without giving him a reason to *stay?*"

Julie rose and padded to the bedroom window. She stared out at the bay. "I should've been reason enough."

***

Chris and Marci had agreed on one thing before beginning their odyssey: they needed to keep a low profile. It would prove critical to their plan—what little plan they had. Thankfully, the west-east route demanded little by way of navigation. Their course took them from Palm Springs to Phoenix on I-10, then north up Arizona State Highway 87 to Holbrook. From there, I-40 stretched all the way to Raleigh. They had calculated the distance. If they pushed it, they figured they could be there in three days.

Playing the designated gopher at gas stations, motels, and restaurants irritated Marci, but they could ill-afford for Chris's fans to catch a glimpse of his well-known face. So, she made a concerted effort to maintain the peace. Never in her life would she have imagined herself stuck with her arch nemesis on a cross-country road trip.

She filled up the Oldsmobile Delta 88 every four hundred miles or so. She obtained their food, often from roadside diners. The time it took the greasy spoons or truck stops to prepare and package their orders gave the would-be heroes a chance to stretch their legs—usually with Marci browsing cheap gift shops attached to the restaurants while Chris paced the parking lot, staying out of sight. She even changed the tire when they had a flat near Henryetta, Oklahoma. At least he shared in the driving. Being his chauffeur on top of his waitress, mechanic, and gas attendant would have sent her over the edge.

Rest stops posed a unique challenge, given the diversity of the people who used them. They required he tuck his long wavy hair into a baseball cap and wear his sunglasses. They took every precaution to ensure Jameson Lockhardt did not catch wind of their impending arrival in North Carolina.

Catering to Chris Grant did not much appeal to her sensibilities, but it was enlightening.

As the miles disappeared behind them, she learned things about him. Things the tabloids would not know. Like how impossible it was to speak to him in the mornings until he had his black tea, which he took without milk or sugar. Or how much it bothered him to listen when one of his songs came on the radio—Mirage or his solo stuff. He consumed an artery-clogging amount of red meat that upset even her stomach. And he snored when he napped in the back seat, often awaking with a start, with Farin's name on his lips.

She did not ask him about his dreams, or nightmares. For 2,442 miles, they did not discuss their mission, their target, or what the hell they planned to do once they found her.

"How long was I asleep?" she mumbled groggily.

Chris yawned and checked his watch. "Hours."

She stretched her arms, adjusting her eyes to the afternoon sunlight. "It's Friday, right?"

He nodded. "All day."

Everywhere she looked, she saw green. Trees, hills. The natural landscape obscured the towns dotting Interstate 40. Nothing but open road, wide, pristine lanes, and green foliage. So unlike California. In LA, one encountered little more than a gray, concrete jungle with garish neon lighting or the occasional sad, withered tree.

The gentle hum of the Olds' engine and absence of conversation had lulled her to sleep. Under better circumstances, she might have enjoyed this trip. Draining, yes. But beautiful.

Guilt over the whimsical thought manifested itself in the pit of her belly. Stuck in a car for days with a man she could barely stand, she had ample time for reflection. It made no sense but, somehow, she believed she should have known Farin was alive.

She stole a glance at Chris. He had said little on their trip, which suited her fine. Maybe he felt the same way she did. They should have come for her sooner.

"We'll need to stop for food soon," he said, his tone as flat as the tire she had changed back in Henryetta. He stared trancelike at the highway, arms locked, both hands on the steering wheel.

She reached down to the floorboard, grabbed the atlas she had purchased at a truck stop near Blythe, and struggled to remember the last vantage point she had noted before passing out. Looking up, she spied a sign for the Oxford School Road exit 138 two miles ahead. "I'm not even sure where we are."

"About an hour outside Winston-Salem."

"North Carolina already?"

"We crossed the Tennessee state line hours ago."

"I don't remember anything since Nashville."

He shrugged, his eyes fixed unflinchingly on the road ahead.

Still disoriented, Marci thumbed through the atlas, stopping at North Carolina. She traced the thick, red interstate line with her index finger.

Her stomach growled. She was starved, yet simultaneously nauseated. Days of stress, coupled with an increasing disgust over Chris's unhealthful eating habits, had taken their toll on her system. She hoped the next place they stopped offered a salad.

When she identified their current location, she nodded. "I think we're close. Maybe a couple of hours or so to Raleigh."

Chris arched his back, winced with discomfort, then twisted his neck side-to-side. "You about ready to take over?"

Suddenly, her eyes bulged. "Not yet."

He shot her a hard look. "Why not?" he asked, his voice clipped with agitation. "You're rested and I'm bloody done in."

She covered her mouth. "Pull over. I don't feel so good."

He swore under his breath, but headed for the exit.

Her brows arched apologetically, but she said nothing. She held her mouth until he exited the highway, turned onto Oxford School Road, then flipped the car around in a turnout just past Wilke Road. The vehicle had barely stopped before she hopped out and scampered to its rear.

Chris remained contentedly out of earshot while Marci hunched over the back of the Olds. He reached across the seat and grabbed the atlas. As he examined the map of North Carolina, his shoulders untensed. Soon, they would reach their destination.

Except for the incident with the tire, their journey had been uneventful. The macabre twist of fate had neutralized some of their mutual animosity. More importantly, there had been no public recognition that he traveled via used car with a bitchy brunette who was not—by any stretch of the imagination—his wife.

In a way, he felt sorry for Marci. This quest had put a heavy burden on her.

He had used the silence of the last three days to ruminate over their circumstances. Something about it felt like a hoax. Grown women were not simply taken without notice. And Farin was not just any woman.

The passenger door opened. Marci peered in at him. She looked pale and weak.

"You know, you haven't had anything since breakfast. It might help if you ate. I saw a sign for a Hardees, whatever that is. I could go for a burger myself."

The door slammed shut as Marci dashed back to the rear of the car.

He watched her through the rearview mirror, hunched down, one hand on the trunk. If she got sick, he might, too.

After her second sprint to the back of their vehicle, she assured him they could continue. They stopped at the Hardees in Statesville, which turned out to be an East Coast version of Carl's Jr. Marci went inside and spent some time in the ladies' room. When she returned carrying drinks, a salad for herself, and a burger combo for him, she looked a little less green around the gills.

"Better?"

She nodded. "I'm just stressed. I don't feel sick or anything. I don't think I have a fever."

He hesitated, then reached over and held the back of his hand against her forehead. Though stunned at the physical contact, she did not move or jerk away from his touch. His hand felt cool against her brow.

"A bit warm, perhaps, but nothing serious I should think." He withdrew his hand.

She stabbed her plastic fork into her salad. "Soon as we get to Raleigh, I need a room and a shower. I'm probably getting sick over my own smell."

"Easy for you to say. I smell like a dead goat."

Somewhere in the Texas panhandle, west of Amarillo, he had removed his shoes to get comfortable. He had quickly put them back on. After, they had found it necessary to roll down the windows to air out the car.

Not thirty minutes after they finished their meal and jumped back on the interstate, Marci had him pull over again. Chris grew concerned. As she purged her dinner, he formulated a contingency plan whereby he would get Farin on his own. She returned to the car and sipped on her Sprite the rest of the way, insistent that she did not need a doctor.

They entered the city an hour later. Rush hour had ended, though its start-of-the-weekend traffic remained heavy. They took the 297 exit off of the 440 beltline surrounding Raleigh onto Lake Wheeler Road and, in moments, passed the Farmer's Market and reached the Dorothea Dix compound. In fact, "compound" was the only word to describe the vast property that made up the institution.

"This is it," Chris said aloud, mostly to prove he had not imagined it. As they motored onto the property, he ducked his head below the visor to eyeball the grounds.

Marci drew in a long, deep breath through her nose, then slowly exhaled through her open mouth. Her eyes welled and her stomach flipped, but it felt different than her earlier nausea.

A tall cyclone fence topped with looped barbed wire surrounded the property, though the main gates remained continuously open, as if inviting—or at least acceding—their arrival. They canvassed the area to get their bearings before planning their next move, mindful not to alert anyone to their presence.

Chris gritted his teeth. "These California plates will stick out like an aardvark at an ant convention."

Marci pointed out a car parked beneath a light pole in one of the parking lots. "I don't know. They don't look too different from the North Carolina plates. Unless someone's paying close attention, we should be okay. Especially in the dark."

The car snaked through the property. "Probably best to back in when we park, just in case we need to make a quick exit. Which building did Ross say she was in?"

"The 'Royster' building?"

"That's it."

"He said it was the building to the right of the main hospital, next to a church."

The Olds' rumbled gently as they motored on. Street lamps peppered the narrow road which, although paved, was riddled with cracks and pitted with mini-potholes. The occasional stop sign was weathered with age, its accompanying roadway paint faded until nearly invisible.

Eventually, they reached the main hospital, an enormous, six-story beige building with dozens of steel windows. To its right, they found the red brick chapel with its towering steeple. Beyond that, they spotted what looked like a condemned building. Despite the absence of illumination in this particular area, they made out the black, upper-case lettering on the white, slatted wood awning above the front entrance, confirming they had the right place.

At the top of the crumbling structure's steps, yellow caution tape roped off its double-door entrance. Several posted signs declared no admittance. Windows throughout the front of the three-story monstrosity looked to have been shattered by rocks, bullets, or the bricks dislodged from its construction.

Marci scooted forward, clutching the dashboard. "She can't be in there. It's a pile of rubble!"

"She'd better be in there," he countered. "We've got nowhere else to look."

They turned left, around a hundreds-year-old oak tree and a broken cement picnic table, to the back. In the rear, the roof over half of the building, mostly the tall, protruding, semicircular façade at its midpoint, had collapsed into the top floor. Signs posted on the three or four doors he noticed warned of asbestos contamination.

They exchanged puzzled looks.

Crestfallen, Marci shook her head. "No one's been inside that building for ages, Chris. Mr. Alexander must have lied. She can't be in there. At least not..." She buried her head in her hands and wept.

He pinched the bridge of his nose, mentally replaying Ross's confession. "I don't know. He said Childs kept her 'hidden in plain sight.'"

She flailed an arm toward the dilapidated structure. "But *this*?"

Continuing down the opposite side of the facility, they reached the back entrance. He exited the campus carefully, making a U-turn across the divided four-lane road called Western Boulevard. In passing, he observed the North Carolina Central Prison, which lay directly across from the Dorothea Dix campus. He wondered if North Carolina had the death penalty.

Marci twisted around in her seat. She watched the facility recede into the dusk behind a cluster of oak trees. "Why are we leaving? We have to get in there."

"You said you needed a shower. Besides, we can't just barge in. I need to think. If we keep driving back and forth, someone will get suspicious."

They passed Pullen Park and drove up Western Boulevard across from the North Carolina State University campus, then headed away from downtown. Chris noted a television station on the left, complete with newscopter. A left onto Avent Ferry Road, then another across traffic, brought them to a movie theater anchoring a strip mall and a Rock-Ola Café. He parked near the theater and killed the engine.

Outside a coffee shop next to a record store, a crowd of mostly students lounged on metal patio furniture, smoking and drinking from enormous mugs. Chris's stomach knotted. He should not be within a mile of a record store. Or a television station, for that matter.

He checked his watch. "It's seven. Want a coffee or something?"

She scrunched her nose. "Let's find a hotel. The sooner we figure out what to do, the sooner we can get Farin and get out of here."

"Right." He hit the ignition, backed out, and turned the car around. "How are you feeling? Better?"

She combed her hair with her fingers. "I can't stand it, Chris. It's taking so long."

He pulled out, signaling to cross the four lanes of Avent Ferry Road into the parking lot of the hotel across the street. Synchronously, they read the marquee above its green-and-burgundy-striped awning. The sign read, "The Jameson Inn."

He gulped. "It's only beginning."

CHAPTER 15

ONE THING ALICIA ALVAREZ DISLIKED about her partner was his insistence on driving them to and from every scene. He opened doors for her. Treated her like a lady. She was no lady; she was a detective. Moreover, she outranked him. Barely.

Sometimes, just to annoy him, she would bolt from the car before he shifted into park, run around to his door and yank it open, then bow as she swept her arm back with a grand flourish. He had responded by disabling all but the driver's inside door handle and installing a switch to re-enable them as he chose. That rested on the driver's side as well. This violated several regulations. She had not ratted him out. Yet.

What Alvarez liked about her partner was that he was not Charles Stark. He was not a slob and he was not on the take, as far as she knew—and usually she knew. She had to admit, though never to him or anyone else, she respected his ability to take all the attitude she dished out and return it to her on a silver platter. And damn if he was not the smartest SOB she had ever worked with.

He had invited her to his home several times over the first year of their pairing. She concocted many excuses, but the truth was she did not easily establish close relationships outside family. Eight months in, however, he wore her down. She disliked Italian food, but agreed to join him and his family for dinner. She even brought wine. That evening marked a change in their partnership and sparked a sort of friendship.

Penny Bridgeman was a hoot. Tall, slender, and flat-chested, with a pageboy haircut, her cheerful disposition lit up any room she entered. Billy adored her. Within seconds of introducing his wife to his partner, any unspoken concerns Penny might have harbored that her husband spent long days, and sometimes even longer nights, in the sole company of an attractive younger woman were put to bed. The women connected immediately. Penny thought Alicia was a scream.

Yet despite the camaraderie, Alvarez felt odd in their perfectly appointed home with its manicured lawn and anecdotal white picket fence. It looked like a television set. No one would suspect a family of five lived there. The girls were well-behaved. Billy and Penny laughed a lot—with each other, and with their children. The harmonic vibe in their household calmed her as much as it frightened her. In the real world, families like theirs did not exist.

"You and the Stepford clan have any plans for the weekend?"

"You mean besides Penny and I pouring over the singles ads, trying to find you a husband?"

She side-eyed him seated behind the wheel of their unmarked cruiser. "Husband? Why you wanna make me hurt you?"

"You know I like the rough stuff."

She scrutinized his attire. "Right. You're quite the wild man. Nice pants."

He looked down at his sharply-pressed Dockers. "What's wrong with them?"

"At least you ditched the wool suits and beard."

"You're just trying to change the subject."

She chased her last mouthful of hot dog with Pepsi. "I told you, Billy, I'm too young for marriage."

"In some countries, thirty's an old maid. What's the matter? Afraid to slip into those bonds of matrimony?"

"They call them *bonds* for a reason."

They had stopped to eat after a long afternoon investigating a stabbing down in Homestead. Their vehicle rested in the shade of a metered space in South Beach as they ate. Besides chips and sodas, they had purchased eight hot dogs, of which Alicia had claimed four. She had greedily wolfed them down and now had eyes for Bridgeman's last.

Bridgeman licked the tip of his right index finger and dabbed at the breadcrumb mess upon the wrap paper on his lap. "You'd be happier if you settled down. Look at me and Penny—"

"Deh-deh-deh." She sliced the air with a stiff, open hand, then pointed to his uneaten frank. "Enough. You gonna eat that last dog?"

He gave her a teasing grin, "You smell it? I'll let you smell it."

She shook her head in disgust. When he picked up the dog and waved it tauntingly in her direction, she attempted to grab it from his hand. He snatched it back, laughing at the failed attempt. "Nice try, Al." He rested the dog on his lap, then squeezed the last packet of mustard across its length. Alicia loved mustard.

Regarding him as she would someone who had dared her to raise her shirt during Mardi Gras, she bent down purposefully to his lap and took a slow, calculating bite from the middle of the dog without once using her hands, except to keep her long black curls out of the condiments.

"Mmm." She straightened up and chewed in exaggerated fashion, running her unadorned ring finger the length of her full lips, then licking off the crumbs and mustard with a loud smacking noise. "You're right, Billy, it smells good, but I couldn't eat another bite."

He moaned seductively against a repressed chuckle. "Oh, Al. Do that again. You know you want the wiener, baby. Take the wiener. Take it."

"You're a real shit." She snatched up the wrappers and stuffed them into her empty soda cup. Peeking out the side window, she spotted a trash receptacle. She jerked her door handle, but found it disabled. With an exasperated huff, she reached across his lap and flipped the switch. "A real shit."

She exited the vehicle, gave a grunting stretch, then bent back inside for the remaining trash. As an afterthought, she plunged her hand into his lap and grabbed what remained of the hot dog, then stomped to the trash receptacle to deposit the waste.

When she returned, Bridgeman reengaged the switch and turned the key. "You know, Al, you shouldn't starve me. I'm a growing boy with active glands."

"Glands," she grumbled, clicking her seatbelt in place. "I'd say those glands of yours are a little *too* active. Three kids?"

"How do you know they're mine?"

"I don't. They're pretty cool kids. Maybe Penny realized you didn't have the right stuff."

"I could prove it to ya," he teased. Then, more seriously, he added, "That reminds me. Penny wants to know if you're coming to her lingerie party next Wednesday."

"Is that it, gringo? You want me to buy a little black lace teddy from your wife and wear it to work for ya? That turns you on, eh? That what you think about late at night?"

She caught a hint of crimson in Bridgeman's cheeks and smirked with satisfaction.

"I don't care what kind of underwear you sport around in, Al." He straightened in his seat and grasped the wheel a bit harder as he concentrated on the road. "I won't even be there."

"And what kind of underwear do *you* walk around in, partner? You a brief man?"

"I've always preferred boxers."

"Figures." Alvarez snickered. She wondered if he made Penny starch them.

Once back at the station, they checked the board and found no pressing cases that would keep them from their desks for the remainder of their shift. Alvarez cozied up to write the report from the Homestead scene. Bridgeman flopped uneasily into his chair.

With marked frustration, he regarded the desk he had occupied for one full year. If most Metro desks needed replacement for one reason or another, he occupied the single desk that needed replacement for every possible reason. He kept a copy of *National Geographic* under one leg and *Guns & Ammo* under another to counter the wobbling. The drawers stuck. In November, he had stripped the top and revarnished it, disregarding his fellow detectives' complaints about the smell. Turned out the desk had originally been cherry wood, not matte black paint. Now, it hunkered in the middle of the room, a two-tone hybrid—odd to look at, like a wood-paneled station wagon, but functional.

He pulled open his top drawer to grab a pen. When he glimpsed the chipped and torn paper lining the desk, he checked his watch. Three hours left on their shift. Plenty of time. He leaned over the side of his chair and grabbed the plastic bag he had brought in and abandoned a month ago. Inside were two rolls of shelf paper Penny had purchased for him in her attempt to shut him up about the less than optimum conditions at his new job.

Overall, the Bridgemans had adapted to the changes in culture and climate between Detroit and Miami. The kids lived contentedly with the Florida sand beneath and between their toes. Still, as Penny had pointed out, Billy had a restless streak. Always seemed to need a project or a puzzle to solve. They viewed this quirk of his as a minor annoyance, but she had purchased the shelf paper anyway.

He emptied the desk drawers, carefully at first, then more enthusiastically, dumping the contents of each drawer atop his perfectly arranged desktop.

Alvarez peered up over her monitor and removed the pen from her mouth. "What are you doing, spring cleaning? I hate to tell you, Billy, but it's only January."

"I can't stand this shredding paper anymore. Every time I grab a pen or pencil, I end up taking a section of a cattle ranch with it. That partner of yours...Stark, right? He was obsessed. Remember all those pamphlets you dug out of this desk?"

She coughed out a snicker of agreement, then returned the pen to her mouth and her attention to her report.

When he came to the last drawer, he found the liner broken in many places. As the paper parted from the wooden base, he found what looked like a document beneath, as if intentionally hidden from view. He examined it at length before motioning to his partner. "How come you never told me you worked a car bomb case with Stark? You know I was EOD in the service."

Having completed her report, she pressed "save," then "print" on her computer. She looked up quizzically as the statement registered. "Stark and I never handled a car bomb case."

He waved the document in her direction. "This says you did. Three years ago. Take a look."

She stood, shimmied to unwrinkle her slacks, then reached across their facing desks to accept the paper. With a frown, she perused the document. She wracked her brain to recall any mention of a car bomb. "Looks like an insurance report from the Farin Grant case back in ninety-one."

Clipped to the bottom of the report was a handwritten note. She read it, shrugged, then passed the document back to him. "It says the fuel tank ruptured. This was part of an accident report, Billy. It doesn't say anything about a car bomb. The adjuster probably clipped this note to the report as an afterthought."

"Fuel tanks don't rupture by accident."

She bobbed her shoulders, unconvinced. "The limo crashed into the K-rail. The impact caused..."

With a slow shake of his head, Bridgeman leaned back in his chair. "First off, we're not talking about a Pinto, here. This was a Mercedes limousine."

She flexed her palms and stared blankly.

He waved her over and pointed out details on the report. "Okay, second. It says right here they identified an accelerant."

She folded her arms in frustration. "*And*? You know, you might try talking English, Billy. Didn't they teach you English in school? What does it matter?"

"What came first, Detective? The chicken or the egg?"

She perched herself on the corner of his cluttered desk and thought for several moments, unable to take her eyes off the document. How had she not seen this before?

Bridgeman rubbed his bald chin as he organized his thoughts. "So, question: why would an 'unknown accelerant' be present? Answer: someone would have used it to cause the explosion, which may have in turn caused the crash—*not* the other way around. Next question: who knew about this report and why was it squirreled away in Stark's desk for three years? Answer: I don't know. But that begs more questions, dontcha think? Who closed this case?"

Alvarez's stomach sank. "We're looking at a double homicide, here."

***

At 2 PM, Lance sat at the bar, nursing his second pint. Every so often, he checked his watch or peered outside the sparsely-populated pub's frosted window into the intermittently bright, then gloomy, day. An hour had passed. He dared not wait much longer. Ivy would do him in if he missed their appointment.

A smiling barmaid of small stature and infinite patience ambled toward him as he upended the glass and swallowed the last drops of lager. "Still waitin' on your mate, are ya?"

He glanced over his shoulder, squinting through the window at the parking lot. A sliver of afternoon sunlight illuminated the blacktop. Dark, pregnant clouds crept across the sky like tumbleweeds rolling in slow motion through an endless blue desert. "Ironically, I'm usually the one everybody's waiting on."

She reached for the empty glass. "Another, then?"

He raised his chin, an almost embarrassed smile stretched across his thin lips. "A half, please...and one for yourself?"

In the six months since Samantha had called about reuniting the band, he had heard nothing from Mirage's former lead singer—*zip*. Actually, despite the fact they lived half an hour apart, they had not talked since the Grammys. When he had spoken with Elliot a while back and, more recently, Faith, both had echoed his experience.

"You don't think something happened to him, do you?" Faith had asked. "You know how he gets."

And indeed, they *all* knew. As with many artistic geniuses, Todd Dalton had a moody, self-destructive side. Over the years, Lance and Chris had often remarked that Todd was the male equivalent of Faith. Both abused their bodies, their fame, and their talent. But where Faith put her bad behavior on display for fans and critics the world over, Todd kept his cleverly hidden behind a mask of feigned shyness and enigmatic sex appeal. In fact, though Chris more notably wore the label of consummate playboy, Todd's base nature made Chris look like a seminary student.

The barmaid placed the lager down in front of him. She raised her own glass his way. "Cheers."

With a curt nod of acknowledgement, he sipped the stout brew.

She gulped down her half pint, then dug a hair tie from the front pocket of her jeans and pulled back her dishwater blonde hair, securing it into a ponytail. Lance looked on as she plunged her emptied glass into, and out of, a basin of soapy water. She rinsed the vessel in a second, clearer basin, then procured a towel from beneath the counter.

"I'm Lance, by the way."

"I know who you are," she said without looking up or pausing her work.

He gave her a clumsy, lopsided grin.

She disappeared momentarily, only to return carrying a heavy box of Tennent's lager. Instinct prompted him to offer assistance, but he feared the gesture might insult her. It was hard these days to figure out whether women wanted men to help or leave them be.

When the other two men in the room made no move to assist, he figured he had chosen wisely. She grunted as she moved behind the bar, nearly dropping the box as she lowered it to the floor. "Whew!" she exclaimed, running the back of her hand across her forehead, eyeballing the patrons scattered about the place. "You're all duffers, the lot of ya."

Lanced looked around. Not one of the others lifted his head from his drink. His cheeks warmed as he faced her. "Sorry 'bout that."

She shot him a wry grin and went about slitting the container open with a box cutter, then stocking its contents. "I certainly didn't mean you."

He ducked his chin. "No? Why do I get an exemption?"

"You don't think I saw that pair of drumsticks sticking out of your back pocket? When's the last time you earned an honest day's wages?"

Her harmless barb struck him as humorous. "I can't say from honest, but I'd like to see you live on a tour bus for months on end, sleeping sitting up more than in beds, never getting a proper meal, isolated from friends and family. It's not for the faint of heart, love, I assure you."

"You bragging or complaining, then?"

He lifted a shoulder and took another sip of lager.

She finished stocking the box's contents, broke it down, and tossed it to the end of the bar. "All right there, Sid?" she called to an elderly gentleman seated near the fireplace at the far end of the room.

The old man waved her off and grumbled, tucking himself into the folds of his coat.

Lance eyed his watch, twisted around to glance out the window again, then turned back.

"You can use the phone."

"If he's not here by the time I'm finished, I'll leave him a message, thanks."

Maybe Todd standing him up told him all he needed to know. Even before the break-up, their lead singer had steadily receded from the group. It had started with Chris's move to Miami. Probably longer, though Lance did not know why. In some ways, Todd had been an outsider since Mirage's inception, though Lance had known him for years before.

Early on, Todd had taken a back seat to the lauded talent of Elliot, Chris, and even Faith. Some might consider it coasting by. Most would blame the drink and drugs. But all that rubbish had started well before Todd's systematic repudiation of his own abilities. With Elliot's quiet public persona, Chris's sexual shenanigans, and Faith's notoriously naughty antics, only those closest to Todd had ever seen him for who he really was: a beautiful amalgam of the three. His image had resonated with the crowds—and with the press—as the golden-voiced, platinum-haired, seemingly gregarious yet unattainable front man. No one had looked deeper. Lance figured Todd had wanted it that way.

The rumble of a car motor and tires on asphalt drew his attention. He straightened in his seat and peered over his shoulder.

The barmaid dried a glass with a dingy rag. She craned her neck up and to the side. "That him?"

The vehicle made a U-turn, drove to the edge of the parking lot, signaled, then turned west onto Brenchley Road.

"Guess not." Lance rested his elbows on the counter.

She busied herself putting away a gray compartment trayful of freshly washed glasses. "Worried, then?"

"Psh. He's all right. Just stubborn."

"Hmm."

He thought about driving the rest of the way into Marden. It was not far. But he had promised Ivy he would meet her at the doctor's office in Chatham for their 4 PM appointment. After months of arguing over Colin's parentage, she had finally saved up the money for one of those DNA paternity tests. He had offered to pay for and arrange it, but she had refused. Nonetheless, he needed to be there so they could test both him and the baby.

"You have any children?" he asked the barmaid, who stood at the till toward the end of the bar making change for a fiver before grabbing Sid his next draught.

"Not a-one," she told him flatly, eyeing him with a look he could not distinguish between insult and regret. "You?"

He took a hearty gulp, then indulged his drink reflex with a satisfied "ahh" as he set down his glass. "Think I'll take you up on that phone call, if it's okay."

She scoffed, probably feeling he had avoided the question, then grabbed the phone and set it in front of him before wandering back to the till.

When Lance lifted the receiver, he hesitated briefly before dialing. Something about tracking Todd down made him feel like a needy teenaged bird who refused to take a hint. Todd's failure to appear had not shocked him. Their earlier conversation had made it evident he had no inclination to meet.

The phone rang six times before the machine switched on. He figured he should hang up and forget it. But it was more than just discussing their glory days and weighing the pros and cons of a Mirage reunion now. Everything inside him told him his friend was in trouble.

"Listen, you tosser. It's one thing to blow me off, but another thing to not pick up when I call. If you're not home, where are you? Bloody well not here, that's for sure! And if you *are* home, I'll assume you're lying in a pool of your own blood, vomit, or piss. So, either pick up the phone or my next call is nine-nine-nine!"

There came a jumble of static and crashing on the other end of the line, as if the receiver had been knocked from its base, fumbled with, and possibly juggled between two people. Lance thought he heard giggling in the background.

That giggling turned to laughter, then coughing as a breathy female voice answered. "Is this Lance?"

He narrowed his eyes beneath a wrinkled brow. "It is. Where's Todd?"

"He, uh..." With a playful squeal, she muffled the phone and told someone nearby to knock it off and to shush. "He can't come to the phone. He's...he's tied up at the moment."

A second voice joined in on the laughter. A male voice. One he knew all too well.

"But he did ask me to give you a message if you called."

"Yeah?" he asked, unamused. "And what's the message?"

"BUGGER OFF!" she shouted before slamming the receiver in his ear.

The inharmonious combination of the woman's shrill of a voice and the sensation caused by the crashing phone sent Lance's head back as if he had received a physical blow. An immediate though short-lived sense of rage rose within him, nearly propelling him out of the bar and into his vehicle.

He dropped the receiver onto its base, snatched his jacket off the seat beside him, and stomped toward the door. Halfway there, he paused, shoulders slumped, hands on hips. A series of inaudible curses, complete with angry head-jerks, ensued. When he had gotten it out of his system, he returned to his vacated stool. "Mind if I make another call?"

She shrugged without looking his way as she handed over a fresh draught to the only other gentleman there besides him and Sid. "I guess there's no harm. But I'll be charging you for the wear soon, so see to it it's a quick one."

He nodded and picked up the receiver a second time, then dialed the Chatham number. Ivy answered on the second ring.

"I've been ringing you for an hour," she yelled into the line. "Where *are* you? We'll miss the appointment!"

The sound of her voice put him right, as usual. "No worries, sweetheart. I'm at a pub in Brenchley."

"*Brenchley*? What in bloody hell are you doing in Brenchley?"

"I told you I was off to meet Todd earlier." A brief pause told him she was trying to remember. Either that or she was refueling.

"Lance Turner, you'd best not tell me you're too pissed to drive. I've waited two months for this appointment and you're not spoiling this for me *or* your son! It's bad enough you're not here to calm him down. He's positively terrified!"

"Are you sure it's the test? He's not even a year for a few more days."

"I know our son! Now get off this phone and come round to get us! And don't tell me you have plans after. You're taking us out for a proper meal tonight like you promised."

"No worries. I'll be there straightaway. In fact, pack an overnight for the both of you. After dinner, we'll all go back to my place for a video. Tomorrow, we'll take Colin for a pre-birthday shopping spree. Maybe a little something for his mum as well. How does that sound?"

Her voice wound down a few octaves to a pout. "There you go again, spending a monkey or two to try and set things right. You think I'm a tart after everything you've got. You know, money isn't everything."

The barmaid tapped her wrist with her index finger several times, then raised her hands, palms up.

"I think nothing of the sort. Now go get your things packed. I'll be there at half three. Plenty of time to get to the doctor."

"And we need to stop at the chemist on the way. Colin's got a right awful sniffle."

"Well, there you go. That's why he's upset. Of course we can stop. Can't have the birthday boy sick on his big day."

Objections addressed, Ivy eased off. Two unmanly kisses into the phone and Lance ended the call. He thanked the barmaid, tucking a tenner beneath the base of the phone before she noticed, then headed out to his car.

Fifteen minutes after he left, a stretch limousine pulled into the parking lot. Sid, the barmaid, and the other gentleman inside craned their necks up, peering wide-eyed at the long, black vehicle pulling up close to the entrance and parking lengthwise across several marked spaces in the front by the door. A sharp-dressed chauffeur exited the driver's seat. He stepped to the rear door, opened it wide, then stepped out of the way.

Bony fingers bearing several large cluster rings and bright red nails shot out, clawing the air, trying to grasp the chauffeur's outstretched hand, missing it four times before latching on. They belonged to a staggering, big-haired brunette wearing a red sequined cocktail dress and a full-length white fur coat. She tumbled from the car and onto the pavement before the chauffeur could prevent the fall. Closely behind her and equally unsteady came a tall, thin platinum blond man in red leather pants, black boots, and a silk shirt unbuttoned to his waist.

When the chauffeur tried to assist the woman, the man waved him away. On feeble legs, he grabbed the woman from behind, hoisting her upright as if standing up a fallen mannequin. Laughing, they stumbled to the entrance of the bar and made their way inside.

CHAPTER 16

WHEN CHRIS AND MARCI RETURNED later that night, the Royster Building looked ominous. Impenetrable. Its broken brick façade and chipped-paint frames of randomly-shattered blackened windows uttered a stern warning that none should attempt to enter.

Dressed for the chill of an East Coast evening after having taken hot showers at the Days Inn, they felt somewhat rejuvenated. While sluggish from three days on the road, their nervous energy counterbalanced their fatigue. They pushed on, parking the Olds around back in the most visually inaccessible spot they could find.

Chris studied their surroundings. Despite the darkness of night and a shortage of working street lamps near the back of the building, he spotted mature oaks with thick, sturdy branches. All, unfortunately, cut too far back from the roof or windows to offer assistance.

A ten-foot-high brick wall, capped with a large cement deck, stood at the base of the semicircular façade. To either side were L-shape stairways, their lose and broken brick reduced to rubble. A dumpster sat at the foot, between them. At the far end of the building, closest to the chapel, another staircase led to a back door. More intact, but almost assuredly locked.

He pointed to the roof and whispered, "Those pipes look pretty stable. I could climb up to the overhang above that door. See? Where it's caved in? I could slip through the top and downstairs."

Marci scanned the area for viable alternatives. "Let's pretend you wouldn't break your leg shimmying up the pipes of a three-story building. Then what? We'll still need a way *out*."

Chris walked the perimeter, searching for a broken window into which he could safely slip. He considered breaking one himself, but their muntins were made of steel, not painted wood. Why this surprised him, he did not know. Naturally, a building on the grounds of a mental institution would use steel grids in the windows and all the rooms would lock. There were probably gates and locks inside, as well.

Idea after idea ended in failure. They could not even confirm Farin was inside this place. If she was, they did not know her exact location. Each moment they loitered the grounds increased the odds someone might see them.

He returned to Marci, who had ascended the one accessible staircase and stood at the back door. "The windows are a no-go. Besides, we don't want to cause a commotion. We don't even know how many people are inside."

Marci seized and tested the doorknob. To their mutual astonishment, it opened.

They froze in unison, each hitching their breath. Hearts racing, they waited for the sound of a blaring horn, or for some security guard to come running in response to a silent alarm.

Nothing.

"Think it's a trap?" Marci asked.

"Even if it is, it's the only way we're getting in this sodding place. Wait here while I relocate the car. Probably shouldn't have it so close to the building in case someone comes by."

When he returned a couple of minutes later, he nudged her side. She looked down to find him passing her one of the two flashlights he had grabbed from the back seat. He had made her purchase them before returning to the hospital. Neither of them knew what to expect. That included the absence of electricity. She accepted the flashlight, then looked at him. With a nod, they stepped inside.

For the most part, they shuffled blindly across pitted linoleum. They crept from one musty room to the next, past abandoned gurneys, wheelchairs, and steel carts scattered like so much debris along their path. Chairs and desks lay overturned. Broken tiles and strips of mildewed or rotting wallpaper mixed into the grit-covered floor along with the occasional pair of discarded crutches and construction tools.

They advanced slowly, aware of each sound, watching for shadowy movements, hesitant to engage their flashlights. The amber glow of parking lot lamps filtered through the front side of the building's dingy windows provided less than optimal lighting. Without a clear navigation point, they stumbled and fumbled, making their way to a main hall, which ran the length of the building.

To either side of the hallway, narrow doorways dotted the walls. They each took a side, checking the small rooms, which appeared to have been cells or padded rooms for former patients. Inside, each housed a narrow metal bedframe, now rusted or broken. Halfway down, they reached the main entrance.

Opposite its double doors, another corridor led back to an enormous alcove, probably a day room. Inside were dozens of stackable plastic school chairs, scattered and unused for some time. Its yellow walls had been inexpertly painted with brightly colored and totally nonsensical collages.

"The dust's giving me a headache," she whispered. She attempted, and failed, to stifle a sneeze.

Chris clutched Marci's forearm. They faced each other, their eyes darting nervously into the darkness as they listened for any hint that they had been discovered.

Again, nothing.

Cautiously, they doubled back to the entryway, then continued inspecting the hall. At the end, they discovered a stairwell. It provided access to the sunken-in top floor or the floor below—perhaps a basement.

He stuck his head in and looked up, then down. When he turned back, he motioned downward with his thumb. She nodded her agreement.

Dim florescent lighting bathed the downstairs hall. At the base of the stairs, to the immediate right, was a door with a sign that read "Utility."

Marci's pulse quickened as they stepped out of the stairwell. To their left, another long hall. Along either side, more rooms to search.

Intuition told her they were close, but each empty room dashed her hopes. The nausea she had battled most the afternoon and evening gave way to unbridled fear that someone would discover them. Or worse, that they had been set up.

A hacking cough came from the utility room. They rushed through the open door closest to them, flattening themselves against the wall inside the tiny room, into the shadows beyond the reach of the garish glow emanating from the hall.

They waited in stillness. Chris leaned forward to peek through the door opening.

Then, the utility door swung open. A woman emerged, donning the obligatory white uniform of a nurse. Shutting the door behind her, she padded toward a rolling podium near the hall's midpoint.

At her makeshift nursing station, she deposited a handful of plastic packaging into a wastebasket, then a syringe into a red plastic Hazardous Waste container, which she then stowed in one of the podium's shelves.

She picked up a metal clipboard, made some notes, then replaced it and headed for the stairs. Her heavy girth caused a distinct waddle in her step.

When she finally disappeared up the main stairway, panting and huffing as she maneuvered her mass, Chris and Marci crept silently down the hall. Unsure if they might encounter anyone else, they eyed potential hiding places.

They stopped at the podium to peruse the notes the nurse had made on the clipboard. All medical jargon, they struggled to decipher much more than the dates listed at the beginning of each entry.

"'Thorazine injection,'" Chris whisper-quoted. "'One hundred milligrams b.i.d.'"

"What's that?" Marci's troubled eyes shifted from Chris, to the notes, to the door from which the nurse had emerged.

He scanned the page. "It's some kind of drug. By the look of the entries, they're giving her this Thorazine twice a day. It says...'patient remains unresponsive. Occasional mild fever is noted. Occasional aspiration of vomitus is indicated. Negative cardiovascular, hepatic, or renal disease. Benign mammary neoplasm "bx" April fourth, nineteen ninety-four. In whole, patient has tolerated treatment with minimal adverse reactions.' What the hell?"

"I don't understand any of that," Marci whispered impatiently. "We don't know if those notes are about Farin. We don't even know if she's here."

He flipped through the pages. "If these are about her, we'll need to know what they've been doing. If they have her on some drug and we just take her, it could kill her. Do you want to chance losing her again?"

She stared back at the closed door.

He replaced the clipboard as he found it. They crept back to the utility room. A notice affixed below the door placard read, "Caution: Do Not Enter."

Chris listened at the door, then tried the knob. Less surprising this time, it opened easily.

Inside, they beheld a marked contrast to the decaying structure encasing them. The large room was clean, sterile, and well-lit. At its center, a circular curtain hung from the ceiling, concealing its contents from anyone who might mistakenly wander inside. Several machines lay scattered about the room. They resembled what appeared to be various physical therapy contraptions. At the far left-hand corner of the room stood a large storage closet.

They stood, transfixed. Everything they had experienced in the last few days came down to this moment. Farin. If Ross spoke the truth, they would find her beyond the curtain—*alive.*

Chris headed for the closet, leaving Marci to verify their search had ended. It was not his place anymore. He could not look. Not yet. He did not want the last three years of his life to intersect in a dilapidated, condemned building on the grounds of a mental institution in Raleigh, North Carolina.

Jameson Lockhardt, I'll kill you. I'll kill you with my bare hands.

Marci reached for the curtain, then stopped. She stared at the nylon drape surrounding the bed. Squinting her eyes, she thought she made out the silhouette of a woman stretched out on a bed. The outline of the forehead, nose, and lips looked familiar.

Tears brimmed her eyes. She stepped back. In her heart, she knew. She watched for some motion, some rise and fall of the chest, or a twitch from the body. Nothing.

We're too late.

Chris opened the storage closet. It was nearly empty. The only thing of interest was a size six ladies' suit, black. A pair of matching black shoes, size eight, were on the floor.

He swallowed hard, then announced through a cracked whisper, "I found her clothes."

It was real.

He vacillated between intense happiness and even more intense hatred—hatred and confusion toward the man who did this to her. The man who had once been closer to him than his own family.

When he turned around, he found Marci hovering beside the curtain. "Hurry. We need to get her out of here before someone comes back to check on her."

A few helpless tears spilled down her cheeks. She shook her head. "I don't think she's breathing, Chris. Look at the shadow on the curtain. I'm afraid to...h-hope."

He nudged her aside, giving her shoulder a tender squeeze. It was the first sign of compassion he had shown her the entire time they had known each other. "I'll do it."

Biting the inside of his cheek, he regarded the curtain. Unlike Marci, he could do nothing but hope. Hope that Farin lay beyond the curtain, alive and well. Hope that Julie could forgive him for taking off and not calling. Hope that she understood his obligation to Jordan, to make right all the years of betrayal.

Slowly, he drew back the curtain. When he glimpsed the face lying still on the pillow, his legs nearly failed him.

Farin lay beneath a thin cotton sheet, eyes closed, a mere wisp of the vital woman he remembered. Dull auburn curls framed her solemn face. The ashen hue of her skin alarmed him. For a second, he feared the worst. Then, he saw the slight rise and fall of her chest. "She's alive."

Marci rushed past him. She beheld the pale, withered body of her best friend. "Farin!" she gasped.

Chris's hand shook as he took her wrist. He felt for a pulse, then rested his ear atop her chest. "Her breathing's shallow. Probably the drugs."

With trembling fingers, Marci brushed hair away from Farin's face, then touched her cheek. "Her skin's so cold."

"We've gotta get her out of here."

"What if that woman comes back?"

He rattled his head. "According to that chart, the nurses and the doctor come in regular intervals." He consulted his watch. "It's ten thirty now. No one should come near this room for hours. But we need to be far away by the time they discover she's gone."

Marci reflected on the dark, debris-strewn route they had traveled to find her. "How are we gonna get her to the car?"

Muffled voices and booming footsteps approach. They faced each other. Chris took Marci's hand, closed the curtain, and piled into the closet. Although a tight fit, they managed to secure themselves inside before the voices entered the room.

He left the door cracked a hair. He needed to see for himself.

The nurse they had seen earlier waddled in with none other than Jameson Lockhardt following close behind. Chris fought the urge to burst out of the closet. Through gritted teeth, he snarled, "Bloody bastard."

Marci looked at him with pleading eyes.

"She's well?" Jameson moved to Farin's bed, jerking back the curtain to inspect his prisoner.

The nurse cleared her throat. "I don't mean to speak out of turn, sir, but after last week, I'm afraid we won't be able to keep her alive much longer. We barely brought her back as it was. The prolonged exposure to the Thorazine could cause irreversible damage. And with Dr. Childs gone, the medication will be difficult to come by."

Jameson folded his hands before him. With a downturned smile of deep contemplation, he nodded as if agreeing with some inner voice, then addressed the nurse. "If the medication fails to do what I want it to, we'll change it."

"Again, Mr. Lockhardt, I mean no disrespect..."

He shot the woman a warning look.

Shifting her ample weight from one foot to the other, she glanced at Farin, then to the floor. "It's just...you've had her here so long, sir. You don't want her conscious and you don't want her dead. Prolonged exposure to *any* medication...well, it could be fatal."

He glared at her with lethal intensity. "You're paid to do a job, Ms. Evans—and paid well, I might add. If it's become too complicated, I'll gladly relieve you of your duties."

Without another word, she lowered her head and waited until he completed whatever assessment he had come to perform.

When finished, he turned back to her. "I'll be moving her to another facility within the next week or so. You'll coordinate with a new doctor. He'll contact you on my behalf. His name is Doctor..." he hesitated a beat, "Doctor Moreau. When he takes over, you'll receive the final payment we agreed upon."

"Oh," was all Nurse Evans could manage in response.

"Give us a moment alone."

She nodded, then exited the door as quickly as her ponderous girth allowed.

Jameson dislodged a chair from a stack of four nested beside a misshapen, overturned walker. He dragged it to Farin's bedside, and sat down. "I wish things hadn't turned out this way, my dear. You might not think so, but I tried to make things better for you. Surely, you realize by now that much of what happened was a result of your inability to let sleeping dogs lie. You spent your life in grief, and through that grief, you bore more grief."

Inside the closet, Marci shut her eyes. Memories of their childhood flooded her mind. How could this man presume to know anything about her? How had it come to this?

"You know, at first, I believed you'd be reasonable. I gave you every chance. But then, all the screaming and crying and trying to escape. We had no choice now, did we?"

Chris's body tensed. When Marci felt him straighten in the cramped space, she grabbed and held him in place. He stared down at her, nostrils flared. She shook her head in desperation.

"At one point, I felt I owed you something, but I've paid that debt many times over. To the world, you died long ago. I'm not even sure why I came tonight. Perhaps to say goodbye in person. I don't know. If you could hear me, I'm sure you'd thank me. I'm doing you a favor. This is no way to exist. Your life is over and has been for years. But I promise you this—and you of all people know I'm a man of my word: the end will be swift and painless."

When Jameson finally left the room, the closet stowaways listened until the booming footsteps vanished back the way they had come.

"The man's bloody insane!" Chris whisper-shouted as he and Marci emerged from their hiding place. "He's been drugging her for *years!*"

Marci hurried to Farin's side, sat in Jameson's vacated chair, and took her friend's hand in hers. "Did you hear what they said? They almost lost her last week. She's not well. And Lockhardt's gonna kill her."

"There won't be anyone here to kill. I'll go upstairs and figure out the easiest way. If anyone comes in, hide in the closet again."

Marci sat, holding Farin's frail hand, for long minutes. It horrified her to see her friend so helpless, so still, so thin. She wondered if they would be able to get her out before someone noticed she was missing. And even if they did, what were the chances she would survive once they left? Would she regain consciousness? Would she be able to walk?

She lowered her head beside Farin's still body and wept. "I should've known. I should have tried to find you. It's just...those last few years, Farin. We were growing apart. I should have...I'm sorry."

Chris returned to find Marci weeping at Farin's bedside. Her tears stopped him momentarily, then he shouldered on. A long road lay before them. If they stood a chance of success, they needed to act quickly.

"You should've hidden in the closet," he said. "What if it wasn't me?"

She sniffed and moved from the chair, allowing Chris easier access. "I knew it was you by the sound of your footsteps. That nurse weighed three hundred pounds and Jameson's wearing dress shoes. You're the one who should've been careful. If someone besides me had been in here..."

"I found a way out. If we hurry, we can use the back entrance we came in through. The nurses are changing shifts right now. It should be okay. I found some supplies of that drug and some IV bags. I loaded them up already. If we're careful, we should be able to get her some help before it runs out. I just don't want to chance taking her off something cold turkey. You heard that nurse."

Marci collected Farin's shoes and clothes.

He stepped forward to gather Farin into his arms. "Unhook her IV bag from that stand, will you? In fact, let's take the stand. And, oh—I forgot the chart notes. Grab them for me on the way out. Everything you can find. And don't forget the flashlights."

For the second time that evening, his legs nearly failed him. The feel of her body against his left him reeling. Thin. Fragile. Cool. But alive.

There came no movement, no sound from her beautiful mouth, just the shallow breathing of her lungs as he and Marci hurried down the hallway, up the stairs, across the corridor, and out the back door.

With gentle, lightning-quick movements, Chris slid her into the back seat of the Olds and positioned her IV while Marci started the vehicle.

They would not return to the Days Inn. They headed out the main gate, made a right onto Lake Wheeler Road, and took the 440 outer-loop exit. Five minutes later, they merged onto I-40 East. In less than an hour, they hit I-95 South, driving as if their lives depended on it.

At least one did.

***

Ben's reaction to the news had surprised himself even more than his wife or Julie. They had told him the day Julie arrived from LA, after dinner and after the boys had gone up to bed. A mild storm had settled over Southern Florida, chasing them off the back patio where they habitually enjoyed lazy evenings with their houseguests.

They opted for the dining room, leaving the patio doors open so they could enjoy the cool, if humid, breeze. Cheryl had poured after-dinner drinks. To Ben's relief and amazement, Julie had declined to partake. She sat opposite him at the table and waited for her iced tea.

He should have known by the absence of dinner chatter something was up. The boys had probably felt it, too. They had finished their meal quickly and headed upstairs to voluntarily finish their homework. Kyle, maybe. But Derek? The tension in the room must have been palpable if it motivated his oldest to crack open a school book.

Cheryl had broached the conversation delicately. She had prepared two small tumblers of Courvoisier and one glass of iced tea, then settled herself next to him at the table. Julie had sulked opposite them, arms crossed. "Darling, I...um, rather, *we*—Julie and I—need to talk to you."

Ben could not recall a time when Cheryl had acted so odd. Rarely did his wife struggle for words. "What is it? Are you okay? Julie?"

It had occurred to him that perhaps things had not gone as well for Chris and Julie as he had assumed. He hoped Cheryl would not announce they planned to divorce. No matter what problems he continued to face with his brother, he wished him well.

After a few awkward moments, she had told him plainly, "Farin's alive."

He had looked at her expectantly, waiting for her to say something. As if she had not said a word. As if he had not heard. She repeated herself four times before the news sunk in.

For the next twenty-four hours, he paced, room to room. He needed something to occupy his time and thoughts. What, he did not know. His mind ran the gamut of emotions: confusion at the bizarre and sketchy details the women had relayed; anger Chris had not told him personally; pride his brother had taken charge; regret he had not accompanied him on his journey; and mostly, concern for Farin. He hoped Chris would call soon to tell him what unimaginable circumstances had taken her from their family.

A part of him wondered whether that would happen. Had their personal problems created such an aperture between them that Chris would merely pass through it without sharing this most important news? In all the years Chris had traveled the hard road—alone, without a thought for the rest of the family—never had this reality come so succinctly to Ben.

He did not retire until midnight Friday. Even then, sleep did not come easily. Filled with questions, he tossed and turned until nearly three.

Minutes after he drifted off, the phone rang. He picked up and answered on the first ring, before his conscious mind registered the call.

"Ben," came his brother's voice.

He shot up in bed. "Where are you?"

"Did Julie call?"

"She's here. We know. Where are you?"

"South Carolina. We should be there tomorrow afternoon." His voice broke with his last words. "I'm bringing her home."

The line went dead.

CHAPTER 17

DEREK COMPLAINED AS HE STALKED his mother from the laundry room, down the hall, and into his room. "But Summer's coming over to study. What's going on? You can tell me. I'm not a kid anymore."

"I figured you'd be thrilled to spend the weekend at Peter's. They're sailing up to Alice Town. You love it there. Should be a lovely day. Peter's mum says they may even spend the night. I packed you some warm clothes, just in case."

He flounced on top of his bed next to the duffle bag his mother loaded with shoes, three pairs of jeans, several shirts ranging from tees to long sleeves, and five pairs of underwear. "Am I staying the weekend or a month? This is way too much stuff."

"You need to be prepared, Derek. Things happen in life. Unexpected things."

Her unconvincing smile puzzled him. His mother usually had it together. He could not think of a time he had seen her hands shake. He lay on his side, his head propped atop his elbow. More gently, he asked, "What's wrong, Mom?"

She smoothed the clothes in his bag, double-checked his shaving kit, then stepped back to survey his room. Once satisfied she had not omitted anything important, she brought her hands to her hips, drew in a deep breath, then blew it out through puckered lips. "I think you're ready. Your father will be back soon from dropping Kyle off. He'll get you to Peter's."

Derek scampered upright. "*Dad's* driving? Why can't I drive myself? What'd I do?"

Cheryl hefted the duffle and placed it in the hall, then returned and sat beside him. She rested a hand on his knee. "You did nothing wrong, son. Your dad and I need a wee bit of time to sort—"

"Is Grandma okay?"

"Of course!"

"Uncle Chris?" he demanded, a slight catch in his throat. "Is that why Aunt Julie's here?"

She put her arm around his broad shoulders. "It's nothing like that. Your uncle's fine. Don't be worrying your head, now. I promise. Things're fine."

He bobbed a shoulder and lowered his head. "Then why can't I stay and study with Summer? Or at least drive myself to Peter's?"

She studied him at length, the way mothers do, as if she had not seen him clearly in years. Pride and nostalgia tangoed across her heart until nothing existed but that moment. She pushed back several dark hairs that had fallen forward into his line of vision, then lifted his chin. "When did you get so tall and handsome? You look more like your father every day."

Wide-eyed and brow-creased, he froze in place, looking askance at her.

"All grown up, wearing cologne. What's that you've got on?" She took a whiff. "Isn't that the one you and Summer gave each other for Christmas?"

He nodded but remained otherwise still.

"What's the name?"

"CK One?"

"Aye, that's it! The one men or women can wear."

Downstairs, the front door opened, the triggered ping of the alarm box signaling someone had entered. Seizing his chance to escape his suddenly sentimental mother, Derek shot off the bed and hastened to grab his bag. "That you, Dad?" he called.

"You almost ready?" Ben called back.

He positioned his duffle in front of him like a shield, trudged back over to his mother, pecked her cheek, then hurried off. "Sorry, Mom. Gotta go. Like you said, I don't wanna be late. I'll call when we get back to the marina tomorrow."

Cheryl remained seated until she heard the front door ping once more, then got up and dusted her hands. "Works every time."

She gathered up the dirty clothes scattered around his room, closed his door as she left, then deposited them in the laundry room. With only a few hours before Chris's anticipated arrival, it was all hands on deck. If only she knew what to expect, she might know better how to prepare. Alas, Ben had learned nothing during their brief conversation some hours ago.

Convincing her husband to help her arrange for the boys to spend the weekend away had been easier than she would have thought. With all they had gone through over the last few years, it seemed reasonable to assess the situation with Farin before heaping shock and confusion upon younger minds. At this point, they had no idea what to tell them.

"I think I'll put Marci and Farin on the third floor, above you and Chris," she told Julie as she bustled into the kitchen for her third cup of tea. "That way, they'll have their privacy."

Julie sat at the table, head on her hand, pushing her scrambled eggs around her plate with a fork.

Outside the sheer curtains of the French doors, clouds obstructed the morning light. Cheryl had checked the weather before packing Derek's things. They would not see rain today, but it would remain gloomy until well into the afternoon.

She sat down opposite Julie at the table and blew on her mug. "I need to put fresh linens on the beds before they get here. It's funny. Ben never understood why I put together one of the guest rooms with two queens."

Julie nodded and sipped her apple juice.

"Your food's cold, Jules. You all right? Should I warm it up?"

"No thanks."

She rested her arm atop the table, extending an open hand her way. "You okay?"

Julie leaned back in her chair. "I suppose."

"He'll be here soon, love. No worries. You two will set things right. You'll tell him about the baby—"

"Cheryl, stop."

She drew back her chin. "What?"

Julie stretched her long legs, crossed her ankles, then crossed her arms. "This is no time to tell Chris we're having a baby. Even *I* know that."

"You're wrong, hen. Plain wrong. Chris adores children. People can say what they want about his dodgy past, but he's always been keen for a brood of his own. Why, you've seen him around our boys."

Julie gathered her breakfast dishes and placed them in the sink. "Please don't make me regret telling you. I need to do this my way. And I *will*— soon. Just not here. And not with Farin fifteen feet above our bed."

She pinched her thumb and index finger together across her lips.

The room fell silent. Cheryl gazed again through the curtains, beyond the patio. Various palms, citronella, and elephant ear landscaping swayed in the soft breeze. Mockingbirds, wrens, swallows, and jays flitted about the property warbling, feeding, and playing in bird baths. She missed her morning routine, sitting outside and chatting with Ben as they traded sections of the *Post*. Days like this made her appreciate them all the more.

It was not that she had changed her mind about Farin. She simply saw things differently than Julie. Yes, untold complications would doubtless accompany the woman's return to their lives. But years of experience with the Grants—as one of them—trumped Julie's paranoia and pregnancy hormones. If anything could ensure Chris did not backslide into a sea of emotion, a baby could. Cheryl was certain of it.

She heard the garage door engage, then the rumble of the Land Rover's engine as it pulled in and parked. When the car door opened and closed, she wondered what his disposition might be when he joined them. Instead, he cut through the garage to the back yard. A moment later, he disappeared into his studio.

Julie came up beside her, lowered her head, and stared after him. "I'd hoped he'd come inside. I wanted to ask him what Chris said last night."

Cheryl finished her tea, then rose and placed her cup in the sink. "He doesn't know any more than he already told us. I realize it's frustrating, but we'll find out soon enough. Now, come help me get the room ready."

Julie sucked her cheeks and followed Cheryl upstairs.

***

Ben spent the balance of the morning in his studio. He had no legitimate excuse to withdraw into his lair of soundproof walls encasing expensive recording equipment and boxes of stowed memories. No justification to leave the lion's share of house preparation to his wife and sister-in-law. But, as was his practice when thoughts weighed him down, he spent his private moments here.

Unlike busier times, he produced nothing all day. In fact, he did not so much as switch on one piece of equipment. Several boxed tape reels cluttered the counter of his console. Dozens of versions of his compositions sent him by various artists he had agreed to work with. Production work. He had found himself a new niche. Even better, after two decades of success, he enjoyed the luxury of cherry-picking his projects. They came to him. And with modern conveniences ranging from email to video conferencing, he rarely had to travel. This appealed to him more and more—which concerned Cheryl.

They had discussed the matter several times. She would say, "I don't need to remind you, love, there's no substitute for being there. We're capable of managing without you for a few days at a stretch."

He would counter, "It's fine. If anyone needs me, they know where I am. Besides, they can always come down here. Who could beat the tropical ambiance of south Florida?"

"Your wee semi-pro studio's no match for the larger ones. You don't have the space or the equipment."

"I have great equipment. When I need something bigger, Keys Studio's five miles from here. And we can always book Tympanum, Standards, or Criteria."

"Aye, but when's the last time you booked an outside studio, Benjamin?"

He understood her point. And concern. They both knew the heart had gone out of his music. The full bloom of his beloved career had withered into something he did out of habit. It was all he knew. It paid the bills. It kept him busy. The busier he stayed, the less time he had to dwell on the past.

Except days like today, when he spent hours staring at an unoccupied isolation booth, picturing his baby brother singing, eyes closed, cupping headphones with his hands.

The morning dragged on. Nine. Ten. Eleven. Chris had said they should arrive "tomorrow afternoon." Ben mentally calculated the distance between South Carolina and Key Biscayne. Depending on where they had called from, the drive would take about ten hours. Adding in gas, food, and restroom breaks, it could be dark before they reached the house.

The silence he had encountered at dinner last night finally made sense. The next few days, weeks, and months would dictate what road the Grants—*all* the Grants—would travel from this point forward.

Farin's presence would test Chris and Julie's marriage. No surprise there. Hopefully, it would not strain his own.

At noon, he decided he had better at least pretend to work. Cheryl would probably bring him lunch. If she found him just sitting there, it might prompt a conversation he would rather avoid.

He went to the kitchenette he had added a few months back. While his tea steeped, he organized tape reels according to their importance and deadline. He was ahead of schedule. Unless he encountered something truly disastrous, he would complete everything by the end of the following week.

Masters beckoned him as he hovered between the storage room and the kitchenette. For all his failures as the oldest sibling, he now protected each of his brothers the only way he could: their laughter, talent, and work preserved forever on narrow strips of magnetically coated polyester film.

They captured them all at their best. Happier times. The three of them working various projects—a new song for one of Jordan's upcoming albums, or a piece Chris wanted to perfect before sharing with Mirage. How many times had they pestered him to join them, insisting the three of them cut an album together someday?

He doctored his tea, then walked back to his seat. Blowing steam from the mug while taking short sips of the hot beverage, he swiveled around and scanned the shelves.

The masters illustrated Jordan's career, from his self-titled debut album to his unfinished last. Most tracks were unreleased. LSI had rejected several songs Ben thought would have been brilliant choices. But such choices had not been his to make. Once his celebrity gave him a certain amount of control over the material, Ben and Jordan had discussed the possibility of releasing them someday.

He swung around in his chair and slammed his fist onto the console. The smaller of two stacks of tapes leapt and shifted in response.

Someday. The word tasted as bitter as his last sip of tea. He scowled at the ceiling-mounted condenser mic in the sound booth. Why did it always take loss to realize the most important things in life? Every tired, over-quoted maxim in the world warned of such truths as, "you never know what you have until it's gone," or "don't put off until tomorrow what you can do today." At times, he felt his life had become nothing more than an old cliché.

Alas, someday never came.

Ben stood and ran his fingers across a row of tapes. One particular dust-covered selection caught his eye. He removed it and eyeballed the cover. It was unlabeled, which struck him as odd considering his recent diligence in cataloging his inventory.

He swiped his hand across the large box to remove a layer of dust, then lifted its lid. The inside reel was also unlabeled. Intrigued, he threaded it into his Tascam ATR-60-16 and, with the flip of a few switches, brought his system to life.

At first, he heard little more than noise—the muffled creak of a microphone stand being manipulated into place. Ben lowered himself into his seat, resting his chin upon his laced fingers. Next came a shuffling sound, followed by a discordant twang of strings as an accidental thump echoed inside the hollow body and emanated out through the sound hole of a guitar. A vinyl stool deflated as an unknown musician sat upon it and positioned the bulky instrument on his or her lap. Finally, the music began.

A mournful riff of melody echoed through the control room walls. It caught Ben in a state of disbelief. He knew. He knew by the unpolished sound of the acoustic guitar, the inelegant chord changes. The shy clearing of the throat.

Jordan.

While neither accomplished nor comfortable playing the instrument, the melody was lovely. A ballad. A love song. A haunting profession of devotion.

> *... Everything I never knew I wanted ...*
> *... I found in your eyes ...*
> *... And every word that ever went unspoken ...*
> *... Echoed in your sighs ...*

Ben heard beyond the ungraceful guitar. Trapped inside the unexpected purity of the piece, he imagined beautiful arpeggios on piano, a soft rhythm of drums, a symphonic string arrangement.

> *... Every man I ever hoped to be ...*
> *... I am when you're around ...*
> *... So, everything you ever need from me ...*
> *... Will always be found ...*

Jordan poured himself into the piece. His voice soft, tender, almost a cry. A verse, a chorus, a bridge. Such touching lyrics, such a personal message. He reached out through the notes and caressed the heart of the listener.

A fleeting twinge of guilt washed over Ben as he listened, as if he were a voyeur trespassing through an intimate exchange.

The piece ended. Another fumble as Jordan replaced the guitar on its stand. Footsteps across the live room floor. The opening and closing of the studio door. Then, silence.

Ben did not move. The impact of finding the tape on this day challenged his disbelief in all things providential. Not that he did not believe in God. As a good Catholic, he attributed little to divine intervention. But how he had missed this particular tape after taking such careful inventory, he could not know. He was just thankful to have found it.

He grabbed a pad of paper and a pen, then replayed the song several times. Ideas on ways to clean up the recording and enhance it soon filled two pages. Unfortunately, Jordan had recorded it as a single track. He had only started taking an interest in the technical aspect of recording before his death. In order to maintain the vocals and lose the poor guitar, Ben would have to build around the vocals while snuffing out the instrument. Not easy. But it gave him something to think about. Perhaps someday, when he completed his current projects.

The buzz of the intercom stole his attention. He checked his watch, then pressed the button. "Are they here?"

"No," came Cheryl's strained voice. "I was just wondering if you intend to spend your whole day out there. Everything's ready. Julie didn't want lunch and I had a late breakfast. You hungry?"

"I could eat. Maybe a sandwich, if you don't mind."

"Not at all. I'll be running to the store in a bit. We need a few things."

"Sounds good. I'll be in straightaway."

"Ben?"

He frowned at her flinty tone. "Yes, love?"

"It'll be a rough day."

"It will."

"For all of us."

"I understand."

"Don't hide. Not from me."

He leaned back, palming his temple. "I won't."

"You already are."

He parted his lips as if to speak, then thought better of it. Who did he think he was fooling? "I'll be right in."

When she disconnected, he glanced at his notes before powering down his equipment. He removed the tape with care, labeled it, and returned it to the shelf.

***

The Oldsmobile pulled into Ben's circular driveway at dusk. Chris parked as close as he could to the tall hedges, hoping to mask the older model car in such an affluent neighborhood. Concealed landscaping lights dotted the estate. Little had changed since his last visit. On some level, it felt as if his family had welcomed him back.

Feelings he could scarcely process filled him. He had returned, in every sense of the word, to the place he belonged. It was more than geography. His fate, and Farin's, were one—their common thread far from what he could have ever imagined it would be.

Marci piped up from behind him. "Mr. Lockhardt has to know she's gone. Isn't this the first place he'd look?"

"Right now, we need to get her out of this car." He twisted around for a better view of the back. Farin lay across the back seat, still unconscious. Marci crouched sideways in an uncomfortable position, practically on the floor, between Farin and the front seat. "She doing okay?"

Marci gathered packaging and litter into a used Hardees bag. "I hope so. I—I just don't know. She's breathing, but she still hasn't moved."

"This isn't good."

"None of it's good, but my six-month career as a candy striper in nineteen eighty didn't prepare me to decipher medication labels."

"We okay on the thora—what's that stuff called again?"

"There's plenty. The notes show they give it to her twice a day. That 'b.i.d.' must be 'twice a day.' That's it. That's all I got. I couldn't read much of their scribble as we passed beneath street lights. Anyway, we've got tons of the stuff. If we keep giving it to her, we're either keeping her alive or helping to kill her. I don't know. I'm worried about running out of the IV bags. Once they're gone, we can't give her the medication anyway."

"Maybe Cheryl can help."

"She's not a doctor, Chris."

"If we take her to hospital, she'll be recognized. Lockhardt would find out, for sure. Even if by some miracle we managed to keep it from the press, the cops would want to question her—and trust me, I know Miami cops. I'm not letting them get their hands on her."

She fused her eyes as her hand shot up to cover her mouth.

He winced sympathetically. "Looks like you may need a doctor, too."

She held up a finger for a few seconds, then moved her hand from her mouth to her belly. "I'll be okay. It comes and goes. It's just stress."

He turned back and scanned the grounds. "You wait here. I'll go get Ben. He can help me carry her inside."

She nodded, then grabbed a travel size package of baby wipes from the floor. She removed a single sheet to use as a cold compress to wipe Farin's forehead, as she had done throughout their long trip south.

Before Chris could unbuckle his seatbelt, the front door of the house swung open and Ben rushed toward them. It was as if time had melted. Years of conflict dissolved into an ocean of meaningless encounters, futile rivalry, and bitterness that no longer mattered. He hesitated at the weightiness of the moment, then exited the car to face his brother.

Ben stopped dead in his tracks as the near-unrecognizable form of his younger brother emerged from the vehicle. Chris's brows pinched together in worry. Dark circles beneath his glassy, bloodshot eyes stood out like black cork charcoal used by high school football players. Untidy strings of unwashed hair hung about his stooped shoulders. The burden of the journey and everything it signified seemed to churn and settle in his mouth, his whiskered jaw clinched as his teeth ground from exhaustion.

Despite the disheveled image standing before him on weary legs, Ben could still make out the bend in Chris's nose. So much bad blood had spilled onto the table of time. Though he assured himself it no longer mattered, three words echoed through his consciousness as they met: *I did that*.

"I need your help." Chris hastened to the rear passenger's door and lifted the handle.

He nodded. "Where is she?"

When Chris jerked open the rear passenger's door, Marci tumbled backwards, startling her and causing both men to rush forward to catch her. Before they reached her, she shot her right arm up and wrapped it around the headrest while thrusting her left hand backwards onto the driveway to avoid impact.

Ben squinted into the darkness of the vehicle's interior. Inside, he saw the emaciated, motionless form of his sister-in-law, lying prone across the seat. An IV bag dangled from a coat hook above the driver's side passenger door.

His breath hitched in shock. "Is she still alive?"

"Yes."

"What happened?"

"Long story."

He had always considered himself a strong man. It was his place to remain an island of strength in a sea of tragedy. Despite deep feelings for those he cared about, tears did not come easily to him. But as the full impact of the situation overcame him, he wiped angrily at the hot moisture brimming his eyes.

Chris's voice sliced into the surreal moment. "I'll go around and get her by the arms. You pull her out your side. Marci, jump in the front seat and grab the IV. You can slide along to the other side as I move her through."

They maneuvered gently through the vehicle. Marci knee-scooted across the cloth upholstery ahead of Chris to ensure the IV tubing did not snag as he exited through the rear passenger door.

"You got it?" He kept his eyes focused ahead to ensure they did not scrape or bump her body against the door as they pulled her through.

"Hold on a sec." She grasped the IV bag in her right hand, curled her left up and out the passenger's door, then over the top of the rear door. Carefully, she transferred the bag from her right to her left. "Okay, bring her out slowly so I can get out. Don't go too far ahead of me. There's not much give."

When they had safely extracted her, Ben shut the car up while Chris carried her across the flagstone driveway. Marci hurried alongside him, holding the IV bag aloft as they moved.

Halfway up the front steps, Chris spotted Julie and Cheryl huddling together in the doorway, wide-eyed and curious. They gasped and covered their mouths as he approached, then stepped aside as he crossed the threshold.

They headed up the stairs. When they reached the second floor, Chris paused to catch his breath.

Ben edged up from behind and held out his arms. "Here. I'll take her. You're beat."

"I'm fine," he insisted. He looked at Cheryl. "Which room?"

She patted his shoulder. "Upstairs, I'm afraid."

Without complaint, he pushed on. Cheryl and Julie went before him to direct the way. He did not know why Julie had flown out, but he could not have been more relieved to find her waiting for him. She was all that remained of his sanity, the only thing that made any sense.

When they reached the bedroom, Chris lowered Farin onto one of the two beds. As he backed away, he stumbled to avoid Marci, who stood close behind with the IV bag.

Ben lifted his hands to his hips and eyed his brother. "You okay?"

He nodded, sat down at the foot of the second bed, and leaned on his right thigh. "I'm so glad to be out of that car."

Marci sat beside Farin and continued to hold the bag of fluid high to ensure proper flow.

Chris looked at Julie. "Can someone go and grab the IV pole out of the trunk?"

"I'll go," Cheryl whispered.

"And Julie, do you mind getting my shaving kit?"

"Of course." She nodded at Cheryl and they headed out for the bags.

Ben inched closer to Farin, his face pale and drawn as the gravity of the situation hit him. "We should call a doctor."

Simultaneously, Chris and Marci barked an adamant and automatic, "No!"

Chris dropped his head and pinched the bridge of his nose. His tone had come out stronger—and louder—than he had intended. He rubbed his gritty eyes with his thumb and index finger. "We need to talk."

Ben shook his head. "Get some rest first. We've got time."

"I'll take you up on it. I can't remember the last time I slept."

Arm strained, Marci switched the bag from one hand to the other. "You haven't slept since Thursday."

Ben looked at Chris, astonished.

"We had to move fast."

Cheryl and Julie returned with Marci's overnight bag and the IV pole, which Marci grabbed with a grateful nod and put to immediate use.

Julie sat down beside Chris. "I put your bag and shaving kit in our room."

He draped his arm around her shoulders and drew her in to kiss her cheek.

"You two must be exhausted," Cheryl said. She went to Marci's side, placing a delicate hand on the woman's shoulder. After a moment's hesitation, she bent down to touch Farin's cheek and forehead with the back of her hand. "We should probably call a doctor."

"*No!*" a trio of voices barked in unison.

Ben wrapped his arms around Cheryl's waist. "We're not doing anything tonight, love. We'll sort it later. It's been a long day. They can fill us in on the details tomorrow."

Chris gave Julie a weak smile. "I need a shower right now more than anything else." He embraced and held her with the last ounce of strength he possessed, wishing he could melt away into the feel of her arms.

"Of course." Cheryl nodded at Chris, then Marci. "You both need to clean up and get some sleep."

Marci stared at her friend. "I'm fine right here."

"Collapsing from exhaustion won't help her," Ben said.

Cheryl pointed out the attached bathroom. "You'll be right next to her. Ben's right. Besides, Julie and I can help. Right, Jules?" She turned to Julie for acknowledgment.

Julie manufactured a warm, patient smile. "Absolutely."

Cautious to the point of near-paranoia and careful to conceal the sheer loathing welling up inside her, Julie calculated every movement she made and second-guessed every word she spoke. She had never considered herself much of an actress. Tonight, however, she gave an Oscar-worthy performance.

Of course I can help. Just leave me alone with that bitch for five minutes. I'll help. I'll help us all.

CHAPTER 18

THE FRENETIC BUSTLE OF NEW York City's weekend traffic thinned only slightly compared to the average weekday crawl. Hours ago, the dawn had heralded a new day. The sun crept slowly across the loft's wooden floorboards. Its rays streamed through overhead panes dusty with age and grit. The light fell across the foot of the bed, covering Faith Peterson's legs like a blanket.

She awoke to the unmistakable sound, and smell, of Henri exhaling smoke. Glancing down to the foot of the bed, she noted that he had brought the easel into the bedroom—something she had complained about innumerable times. His hands busily covered a canvas with paint. Occasionally, he swapped brushes and colors. His enormous, precise movements crafted a scene only the depths of his imagination could see, translating his vision through sculpted oil and pigment on stretched canvas and wood.

Faith watched Henri send dual streams of smoke toward his chest through his nostrils. Smoking was one habit she had never picked up. What with the drugs, promiscuous sex, a penchant for older men, and a boisterous disposition that had landed her in more precarious positions than she could count, she figured she had amply filled her self-destruction quota.

Henri's smoking was as much a part of him as breathing. The ashtray on his worktable overflowed with extinguished butts. Sometimes, she imagined him as a steam locomotive, puffing and spewing smoke as he raced with bridled power toward distant destinations.

When she wriggled out of the covers and attempted to sit up, Henri held up his hand. "No, please. Not yet."

She lay back and resumed her sleeping pose, an automatic response over the time they had lived together. "I have to pee."

"Me too," he peeped softly.

She battled her throbbing bladder and lay as still as possible. Hopefully, he had started this piece hours ago and would soon finish. If only he would sketch her first and paint from that. She had suggested it several times but his argument never changed. He preferred the intimacy of a live model.

Whatever. All she knew was his artistic purity spelled aches and pains for her legs, arms, back, neck, and bladder.

"When did you get up?" she probed.

He chuckled soundlessly, puffs of smoke escaping his nostrils with each snort. "Quiet now. The light's changing. I have to hurry."

She closed her eyes and awaited permission to move.

The day Elliot had called with the Las Vegas wedding rumors, she had confronted Henri about his past. He had grown hostile at first, pitching a fit as if doing so might redirect their conversation. Then, he had threatened not to accompany her to the party in the Village if she pressed him. But when she feigned indifference and hinted she might find a more mature date, he caved.

Beyond the initial astonishment that she—born and raised Catholic—now shared her life and her bed with the son of an Orthodox Jew, it did not matter to her. In fact, given her past, she found it comical. Only after making her swear not to make an issue of his confession did he tell her what he had shared with no one since he had left his boyhood home.

Born on the Lower East Side, the seventh son and youngest child of a well-respected rabbi, Melvin Leberwitz had felt out of place his entire life. While his brothers and sisters planned pilgrimages to the Holy Land, he had dreamed of traveling to Europe to study art in cities once inhabited by the masters. His fondest childhood memories involved days spent in the Metropolitan Museum of Art.

"Damn it!" Henri cursed the canvas before him. He squirted a glob of Prussian green on his palette, then mixed it expertly with a palette knife.

Faith's eyes darted out the east window of their warehouse loft. The sun crested the upper edge of the frame, causing the shadows upon their floorboards to recede. Soon, they would vanish altogether. She closed her eyes, ignored his outburst, and prayed she would not soil their bedsheets before he finished.

Rabbi Leberwitz had considered Melvin's artistic passion a colossal waste of time. He insisted the boy would bring home better grades if he would use his pencil to write history essays and solve math problems instead of doodling.

Conversely, Barbara Leberwitz had adored her son's creations. She dressed their refrigerator with his sketches and watercolors, and bragged about him to her friends. Whenever possible, she would cajole someone to pose for him—usually a young girl about his age and always from a prominent Jewish family. Melvin acted oblivious to his mother's motive, thankful for someone to paint, sketch, or both.

"Are you almost finished?" Faith asked. "Sorry. My bladder's about to explode."

"Yes, yes. Almost," he replied softly.

As he grew, problems surfaced. He often skipped Hebrew class, which jeopardized his eligibility to read from the Torah at synagogue. When his father arranged for a tutor, Melvin routinely skipped his sessions. His parents later discovered he spent his after-school hours at the library, studying biographies and books on craft.

By his thirteenth birthday, even Rabbi Leberwitz grudgingly conceded that God had gifted his youngest with talent. He accepted the fact that the boy's paints, charcoals, and smelly thinners were more than a passing fad and adjusted his prayers for his son's future. Instead of religious and educational books at his bar mitzvah, friends gifted young Melvin with art supplies as well as the traditional stocks, bonds, and cash. Rabbi and Mrs. Leberwitz maintained tradition by presenting their son with his first tallit.

Problems continued through high school. Rabbi Leberwitz finally accepted that none of his sons would follow his rabbinical calling. Indeed, his daughters had more interest in such things than any of the boys. But Melvin also refused to consider a vocation as a doctor, a lawyer, or a stockbroker. Instead, he had worked at Katz's Deli and spent his earnings on art supplies.

"Is this another one you're not gonna let me see?" Faith asked.

Engrossed in perfecting some detail or another, Henri did not answer right away. When the question registered, he mumbled, "Yes. Hush now."

Shortly after turning eighteen, he had cashed in every stock certificate, every bond and, in one last impulsive stroke, emptied his bank account. He purchased a one-way ticket to France and left without *au revoirs*.

Four months later, he found himself strolling along the banks of the Seine outside the *Musée du Louvre* in Paris. He trampled the same grass the masters had in their day. He drank the same bitter coffee, ate the same unpasteurized cheese. Each night, he allowed himself a single glass of chateau wine. He found a small apartment and paid for one year's rent in advance.

A week later, he returned to his apartment late one night to find he had been robbed. Suddenly, he was without means, a stranger in a foreign land.

"Henri?" Faith whined.

"Shh."

From that point on, he got by as best he could—waiting tables, bell-hopping, cleaning toilets—but he never stopped painting. When not working, he learned about craft from fellow painters and more about life than he ever suspected he would. Good thing, since the robbery had quashed his hopes of registering for *École des Beaux-Arts* that next February. He also learned conversational French.

Three years later, he signed up for a six-port tour on a merchant marine vessel. He made his way back to New York over the next few months. Sometime after his return, when he had gathered the courage to confront his parents, he went home. Unfortunately, he arrived too late.

The year before, Barbara Leberwitz had suffered a stroke and then an embolism. She had never regained consciousness. Henri had to find out on his own. No one in his family would talk to him. When Rabbi Leberwitz had opened the door and saw his prodigal son, he turned his back, disowning him with a gesture.

"Why are you doing all these when you won't sell them and you won't even show me?" Faith asked without opening her eyes.

Henri chuckled and lit another cigarette. He exhaled slowly. She imagined the smoke spreading over and rolling off the canvas.

A quintessential starving artist, he had struggled for close to five years. Some months, after squeaking out rent money, he had to choose between buying paints and canvas or food. People liked his work, but no one wanted to pay for it—and who could blame them? What credibility might a name like Melvin Theodore Leberwitz imbue? Eventually, his pursuits morphed into a sort of divine irony.

One dreary January evening, he caught the J train to Cypress Hills, then hoofed it half a mile to the Beth Olam Cemetery to visit his mother's grave. He had put off his visit for some time, as if even in death she would see his failure. In his jacket pocket, he carried a Smith & Wesson .22 long rifle. He fancied himself a modern-day Jewish George Bailey without the family, the guardian angel, or a bell-laden Christmas tree, and fully intended to succeed where George had failed.

Fortunately, Melvin had not thought his plan through.

First, he had arrived after 5 PM—an hour after the cemetery closed.

Second, he had attempted his visit on a Saturday. As he stood and peered through the iron bars of the gated entrance, it dawned on him he did not even know the location of his mother's grave.

Broken and bitter, he had withdrawn the gun from his pocket, inserted the four-inch barrel into his mouth, and attempted to pull the trigger before realizing he had not switched off the safety. His second unsuccessful attempt reminded him he had not loaded the pistol, and that he had left the bullets at his Ludlow Street studio. He cursed the entire subway ride back to the Essex Street station, then painted all night.

The next day, he rummaged through his belongings until he located the tallit his parents gave him years earlier. He wrapped it around the .22, walked down Grand Street to the Promenade, and threw them both into the East River.

In the end, the dissolution of his life, the death of his mother, and the disowning by his father resulted in his rebirth. He emerged a man who lived and breathed to create great works of art, a man with no last name and no past, a man with no home—a man called Henri.

"Voila!" he proclaimed seconds before carefully draping a torn bed sheet over the rigged ribs he had fashioned atop and below the frame of his easel.

Faith's eyes flew open. She bolted out of bed and scampered to the bathroom. As she took care of business, she thought about the similarities between Henri's past and her own. She stared at the Grammys arranged on a shelf before her. *Exactly where my music career belongs—the toilet.*

She pondered the actions of her lover over the last several weeks. He would catch her eating or sleeping, playing a concerto on her baby grand, or something else mundane, and paint her. Then, for the first time since she had begun posing for him, he refused to show her the finished work. At first, this new wrinkle in his behavior annoyed her. Now, she was simply curious.

Dozens of nudes arrayed the loft, all of which he had painted during the months before he had acquired this new eccentricity. She wondered what might be different about these and hypothesized they might be so obscene even the fearless Henri worried over her reaction. She figured he would show her when he felt the time was right.

A gentle knock came at the door. "You almost finished, *mon trésor?*"

"Almost. I told you my bladder was about to burst!"

Henri padded away. The sound of gathered paint brushes and the dragging of his easel made her smile.

Part of her wondered how long their relationship would last. She could count the number of her serious relationships on one hand. Only two had existed outside her imagination. Until Henri, her longest relationship had also been her biggest mistake—an affair with a man thirty years her senior. They had met shortly after her seventeenth birthday. It had changed her life, but stole more from her than it gave.

The unwelcome thought of him soured her. She swiped angrily at the toilet paper roll, then ripped off several squares.

Resentments are toxic, shithead. Get it together.

She washed up, then headed out to make the bed. Henri rushed past her to use the restroom. Glancing right, she noticed he had returned the easel to its proper place. A fresh canvas sat upon it.

As she pulled the bed together, the sputtering of the coffee pot and its resultant aroma filled her senses. When Henri returned to the kitchen, he poured them both a cup. She joined him at the kitchen table.

"You let me sleep late this morning," she said.

Henri nodded. "The light was perfect."

She dragged her mug to her and blew on it. "My little secret agent." It had become her nickname for him since he stopped showing her his work.

They enjoyed their coffee as the sun flooded the loft.

When Henri rose for a second cup, he asked, "You feel like playing this morning?"

She looked over at her baby grand, located on the extreme southern end of the loft, directly opposite Henri's designated studio. "Maybe in a bit. When I talked to Gale last night, she asked if I wanted to catch a meeting."

He nodded. She could not tell if the idea pleased or disappointed him. "Don't forget. My show's next Friday."

"How could I possibly forget? You tell me every day."

He grunted. "Becky called earlier."

"I didn't hear the phone."

"I turned down the ringer. I wanted you to sleep."

"What did she want?"

"Something about forgetting to tell you your order came in Friday afternoon. She said it's at the faggot's office."

Faith had given up trying to make Henri stop calling her designer by that offensive epitaph. Shooting him a look of disapproval, she hopped up from the table to return the call. On the way, she topped off her coffee and attempted to add milk. The carton dribbled out a few pathetic drops. She made a disgusted sound, abandoned her cup, then hunted for the cordless phone.

"I need more black and orange anyway," Henri said. "I'll get some milk after I run by the art supply." He grabbed his house keys and headed for the stairs, then turned back as she grabbed the handset. "Need anything else?"

"I can't think of anything."

He kissed her cheek and headed out the door.

***

Outside the floor to ceiling window of Samantha's master bedroom, the sun cast the first blue hues of dawn across the sky. The Hollywood Hills estate sat perfectly positioned, boasting a grand view of Los Angeles below. Stray city lights dotted the valley as daylight approached, their luminescence haloed by the fog settling in from the coast.

Sam was an early riser. Even on weekends. But this morning, something more than habit roused her. Today, an uneasy feeling held her in its grip.

Of all times for a panic attack. The first weekend in months where she did not have to share Ethan with nurses, interns, or attendings. Come April, he would complete his residency. Maybe after he joined his uncle in his Beverly Hills office, weekends like this would become the rule instead of the exception—minus the anxiety.

She yawned and stretched, then rolled over and propped her head upon her hand to contemplate the man slumbering beside her. Thirty years old and not a blemish on his skin. She paid handsomely to maintain her complexion. It sort of ticked her off. This gorgeous blond Adonis—he did not even snore. She squinted and leaned in for a closer look, hoping to at least find a dislodged eyelash or the hint of a laugh line. Nada.

"You can't sleep, so you stare at me so I can't sleep," Ethan muttered groggily, eyes closed. "You're like this creepy, staring bed stalker."

Grinning, she bit her bottom. "You're young—you can take it."

He opened one eye and looked her over. "Are you still wearing my shirt, Ms. Drake? No wonder you can't sleep. Do you realize how much starch the cleaners use on those things?"

Sam pulled on the stiff collar for a whiff of his scent. She loved the smell of his body. On occasion, she stole a shirt from his laundry to cuddle when he worked nights.

He maneuvered her over and on top of him and kissed her. "Maybe you need to continue where we left off last night," he groaned seductively. "Seems I haven't done a very good job of wearing you out."

An immediate hunger for her fiancé rose within her. She rose to straddle his waist, then lowered herself to take his lips in hers. They melted into one another, surrendering to desire as they had the previous night.

Ethan fulfilled her, both in and out of the bedroom. Until he came along, she had never explored what it meant to be a woman. She had only considered herself a business professional.

Now, she had it all. Her life's work. The success she had labored for. All the power her position entitled her. Moreover, she had a sense of self-worth she had never achieved at LSI. Those dark years had disappeared. Jameson Lockhardt would never again...

As she climaxed, a sudden, inexplicable feeling of dread overcame her. Rising to her knees, she arched her back, tensing every muscle in her body, sending Ethan into waves of elation that wracked his body in indescribable pleasure. She strained against foreboding thoughts as she tried to focus on her lover and her own pleasure. Finally, she collapsed atop her lover's chest, panting and sweating with exhaustion, liberation, and fear that gripped her very core.

She flattened herself against his body. He threaded his fingers through her cropped black hair. Lips parted, she opened her eyes and stared at the far wall of the bedroom.

The sound of Ethan's thunderous heartbeat beneath her usually calmed her. She focused on the symbiotic rhythm their hearts had created through their mutual release, hoping it would tranquilize her. But try as she might, she could not shake the feeling of impending doom. At last, she moved aside and stared at the ceiling.

Ethan turned on his side and touched her cheek. "Something's wrong," he said, more in fact than concern. "Tell me."

"I'm not sure. But yes, something's wrong. I can feel it." She faced him, regret etching her features. "I'm sorry. It's not you."

"Well, that's good news." He gave her an asymmetrical grin. "What do you think it is?"

"I'm not sure. Probably nothing. I just can't help feeling...I need to make a call." She wriggled out of bed and slipped on her white lace robe and house slippers.

His expression told her he had learned to roll with her random moments of urgency. "Don't keep me waiting too long," he called after her. "If I get lonely, I might just head on back to the hospital."

"Don't you dare!" she called back, giggling over her shoulder. "I'll be right back."

His groan of playful frustration filled the hallway as she descended the stairs.

She strode across the exquisitely decorated living room and into her den. Few associates had received an invitation to Samantha Drake's Hollywood Hills domicile. Oriental rugs, crystal and brass fixtures, and overstuffed, oversized furniture revealed a warmth to her personality no one would suspect, given the sterility of her business demeanor. Tall indoor trees, lush plants, and enormous floral arrangements scattered throughout the house evoked an air of freshness that soothed her after a particularly trying day at the office.

She lowered herself behind her antique desk and flipped open her PDA, which Deborah had purchased on her behalf and trained her to use. The tiny device was her telephone book, appointment minder, personal information manager, and contact organizer. These days, she had no idea how she had ever managed to get anything done without it. She made a note in her memo section to see about getting that girl another raise.

Her fingers quivered as she held it to the receiver of her telephone, allowing it to dial the Palm Springs number. She tilted her wrist to consult her watch, then realized she had worn little more than a smile since ten o'clock last night. She touched the screen of her PDA and activated the clock, closing her eyes in regret as she read the display: 6:31 AM.

"I'm being ridiculous," she admonished herself in a stern whisper.

Before she could hang up, a hoarse, sleepy voice managed a groggy, "Hello?"

"Ross, it's Samantha." She winced. "I'm sorry I woke you."

"Sam?"

"I'm sorry. Something told me I needed to call. Is...is everything okay?"

"Everything's fine here."

She heard the rustling sound of him sitting up and adjusting himself in bed, then the click of what she assumed was a light on his bedside table. She lowered her head to her free hand, realizing she would owe Josephine an apology as well.

"What's going on? Did you hear something—?"

"Nothing," she said. "You?"

"Not a peep."

She sat straighter and prepared to end the call. "Josephine must be furious. I'll let you get back to sleep. Please send her my apologies."

"Actually, Josephine spent the night in LA with some friends. We're leaving tomorrow afternoon. Her sister's fallen ill. She wanted to get back right away, so her friends threw her a going-away party. They're going to church together this morning."

"Without you?"

"I begged off," he confided. "I wanted to stay close to the phone."

Her eyes flitted about her study. "It's been days."

Ross smoothed back his thinning hair, then massaged his jaw where Chris had parked his fist earlier that week. The swelling had subsided, though a deep bruise remained. Josephine had appeared more perplexed than convinced of his account of slipping on the kitchen rug and slamming into the refrigerator door while trying to get some ice cubes. "You'd think he'd have called you by now."

"Have you talked to Jameson? Might there have been some trouble?"

"I talked to him after Childs's funeral. Everything seemed fine. He and Bobby are out scouting bands. But they were headed for Raleigh on Thursday."

She leaned back in her chair, crossed her legs, and fussed with the folds of her robe. "I don't understand."

"Farin's in Raleigh," he stated flatly. "Chris and Marci left here Monday night."

She gasped.

"I wouldn't worry. As I said, Bobby's with him. The boy knows nothing about this. It would ruin everything if he found out. Jameson won't let that happen."

"You're going to fill me in on the whole story someday," Samantha said, her voice stern. "I have a million questions."

"When Jameson's no longer a threat, I'll tell you everything I can." As a grim afterthought, he added, "I imagine Farin will have a few questions as well."

She paused. "What do you think Chris will do when—*if*—she comes back?"

Ross rubbed his eyes with the ball of his hand and yawned. "What do you mean?"

"Do you think it'll affect Chris's focus? I'm sorry—that's selfish, I know, but *Aftermath*'s been such a success. He's got a summer tour to work on, and we'd talked about him getting back into the studio. I don't know. I worry."

"You're practical, Sam, not selfish. I'd say, at this point, we all have a lot to worry about when...*if*...Farin comes back."

As they ended the conversation, it occurred to Ross he had spoken carelessly. He should not have taken a call from Samantha, Chris, or anyone related to this situation on a traceable line. Jameson had been known to bug phones. His sole comfort was that, to this point, Jameson did not appear to suspect him of any wrongdoing—despite the one luncheon with Samantha a year ago.

Too awake to try to go back to sleep, Ross got up, brewed a pot of coffee, then headed out onto his patio to enjoy the dawn. He considered a swim, and thought how much he would miss Palm Springs. How much he regretted cutting his vacation short this year. Still, Josephine's sister needed her.

With every passing year, Ross found it more difficult to leave his desert hideaway. Sometimes, he wondered if he could wait the ten months before Jameson retired. He wanted to leave New York. Permanently. Josephine had many friends as well. She looked so happy during their annual visits.

Soon, he told himself. *Soon.*

He finished his cup and went for a refill. A knock at the door rerouted him from the kitchen to the front door. What a curious vacation this year. The last time he opened his door to an unexpected guest, he had almost ended up in the hospital with a broken jaw.

A second, more insistent, series of knocks made him think twice before answering at all. He hastened into his bedroom and retrieved his .32 caliber revolver from his nightstand, then plunged it into his robe pocket and held it fast as the knocking turned into a repeated ringing of the doorbell.

Having wised up a bit in the last few days, Ross peeked through the peephole. When he recognized the looming figure outside, his heart dropped into his stomach. His grip tightened around the pistol.

He fumbled with the chain, the dead bolt, and finally, the door lock, enduring the repeated and insistent ringing of the bell. He threw open the door. "J-Jameson!" He stepped aside to welcome his friend. "You startled me. What are you doing here? I thought you were in Raleigh."

Jameson strode inside, eyeballing the place with a blend of suspicion and curiosity. Though unfamiliar with their home, he trudged down the foyer, found the living room, and then sat upon Ross's couch. "Where's Josephine?"

"What?" Feeling vulnerable as he stood there in boxers and a thin cotton robe, while Jameson donned a crisp suit and polished leather shoes, he cursed himself for uttering Farin's name aloud on the phone earlier, as if doing so had conjured forth the old man.

He stood beside his recliner but did not sit down.

"I'm hoping we can talk in private." The statement was more demand than request. "Josephine disapproves of our meeting outside office hours. Is she here?"

"Uh, no...no, she's not," Ross stammered. "Why are you in Palm Springs?"

"I'd been riding around LA all night, then decided to venture further out. Bobby and I have meetings next week."

"I see. Well, I was just refilling my coffee cup. Can I get you anything? Coffee? Tea?" *Scotch?*

Jameson held up his hand. "Farin's missing."

Ross blanched. "Missing?"

Jameson signaled for Ross to sit down, then stood and paced the room as if back in his Manhattan office. "I received word during my flight out here. I'd just seen her. I believed her to be sedated, but I'm afraid I've misjudged her strength. She's tried to escape before."

Again, Ross plunged his hand into his pocket and gripped the pistol, his every sense on high alert. Jameson had to suspect him. Otherwise, he would have returned to Raleigh instead of staying in California and driving two hours into the desert to discuss a matter easily dealt with over the phone.

The phone.

"She can't have gotten far, if she was sedated."

"One would think."

"Any idea where she went?"

"A weak woman with no clothes, no money, and—hopefully—little memory of the past several years? I don't know."

Ross wondered what he had in mind. Poison? A gun? A knife? A car accident that would turn him to charcoal? Jameson excelled with accidents.

He considered shooting Jameson himself, then claiming self-defense. "How did it happen?"

"If I knew that, I'd know where she is, wouldn't I?"

Relief washed over him despite his terror. Chris and Marci had successfully rescued Farin. She was safe. For now.

He could not say the same for himself.

"If she's on her own, she couldn't have gotten far. What about the woods surrounding the property?"

Jameson fixed his eyes on his colleague. "Did I say she was alone?"

Ross's insides quaked. "Well...wasn't she?"

The old man stopped pacing and headed for the door. A look of intense contemplation shrouded his features as he crossed the foyer. "I haven't decided. I didn't anticipate something like this happening. Not only have I misjudged Farin, I'm faced with the possibility I've also misjudged someone I thought I could trust."

Ross followed Jameson to the door. The man paused before turning the handle. He shot Ross an eerie, knowing glare. "Have a safe trip home. My regards to Josephine."

Before Ross could open his mouth to speak, Jameson stepped out into the dawn and marched down the walkway to his waiting limousine.

Ross's throat constricted as he shut the front door. He rushed into his study and seized the telephone, then slammed it back onto its base, eyeing it with fearful suspicion. Might it be bugged? If so, the damage was already done.

Defying his paranoia, he picked up the receiver again. He stabbed the buttons with icy fingers.

"Reservations. How may I help you?"

"M-My flight." The words caught in his dry, tightening vocal cords. "I have tickets for a flight out tomorrow afternoon—going to New York City. I need to change my reservation."

Sometime during the call, he lifted his hand out of his robe pocket. Only then did he realize he still gripped the pistol in a fist of steel.

CHAPTER 19

CHRIS SAT AT THE KITCHEN table, debating with Ben. For two hours, he had relayed the events of the past week to his brother, his wife, and his sister-in-law. "We need to leave as soon as possible. He must know she's gone by now."

"You can't take her back on the road. She'll never make it."

"He's trying to kill her, Ben. We both know this is the first place he'll look. I'm not putting you, Cheryl, and my nephews in danger by keeping her here. And Julie, I want you back home as well."

The group congregated around the table, sipping their morning tea. Cheryl had checked in on Marci and Farin earlier. "I don't think Marci got much sleep. And Farin...well, there's no change. I don't know if that's good or bad. I'm no nurse, but I don't like her color. Without a doctor, the least she'll do is waste away to nothing. That IV solution only keeps her hydrated. She's probably starving to death. How have they fed her all this time?"

"I don't understand why we're not calling the police," Ben pressed. "Or why we can't get her to hospital. And *why* does Lockhardt want her dead?"

Chris peered out the French doors. "I wish I knew. I don't. I don't know why he took her. I don't know why he kept her alive just to keep her unconscious. I don't know why he wants to kill her now. I don't know, Ben. All I know is, if we take her to hospital, the cops will get involved."

"Don't we *want* them involved?" Cheryl cut in. "If Lockhardt's gone mad, I'd think we'd be grateful for the protection."

Chris scoffed. "They don't want to protect her. They want to question her."

"Aye, but once they question her, they can sort this out."

"If the police were our allies, why didn't they know it wasn't Farin's body they had? You don't think Jameson has those bobbies in his back pocket? We'd be leading him right to her."

Ben stared at the table as if trying to mentally assemble the pieces. "Am I the only one wondering if this has something to do with Jordan's death?"

Chris sprawled in his chair, one arm hooked over the back of the seat, his aspect bitter and doubtful. "Have they made any progress finding the killer? Have they even tried?"

Cheryl stood and bustled nervously about the kitchen, rinsing cups and breakfast dishes to load into the dishwasher. "None of us are safe now, are we?"

"That's why Marci and I need to take Farin and leave. *Today.*" He stabbed the table with his index finger, punctuating his determination.

Ben stared absently at his cup. "Cheryl's right. Farin's probably starving to death. One way or another, she needs professional help. We're in way over our heads, here. I'm not sure she can survive a cross-country trip."

Julie rose from the table to hand Cheryl her teacup. She congratulated herself on not having thrown it across the room. Everything inside her cursed Farin and her pathetic drama.

She had listened to the tragedy and the heroism of her husband's story with interest and feigned horror at their narrow escape from North Carolina. Inside, she wished Farin had died in the car before arriving in Miami. For a moment, she considered calling Lockhardt herself, but thought better of it. If the man was ruthless enough to kidnap her in the first place, who knew what he might do to Chris for helping her escape?

"I have to make a call," she lulled softly into her husband's ear as she bent down and kissed his cheek.

Chris reached up and gave her arm a gentle squeeze. "Ben and I have to finish ironing this bloody thing out anyway. I'll need to pack soon, though. See you in a bit?"

She stroked his hair, then headed upstairs.

"Hold on, Jules," Cheryl called after her. "I'll go with you. I want to get this upstairs for Marci anyway." She cut eyes at her husband and brother-in-law, then grabbed the breakfast tray she had prepared.

When the women left, Chris folded his arms on the table, dropping his weary head atop. "I'm right about this, Ben."

"But why California?"

His eyes flickered with remorse. He stared again through the sheathed French doors. "It's my responsibility. I owe..."

Ben hung his head as his brother's words echoed into nothingness. Chris's proclamation two nights ago that he was bringing Farin "home" had left him worried that his brother had lost his mind. He envisioned Chris abandoning Julie without a thought, as he would have years ago.

With Jordan gone, what prevented Chris from falling into old patterns?

They had not discussed it, but Ben knew Julie well enough to know she struggled with the same fear. Yet as he studied Chris now, Ben believed his brother no longer existed in the same reckless state.

He fidgeted with his teacup. "It wasn't your fault."

Chris lifted his head. His eyes misted with regret. "Wasn't it?"

"You didn't kill him, Chris."

"The last time I saw Jordan alive was in hospital with Farin. Before that, you had to tear us off each other. And the time before that, he basically said he never wanted to see me again."

Ben did not respond.

"I'm sorry." His voice came out thick with spit, his throat tight. "I'm sorry for everything, and I never got a chance to tell him."

"You have to let that go. Jordan wouldn't want you to—"

"Jordan wouldn't want me to abandon the only woman he ever loved!" Chris shot out of his chair, stalked to the counter, and braced himself on the tiled counter. "This is *my* responsibility!"

"We're family. We're in this together."

Ben fell silent as Chris's shoulders began to quake. In that moment, he realized how little he knew about the inner workings of his only living brother's heart. Ben wondered if he could have held up so well for so long. The strain had to be tremendous.

Chris's chin bowed to his chest. Deep sobs shook him. Ben rose and went to put his arm around his shoulders. To his astonishment, Chris turned into him, muffling his sobs in Ben's chest.

The idea that Chris had lived through the horror of discovering Jordan's brutal murder, and now Farin lay upstairs dead to the world, clicked into perspective. The situation looked hopeless. The exertion, crushing. Yet, he bore it—his own personal cross.

Without notice or fanfare, Chris had become not just a man, but a *good* man. The seeds of nobility sewn in their childhood had bloomed late inside him but, for all their tardiness, they had blossomed more glorious and fully developed. For the first time, Chris clung to him, needing his strength and support. Ben held him close, ensuring any fears of possible rejection Chris might have anticipated vanished.

Chris cleared this throat and pulled away, collecting himself as if nothing had happened. As if he was not knuckling his eyes dry with his shirtsleeve. As if they had just finished a conversation about work or sports. Then, briefly and unexpectedly, Chris reached for Ben once more, this time with a hearty measure of strength and a token slap on the back. At last, they resumed their places at the table.

Chris mumbled, "I can't believe my nephews are men now. I wish I could see them while we're here. But you're right—too risky."

Ben shot his brother a wry grin. "You know Derek's driving."

"I saw that white Blazer out front and figured." The side of his mouth rose into a knowing smirk. "Chasing bird I imagine, too."

"He's set his sights on the head cheerleader."

"Really?"

"It was quite the sixteenth birthday. He woke up to find out his persistence had paid off, what with the car and all. Later, he had a pool party. We must have had thirty teenagers at the house. After the lot of them left, Summer stayed behind and gave him this braided gold chain. We heard him tell her he'd never take it off. And he hasn't."

"Sounds like she fancies him as well."

"I'll be adding another phone line in July for his birthday, I think. Keep him off our main line."

They both chuckled, enveloped by youthful memories or the temporary respite of whimsy.

Chris drew invisible lines on the table with his index finger. "I'm a relic."

"Not me. I found Ponce De Leon's map to the fountain of youth. Why do you think I live in Florida?"

Silence settled over them, the only sound an occasional "clink" as they returned teacups to saucers. Chris raked his fingers through his hair. "It's a bloody mess, isn't it?"

Ben nodded. "There must be something we can do."

"There is. We're taking her back to California."

"How can I let you leave here with no one to help get Farin across the country but a pregnant woman?" Ben instantly reprimanded himself. Cheryl had made him promise.

Chris froze. "*Pregnant?*"

***

Upstairs, Farin lay unmoving, as she had from the minute Marci and Chris freed her from her hospital prison. Marci changed Farin's IV bag. She kept the Thorazine injections pumping through the plastic tubing into her system. If only she could go to a library to research its purpose and side effects. Not knowing killed her, but it was Sunday. Besides, Jameson might be watching them. So she sat, waiting, hoping for some movement or sign of life other than shallow breathing. It could not go on indefinitely.

They had developed a collective paranoia. Their every thought involved some diabolical scenario in which Jameson discovered them in Florida. A tracking device planted in the car while they were inside the Royster Building. A shady private eye. A hitman.

The sooner they headed back to LA, the sooner Chris's family would avoid the repercussions of what they had done. Once home, they could find a proper hiding place and assistance.

"Anything?" Cheryl asked.

Marci flinched at the sound of her voice.

"Sorry for startling you." Cheryl set the breakfast tray down and handed her a cup of tea.

Marci nodded gratefully. "Let's hope I can keep this down, huh?"

Cheryl sat cross-legged on the floor, facing Marci. "Ben told me you asked him to get you a pregnancy test earlier. I take it you're pleased?"

Marci smiled for the first time in days. "At least I know why I haven't been able to keep all the food Chris keeps trying to stuff down my face in my stomach."

She gave her arm a sympathetic squeeze. "Aye, it's a struggle at times."

Cheryl liked Marci. After the funerals, they had kept in touch. Eventually, they had adopted her as part of their extended family.

"I wish I could call my husband." Marci sipped her tea. "Then again, I'd rather tell him in person. Tell me this nausea won't last forever."

Cheryl giggled warmly. "Every pregnancy's different, pet. With Derek, I was fine. I thought all the horror stories I'd heard had been fabricated as some sort of conspiracy to stop the world from reproducing. But then with Kyle, I thought I'd never recover. Nothing helped. It lasted a full four months. The doctor almost hospitalized me."

"We tried for so long. I was about to give up hope. You know, before Jordan...died...Farin said they wanted to try to have more children."

"I thought she couldn't. What about Melody's delivery?"

Marci glanced at the bed. "They were getting a second opinion. But then everything happened. They would've been great parents. I know Jordan was. I think Farin would've been a good mother."

"I never knew her the way you do. I only knew her effect on my family. I'm sorry if that upsets you. I don't mean it to. I've been sick with worry since Chris called and said he was bringing her here. We didn't know what had happened or what to expect. I thought..."

Marci sipped her tea, then stared into her cup. "I'm not upset. Things were messy. But now they're different. You and I'll make sure of that, huh?"

They stifled guilty giggles.

"They would have made a dreadful match—even if Jorie hadn't been a factor," Cheryl said, her smile fading.

Marci studied Farin's face. A raw longing to share her good news with her best friend overwhelmed her. "I think they were just too much alike. Strong-willed. No self-control. Immature."

"Aye, you've certainly pegged our Chris."

"It was such an ugly time. I'm sorry for the pain she caused Jordan. There was a lot of hurt going around back then."

Cheryl rested her back against the nightstand. She fidgeted with her wedding ring. When she looked up, she studied the stationary form atop the bed. "I don't know how to feel about all of this. It's shocking. I guess it's partly guilt. I don't want Chris losing his mind again."

Marci rocked upward on her knees to slide her empty teacup onto the nightstand, then sat back down. "He and I've never gotten along. I don't know if we ever will. But I'll give him this: he really came through for Farin. Sometimes I forget. This isn't the first time he's saved her life."

Outside the bedroom door, undetected by a soul, Julie eavesdropped on their conversation. She seethed as her sister-in-law and the bitch's friend talked about Chris and Farin, never really admitting what they both knew. Julie knew, though. The writing was on the wall.

It infuriated her to hear Marci and Cheryl talk openly about Marci's pregnancy. Yet, a part of her wished she could join them and share her own thoughts and feelings. When Chris had come to bed last night after showering and wolfing down two ham sandwiches, three glasses of milk, and a piece of cherry cobbler, he had fallen right asleep. He had barely kissed her good night. She had not told him their news.

***

Chris showered one last time, then packed his shaving kit. The sweet aroma of Julie's perfume lingered in the air of their borrowed bedroom. He shook out his dark mane, swiped on deodorant, tossed his toiletries into his kit, then zipped it shut.

It occurred to him he had neglected his husbandly duties since that fateful day in Samantha Drake's office, when he learned the last three years of his life had been built on a lie. It tore him in two opposing directions. Each made little sense.

Julie had been noticeably quiet since his arrival. Chris figured it must be uncomfortable with Farin upstairs, unconscious, and them in such close proximity to the home they had temporarily shared. Fear overran him—fear that Farin's death would strike them a second time.

He had spent last night in a surreal state of half-sleep, half-paranoia. Though exhausted, every sound, no matter how insignificant, woke him. Ben's house could not keep Farin safe, at least not for long.

Ben and Cheryl's insistence on getting Farin to hospital frustrated him. He wished they could. Not only had her condition not improved, she steadily declined. With no sustenance, a dwindling supply of IV bags, and no sign of consciousness, they had to do something.

But he would not surrender her to doctors or police. Not yet. He had seen her through two dreadful hospital stays. The first rendered her unable to have more children. The second nearly had her committed. There had to be another way. Once home, he would decide their best course of action.

When he left the bathroom, he found Julie seated on the bed, leaning against the headboard, arms crossed. Her staid expression told him she was unhappy...and wanted to talk.

He smiled weakly, checked the room to ensure he had not forgotten anything, then zipped up his bags and stacked them by the door.

"What should I do? Is there anything you need to get ready for...*her*?"

"I'm not sure yet." He crawled up beside her and gathered her into his arms. As he nuzzled her neck, he enjoyed the scent of citrus in her hair. "I've missed you."

Julie's hatred defied communication. She felt cheated that Farin had not yet died a real death. Last night, she had again prayed to a god she did not believe in for ill fate to prevent Farin from returning to LA alive.

She cuddled into him. "When will you be home?"

"If Marci and I share the driving, we can probably go straight through. I can't wait to sleep in my own bed again."

"Have you talked to Sam? It may sound heartless, honey, but...you have a life to get back to."

He kissed the top of her head. "Bother work. I just want some time with you before I go. The rest will work itself out. It always does."

She wished she could freeze time. That they could stay in each other's arms forever. Their marriage had never lived up to what it should have, but they had enjoyed a happy illusion for a while. "Has there been any change?"

"None." He collapsed back against the bedframe, his arms falling to his side. "She's hardly moved the entire time we've been here."

Good. Maybe the universe or God or whatever does answer prayers.

"So...three days back. I'll book a flight so I'm can be there when you get home."

He stroked her hair. "I'm sorry you have to fly."

She frowned through pursed lips and shrugged.

"You'll be back before you know it. Have a couple for me on the plane."

She looked down at the comforter and focused on a stray piece of string. Despite her promise to Cheryl, she could not tell him their news. Not while another woman owned his thoughts.

He scooched down the bed, leaning back on his elbows. "I know you, Jules. You're not doing as well as everyone thinks. I hope you understand— I mean *really* understand. If Jordan were here, things would be different. But he's not. This is on me."

Studying her husband's forlorn features, a part of her was swept away by the heroism of it all. Had he never pursued Farin, everything would be different. No affair. No separation. No breakdown or overdose. Maybe no reason to be at Bobby Lockhardt's house that day. Who knew?

"Nothing you do will bring him back."

He jerked himself upright and swung his legs over the edge of the bed, clutching fistfuls of his damp hair. Julie watched him, unmoved. She would not comfort him. Truth was, there had been an affair. Chris had loved Farin. He still did.

It was 1991 all over again.

Chris had gone half-crazy when Farin and Jordan reconciled that summer, fleeing to Switzerland to get as far away from his life as possible.

The night they met, Julie had been as high as he was low. They had both checked into the same chateau under assumed names. She had registered under the name Jade Johnson; he had registered as Rhett Butler.

Julie had had a year for which most models would sell their souls, the result of which was signing a multimillion-dollar contract with the largest cosmetic manufacturer in the United States. *Good riddance, North Platte, Nebraska,* she had thought as she boarded her flight and wrestled down a flight attendant for a celebratory gin and tonic.

They had met in the restaurant the night she arrived. Chris sat alone, long after the dinner crowd had left. His back to the large, empty room, he faced a floor-to-ceiling window that, in the daylight, boasted a picturesque view of the Alps.

Julie had been disinclined to interrupt his liquid dinner. Everyone on the planet knew about the affair by then, as well as the news of Farin's overdose. Given his presence at a chateau some five thousand miles from Miami, Julie deduced the torrid romance had ended.

They knew each other by reputation, an advantage to Chris. Julie had a penchant for playboys. She had left an impressive string of men by the wayside on her journey to the top. Businessmen, photographers, agents, millionaires—her cup had overflowed, and she had a reputation for draining it dry.

"Funny thing about windows," he had said, startling her as she stared at the back of his head. "During the day, you see what's before you. At night? You notice what's behind."

"Sorry. Didn't expect anyone else would be here."

He watched her as if through a mirror. "That makes two of us."

Part of her wanted to leave him to his whiskey. Most of her wanted to stay.

"If you're waiting for an invitation to join me, darling, I'm afraid you'll be disappointed. I'm in no mood to socialize."

The astute observation had embarrassed her. She yanked out a chair from the table behind him and plopped down, her back to his. "Good. I'm too happy and too drunk to hear your sob story."

"And I'm too drunk and miserable to indulge your cheerfulness."

They ignored each other while she enjoyed her appetizer of Gravlax on rye with horseradish and roasted dill. She lingered for another two gin and tonics while a patient waiter stood inconspicuously nearby, probably hoping to close up the restaurant for the night. During that time, Chris had ordered a bottle of Glenlivet. She cursed her inability to conjure up a biting remark to crash his drunken pity party.

When her dishes were cleared and she could think of no excuse to stay, she left. An hour later, after a relaxing soak in her tub had calmed the last of her post-flight nerves, she decided to turn in for the night. A triplet of knocks at her door stopped her as she crawled into bed.

She answered the door wearing nothing but an anticipatory smile. Chris leaned casually against the doorframe, a bottle in one hand and two glasses in the other. Seemingly unfazed by her naked greeting, he had said nothing as he brushed by her into the room.

He had tried to play down his pain, but instructed her to extinguish the lights and refrain from conversation as he poured the drinks and stripped off his clothes. Something about the way he made love to her told a story that differed from the tawdry accounts of the gossip magazines. The intensity of his passion bordered on frightening. She knew it was not meant for her, but considered it a challenge more than a rejection. From her first taste, she was hooked.

It took a week to capitalize on his suffering. She showered upon him every ounce of love she could manufacture. In the end, they had returned to America together.

Now, more than three years later, she questioned whether she had made a mistake opening her hotel room door.

Chris twisted around and looked at her with downcast eyes.

She studied his face. It was only a matter of time now. Nothing would stop Chris from returning to his one true love. "Is it time to go?" she asked mistily.

"Soon," he said, moving to take her into his arms.

She drew in the spice of his cologne. Her heartbeat quickened at the feel of his lean, firm body against hers. She held him closer, committing to memory the warmth of his hands wrapping themselves around her.

"I'll be home shortly," he promised.

Julie cupped his face and pulled him closer, melting her lips into his. She wanted him now, just once more before she lost him forever.

He slipped away, shut and locked the door, then removed his shirt and trousers, his desire evident through the thin cloth of his shorts. He held her eyes with his as he returned, hungry for her, sensing her uncertainty in the silence.

"I love you so much." She sighed as she surrendered to her husband's touch. "Hurry home. I need you with me."

He cooed endearments in her ear as he took her. "Wait for me. I'll be home soon. We'll be together."

Julie made love to Chris as if it were the last time. Though heartsick, she battled her ready tears.

When he and Marci left with Farin two hours later, she gave him one last, lingering kiss at the front door, then waved goodbye.

CHAPTER 20

THE STENCH OF PROCESSED MEAT, sour condiments, and hours-old coffee assaulted Jameson when he entered the deli. As usual, he stood in back between the restrooms, listening to the endless ringing of an unanswered call. A whiff of pungent urine as a blue-collar forty-something exited the men's room prompted an automatic wrinkling of his nose.

A synthetic voice answered at last. It directed him to another number. Curious, he complied. When that call finally connected, a woman's voice answered, "Z-Master Imports. How may I help you?"

He jerked his chin and scowled, fearing he had the wrong number. Then, it hit him. Obviously, his associate had decided to infuse some credibility into his felonious vocation. He played along, impressed with the ruse. "I'm calling about the status of an order for Raleigh, North Carolina."

"One moment." Tinny hold music filled the line, its sound like warped LPs played on an unserviced turntable. The female quickly returned. "I see you placed the order Thursday. Are you calling to cancel? The full charge still applies if it turns out the package has already been delivered. And I'm sure you're aware of our restocking fee."

"No!" Jameson shouted. A few heads turned his way, rudely curious as to the source of the outburst. He scanned the dingy restaurant with suspicious eyes to ensure no law enforcement types had taken an interest, then turned his back to the patrons. Stern but quiet, he continued, "I most certainly do *not* want to cancel. I'm simply trying to...confirm delivery."

"I see. Sir, Z-Master Import's policy is clear. We cannot confirm delivery for a minimum of two weeks after the order is placed. Today's only Tuesday. We'll be unable to trace your package until next Thursday. But don't worry, I'll have my manager reach out to you with a status in a few days. It should be no problem."

Unceremoniously, the line went dead.

***

Dr. Ethan Maxwell flumped into the front seat of his car and shut his eyes. With an audible yawn, he dragged his tired legs onto the floorboard and positioned his body to start his vehicle. The end of another double shift in Cedars-Sinai's Emergency Room. Only three more months left in his residency, then his schedule would stabilize—and not a moment too soon.

The gritty buildings, gigantic billboards, and periodic blaring of horns faded to white noise as he traversed the busy LA streets, willing away the tension in his shoulders, face, and arms. Barring unforeseen traffic snafus, he would be home in about twenty minutes. He longed for the tranquility awaiting him.

Sam respected his need to decompress before discussing his day. In fact, they seldom discussed it at all. The strain of life and death decisions. Restrictions placed upon him by oppressive state and federal regulations. The constant tap-dance between quality of care and reimbursement. Struggling to be a good physician amid unspoken threats of a malpractice suit should a patient dispute his competence or integrity. These things did not exist in their Hollywood Hills home.

He loved that Samantha did not need to crawl under his skin to feel its warmth. Her strength of character overrode the typical female insecurities he had experienced with other, less mature women in the past.

Certainly, theirs was no old-fashioned romance. Two upwardly mobile professionals whose careers made enormous demands on their time. They had agreed early on to prioritize the most important things in life. Often, that meant establishing reasonable work boundaries. Sometimes, it required an apologetic call home, followed by a bottle of Chardonnay and a bouquet of calla lilies.

He saw beyond Sam's exterior gloss and polish to her base needs. Needs she had sacrificed on the altar of success. He pampered her, left cards in unexpected places around the house, and never forgot anniversaries—theirs or their families'. Twice a month, they had a date night, where they danced, drank champagne, and enjoyed each other's company to the exclusion of the outside world.

All in all, they enjoyed a serene, happy existence. Deciding on the wedding date was the only remaining wrinkle. He could not wait to see her walk down the aisle on her father's arm. Knowing Samantha, it would appear more like a resolute stride mixed with the idiosyncratic smoothing down of the fabric of her dress.

The thought made him smile. A second later, that smile became a frown. He gripped the steering wheel with a heightened sense of purpose as he recalled her earlier message. "Hurry home. I have news."

News. Her tone told him she had finally heard from Chris Grant. Whatever that meant.

Ethan had never thought much about Samantha's professional past, though he knew she had struggled. He assumed that whatever turbulence had prompted her to leave New York was behind her. But recently, her phlegmatic persona had changed.

For the last year, she had jumped at the chime of the doorbell or the ring of the phone—sometimes even at the sound of his voice if he entered a room unannounced. She offered no explanation why. He overheard occasional bits of muffled conversation through the closed doors of her home office. Invariably, they centered around three names: Ross Alexander, Chris Grant, and Jameson Lockhardt.

The significance of these names was lost on him. People came and went in each of their chosen professions. He only hoped that Sam's news would signal the end of whatever issue had unsettled her.

He backed his Lexus into the two-car garage, beside her silver BMW convertible. The day's tension loosened as he killed the engine and exited his vehicle, but the weariness from lack of sleep clung to his body like static electricity. He closed the automatic garage door, then climbed the winding set of steps that led to the kitchen. Halfway up, he heard the muffled echo of KTLA's evening newscasters on the television. His nostrils flared, an involuntary response to the smell of focaccia bread wafting from the oven.

"Sam," he called, dropping his keys on the kitchen table. "I'm home."

She entered the kitchen with a smile and a bounce to her step. Clad in her favorite sweats and a threadbare Wharton T-shirt, she appeared relax, maybe even happy, as she collected his suit jacket, draped it over a kitchen chair, then wrapped her arms around his neck. "Welcome home. I've missed you."

He rubbed her back. "I tried to head out sooner, but an MVA came in as I was getting ready to leave. I didn't have a chance to call. Sorry about that."

"It's okay." She pecked his cheek, mussed his hair, then went to the stove to stir and test a pot of boiling fettuccine noodles. "You're here now. Besides, dinner won't be ready for a few minutes."

He walked up behind her, wrapped his arms around her slim waist, and nuzzled her neck. "Only a few minutes? You know that shirt drives me crazy."

She wriggled out of the embrace, shooing him away with a slotted bamboo spoon. "You smell like a hospital, Doctor. You have time to shower. But I'm making the pesto fresh, so don't take too long."

"You know I love it when you talk like Wolfgang Puck. I love it even more that you don't look like him."

"Go!" she scolded playfully, pointing the spoon at him.

Hands raised in surrender, he back-stepped, turned, then jogged up the stairs. He removed his shirt and tossed it into the laundry on the way to the bedroom. Sam was in a good mood, which pleased him. Even better, he noted she had set out his clothes.

He showered and shaved for the first time in two days, ridding himself of the ER's potent stench while considering the logistics of their wedding—which he hoped to discuss over dinner. Most of her family resided between LA and Carlsbad, but her friends lived in New York. He had the exact opposite dilemma. No matter where they held their nuptials, it would involve travel. The date would likely dictate location. He doubted either of them wanted a soggy ceremony and, in all honesty, he did not relish the idea of going home.

Ethan had enjoyed an easy existence. His prominent Connecticut family had afforded him the luxury of private schools and summer homes. Until his graduation from Yale, he had almost never set foot outside New England. The announcement of his decision to complete his residency in California had, therefore, understandably shocked his parents.

"But son, why California?" they had asked, horrified.

"I just want something real," he explained. And what could be more real than Los Angeles?

Those who knew him labeled him a courageous, level-headed man. He had mercifully dodged the Maxwell family's "pretension" gene, which his siblings had inherited. He eschewed following his father's path to Wall Street to solidify the family's inveterate legacy of wealth.

Instead, he chose a nobler, more challenging profession. He spent his residency atoning for the sins of a privileged upbringing, caring for those his parents often scorned. Now, his debt to mankind nearly paid, he would settle down somewhere between his past and present, creating a future and a family of his own, on his own terms.

He toweled off, skinned on the lounge pants and T-shirt Sam had laid out, then trotted back downstairs. The kitchen table was cleared of his keys and the daily stack of mail, replaced by candles, wine, and two table settings. The focaccia bread sat nestled in a basket at its center, wrapped in a cloth napkin. Enticing scents of basil, parmesan, pasta, and fresh bread wafted in the air, commingling in a perfect combination that set his empty stomach rumbling.

Relaxing into a kitchen chair, he sipped the glass of Chardonnay awaiting him as he watched her finish cooking. "You mentioned you had news."

She glanced over her shoulder. "Yes. Chris finally called. They should be back sometime on Thursday."

"And that's...*good*?"

"It's wonderful." She spooned fresh pesto into the fettuccine, then tossed the mixture with metal tongs. "It means everything can go back to the way it was. Only better. I may be looking at the president's seat if things go according to plan."

"President?" He whistled, slouching casually in his seat. "Well now, that *is* news! Will that make me First Lady?"

She turned, a hand planted to her hip. "You know what I mean."

"Not really. It seems I've misplaced my super-secret invitation into your circle of trust."

A tinge of guilt flushed her cheeks. "It was for your own good, Ethan. If something had gone wrong, or if Chris hadn't made it back safely, it would've been my neck. I didn't want you to be caught in the middle—"

"Wait-wait." He waved a hand, straightening in his chair. "Hold up. I knew you'd been edgy lately, but I didn't think...this isn't something dangerous, is it?"

Samantha tapped the tongs against the pot. "Maybe. But now that I know everything's going to work out, I can explain." She wiped her hands on her apron, then hung it on a hook beside the fridge.

Their earlier whimsy faded as she grabbed serving bowls of pasta and salad, set them on the table, and slid into the chair opposite her handsome fiancé. She brought her wineglass to her lips, then set it down again, tapping its stem with the tip of a slender finger.

Ethan made no move to fill his plate. He slid aside the Chardonnay, steepled his fingers on the table, and looked at her expectantly.

Sam deflated under his patient scrutiny. In his dark eyes, she saw confusion, concern, and exhaustion—as if his day had felt like a year.

Once again, she cursed her power play for Chris's tapes. Motivated by greed and hubris, she had wanted to best Lockhardt once and for all.

"You know I worked for LSI," she began.

"I know you were unhappy. You'd mentioned being concerned your old boss might try to sabotage your new position."

She nodded. "But he didn't. And I always wondered why. That is, until about a year ago. Do you remember Jordan Grant?"

"Maybe. The name. I'm not much of a music person."

"You know he and his wife, Farin Grant, were on the LSI label."

He flexed his hands, frustrated with the protracted explanation. "Only because you told me."

Her eyes glanced down at his hands, then back to his eyes. He caught her bristle of displeasure at his response and decided it best if he back down. Calmer, he added, "I do remember them dying. It was all we saw on the news for days."

"Well, until recently, I believed those stories. But things have...taken a bizarre twist." She scooted her chair closer. "Look, I'm not sure what's gonna happen, so you have to swear you won't tell anyone what I'm about to say."

Ethan pinched the bridge of his nose. "We're not in grade school, Sam. Do you really need to question my discretion? I'm a *doctor!*"

She folded her hands atop her lap, allowing his sarcasm to breeze past her. "This is serious."

"It sounds like you're in over your head. You need to tell me exactly what's going on."

"That's what I'm trying to do."

He rested a forearm on the table, lifting a thumb as he dipped his head, motioning her to continue. His stomach audibly protested its empty state.

Sam smoothed the fabric of her sweatpants with her thumb and index finger. "It wasn't like Lockhardt to let someone leave the way I did and not seek some sort of revenge. But apparently, my crimes weren't as severe as someone else's. Ethan...Farin Grant's alive."

A tease of a grin lifted the corner of his mouth. He stared at her as if waiting for a punch line. "That's impossible."

"I know."

When Sam did not elaborate, he paused to consider her words. "Okay, let's say for argument's sake it's possible—which it's not. What are you saying? You think Lockhardt had something to do with it?"

"I know he did," came her laconic reply. "He kidnapped her."

"This *multimillionaire businessman?*"

She nodded.

He coughed out a burst of doubtful laughter. "I see. He kidnapped her. Then what? He just hid her away all these years?"

"Yes."

"Was there a dungeon involved?" he mocked, his tone low and conspiratorial.

Her head tilted to the side.

He leveled upon her a look of unrepentant disbelief.

"Are you done?" she asked.

"Are you?"

"No, actually."

"There's *more*?" He studied her stoic expression for some sign that she had invented this bizarre tale. "Look, Sam. If this is a joke, I'm not in the mood. I'm starving. Exhausted. And what you're saying...things like this don't happen in real life—not even in celebrity fantasyland."

She picked up her wineglass and took an impressive gulp. "I'm sorry. I should've told you sooner. I didn't know what to say."

"How did you get involved with this? How did you find out?"

"It's a long story. What's important right now is that Chris went after her. He's on his way back right now. The problem is, Jameson knows she's gone."

He peered at her as the implications beset him. "And that's why you've been talking to Ross Alexander every night this week? Sam, if this guy did what you claim he's done, he's insane. You need to call the police."

"He *is* insane. Unfortunately, it's not safe to call the police yet."

His jaw slacked.

She clutched the sides of her head. "*Money*, Ethan. He could...it's complicated."

"And Farin Grant...she's okay?"

Head low, Samantha recalled hating Farin with such intensity that, at one point, she had wished she would drop dead. "I'm not sure. That's where I need your help."

"*Me*? What do *I* have to do with any of this?" He sank back, stupefied. "Sorry, babe. I love you. You know I do. But things like this don't happen in the real world. And if this *is* real, you're putting yourself in danger. I can't have it. I won't have it."

Ethan jerked himself upright. He helped himself to a heaping bowl of pesto fettuccine. Without waiting for her to join him, he stabbed angrily at the pasta, twirled a large forkful, and shoveled it into his mouth. As he chewed and swallowed, he shot up and stomped to the cupboard. He grabbed a large tumbler, let the cupboard door slam shut, then marched to the fridge and filled the glass with milk.

"You took an oath, Ethan."

He replaced the milk carton. "Oh-ho-ho. Don't start, Sam."

"If she needs help, you can't tell me you'd refuse it. That's not you."

He dropped heavily into his seat and resumed his ravenous assault on his meal, his eyes fixed sullenly on the table. "How long until they're here?"

She straightened and, with a slight shoulder roll and a measure of nonchalance, spooned a helping of pasta into her bowl. "Unless something goes wrong, I'd say this weekend."

His leg bounced as he continued skewering his meal. "I'll see if I can get anyone to trade a couple shifts with me."

Lips curled into an inconspicuous smile, she nodded. "Thank you."

***

Tami Evans's commute from the hospital to the driveway of her Dorothea Drive home took approximately ten minutes. He watched her park and extract her wide, frumpy form from the vehicle, lock it, and waddle heavily to the front door.

Her overstuffed purse slung over her shoulder and a bag of Doritos in her hand, she fumbled with her keys. She grabbed the bag with her teeth, freeing her fingers to juggle the keychain until she identified the proper key. Then, she disappeared inside, closing the door behind her.

He checked the rear-view mirror, then eyed the neighborhood for any pedestrians out for a late-night dog walk before bed. Finding the streets clear and most porch lights extinguished, he exited the rented Town Car he had parked three houses down. He tucked and smoothed his shirt neatly, then reached inside the car to extract a well-pressed white lab coat.

Plunging his arms inside the sleeves, he cased the street with untrusting eyes. He straightened his collar and slipped back inside the vehicle long enough to check his image in the visor mirror, then grabbed a leather bag from the passenger's seat and stalked to the house he had surveilled for the last hour.

Inside, Tami Evans changed out of her nursing uniform into a house robe. She settled on her living room sectional with her Doritos, a rum and Coke, and the television remote.

Tami had lived in a beat-up double-wide in rural Johnson County until two years ago. She had purchased the house on wheels as a bank-repo eight years before at the age of twenty-five, when her husband had split without a goodbye. He took their three-year-old son and left her bills that never stopped. To this day she would not acknowledge, even to herself, that her drug abuse had preceded his abandonment.

At the time, she could barely afford insurance on her fifteen-year-old Chevy Citation, much less a house payment and tuition for classes toward her Associates degree. Now, she lived in a two-story brick with a basement. She had recently paid off her '94 Mustang GT Convertible.

When the bell sounded, she scowled at the front door. Years of working swing shift had resulted in few friends and even fewer visitors.

She consulted the wall clock, considered her attire, then shrugged. Maybe a neighbor had come by with an update on the status of the feral cats that had rummaged through their garbage cans for the last several days. She dusted off her hands on her robe, then ran them through her short, untidy mane as she crossed the room. "Who is it?" she called, checking to ensure she had secured the chain earlier.

"Nurse Evans?" came an unfamiliar voice from outside.

Tami peered through her peephole, then realized her porch light was off. She flipped the switch and discovered a tall blond man waiting on her front steps. "Who're you?"

"I hate to bother you at home. I'm Dr. Moreau."

"Oh, for Heaven's sake!" She hastened to unlock the door.

Since her conversation with Mr. Lockhardt last week, she had heard nothing. She had assumed another nurse had handled the matter.

Others were involved, though she never knew their names. Dr. Childs had maintained strict confidentiality. In her time on the job, she had been paid well—paid to do a job, keep her mouth shut, and ask no questions. Now, job complete, she could barely wait for the payoff Lockhardt had promised. She had stopped off at a local travel agency in town last weekend to pick up brochures on Hawaii.

"Dr. Moreau," she greeted with a subtle blush, grabbing the folds of her tattered pink terry-cloth robe and ushering the man inside. "I'm sorry. I wasn't expecting company. Please, come in."

He stepped inside, sizing up its contents as well as its owner. Typical middle-class dwelling. Bargain-basement furnishings. Untidy. The nurse, round in figure and trusting in nature, did not seem to find it odd he would make a house call—especially so late in the night. *Good. Very good.*

"Won't you have a seat?" She scuttled to her sofa and relocated several sections of that morning's newspaper to accommodate her unexpected guest. The folds of her robe fell open at the chest, revealing ample fleshy cleavage as she bustled about. "I was just having a night cap. Can I get you anything?"

Moreau focused narrowly on her every move. When she looked at him and gestured to the couch, he painted a broad smile across his face and nodded his thanks, accepted the hospitality, and set his leather bag on the cluttered coffee table in front of him. "Nothing for me, thanks. I'm still on duty and can't stay long."

She had not yet finished her first rum and Coke, but found herself flustered as she beheld the physician seated next to her. Subtle laugh lines added a roguish quality to his clean-shaven face. He resembled a perfectly sculpted, brown-eyed Brad Pitt.

A bit young, in her opinion, to be a physician. And handsome. So much so, Tami wished she were ten years younger and many pounds lighter. She worried her dark roots were visible, then realized with some embarrassment that she had not combed her hair.

"When I saw Mr. Lockhardt last week, he said you'd be in touch. But when I came in the next night, she was gone. You must have coordinated with one of the others, huh?"

Moreau nodded. "Exactly."

"I must admit, I'm relieved she's gone. As you could see, she wasn't well. I tried to tell Mr. Lockhardt. The poor girl wasted away to practically nothin'. She doesn't tolerate the medication very well. I hope the new facility gives him what he wants." She shook her head. "To be honest, I think he's gonna kill her if he doesn't let her come to soon. Don't you agree?"

He listened as she jabbered on. A big mouth. Not good. His client had rightfully expressed concern when hiring him last week.

Upon discovering his mark had been moved prior to his arrival, he had scouted the facility, unsure whether another party had become involved in her disposal. Nurse Evans was the obvious one to question as she was likely the last shift nurse to see his target. Her assumption that he had completed his mission meant something had gone awry. No matter. Not to him, at least. Either way, Lockhardt would pay.

Still, she had seen his face.

He smiled with calculated warmth, leveling his eyes upon hers. "Don't let it worry you. She's doing well in the new facility. You did a fine job."

Tami blushed under his stare. She pulled the folds of her robe tighter. "Are you sure I can't get you something? A soda? Water? I may have some orange juice in the fridge."

"To tell you the truth, I shouldn't have even come inside. I just wanted to let you know the patient's transfer was complete. I'm sure your husband wouldn't approve of my visiting so late at night. I should get going."

"Oh n-no." She reached out as he rose from his seat. "I'm not married. Divorced, actually."

"Really?" Moreau lifted his brows and inclined his head, offering her a sideways grin. "Me too. Only for about a year or so, though. It's tough, isn't it? How long were you married?"

A floodgate opened inside Tami Evans. So few visitors. Even fewer male visitors. She had not dated in months. Was it possible the blond Adonis beside her was flirting?

In five minutes, she relayed a summary of her failed marriage, leaving out the more private details of her own failings and addiction. Moreau asked all the appropriate questions, at all the appropriate times. Meticulously, he lured Nurse Evans into his web. He listened to her woeful tale with convincing interest, inched closer, rested his arm on the back of the couch, and crossed his legs.

Yes. Tell me everything, dear. Get it out now. While you still can.

CHAPTER 21

S EÑOR FROG'S CANTINA NESTLED DOWN on Collins Avenue in South Beach amongst a string of trendy clubs and eateries serving the millions of tourists who visited the swank and impressive Art Deco District. Miles had eaten there many times. The first time, some four years ago, he had taken Sandra. In fact, they had gone back the night he arrived in Miami.

Sandra. What a piece of work. He had gone by her house after checking into his hotel and freshening up, eager to get his hands on the phone records she had procured for him. She had met him at her door naked as the day she was born.

He had dashed inside her apartment and shut the door behind them. "You want the neighbors gawking at you? Are you crazy?" Stupid question.

A dinner out notwithstanding, he had not left her apartment for two days.

When he called Detective Alvarez Monday morning, she was surprisingly willing to speak to him, but insisted they meet at a neutral location away from the station. They agreed to meet at Señor Frog's Wednesday at 4 PM. He did not elaborate on the information he had obtained, but figured once she saw what he had, she might be willing to discuss its implications.

He motored his rented Chevy Geo over the MacArthur Causeway and onto Miami Beach, tooled down Washington Avenue, made a right on Sixth, then another on Collins. Nearing the restaurant, he searched for parking. The closest garage was full. In fact, he could not get within five blocks. This left two options. He could either periodically interrupt his meeting with Detective Attitude to feed a parking meter on Ocean Drive, or risk a parking ticket. Neither appealed to him. In the end, he pulled into a hotel off the beach and charmed his way into paying for a day's parking there.

Señor Frog's was four blocks away. Miles rolled up his sleeves, grabbed the manila envelope off the passenger's seat, triple-checked the rental was locked up tight, and hoofed it. Blocks of vintage cars occupied most of the curbside parking in front of the cafés and hotels. He checked his watch. With a few minutes to spare, he admired a souped-up '59 Corvette.

Miles had never seen Detective Alvarez. Though he had met with her deceased partner many times, it was always alone. Whenever Miles had found himself at a crime scene with other reporters, Stark habitually positioned himself between Metro and the media.

Alvarez had told Miles to meet her at the bar. Scanning the area, he found no fewer than three Cuban females who fit the mental image he had concocted based on their strained conversations. He scrutinized each of them, curious which he should approach first.

"Confused white boy checking out *las chicas plásticas*," a clipped Cuban accent called from behind him. "You must be Macy."

He nearly tripped as he spun around and faced her. Somehow, her truculent demeanor had painted a taller, heavier, less attractive image in his head. A stern type with a constant scowl stretched across an unpleasant face. The miscalculation pleased him, though for the life of him he did not know why it mattered. His eyes widened as his brain recalculated. "It's...uh, you're..."

"I'm...I'm...spit it out," she teased with an overweening simper as she perched an impatient hand on one hip and drew her sunglasses down the bridge of her nose.

The top of her head barely reached his shoulders. Far from heavyset, she possessed a trim physique with a narrow waist and perfectly widened hips. Behind onyx eyes he saw cunning and intelligence. Inexplicably, he recalled sitting in the House of Blues some months back, enjoying a guitarist play a set of songs dedicated to "Anna," a woman for whom he pined. As Miles regarded the no-nonsense cop before him, impatiently tapping her foot, one of those songs screamed into his mind.

... Anna's like a stretch of highway ...
... Soft shoulders and dangerous curves ...

Alvarez was stunning. Not that he cared.

Shaking off a sudden lightheadedness, he squared his shoulders and cleared his throat. "How did you know it was me?"

"What's the problem, cowboy? Don't think I know how to spot a reporter? You didn't think I'd have you checked out?" She snickered, then turned on her heel and stomped off toward the back of the restaurant before he could shake her hand.

She wove in and out of the expanding happy hour crowd as he blindly followed. He stumbled to keep pace, training his eyes on the impossibly thick, wavy hair spilling down her back. "Thanks for meeting me. I think you'll be interested in what I have to say."

"I'd better be," she shot back over her shoulder. "I've got plans tonight. And you, Miles Macy with the *Chicago Chronicle*, have exactly," she checked her watch as she slid into a booth and jutted her chin at a passing waiter, "...one hour and fifty-two minutes before I walk out of this place and leave your Windy City butt behind. So, order up and let's get to business."

Miles flattened his tie to his chest and slid in opposite her at the booth. "Got a hot date or something?" He inclined his head toward the waiter and told him they would need a few minutes to decide.

Alvarez ignored the question. She had not come to Señor Frog's to discuss her personal life, such as it was. And even if she were so inclined, she would never reveal she had let Penny Bridgeman convince her to attend a lingerie party.

Squinting at Macy, she shot out her hand and grabbed the waiter's wrist before he could retreat. "We want two orders of the grilled steak fajitas with double sour cream and two guacamoles. And bring extra tortillas with that. Also, I want a margarita. On the rocks. No salt." She nodded at the reporter. "What's your poison?"

Miles gave her a lopsided smile, as if accepting some unspoken challenge. "Corona with lime," he said. "And go easy on the fajita spices, will ya?"

"Lightweight." Alvarez scoffed as the server disappeared to submit their order. "Didn't you used to live here? How'd you survive? Anyway, you called me. You wanted to discuss the Grant case—"

"Hold up." He raised his hands. "There's no need to be hostile. When I called, you seemed a heckuva lot more interested in meeting me than you do now. What's changed?"

She snatched her napkin off the table and unscrolled the silverware inside. "Cut the chitchat. What've you got for me? You'd said you got something on Stark relating to the husband's murder. That case is a dead end. Now, I read your little séance piece on the wife. Sounds like you're starstruck, cowboy. You two have a little thing on the side? From what I heard, she had quite the love life for a while."

Miles sank back, mouth agape. Clearly, she had hit a nerve. Watching Farin Grant drown in a pool of flames had doubtless shaken him up.

"I get it. I'd be bitter, too, if I'd been saddled with a crooked partner. And it doesn't make you look too good, either, since you were on the case with him." He flaunted the envelope he had set beside him in the booth, the corners of his lips lifted into a self-satisfied smirk.

Her nostrils flared at the sight of it.

Miles stood and tucked the folder under his arm. "I think I'll take off. I wouldn't want to waste your time. You can read about my little discovery in the papers. Good evening, Detective."

Alicia blanched as he turned away. For days now, she and Bridgeman had poured over an embarrassingly flimsy case file on Jordan Grant's murder. They had no motive and no suspects. For all the ribbing she had given Chris Grant during his interrogation, she now questioned his involvement.

Macy's call, proclaiming a cover-up involving the police and a big-name entertainment guru, had seemed timely and fortuitous. She figured she would manipulate him into handing over what information he claimed to have. But he had come to barter. Thanks to her stubbornness, a key piece of information might slip through her fingers. And worse—if that information went public, she and Metro would look like fools.

"Wait," she called at his retreating back. When he stopped and turned around, she bit the side of her cheek. "Give me a break here, huh? It's been a long day. You know how it goes. Sit and have some chips and salsa. Best in Miami Beach."

He studied her warily, then dropped the folder on the table and slid back into the booth.

Their waiter returned with their beverages. Alicia and Miles eyed one another as their nodding, smiling server deposited their drinks before them. A victorious grin stretched across Macy's thin lips.

"Anything else?" the waiter asked with a thick accent.

She considered a moment. "*¡Oye! Quiero que haga esas fajitas lo más picante que pueda. ¿Entiendes?*"

Wide-eyed and open-mouthed, the server hitched his thumb toward her seatmate. "*Pero él dijo que no le gustaba la salsa picante.*"

Alicia rolled her eyes impatiently, then shot him her most intimidating look. "*¿Necesito volver con mis esposas y placa?*"

"*¿Usted lo quiere más picante?* No problem!" he answered with fearful obedience, then scuttled off to the kitchen to inform the cook. But something told him the white boy seated at the table would regret having extra spices mixed into his food.

Alvarez sucked in her lips to quash a burst of laughter. That ought to wipe the smug look off Macy's face.

She pinched the lime out of her margarita and tore the membrane from the rind with her teeth. When she bit into the skin, the explosion of tang and sour juice contorted her face. She sipped the cocktail through two thin straws to wash down the pulp.

Running a finger across her chin to wipe away a drop of juice, she caught Macy smiling. He leaned across the table and lowered his voice. "Bottom line here: Stark was a dirty cop."

She crunched a tortilla chip piled high with chunky salsa. "Now tell me something I don't know."

"He was paid to let the Grant case go cold."

Bingo.

She locked eyes with the reporter as the words hit her ears. "And what makes you think that, cowboy? You do another one of those computer séances? Did Farin Grant tell you this, or did you summon up ol' Stark, too?"

He dismissed the barb with a chuckle and a shake of his head. "N-n-no, Detective. That's not how this works. I gave you something. Now you give me something."

"What have you given me, eh? You think Stark let the case go cold? Newsflash, Paper Man—he *did*. You think he was a bad cop? No kidding. How long did it take to figure that out? You've given me *squat*, gringo," she scoffed. "Now tell me something I don't know and maybe we can deal. That's the way this thing works. You know it, and I know it."

He nursed his beer and snacked on chips. "What if I had evidence to link your former partner with a suspect?" He moved his hand to the folder, giving it a protective pat.

Her eyes darted first towards the package, then back to his stare.

He winked. "Your turn. Last time we spoke, you disregarded me with that indignant little snarl of yours. This time, you agreed to meet. You know something you didn't a few months ago. I'd bet my career on it."

She scrutinized him with untrusting eyes. About her age, if she had to guess. Polished. Probably bought his clothes at the same place as Bridgeman. She had imagined some celebrity-chasing alcoholic. A sleazy journo in stained khakis, Hawaiian shirt, and a permanent three-day beard, moving from one salacious gossip-fest to the next, jotting slanted half-truths on a dog-eared pad with a stubby, chewed-up pencil.

Macy was none of these things. Maybe she should have let Bridgeman come after all. But it was too late. Her partner would spend the bulk of his evening elsewhere, gathering evidence from another source. Hopefully, he would make out better than she.

"Why are you so involved, anyway?" she asked around a mouthful of chips. "You don't even live here anymore. What—did witnessing Farin Grant's public cremation mess you up in the head or something? They have doctors for that, you know."

He rested an elbow on the table. "You're stalling. I thought you didn't want a lot of chitchat."

She dusted her hands on her jeans, then reached across the table to snag the envelope.

He jerked it away, relocating it beside him on the seat. "Nice try."

"Enough of the games, Macy. How 'bout you fork over what you have before I get a warrant or arrest you for withholding evidence in a murder investigation?"

"And give up a perfectly good story about the death of one of the biggest pop stars in history and the cop who conspired with the murderer? Fat chance."

After discovering the insurance adjuster's report, she and Bridgeman had agreed to keep their newfound interest in the investigation under wraps. So far, they had trusted no one else. Now, she had to decide if she could trust a virtual stranger.

She gripped the table with both hands, her dark eyes seething with frustration. "We both know if you had anything worth publishing, you'd have done it already."

He bobbed his shoulders. "Maybe. Maybe not. But I'm protected under shield laws, so your threats are pointless. The only way you'll get a look at what I've got is through trade."

She jerked back into the booth and shot him an icy stare.

"This doesn't have to be so hard." He chased a chip down with the last of his beer before lifting the empty bottle in the air to get their waiter's attention. "We could help each other. Think about it. I'd wager there would have to be some satisfaction in getting to the bottom of it."

Her reputation conspired against her suspicious nature as they traded challenging glares. Yes, she felt responsible for reopening and solving this case. She did not want to think Stark's refusal to let her get more involved resulted in a murderer walking away. Who knew what information might be in that envelope?

At last, she made her decision. She hoped her instinct would not prove her wrong.

"We found some evidence that was omitted from the files when Stark stopped working the cases. We think he hid it in an attempt to avoid implicating a possible suspect. It may indicate a second murder."

An irrepressible grin stretched Miles's lips as Detective Alvarez's fortified barricade crumbled. They needed each other. She realized it, too.

At first, he had determined not to let her get the better of him. Now, the image of her pulling that lime skin from its rind with her teeth distracted his thoughts. Her full red lips pulled at his like a magnet. Her almond-shaped eyes sparkled when she found herself up against a wall. He wondered if her later plans included some lucky sap who planned to peel away that tough exterior between a set of sheets.

He decided he wished he were that lucky sap. When the waiter arrived with dinner, he ordered a shot of tequila and another beer.

***

Detective Bridgeman drew deep breaths of clean, salty air as he drove, windows down. Two days in Michigan had nearly frozen him solid. Florida had grown on him. He was glad to be back. Ready to go home to his wife. A downward glance at the dashboard clock, however, told him two things. First: Penny's party would not have ended so early. Second: it was too late to call Alicia.

He wondered how the meeting with her informant had gone. With equal curiosity, he wondered how the lingerie party was going. More than anything, he wondered what, if anything, his partner had purchased by way of sexy undergarments. Neither Penny nor Alicia would tell him, of course, but how could he tease her if he did not know?

William spent an hour fighting traffic before finding a place to stop for a late dinner. The return flight from Detroit had left him famished for anything other than airplane food.

Their clandestine investigation had identified the final resting place of Farin Grant's limousine carcass near his hometown. The pop princess's rabid fans had bid for ownership of the wreckage after Metro released it for salvage. Eighty-five thousand dollars later, it sat painstakingly preserved in a glass case atop a cement slab in the middle of a large backyard in Redford Township. It remained forever free of future damage brought about by time and, thankfully, the elements.

"You wanna do *what*?" the owner had asked when his unexpected visitor made the request.

Bridgeman offered a brief explanation. "It won't take long."

The man had scratched his head as he contemplated the request. "You got a warrant or something?"

"Afraid not."

"Can I watch?"

"Uh, no."

He agreed anyway, and showed the detective to the backyard.

William's initial impression warned him not to get his hopes up. The engine and drive train were gone, as were the door skins. Slag and ash still filled the interior, which had been largely destroyed. The frame was crushed from the weight of other vehicles during its temporary stay at the Cairo Lane salvage yard in Miami. But Bridgeman's primary concern was whether the fuel tank had been stripped.

Bundled in layers of winterwear, each breath visible in the frigid mid-morning, he circled the slab three times, his insulated boots crunching snow as the owner engaged the protective glass, raising it to give him access. He mentally reconstructed the damage, observing details explosives experts notice: scratches, marks, indentations, burned paint patterns.

He crawled in and out of the aft cabin, making similar observations. His thick gloves were an impediment to taking photos with the disposable camera he had purchased, so he removed them, snapped some exterior shots, then crawled inside and took pictures of what was left.

Eventually, he would need to get under the vehicle. At least he would not have to lie down in snow to do it. God bless obsessive fans.

The back seat had been burned away; the spring material had run to slag. What remained had rusted. Judging its condition, William estimated the peak temperature from the fire had exceeded 2,500 degrees Fahrenheit. There could not have been much left of the passengers. Heat like that would melt fillings.

Having assessed the vehicle's perimeter and interior, he turned his attention to the matter at hand. He lay down on his back, slid beneath the vehicle, and navigated past the rear axle. Mostly immobile in the cramped space, he relied on his sense of touch to answer the $64,000 question. Soon, his freezing fingers encountered the jagged metal atop the fuel tank.

"Bingo," he whispered aloud. As suspected, the rupture had originated inside the tank, causing splintered, fragmented ends of the breach to burst and curl back over on themselves like a blooming metal daisy at sunrise.

He inspected his fingers for residue, then sniffed, hoping his numbed nose would not fail him. If used, a professionally-milled explosive like military grade C-4 or even TNT would leave a distinctive odor, even years later. These items were easy to trace to their source.

No such luck.

Were they free to formerly reopen the Grant case, Bridgeman could have subpoenaed the vehicle for further inspection at a qualified lab. Without a car lift or garage pit, it took an hour to free the fuel tank from its mechanical restraints. His face and hands ached from the biting cold, but he soldiered on.

After several sniff tests from the sides of the perforated container, he lowered his arm fully inside and dipped a finger into the oil-slicked water at the bottom. He scraped a bit of rusted material under his nail, sniffed, then touched it to his tongue. Whatever initiated the chemical reaction had not been pure diesel fuel. An accelerant of some kind had been used. Not gasoline or anything obvious—possibly something exotic.

More difficult to trace, but maybe I'll get lucky.

As he withdrew his arm from the tank, mindful of its sharp, jagged edges, the heel of his foot slipped on an icy patch of cement. His shoulder bumped the metal container. The motion made the tank shift.

He heard something.

Twisting into an impossibly uncomfortable position, he reached back inside and felt around for loose objects. His fingers made contact with an unfamiliar ripple along the wall at the far end. He strained to reach further inside. With a combination of determination, care, and brute force, he broke the piece free.

The charred black clump of plastic slag crumbled in his hand as he inspected it, revealing what resembled part of a battery. He studied the pieces intently and realized he likely held the casing used to protect whatever had triggered the explosion.

William bagged the pieces, then scraped samples into pill jars and plastic baggies. He worked methodically, documenting his findings with detailed precision. Alvarez had put him in touch with a buddy of hers who worked over in the Forensic Services Bureau. The lab rat had agreed to check out any samples and keep things under his hat.

Excited that his investigation might bring something substantial to light, he hurried back to Miami without stopping to visit his family. The sooner he returned, the sooner he could send his samples to the FSB. Plus, he needed to thaw out.

Around ten that evening, he pulled his unmarked into the parking lot of his favorite greasy spoon. He still had an hour to kill. Before exiting the vehicle, he checked for messages. His voicemail box was empty.

He strolled inside, visited the rest room to wash his hands, then found a booth and scoured the laminated menu for something appetizing. Eventually, he settled on steak and eggs.

As he ate, he wondered what accelerant the bomber had employed. The details his trained eye had taken in puzzled him. He struggled to recall the ignition temperature of diesel. His mind churned, analyzing facts and figures as he filled his mouth and chewed mechanically. Occasionally, the waitress refilled his coffee. He thanked her with a grateful grunt.

When she had cleared his empty plate, he used his napkin as a sketch pad. Vectors and lines of force overwrote crude diagrams of the vehicle and its occupants. He needed access to more sophisticated gear but made do.

At eleven, he headed out, leaving a healthy tip and his crumpled napkin behind. Penny had forbidden him entrance before eleven-thirty, so he took his time driving home. When he pulled into his driveway, none of her guests' cars remained. Inside, he found his wife shuffling around the living room, picking up paper plates and cups.

"How'd things go?"

Penny set down her armload on the coffee table and wrapped her arms around his neck. After a lingering kiss, she waggled her eyebrows. "My man's home."

He laughed and kissed her again.

Her voice lowered to a seductive purr. "I bought something for myself. Show ya later."

"Mmm...I can't wait. Want help straightening up?"

She moved out of the embrace and returned to the task at hand. "Sure! It went great. I'm having another party next month. One of the girls wants to become a distributor and they all want to bring friends."

He fought the urge to ask what Alicia bought.

Penny glided around the living room the way she always did when she felt romantic. Her hips moved and her breasts swayed as she retrieved an ashtray from the floor next to the couch. She caught him staring and grinned.

Later—much later—in bed, Penny cuddled into his chest. "I like it when the kids aren't home."

William rubbed her back. "You get to make all your noises."

She gave his chest a playful slap. "You're louder than me."

"Ha!"

They giggled together while he caressed her skin. She peppered his chest and neck with soft kisses. His free hand fell on the garment she had worn under her dress. He picked it up and rubbed the fabric between his fingers and thumb, vaguely remembering having peeled it off her earlier.

"So, I have to ask," he coaxed. "What did Alicia buy?"

Penny lifted her head and peered at him. "None of your beeswax, Mr. Man. You need to think about how good your wife looks in a teddy, not your single female partner."

"It's not like that, Pen. C'mon. Give."

She snuggled contentedly back into his arms. "Nothing."

"Really?"

He contemplated how best to tease Alicia about her aversion to intimate underwear.

"She didn't even show up."

"What?"

"She never came."

"Did she call?"

"Nope."

A chill unrelated to his wintry sojourn ran his spine. They had only known each other a year, but he knew her habits pretty well. Surely she would have called if something came up. "She interviewed an informant this afternoon."

Penny nodded against his chest. "See? Something probably came up and she went to check it out."

He repositioned himself to check his bedside clock, debating whether to call dispatch or chance calling her at one in the morning. Or, maybe he had best calm down. "Yeah," he mumbled. "But when her last partner went to interview an informant, he turned up dead the next day."

***

Marci barely recognized the stranger driving the car. He resembled Chris in appearance—from his long hair to his slightly crooked nose. He even sounded like Chris. He spoke with the same British accent as her husband. But despite these things, she suspected the man behind the wheel was, in fact, an impostor.

At first, she had chalked up his sudden helpfulness to relief over having freed Farin from her captivity. Then, she thought maybe it had to do with seeing Julie at Ben's house. Or maybe the fact that, after three years of not speaking to one another, he and Ben had mended fences.

Whatever the cause, the result was...well, weird.

It started back in Key Biscayne, when Chris offered to load her luggage. She had only two small bags, but still—*he had offered to load her luggage.* When she declined the assistance, he had taken them anyway and placed them in the trunk. He had not even argued about it. She probably should have realized something was afoot.

Along their journey back across Highway 40, she had spent most her time crouched on the back seat floorboard, in close proximity of Farin, who had still not regained consciousness. She administered the Thorazine, regularly cleaned the IV site, changed the adult diapers they used to avoid her soiling her clothes, and used baby wipes to mop her brow—the same routine she adopted on their drive between North Carolina and Florida. The difference between their southbound trip and the journey west? Chris's chatter. And not just chatter...*friendly* chatter.

"Do we need to stop?" he asked at every exit, rest stop, and gas station along the way. "Are you comfortable? Do you need to stretch? Are you thirsty? Hungry? Tired? Bored? Want me to pump the gas? Need anything at the store? Are you okay? Do your feet hurt? Your legs?"

If the man driving the Oldsmobile *was* Chris, Marci worried she should have checked him into Dorothea Dix before leaving Raleigh.

They hit Winslow, Arizona at midnight on Wednesday. They had made good time, though they had taken the drive home to LA at a safer pace. They traveled by day and slept in modest motel rooms at night. The weather had been kind for late January, save a thunderstorm earlier that morning near Amarillo.

"We should stop here," Chris said, turning off the Winslow exit near a Howard Johnson's Express. He pulled the car into the parking lot far from the motel lobby. "I'll register us. You're probably exhausted."

Marci rolled her eyes. She crawled out the rear passenger's door on cramped legs, then stretched and bent her body left, then right, to work out the kinks of the last few hours. "You can't risk showing your face. Don't start taking chances now. We're nearly home."

He joined her at the door and peered in to check on Farin. "I've got my handy-dandy disguise. Besides, you shouldn't have to do all the leg work. You sure you're all right? You must be starved."

She huffed, then proceeded to the lobby. When she returned with two room keys, they performed their usual dance of transferring Farin and the IV to Marci's room.

"We're out of Depends and baby wipes," she announced as they settled Farin on one of two queen sized beds. "I'm gonna run to the store. I saw a K-Mart down the street. Can you stay with Farin?"

"I'll go," he said. "You shouldn't be running around so late at night in your...at this time of night. Make a list. Are you hungry? Should I stop and pick up food?"

Marci planted her hands on her hips and glared at him. "Okay, *who* are you and *what* have you done with Chris?"

He cocked his head. "What do you mean?"

She blew out an exasperated breath, snatched up the car keys, and stomped out the door.

CHAPTER 22

T HE FIRST THING ALICIA ALVAREZ noticed when she came to was that she was stark naked. The second was that her face was plastered in a puddle of drool on someone else's bare back. Her right arm was trapped beneath him—at least, she hoped it was a "him." Intense snoring had startled her out of her alcohol-induced unconsciousness. She glanced through slit, bloodshot eyes at the digital clock on her nightstand. Seven AM. She had overslept by more than an hour. A condom wrapper lay beside the clock.

"*Madre*—!"

She tried to move, which triggered sharp pain behind her eyes and a sick feeling to her stomach. How she had managed to subject herself to what felt like the worst hangover of her life, she could not remember. In fact, the last thing she remembered was talking to Miles Macy, trading tequila shots...

"Oh, n-n-no! Get up! *Get up!*" She yanked her arm from beneath him, then wriggled off his back and onto her regular side of the bed.

Miles yawned, rolled over, and encircled her in a sleepy embrace. "Take it easy, sweetie. It's still early."

She pushed on his chest. "Get off me! Get up, get dressed, and get out of here!" As an afterthought, she added, "And don't call me *sweetie!*"

Miles opened one eye, then the other. He sat up and stretched his arms, momentarily glimpsing her unclad body. Even hung over, he marveled at her beauty, from her perfectly formed teardrop breasts to her hard, flat stomach. His admiration turned to amusement when she snatched up the comforter and covered herself. "Running late?"

She spit a stream of invective that might have impressed him had he understood a word of Spanish. He yawned once more, kneading his temples. "Not much of a morning person, huh?"

Collecting herself, she bounded out of bed with a disgusted scoff. She teetered on unsteady legs toward the bathroom. Before closing the door, she hissed, "I'm gonna shower. You'd better be gone when I get out."

"Whatever you say." He wondered what he would make them for

breakfast.

Inside the bathroom, Alicia dropped the comforter on the floor. She peered at her reflection in the medicine cabinet mirror, horrified. Her hair would take forever to untangle. Her bloodshot eyes begged for more sleep; her head screamed for aspirin. To heap humiliation upon painful regret, the numb fullness between her legs confirmed last night's activities. She hung her throbbing head and spied another condom wrapper on the sink.

Twice?

She engaged the shower. For the second time in her life, she would be late for work. The first time, she had broken her arm riding a motorcycle with her oldest brother.

Murky memories of the night before oozed like sludge into her conscious. It had started with Macy ordering a tequila shot. She had made a wisecrack remark. That led to them trading shots. He had insisted she could not out-drink him. Turned out, he was not merely bragging.

She derided herself for challenging him or for letting him challenge her—whichever the case. The details were hazy. She could not remember them any more than she could remember bringing him home...*to her house*! She cursed and stepped into the shower.

Miles rolled out of bed and hunted for his pants. When he came up empty-handed, he figured they lay on the bathroom floor. To improvise, he wrapped a sheet around his waist, knotting it low. He smiled as he left the bedroom, the kind of smile men only wear after achieving complete sexual satisfaction.

He went to the kitchen and located her coffee maker. Next, he searched cupboards for coffee and filters. He glimpsed around the small house as he prepped the filter, scooped in the coffee, and measured water into the reservoir. The Castilian décor suited her, he decided. With a tuneless whistle, he engaged the brewer, then rummaged through the fridge for eggs and some sort of breakfast meat.

An insistent series of knocks resonated from the front door. Then it came again, louder.

"Okay, okay. Keep your shirt on. I'm coming," he called. He trudged through the living room to answer the door, holding the sheet with his left hand. A well-dressed, if tired-looking, man stood out front, poised to knock a third time. "Morning," Miles greeted cheerfully.

The man stared at Miles. In a low, uncertain voice he replied,

"Morning."

"Can I help you?"

The man's eyes bulged, then narrowed in confusion or concern. "Um…I'm Detective Bridgeman with the Metro-Dade Police. Is…Detective Alvarez in?"

"Ah hell, Bridgeman, glad to meet you!" He unlatched and creaked opened the screen door, then extended his hand. "Miles Macy. *Chicago Chronicle.*"

Bridgeman stared at the sheet as he shook his hand. "Right."

Macy stepped aside to welcome him in. "Java's on if you wanna wait in the kitchen. She's in the shower."

"O-kay," Bridgeman replied slowly. He followed Miles into the kitchen, and helped himself to a dinette chair, deliberately clamping his mouth shut.

Macy dug in four cupboards before he found the coffee mugs. He poured them each a cup. "Need milk? I didn't see any creamer or anything."

"No, uh…black's fine." They sipped in silence. When the curiosity became unbearable, Bridgeman dared to ask, "So, how long have you known Alicia?"

Miles blew on the top of his mug. "Who?"

Bridgeman dipped his chin. "My partner? Detective Alvarez?"

"Hmm." His brows raised above a downturned smile. "Uh-LEE-cee-ah," he said, annunciating each syllable separately. "I like it. It's nice. We met last night."

"Last night?"

He gave a sideways shrug. "Well, yesterday afternoon."

"I see."

"You hungry? I was gonna make some breakfast."

"Breakfast," Bridgeman echoed, drumming his fingers on the table. He leaned back, smirking as the worry and tension of the last six hours gave way to the humor of the situation. "Sure."

Alvarez emerged with one towel wrapped around her body and another surrounding her head like a turban. She detected a male voice from the vicinity of the kitchen. As she crept down the hall, the smell of bacon, eggs, and coffee filled her nose.

Poking her head around the kitchen doorframe, she spied Macy at the stove, scrambling eggs and flipping bacon. He wore nothing but her sheet.

She clutched her body towel at the chest. "You were supposed to clear out. What're you doing?"

"Hey!" He smiled through parted lips and pointed his spatula at the pan. "Want some breakfast?"

"*No!*"

"Aw, c'mon. Have a bite. It won't kill ya."

Before she could utter a venomous reply, a second male voice outside her field of vision chimed in with a sarcastic, "Yeah, Al. Come have breakfast."

She peeked around the refrigerator and found her partner sipping coffee at her kitchen table. He lifted his eyebrows up and down.

"Oh sh—" she breathed before scurrying to the bedroom.

"She's a little hung over," Macy explained.

"I'm sure," Bridgeman agreed.

She rifled through her closet for something to wear. A new suit she had picked up last week while shopping with her mother still had the tags on it. She bit through the tagging barbs, then went to throw them away in the bathroom. A condom wrapper lay in the wastebasket.

"*Three*? Who does it three times?" In answer to her own question, she resigned herself to the fact that she had.

As she hurtled into her clothes and made a pass at her hair and makeup, she strained to remember more details. From somewhere, she recalled finding him attractive in a boyish sort of way. There might have been a kiss at the restaurant before he confided that his insides felt like they were on fire.

He must have followed her home. The thought incensed her. And worse—he was in her kitchen, wearing the sheet they had done who-knew-what under the night before, using her fry pans and utensils to make breakfast for her and her partner as if either of them were regular visitors.

Until last night, she had only invited a few close friends, family, and Father de Ulloa into her home. She guarded her privacy like a precious jewel. Not even Bridgeman had been past her driveway until this morning. She wondered what brought him over, then recollected the lingerie party. She shook her head at her mirrored image. "He'll never let me live this down."

She stomped back through the bedroom to slip into her shoes. The room reeked of sweat and sex. If only it were a figment of her post-inebriated imagination. Unfortunately, her luck did not run so pure.

When she returned to the kitchen, sheathed in her new suit and an updo intended to compensate for her lack of enthusiasm for properly fixing her hair, she found the men halfway through a plate of bacon, eggs, and toast. Macy looked ridiculous sitting there in her sheet juxtaposed to her partner, who had tucked a paper napkin in around his collar to cover the knot in his silk tie, which he had flung over his right shoulder. Out of long habit, she wanted to rib him about his compulsive cleanliness, but decided it best to hold her tongue.

A loaded plate sat at an empty place near a steaming cup of coffee and a bottle of Tylenol. She wished Miles would leave her house.

"So, it was definitely a bomb?" Macy asked through a full mouth. "I knew it."

"I think we've got a shot at proving it."

Her presence registered with both men at the same time. Bridgeman winked at her. Macy looked her up and down. Cheek stuffed with toast, he pointed to the plate with his fork. "It's still warm."

He gestured with his fork again, this time at Bridgeman, "I can get those pictures printed, no problem. Give me an hour. I can do it myself at the *Post*."

"No." Alvarez jerked out and fell into her chair. "We'll do it ourselves. I'll brief Detective Bridgeman as soon as you leave."

Mouth full of eggs, Miles replied with a noncommittal, "Hmm."

"You never said you were intimately acquainted with a material witness in our car bomb case, partner," Bridgeman observed deadpan.

Alicia said nothing. His smile was so enormous, she wondered how the coffee stayed in his mouth. It should have spilled out between his pearly whites and onto his bib.

She addressed Miles with marked annoyance. "Shouldn't you get dressed and be on your way?"

Unaffected, he washed down his food with the last of his coffee. He refilled his mug from the urn and asked, "Mind giving me a ride back to Miami Beach? My rental's still parked there."

Alicia dropped her forehead into a sweaty palm. Not only had they arrived in her home as a couple, but someone had driven her car while well over the legal limit.

"Sure." Bridgeman beamed at Alvarez, then turned to Miles. "No problem at all."

"Please get dressed," Alicia pleaded.

Macy washed down the last of his toast with a slurp of coffee and nodded. "I couldn't find my pants. I think they're in the bathroom."

Bridgeman looked away to stifle a laugh. Alvarez's warning glare only further amused him.

When Miles stood and headed out of the kitchen, they both noticed the angry, red scratch marks running the length of his bare back and disappearing beneath the sheet. Alvarez's hand shot up to her mouth.

Bridgeman leaned across and whispered, "You know, Penny's a nurse. She could take a look at that for him if you want. Wouldn't want loverboy to get an infection."

"Shut-up," she growled, stringing the two words into one.

***

Four twenty-foot walls engirdled a career every record company in the world coveted. They boasted great works of art and encased priceless antique furniture, cutting edge technology, and dozens of silver, gold, and platinum trophies—none recent.

At the apex of the Lockhardt Sound offices, Jameson stood statuelike at his scenic window. He stared past his reflected image, beyond the cityscape where early evening lights dotted the surrounding office buildings, into the amber twilight. On the street below, a multitude of people scattered like insects, fleeing their corporate prisons and flocking to the city's myriad restaurants, clubs, and shows.

Hands clasped behind him, Jameson wondered where Farin would spend this Friday evening.

He concerned himself with precious little outside these corporate walls. Encouraged by an emerging new stable of talent and the promise of financial recovery, the stranglehold on his company had begun to loosen.

Ultimately, LSI's decline was his fault. He had lapsed into old patterns, betraying his fervid business discipline by letting personal motives dictate professional decisions—with near-fatal results. But Jameson, never a man to cry in his martini, had rallied.

In ten months, it would no longer matter. Not to him. Bobby would seal its fate. One generation passing the yoke of responsibility to the next. A rite of passage. A right of inheritance.

A sham, but no matter.

LSI had served its purpose. Jameson would not wax nostalgic over a ruse, though he sometimes fretted over its fate. Habit, he supposed.

"I win," he announced to his reflection.

Time to declare himself the winner of a decades-old game. No Scotland Yard, no FBI, and no jail...well, as soon as he eliminated the two final threats to his freedom. Hours ago, his fax machine had confirmed a betrayal. But whose?

Hesitant footsteps approached his office, then halted outside. A knock sounded against the thick mahogany doors, severing the silence of the early evening.

Jameson's voice boomed an authoritative, "Come in."

Ross entered, creeping soundlessly over to the uncomfortable 18th-century sofa he had occupied for over two decades. Jameson acknowledged him with a distracted grunt. For eight days, he had questioned if Farin was dead or alive. At ten o'clock this morning, he got his answer.

A facsimile of a Raleigh newspaper clipping had come in from an anonymous source. That morning's *News & Observer* had reported how one Tami Evans, RN, had been found dead in her Dorothea Drive home—a victim of an apparent overdose. Evidently, Nurse Evans had a long history of drug abuse.

In the margin of the facsimile, a hand written note read:

Greetings from the Amarillo trail. Consider this one gratis.

The phone had rung almost simultaneously. "Your package wasn't at the warehouse," came the distorted voice. "I'm afraid you've forfeited your deposit, old man. And there'll be a rerouting fee for delivery to its final destination."

"Then perhaps you should concentrate on tracking this package," Jameson had seethed.

The suggestion had irritated the caller, who twice declined, insisting it might prove more fitting to hire a tracking specialist. Jameson used every ounce of persuasion to change his mind. In the end, the caller acquiesced. "Very well, but the fee just doubled."

"Agreed."

For the rest of the day, Jameson had pondered the possibilities. A weak link had emerged in his chain of deceit. Soon, he would remove it.

"There's been no sign of them," he announced in a muted explosion of fury and frustration.

"I've checked the airlines, the bus lines, all the rental car agencies."

Still facing the window, his jaw rippled as he ground his teeth and muttered, "Chris must have someone helping him."

"You're positive she couldn't have escaped on her own?"

"I saw her myself. Even if she had regained consciousness, she was too weak to escape on her own."

"Well..."

"Well what?"

"Might someone at the facility have intervened? A disgruntled nurse or someone concerned about potential exposure after Childs's death?"

He harrumphed, unclasped his hands, and began pacing. Over the past several hours, he had considered similar scenarios. So few within his web of lies knew of Farin's kidnapping. "Initially, I wondered about the possibility of Childs committing a deathbed betrayal."

Ross unbuttoned his suit jacket and draped his arm along the top of the sofa. "I hadn't thought of that. It happens—a farewell act of contrition before meeting one's Maker."

His Berlutis trampled the worn path in his Oriental rug. "A crisis of conscience seems doubtful after all he did. Farin, Bobby...he helped us avoid many a scandal in his career. As for the staff, they've surely heard the news by now."

Ross frowned. "News?"

"One of the nurses met an unfortunate end a couple of days ago."

Ross's arm slid off the back of the sofa. He peered down at the floor.

"It's fair to say the rest will keep their silence."

"S-so, then, someone else must be involved."

Jameson wondered if he had let something slip to Bobby while in Raleigh. Had his son followed him to the hospital? As many times as he had questioned himself on the matter, he dismissed the possibility. Had Bobby known of the happenings on the Dorothea Dix campus, the boy would have confronted him, if only to cry over the injustice of the situation.

That left only two people in the world who knew of the crime. He was one. The other sat before him.

Stealing steely-eyed glimpses of his longtime colleague, he noted how small and vulnerable he appeared. Nervous. Almost withering in his seat. Odd. What if...

No.

Certain realities existed in the world. Without them, nothing made sense. The sun rose in the morning. Rain fell on the wicked and the righteous alike. And he could trust Ross Alexander with his life. He had solidified that loyalty decades ago.

He went to the wet bar and poured two Baccarat snifters of Macallan, handed one to Ross, then continued his stride as he drank. "She couldn't have made it on her own," he repeated almost to himself. "And I was told no one was seen in the vicinity that evening."

Ross cleared his throat. "What I don't understand is that you were there that night and didn't see anyone, either."

Jameson sat down and mentally retraced his steps. Prime rib and lobster at the Angus Barn with Bobby earlier that evening to discuss LSI's future. Later, he had slipped out the hotel's side entrance and gone to the hospital. He remembered observing the mostly-empty parking lot, few vehicles dotting the asphalt.

He slammed his fists onto his desk. "I can't remember anything unusual."

Ross sipped the thirty-year-old Scotch with a tremored hand. "Have we considered the possibility she didn't make it? If she was as weak as you say, maybe she—"

"One can only hope." Jameson snorted, rubbing his bald chin.

His thoughts circled back to his most trusted colleague. Ross knew all there was to know about his business dealings—legal and otherwise. Under no circumstance was he the weak link. Besides, at the time of Farin's escape, he and Josephine were on their annual Palm Springs vacation. In fact, the year before, he had met with Samantha Drake to deliver Chris's unreleased master tapes. They had caught up on...

In an abrupt moment of clarity, Jameson rose and returned to the window. His hands gripped one another in the small of his back.

Ross Alexander. Lockhardt Sound's moral compass.

The scenario played out like a motion picture. Using the masters as the perfect ruse, Ross met with Samantha. He relieved himself of his guilt, along with the tapes. Samantha transferred the material, and the news, to Chris. Or did Ross meet with Chris directly? Who knew? Who cared?

Enter the fool. Racing across the country to rescue his tormented damsel in distress. It was laughable. Notorious playboy, Chris Grant, struck down by the one woman who could never return his feelings— especially if she knew the truth about him.

Jameson's facial muscles transformed from tense to tranquil. He shot himself a sinister grin in the reflected glass, then peered down at the street to watch the taxis ferrying customers through busy evening traffic. For a moment, he indulged himself memories of simpler, albeit poorer, times.

Did he regret his life choices? Never.

He smoothed his thinning, slicked-back mane, turned to his unsuspecting "friend," and squared his shoulders with a confident stretch of his neck. "Call Ben. If Chris did help Farin escape, he'd take her there."

"What excuse could I possibly give for calling? If they *are* there, they'll know you're onto them."

The subtle quaver in Ross's voice brought Jameson immense pleasure. "Tell him we need material for one of our new bands."

"He'd never buy that. It's no secret how he feels about you."

A mad cackle escaped Jameson's mouth. He had regained control of this fragile game. What a fool he had been. Was it really so long ago he had had to twist fate to his advantage, to manipulate Ross onto this dark path?

As soon as he located Farin, he would no longer pretend. He knew the odds, the stakes, and how to beat them. Soon, Ross would pay.

They would all pay.

***

Leaving the shop late that evening added to the aggravation of Faith's day. She had hoped to make Henri's show early, or at least on time. No such luck.

She had spent the better part of the morning meeting with Basilio Acardi, her very talented, and very gay, designer. Their thorough review of the plans for the fall line had lasted through their catered lunch and well into the mid-afternoon.

Basilio had a high-end label of his own, but had taken Faith under his wing some months back, agreeing to help transform her concepts into creations. She had not wanted to trade on his impressive reputation, though his involvement would lend a certain level of credibility to her designs which were, to quote her upcoming press release, "...a unique marriage of linen and leather, capturing the sexy, sophisticated vibe reverberating from Greenwich Village to the Upper East Side."

It was pure sleaze. Tasteful sleaze. In any case, Basilio had insisted. Now, Faith stood poised to draw the high dollar price tags in all the right shops.

On his way out, Basilio left dozens of swatches for her approval. Over the next three months, she would plow through her sketches and finalize the plans for her first major show this coming October. It had already generated a lot of buzz and promised to bring her designs to the forefront of the fashion industry.

If Walt and Millie Peterson thought their oldest daughter's *first* career was a disgrace, this second one might shame them into never leaving New Rochelle again. Faith could only hope.

Most people regarded leather as either cool or kink. Faith supposed it was both. She had certainly used it as both. But now, she intended to bring an element of class to her favorite fabric.

Before leaving for the exhibit, her assistant Becky requested a moment to update her on pressing business matters. She gave an impatient Faith the rundown on repairs to a faulty heater, handed her a folder of catalog proofs, and told her she had received a call from the Monroe Agency. Apparently, Julie Swanson Grant had made overtures about walking the runway at the premiere.

Faith flatly refused.

"Are you sure?" Becky asked, astonished. "Julie's hot. And with your and Chris's history?"

Faith pinched the bridge of her nose. "I'm positive. Don't bring it up again."

"But Faith—"

"I said fuckin' *no*, Becky! What part of that don't you understand?"

Her assistant withered and retreated to her office.

Faith considered going after her. The day had taken its toll. But when she saw the time, she bolted for the front door, swearing aloud. She grabbed one of her design prototypes off the rack on her way out—a mostly black leather job with metallic flakes sprinkled in key areas. It bordered on trashy but would have to do. She skinned it on half in the hallway and half in the ladies' room. Friday's hyper-congested traffic guaranteed a tardy arrival unless she changed en route.

The sky had begun to drizzle as she climbed into an obliging cab. She slid along the bench seat, weaving her head and shoulders to check her image in the driver's rearview mirror. Beholding the red-frizz result of the humidity, she groaned and made an abortive attempt to tame her hair. In the end, she gave up in frustration, leaving it to fall in puffy orange ringlets that screamed '70s afro. As if the Mod Squad's Linc Hayes and Julie Barnes had had a red-headed love child.

The taxicab wended through the thick stop-and-go—mostly stop—traffic on its way to SoHo. Gratefully, the cabbie did not speak much English and was disinclined to try what little he knew on her. As a bonus, he either did not recognize her or did not make a fuss. She beheld her ensemble and snorted. He probably figured she was a hooker. In younger days, she would have had fun encouraging that notion. Tonight, she felt every one of her forty years.

As the cab passed the towering LSI building on 6th Avenue, a shiver crept up her spine. She imagined Jameson staring down at the street from his office window. Had he ever broken that creepy habit? Who was she kidding? She knew his creepy habits better than most. The old man would never change.

She arrived at the exhibit to a mixed response. Some welcomed her with gasping enthusiasm. Others peered down their noses in disapproval. She had gotten used to it.

Elites donned formal attire. They swept past displays with a pretentious promenade, indulging on the gallery's complimentary wine and hors d'oeuvres. True art lovers mingled and fussed over various works. A handful of loyal Mirage fans huddled together in a small group, side-glancing her every move. She always recognized them. They dressed like her.

Her secret agent stood trapped at the back of the room. At first, she worried his social anxiety had overtaken him. Then, she spotted the art critics from the *Times* and the *Post* standing between him and the rest of the crowd, blocking his exit. She recognized them even faster than her stalkers. They were the ones in the rented tuxedos.

Henri nursed a glass of chateau, holding it before him like a shield to increase the distance between them and hopefully limit conversation. The sight of him lightened her mood. When he saw her, his brows lifted up and out beneath a desperate frown, signaling for help. She beelined for him, scanning the walls as she passed. Maybe tonight he would unveil his secret work.

To her disappointment, she recognized every piece.

As she approached, she noted Henri's mysterious and uncharacteristic smile. His long hair had received little attention, obviously combed back after his shower, then left to hang about his stubbled face and shoulders as it dried. He wore black jeans spotted and streaked with paint, a dingy white T-shirt, and the Burberry pea coat she had given him for Christmas. Defying fire codes, he chain-smoked from a pack of clove cigarettes.

She kissed his cheek. "How goes it?"

Henri maintained eye contact with her as he chatted with his thick, faux accent. "Bert and Joella seem happy. It's their show. I think three've sold so far."

Faith studied him as he exhaled smoke and sipped his wine. "Happy?"

He nodded his goodbyes when the critics excused themselves, then glibly bobbed a shoulder. "Parties. People."

Their inside joke evoked a smile. "I know. What a farce."

They stood silent and watched the crowd. Faith nibbled the fruit she had snagged as she passed the buffet on her way back. Henri eyeballed her attire. "I'll paint you in that. It's new, no?"

"Hot off the sewing machine." She ran her palms along her midriff, grateful he had ignored her hair.

"You didn't go home first."

"The meeting ran late."

Henri grabbed two glasses of champagne off the tray of a passing waiter and handed her one. "I think Becky has a crush on you."

"I know Becky has a crush on me."

The critics soon returned, prompting Faith to adopt her celebrity face. No matter how many times she answered the same inane questions, she pitched her voice as if it were the first time. Which of these penguins would be the first to ask if she was still sober? She gave the short, fat one two-to-one odds.

"How long have you modeled for him, Faith?"

She locked her arm in Henri's and pretended they had not asked the same question the last time they saw each other. "A couple of years or so, I think. Maybe longer."

"It looks more like your show than his. Everywhere I turn, I see your face."

"I—"

"And everything else too!"

"Yes, well—"

"Are you comfortable with all these nude portraits of you?"

"It doesn't—"

"Do you pose live or does he paint from photographs...or memory?"

Faith opened her mouth to speak.

"And how are you doing, Faith? Still clean?"

Ah-ha...so tubby wins after all.

Time crawled by like a panther stalking prey. Henri sold four more paintings and talked to prospective patrons—all boring. At the direction of his manager, he worked the crowd. He stared woefully at each purchased piece, as if surrendering one of his organs on the black market. He was perfectly authentic. Faith chitchatted with Bert and Joella while a major art dealer from Boston momentarily sequestered Henri.

Joella said, "We *so* love when you drop by the gallery, Faith. I grew up listening to Mirage."

The last thing Faith needed to hear. Ever. She anticipated Bert's question and readied her answer.

"So, Faith," he gossiped as if they were childhood friends. "Do you think Mirage will ever get back together? Even for a live album? Another tour would be awesome."

She pretended to mull the question over. "I really couldn't say. We're all doing different things right now."

"Too bad." Bert frowned. "It'd be great."

She chin-pointed in Henri's direction. "How's the show going? I figure it's good or he'd have bowed out by now."

"Wonderfully," Joella said. "I'll be surprised if he doesn't sell out. I can't remember a bigger turnout. There're buyers here from all over."

Bert winked. "It doesn't hurt that you're here."

"True, true." Joella touched her champagne flute to her colleague's.

Faith caught Henri's attention long enough to tell him she wanted to go. "It's been a long day. Is it okay?"

He lit a cigarette and exhaled smoke into the air above her head. "I can't leave yet."

She noted the "sold" tags on the corners of several oils. "I'm fried."

Henri kissed her forehead. "I'll see you at home."

"Wake me when you get in and tell me what I missed."

"See you then." Again, he gave her his mysterious smile, then walked over to a couple who were contemplating a portrait of a nude Faith Peterson doing a handstand.

Bypassing the freight elevator in favor of a little exercise, she took the stairs up to their loft. She unlocked all five deadbolts at the door, then entered and secured them behind her. Moonlight broke through clearing clouds, illuminating the open space through the mostly-glass ceiling.

Guided by the artificial light bathing her body and spilling onto the hardwood floor, she wandered across the room to the refrigerator for a drink. She perused its contents, then grabbed a bottle of apple juice and shut the door. The loft smelled musty, like old paint and cigarettes...like Henri. The quiet settled her nerves.

After a moment's hesitation, she ambled over to her baby grand. She straddled the stool, which intersected the keyboard at right angles. She set her juice atop the highly lacquered lid. For the first time in months, she had an unobstructed view of the loft's floorboard runners. The absence of Henri's paintings made the open space feel empty.

Her fingers glided awkwardly across the keys at first as she created music from nothing. A few meandering seconds later, she fell into Bach's Piano Concerto No. 1 in D Minor. Chris had always loved it when she played Bach. She struggled a few seconds in. It frustrated her. She used to know the piece by heart.

As she played, she reflected on how very different her and Henri's pasts were and how similar they had turned out. They had both experienced a personal renaissance of sorts. Henri still seemed so young, while she felt ancient at times. Times when Joella Downs paid her a backhanded comment. Times when it felt like forever since she had tried to reconcile with parents who had banked on a different career for her—a career more conducive to playing a concerto at the Met than a sold-out rock concert at Madison Square Garden.

Who would see Faith Peterson, who wore only black leather and little of that, who battled addiction, who had earned her reputation as an unbridled woman with the face of an angel and the soul of a devil, and remember she had once been a Julliard-trained child prodigy? Who would suspect Faith loved Mozart and Chopin? Who would remember she had won the Leventritt competition at age twelve?

Her fingers stroked the keys until Rachmaninov's Piano Concerto No. 2 filled the empty darkness around her with bittersweet melody. She missed Chris. If anyone had kept her sane during those years on the road, he had. She loved Elliot like a brother, but she loved Chris differently. How long had it been since she had seen him? The Grammys, she supposed.

Rachmaninov was probably not the best choice.

She played a solo from Mirage's last album. The thing she missed most about the band was their time together. She had mothered, even smothered, them at times—especially Todd and Lance, who always seemed to need both. They had put up with it, and with her. In return, they defended and indulged her ferociously. Even when she had been difficult, which had been often.

Since the breakup, Todd had sent her one Christmas card.

Lance had sent her three letters when she had been in rehab. He had even visited once, a couple of years ago. Elliot and Marci called semi-regularly. But Chris's few letters left her unsettled. Something about the return address of "Mr. and Mrs. Grant."

She found herself playing Camille Saint-Saëns, the painful reminder of a childhood sacrificed on the altar of perfection over years of piano instruction. Something she shared with the composer. A rebellious smirk stole across her face as the music dissolved into a simple chopsticks-like version of Jingle Bells, followed naturally by Joni Mitchell's "River." She played as if exorcising a demon, heedless of the stray tear sliding down her cheek.

A long moment passed after the last note faded. She peered out the loft's floor-to-ceiling windows.

With a melancholy sigh, she rose and removed her spike heels. Next, she stripped off her leather ensemble, then draped it over her arm and stacked the heels on top. Down to a black lace thong, she finished her juice and padded into the bedroom. She switched on the bedside lamp and hung her outfit, never suspecting dozens of eyes watched her every move. When she turned around, she saw them.

Hanging on the wall behind and above their bed were some twenty canvases: Faith in sleeping repose; Faith sitting straight-backed, playing her Steinway; Faith peeling an orange; Faith sipping coffee. In each painting, someone was painted in beside her. Someone familiar. His arm draped across her stomach as they lay in bed. Ever near as they laughed over coffee. Eyes shut, smoking as she played.

The masterpiece hung centered directly above the bed. Henri, his back to the world, sitting before his easel, painting a portrait of himself painting Faith as she posed. On the canvas-within-the canvas, before the miniature painted figure, one could see Henri's back as he painted Faith and a mini-portrait of Faith herself. The perspective went on and on into infinity, like cascading images between two parallel mirrors.

For possibly the first time in her life, the ever-loquacious Faith Peterson was speechless.

CHAPTER 23

ROSS DROVE HOME IN A state of numb resignation. He made turns, stopped at red lights, navigated between white or yellow lines, all from habit. He was no more aware of his driving than he was of the other cars on the road. Tonight, he had realized his fate.

No longer did Jameson seemed confused, frustrated, or even curious about the events surrounding Farin's escape. The fog obscuring his evil blue eyes had cleared. Ross had witnessed the change live and in-person.

Jameson smelled blood. And like any murderous shark, he would follow the scent to his helpless, albeit suspecting, prey. Ross treaded bloody water, and was going down. Though immune now to private meetings, thinly-veiled threats, plots, and plans made behind the imposing closed doors of his old friend's domain, soon the truth would surface.

Farin's escape from Dorothea Dix was his doing. *He* had relayed the news of her fate. *He* had told her rescuers where to find her.

An overwhelming sense of dread had filled him tonight in that office. He feared he would die in that room and never see his bride again.

He parked his black Lexus in the garage and trudged upstairs, feeling his way through the dark, ruminating over every chair, every wall, every vase and tiny figurine. Careful not to wake her, he shed his suit in the guest bedroom, then padded into the master wearing only the silk boxers Josephine had stuffed into his stocking last Christmas. Before climbing into bed beside her, he studied her still, moonlit form as she slumbered. He swallowed against the catch in his throat as he slid in next to her, moving his body close and slipping an arm around her slender waist.

Josephine was a good woman. The best wife a man could ask for. She maintained a beautiful home and dutifully served the church. Along with a quick wit, she possessed wisdom and a fullness of life that had calmed him during the most chaotic of times. She made him laugh despite Jameson and the hellish underworld of circumstances surrounding the Lockhardt name.

Ross's arm tightened around her. Though he did not know when or how, he knew his days with his beloved bride were few. Pointless, he figured, to tell the truth now. Josephine was strong. Somehow, she would find a way to live without him.

***

At first, it seemed like a good plan. The only plan that could bring them home safely. But as they neared the Arizona/California state line, Chris realized they had overlooked a significant detail.

Agricultural inspection sites blocked entrances to the state of California. Unsure if the uniformed inspectors were law enforcement, forestry agents, or what, he could not imagine how they would avoid attracting attention. Someone might recognize him. Worse, how could they explain carrying an unconscious woman attached to an IV bag hanging from a coat hanger in the back seat? Or the vials of unprescribed drugs in the trunk?

They stopped in Yucca, Arizona at a run-down gas station some forty miles from the border to fill the tank and formulate a plan for completing their long and taxing journey. For the first time in days, Marci called Elliot, assuring him things, thus far, had gone more or less according to plan.

"I've been worried," Elliot said.

She recognized the strain in his voice as she studied the highway for suspicious vehicles. "We didn't know when it would be safe to call. We're flying without wings here."

"When will you be home?"

"Tomorrow, unless something unforeseen happens. We've got about five hours or so left."

"She holding up okay?"

Marci glanced at the car's rear passenger door, then back to the road. "She hasn't woken up, El."

"What?"

"I'll explain when we get back. I can't talk long. We're trying to stay off the phone and avoid anyone figuring out where we are."

"I understand. But Zoso, you know it wouldn't be hard to do, right?"

"I know." Her voice came out sad and low. "Hey, do me a favor?"

"Anything."

"I need you to go to the library and research a medication for me. Write this down." She spelled out Thorazine and gave the dosage they had been dispensing. "We haven't taken her off it because we're not sure about any side effects. Will you look into it for me?"

"Sure thing," Elliot told her. "Be careful. Is Chris being good? You two aren't fighting too much, are you?"

"He's okay."

"Good."

"I have to go now."

"I love you, Zoso. I can't wait to see you."

"I love you, too."

She waited outside the car while Chris went inside the station to get change from their fill-up. He had donned the dark glasses and baseball cap get-up. Not glamorous, but it did the job.

As she climbed into the cramped back seat, she studied her best friend. Still safe, but still unconscious. She resisted panic, but Farin looked worse. The longer they drove, the more she seemed to vanish into the back seat.

"We should stop for the night," she suggested when Chris returned.

He secured his seatbelt, removed his cap, and then shook out his hair. "I was thinking the same thing. You okay? Did you want something to eat? You look tired."

The questions did not bear answering. She had abandoned any hope of understanding the change in his personality. "We need a room, and we need to find the local hospital."

He frowned at her through the rearview mirror.

"She's not gonna make it, Chris."

"Yes, she will. We're close." He twisted around in his seat. "You don't want Lockhardt to—"

"He won't be much of a threat if Farin's *dead*. Look at her!"

Chris bit the inside of his cheek as he studied Farin's still body. His throat felt constricted. "We can be in LA before noon tomorrow."

Marci propped herself up against the edge of the back seat. "She'll be dead before noon tomorrow."

"You don't know that!" He whipped back around and fumbled with the keys.

"*Please*, Chris."

He fixed his jaw and peered again through the rearview.

Marci shook her head. "Please."

"Maybe we should just keep going. It's only four."

"She's traveled enough for the day. Let's do the right thing, here."

"I'm trying, Marci. I'm doing every right thing I can think of. And right now, I'm trying to keep her as safe as I know how—the only way I know how. If we take her to hospital, I can't protect her."

She gazed down at Farin. "Let's get to a motel before someone notices us. We can discuss it more there. Elliot said he'd look up Thorazine for us. Maybe that'll give us some idea of what we're up against."

Chris started the engine and navigated the Olds toward the exit. "There's a motel about a mile from here. We'll stop there for the night."

The motel was deserted, save its owner—a squat, balding man with leathery skin, a potbelly, a permanent five o'clock shadow, and few teeth. Railroad tracks ran parallel to the single-story establishment on the eastbound side of the highway, between the access road and the motel. The proprietor registered them in Marci's maiden name and gave them the keys to rooms 26 and 28 on the west side of the hotel, farthest from the lobby.

The weathered doors of their rooms were in sore shape, in need of replacement or at least a fresh coat of paint. Chipped furniture in shades of avocado and harvest gold dressed the rooms. Bed sheets covering the cheap, lumpy mattresses were worn thin. The sort of rooms where the wallpaper did not match the wallpaper. Thankfully, there were no bugs...or snakes.

"Uh-uh. No way," Chris said as he carried Farin into Marci's room. He pivoted around to leave. "She's not staying here."

Marci bounced a few times on one of the two beds to test the springs. "It's not much, but it's clean. It'll be fine for the night."

"There must be something better in town."

"It's a small town, Chris. There's no Four Seasons here. Just put Farin down and go get dinner. I'm gonna find a phone book."

A half-moon shone down on the motel that evening. After discovering the closest hospital was twenty-four miles back in Kingman, they ate dinner in Marci's room to monitor Farin for further decline.

"There's only one IV bag left." Marci swallowed the second and, she feared, last bite of her salad.

Chris glanced at the IV pole to assess the current bag. "How long does each one last?"

She gave him a grave look. "We need to be in LA before noon tomorrow."

He set down his burger and turned away. "I called Julie earlier. Sam, too."

"Everything okay?"

"We didn't talk long. I just let them know where we are and that things don't look good. If we make it through the checkpoints tomorrow, we should be okay."

"And then what?" Marci dropped her fork and pushed her salad away. She wiped her hands, then sipped her Sprite. "Once we're home, how does that change the fact we need a doctor?"

He chased down the last of his burger and fries with an iced tea, then gathered his garbage and headed out the door. "Good night." He shut the door behind him.

Once settled into his beat-up room, Chris endeavored to devise a plan to make their final jaunt into California. He plotted until his brain numbed with thought. Finally, he crawled into the rented bed to try to steal some much-needed sleep. Twice an hour, a train chugged past the motel, horn blowing. The rumbling shook the bedside lamps and cheap prints drilled into place on the walls.

He missed his wife. He missed his clean, simple existence. Samantha had filled him in on all the news of *Aftermath*. He needed to get back and fulfill the commitments of his publicity campaign. Then, he needed to get back into the studio. The tapes she had recovered from LSI would give him a good jump on his next album.

He wondered if Farin would ever sing again.

For hours, he tossed and turned in bed, which vibrated violently with each passing train. Resigned to the fact that sleep would evade him, he showered and shaved. The dingy, mildewed bathroom tile was chipped and broken in many places. The tub leaked a large puddle of water onto the floor. When he emerged from the shower, he noticed only one thin cotton towel hung from the rusting metal towel rack on the bathroom wall.

He dried off, stepped into his jeans without zipping or buttoning them, then tossed the towel down to mop up the floor. As he shaved, he considered the toll this trip had taken. No tour in his entire career had left him so exhausted. His bloodshot eyes, sallow skin, and harried appearance exposed many a long and restless night.

He wished he could take a walk. But no. Jameson had to have started looking by now. It was a miracle no one had spotted them hauling Farin in and out of motel rooms across the nation.

Alone and restless, he sat on the end of the bed, head in his hands. Marci was right. They might not get her back alive. She had made one fleeting movement their entire journey—a twitch of her hand and a simultaneous flicker of eyelids.

A sudden pounding on room number 28 startled him to his feet. He buttoned and zipped his jeans, then grabbed his shirt off a cheap vinyl chair as he dashed to the door.

Marci stood wild-eyed before him in the same jeans and sweater she had put on three days ago. A plastic clip still held her dark, unkempt hair. "Chris, I think she's dying."

His body froze as the words escaped her wind-dried lips. She paled with fear. Tears streamed down her cheeks. He darted from the doorway and beat her back to room 26, swallowing hard as he crossed the threshold.

Farin lay sprawled atop the sheets, stretched sideways across the rickety bed. Her body glistened with sweat.

Marci sniffed. "See?"

"She's moving?"

She nodded. "All the sudden. She started ripping the blankets away."

Farin's body twitched and convulsed. With each movement, her face contorted in agony. Eyes closed, she licked and smacked her cracked lips.

Chris knelt down beside the bed and tried to still her writhing body. "She's burning up!" he barked, half in shock, half in fear.

"*Jordan!*" Farin rasped in horror. Chris jumped back in surprise. Her body moved weakly, more from memory than muscle control. "*No! Jordan!*"

Marci rushed to Farin's side. She scampered across the bed to sit behind and support her back, cradling her friend in her arms as she shushed and stroked her brow.

"Look at her! She's *dying*, Chris!"

"Quit it," he spat, inching forward. "What if she can hear you?"

"She can't hear anything. Can't you see that? We have to get her to a hospital."

"And then what, Einstein? We've already discussed this."

"It can't be worse than this! We can't do anything. Call an ambulance!"

Farin's outburst soon subsided.

Chris rubbed his neck as he considered their predicament. "This may be a good thing. It's the most she's moved since we found her. Maybe she's getting better. You should go and get some air. Freshen up a bit."

Marci's eyes brimmed with emotion. "I'm not leaving. I have to be here with her."

"Rubbish," Chris scoffed. Defying his own fears, he climbed onto the bed behind Marci, nudging her aside and taking her place behind Farin's body. "She's finally coming around. You need to relax. I'll sit with her for a while. You go—really. It'll do you good."

Marci hesitated. She watched Chris cradle and rock Farin in his arms. He was gentle with her, careful to keep her comfortable.

"Can you get me a cool washcloth before you go?"

She nodded, then went to the bathroom.

Chris was right, she told herself. She had overdone it. Inadequate food intake. Little rest. Refusing assistance. If she intended to help Farin recover while maintaining a healthy pregnancy, she needed to calm down.

She returned with the wash rag. "You win. I'm gonna go take a walk. I'll shower when I get back. I won't be far. Let me know if things get worse."

Chris held and supported Farin, pressing the rag to her forehead and dabbing it against her face. How many times had he begged for one more chance to hold her? So many words had passed between them; so many more remained unspoken.

Their troubled past strobed in his head. He had let her go. He was finally the husband Julie deserved. Now, his thoughts confused him.

"You made me the man I am now," he dared to whisper in her ear, his eyes fused shut against the pain as he rocked her gently. "I didn't know what love was until I met you, Farin. I'm sorry...sorry Jameson did this to you. It's my fault—everything. If I'd left you alone, Jordan would still be here. You'd be well and happy."

Emboldened by the familiar scent of her skin and the feel of it against his, he made apologies he had believed she would never hear. He apologized for manipulating her after Chase died. For destroying her wedding. Robbing her of a honeymoon. He apologized for lying moments before she lost Melody. For the public humiliation the night of Mirage's last concert.

For not coming sooner.

He rocked her back and forth, singing soft melodies in her ear. Songs no one else would ever hear. Written for her ears only. And as he sang, the past and present collided. Regret strangled him as he held her closer.

"Fight," he coaxed with a gentle shake. "You're stronger than they think you are. They were wrong. All of them. But it's up to you, now. Marci's having a baby, you know. She'll need you here with her. We all need you, Farin. *Fight*. Please come back to me."

He should have taken her to hospital like Marci had begged him to—

damn the media, damn the police, and damn Lockhardt to hell. His powerlessness incensed him.

The image of Jordan's bloody, vacated body lying on Bobby Lockhardt's floor flickered in his mind. If Farin died in his arms, he would not survive. Never again did he want to feel death on his skin.

Slowly, she began to stir. She dragged her arm to her stomach and uttered a long slow moan. Tears escaped her closed eyes. Chris watched, stupefied, as the moans intensified. Her head rolled side-to-side, her turmoil mounting as it had before.

"*Somebody!*" she shrilled, jerking out of Chris's arms and bolting up into a sitting position. Her eyes flew open. She stared sightlessly at the far wall. "*Help us! Help us, please!*"

Chris caught her as she collapsed backward, her atrophied muscles too weak to remain upright. Her eyes shut again; her face twisted in pain.

"It's okay," he hushed, pushing back tendrils of dull, unwashed hair from her face. "You're safe. I'm here. Marci's here. You'll be all right."

"*Jordan!*" Farin wailed, weaker now, as tears spilled down her sunken cheeks. "*No! Daddy!*"

Chris held her tight. Her mind was trapped in another time. In a place Chris visited from time to time in his own troubled nightmares. A time when her husband still lived, when Chris had been so obsessed, he would have given his life to win her love. A time when her rejection left him reeling.

Three years. He had made his peace. He had put Julie first. They were happy.

And now, Farin was back.

Everything changed the day Samantha told him. The feel of his arms around her tested his will and found it lacking. Though buried, his feelings had not died. They never could. As he stroked and petted her, he confessed the truth he had disavowed. "It's always been you," he whispered, a cry in his voice.

He burrowed his face into the nape of her neck and sobbed. As clear as his feelings were, he knew what he had to do: reject them outright.

Redeeming himself with the family he had betrayed mattered more than anything, now. He would ignore the memories. Make Julie his priority.

He would do the right thing—come high water or hell.

"Please," he begged as she whimpered in his arms, weeping softly through her grief. "You're safe now. We're taking you home."

"Home," she cooed, her voice no more than a wisp of smoke.

His head shot up at the connection. "Yes, home!"

She moved slowly toward the misty voice at the gate of her consciousness.

"It's me, Farin. It's Chris. You're safe, now. Open your eyes."

She released a pitiful moan. "Help."

"I'm here, love. Come back to me."

"Marce."

"She's waiting to talk to you. Come now, there's a girl."

Farin licked and smacked at her dry lips. She struggled to maneuver herself up. Her eyelids fluttered.

Chris rubbed his face against his upper arms, first left then right, his T-shirt absorbing his tears.

She opened one eye, then the other. Blinking her vision clear, she used what little strength she had to look up, recognizing him at last. "Chris?"

"Yes," he smiled, grateful, disbelieving. "I was beginning to think..."

"Where am I?"

"You're safe. That's all that matters."

"Where's Jordan?"

The question beset him like a physical blow.

Cruel reality assaulted her. Her face squinched in horror. Her body withered. "No," she rasped through her tears. "It isn't true."

He bit his top lip and shook his head mournfully.

Words failed Farin as she relived the trauma. She bolted up as if by reflex, wrapped her arms around his neck with what little strength she could muster, and sobbed. "Oh, Jordan..."

His mind dizzied with questions. Why had Jameson taken her? Why would he lock her up and drug her, leaving her friends and family to mourn her death? Who killed Jordan? What happened that day?

But those questions could wait.

Chris grabbed the damp, discarded cloth. "I'm gonna freshen up this wash rag. I won't be a moment."

He slipped out from behind her, eased her back onto the bed, and rushed to the bathroom. "Here we are," he said as he returned. "A warm compress should set you right."

There came no response. Farin lay still. Her small body looked as if it had dissolved into the bed.

Two minutes ago, she had wrapped her arms around his neck. She was coherent. She had remembered. Now, she was gone again. He felt for and barely detected a pulse. "Farin? Can you hear me?"

Her body felt as cold as the Santa Barbara gravestone that bore her name.

"Marci!" He rushed to the door. Tears blurred his eyes as he grabbed the doorknob. Jameson would pay for his crime. Chris would see to it. He had taken Farin from everyone who loved her. Twice. "Marci!" he called again, jerking open the door.

In the dim shadows beyond the doorframe, a man Chris did not recognize stood with a raised fist, poised to knock. The stranger stood tall, over six feet, with blond hair. He wore a white lab coat. In his left hand, he clutched a leather bag. The man lowered his fist, letting his arm fall loosely to his side.

"If it isn't the infamous Chris Grant."

The hair on the back of Chris's neck rose.

"Who are you?" he demanded, his breath low, scratchy, and fearful. He spread his arms to grip either side of the doorframe, blocking the entrance.

The man offered an ingratiating smile. "I'm here for Farin."

The blood rushed from Chris's face to his stomach. Their luck had finally run out. No one could save them now—not him, not Farin, not even Marci's unborn child. This man, this Doctor Moreau, would kill them without pity. Somewhere along the way, they had been careless. And that carelessness had just cost them their lives.

CHAPTER 24

CHERYL GRIPPED THE STEERING WHEEL as she drove. It was that or wring her sister-in-law's neck. She had good reason for personally driving her to the airport. Namely, amazement.

What amazed her was not Farin's reemergence after all these years. Or Marci's pregnancy. Chris and Ben's unlikely reconciliation—even that paled by comparison.

What amazed her was Julie's behavior.

From his arrival to the second he drove away, Julie had—in Cheryl's presence anyway—treated her husband of three years like a stranger. Instinct told her Julie let Chris leave with no idea she carried their child inside her. This shocked, disappointed, and frankly, disgusted her.

She had tried to bite her tongue. Julie was an adult. A friend, even. Whatever was going on between her brother- and sister-in-law was none of her business. But now, there was a greater consideration. Who would speak for the baby? Today, Cheryl would.

"What did Chris say when you told him the good news?"

Julie sat beside her, fixing her makeup. "What good news?"

"*Your* good news. You did tell him, didn't you?"

She shut her compact with an impassive click. "Of course."

"Well? What did he say?"

Julie tossed her bag onto the floorboard. "Not much."

Cheryl stared ahead at the road, white-knuckling her grip on the wheel. She wanted to confront the obvious lie. Instead, she fell quiet.

The silence between them grew heavier as they exited I-95 and merged onto 836 West. Cheryl had her own husband and kids to worry about. Julie's behavior left her confused. Angry. And a little sick to her stomach.

"You didn't tell him, did you?"

"I can't talk about this now, Cheryl."

"You can. And you need to."

Julie covered her face with her hands.

"Why did you lie to me? And why didn't you tell Chris?"

She crossed her legs, cupping her knee with laced fingers. "Because I didn't want to add to the insanity."

"Och! Insanity? Your *baby*? You listen to me, noo." Cheryl stabbed the air as she spoke, periodically glancing at her and away from traffic. "That man loves children. He'd walk through fire for either of my wee boys, and all the farther for his own!"

"I don't know."

"Don't *know*? Look what he did for Farin!"

Julie's body went rigid. "Yes. *That* I noticed."

"It isn't fair, hen. No matter the circumstances, you find a way to let him know. Promise me—*promise* me you'll tell him the minute you see him."

"I will."

With an irritated flick of her wrist, Cheryl activated her turn signal to make a right onto NW 42nd Avenue. "Not good enough. *Promise*."

Julie set her jaw. "I promise. I'll tell him."

***

The man with the leather bag pushed past Chris and entered the room. Chris's knee-jerk impulse was to attack him from behind. But no. This man could kill him in ways he could only imagine. Besides, Farin was already dead.

He had to save Marci—and her unborn child. He had no idea why the man had not shot or stabbed him, or whatever professional killers did, but he decided in the space of a second to capitalize on the man's mistake.

So, he ran.

"Marci!" He raced toward the car.

"Quit shouting!" Marci appeared out of the shadows from beside the vending machine a few yards away, a Sprite in her hand. "What's wrong? Is Farin worse?"

Chris dashed to her side. "Moreau!"

The Sprite dropped from her hand. It gurgled and bled onto the gravel.

He grabbed her upper arm, hurrying her toward the Oldsmobile.

Terror saturated her voice. "Where's Farin? What are you doing?"

"I'm getting us out of here."

She stopped short of the car while he raced around to the driver's door. "What if there's a bomb?"

He recoiled, dropping the keys as he raised his hands and backed away from the car.

"What do we do?"

"We've gotta get out of here!"

"Where's Farin?"

"We should've bought a gun!"

"He's killed her, hasn't he?"

He visually, and urgently, searched their shadowy surroundings, the dim streetlights offering little by way of illumination. "I need a weapon."

"Let's call the police."

"Tire iron!"

"*What?*"

He picked up the keys and dashed to the trunk.

Marci flailed her arms. "No! There could be a bomb!"

"Get back!" he shouted.

He winced as he sprung the trunk, holding his breath and preparing for the worst.

Nothing.

Marci clutched her chest, her body deflating with relief.

Chris rummaged through shriveled IV bags, repackaged syringes, empty Thorazine vials, an open pack of disposable diapers, and luggage, dumping most of it onto the ground as he searched for the tire iron.

Marci held her stomach. Her eyes darted back and forth between him and their motel rooms. "She's in there with that monster! How could you?"

"Don't you understand? She's already dead!"

"We can't leave her, Chris!"

"And we won't!" At last, he found the tire iron. He brandished it in his hand, acquainting himself with its heft.

"She's really gone, isn't she?" Marci pressed, chin quivering.

He tossed her the keys, then raced across the gravel. "If I'm not back in two minutes, *go!*"

Fear churned in her stomach like a hatching nest of spiders. Spellbound and frozen, she heard muffled shouting from inside the room, but no sounds of a struggle. No gunshots.

After what felt like an eternity, Chris emerged from room 26. He beckoned her over with a wave.

She squinted through the darkness to see if he was hurt or bleeding. "Are you okay?"

He gave a thumbs up and waved once more.

Leaving the door open, he turned and walked back inside. She took three halting steps, then increased her pace until she reached the doorway.

She scanned the tiny, untidy room, unsure what she was looking for, yet afraid she would find it.

Farin lay still on the bed. Her IV had been moved from her right to her left arm. The old needle mark was covered by gauze and medical tape. On the second queen-size bed, an assortment of supplies, wrappers, and pill bottles lay scattered near a medical bag.

Chris knelt beside Farin and took her hand. He whispered something in her ear, then kissed her cheek. On the rickety dresser beside an old, boxy television, she spied the abandoned tire iron.

A stranger stood between the two beds, talking on the telephone. "Yeah. She's stable for now. I'll study the chart notes. We need to get her back to LA as soon as possible. Uh-huh. Uh-huh. Yeah, I think she just got here. Did you need to talk to her? Okay, then." The man smiled into the silence of the room, at no one, as he spoke. "You'd better believe you owe me. I nearly got my head smashed in."

"Don't hang up." Chris reached out, palm down. "Tell her we'll take her to the beach house."

The man covered the receiver with his free hand. "Beach house?"

"In Malibu. Jordan's old place. I can't remember the address, but—" He glanced at her. "Wait. You lived there. What is it?"

In a daze, Marci recited the address where she had lived with Dan Albright until shortly before she met Elliot.

Chris turned back to the man. "You get that?"

The stranger repeated the Malibu address, raising his brows for confirmation. Chris nodded.

Then, into the telephone, the man said, "I'll give her a better exam but if things look good, we'll move her tonight. Uh-huh. No, that shouldn't be a problem. Okay. If we can't move her tonight, I'll call you back within the hour. Otherwise, we're out of here. I know. Do you need to talk to Chris again? No, he's okay now. Ha-ha. Okay. I love you, too. 'Night."

The man hung up, then crossed the room to where Marci still stood in the doorway, hand extended. "You must be Marci. I'm Dr. Maxwell. Sorry for the scare."

***

Friday morning found Detectives Bridgeman and Alvarez pulling into a familiar spot near a Miami Beach street vendor. They had returned to meet up with a key witness to the stabbing they had spent most of yesterday processing while Bridgeman pulled double duty nursing his partner's hangover.

"Feeling better?"

His somber expression fooled no one.

He shifted the car into park and killed the engine. "I threw some old towels in the trunk in case we have any more accidents after lunch."

"Can it, Billy. I had enough of your sarcasm yesterday. And no, as a matter of fact, I feel awful."

"All I said was, you should've taken your new friend up on his offer to print out those limousine photos. I barely had time to walk my samples over to FSB before we headed out."

"He's not my friend," she snapped, pinching her forehead.

He checked his rearview and side mirrors. "Okay, okay...*boyfriend*. I mean, he did call twice yesterday, even after you practically kicked him out of the car at a rolling stop. You could've at least called the guy back."

"Shut-up." She rummaged through her purse for her travel-size ibuprofen bottle, then tapped four tablets into her palm. A quick search of the unmarked left her frustrated for lack of anything to wash them down with.

Bridgeman lifted his chin at the glove box.

Squinting against the light as she slid her sunglasses atop her head, she retrieved a half-empty water bottle. She scrunched her nose. "How long has this been in here?"

He pulled the corners of his mouth and shoulders together in a shrug.

She flung her purse to the floor, swallowed the ibuprofen with the warm, stale liquid, then quick-shuddered. "*Ack!* When are we meeting up with this witness? Do we have time to grab a drink?"

He checked his watch. "She shoulda been here already. It's past noon."

"Great. Now we have to track her down." She yanked her seatbelt across her shoulder and waist.

"Hold up. Let's give her a little more time. Maybe she's spooked."

She opened her hand. The belt self-retracted with a zip. "So, we sit here all day? The sun's killing me. And I'm starving."

"You know what they say about patience."

A single, painful jerk of her head caused her sunglasses to fall forward into near-perfect position.

He turned around in his seat, scanned the street, then righted himself and eyeballed his mirrors. "If she's not here in ten, we'll go."

"Deal. Now go grab us something cold to drink before I need your towels."

He peered beneath the visor at a camera shop three doors down. "See that? We can drop that film off while we wait."

Ten minutes came and went. Their witness never showed. Bridgeman radioed the station and let dispatch know they would canvass the area to see if they could locate her or anyone else who might have seen something around the time of the murder.

As they awaited their photos, he procured two iced sodas, two bottled waters, and three hot dogs from the vendor. He balanced the order in his hands, signaling with a dip of his head for Alvarez to help with the drinks.

Her door would not open. With an innocent simper, she raised her hands. "Guess you shouldn't have rigged the door, huh?"

He teetered and shifted his way around to the driver's side, set the majority of his armful on the roof of the car, then handed the drinks in two at a time. Alvarez had downed the first water bottle before he settled in with the food.

Inside, he turned and asked, "You want a wiener today, partner?"

"No, thanks. I need something a little more substantial today."

"Had your fill of wiener, eh?"

"Shut-up," she replied automatically. "I can't wait forever for you to act like an adult long enough for me to tell you what I got from Macy."

Bridgeman coughed, nearly choking on his dog.

She shot him a look of patient irritation. "In late January of last year, Stark sent a fax and made a six-minute call to Jameson Lockhardt in New York City. A month before that, Macy had published that séance article about Farin Grant."

His forehead creased. He flattened his lips to speak around a cheekful of food. "You sure?"

"Yep. The idiot used his desk phone and the station's fax machine. Stupid, but ballsy. Anyway, less than two months later, he made *another* call to Lockhardt—only thirty seconds. Probably left a message. The next day, he was dead."

Bridgeman slurped his soda. "It's thin. Circumstantial at best, but it does tie Stark to Lockhardt. Interesting."

"Especially when our vic was murdered at the son's place."

He ran his tongue along his top teeth. "Then there's the evidence from the limousine. I don't know. Something's missing."

They sat in silence while he finished his pre-lunch snack. Foregoing their normal quasi-flirtatious banter, she reached across and disabled the door lock. She gathered up her trash and dumped it in a nearby waste receptacle, then bought four additional water bottles from the vendor.

Back in the vehicle, she did not comment when he re-triggered the lock. She placed two of the bottles in the vehicle's cup holders, opened the third and drank half its contents, capped it, and set it between her legs. The fourth she pressed against her face, alternating between her cheeks, forehead, and neck.

Bridgeman finished his dogs, then swiped away crumbs from his lap. "So back to the matter at hand. I trust you didn't reveal anything you shouldn't have when Macy probed you the other night?"

She dropped her head back, rolling it side-to-side against the headrest. "Shut-up."

"You know, it's okay to be a woman, Al. You're sorta impossible to mistake for a guy anyway. And as guys go, you could do worse. Macy's kinda good looking in a hinky sort of way. And if you don't mind his ego, which apparently you don't…"

"If you like him so much, why don't *you* date him?"

His eyes brightened over a huge smile. "Oh-*ho*! I was right!"

"Actually, you're wrong. He left two messages. In the first, he left his hotel and room number. The second, he asked me to dinner. I didn't call him back. Hopefully, he got the hint."

"I dunno. It might not be that easy. Don't forget your little sleepover."

"Didn't I tell you to shut up? I distinctly remember telling you to shut up."

His expression turned sincere. "I like him is all. Something tells me he'd be good for you."

She pressed her water bottle compress to her forehead. "Too bad."

Bridgeman gave up and headed back to the camera shop.

Hours later, they returned to the station without a witness statement, but armed with Bridgeman's photos and copies of the phone records from Macy. When they stepped out of the elevator, their peers noticed their arrival.

A handful of officers stopped mid-task to applaud, whistle, cheer, and catcall. The closer they got to their desks, the more insistent the jeers and hoots became. Then, they saw Alicia's desk.

Bridgeman nudged her with his elbow. "See? He's a good guy."

Atop her desk sat the most audacious arrangement of flowers she had ever seen outside a funeral home. The card, long since opened and passed around the department, surely said something she would find eternally embarrassing. She covered her face with her hands.

He leaned in and whispered, "Should I go get the towels?"

"Shut-up."

***

The killer had grown bored with the chase days ago. Unchallenging. Little risk. His target obviously traveled by car. Based on his primitive investigative skills, he narrowed down the vehicle's identification to one of two possibilities: they were in an older model silver sedan, either a Buick or an Oldsmobile, with California plates. In Amarillo, he had lost the trail.

They were likely headed back to Los Angeles and might have turned off Highway 40 somewhere in Arizona. He drove to the state line and waited. And waited. Then waited some more.

The delay in North Carolina had cost him time, so he had caught a flight from Raleigh to Oklahoma City. From there, he had hit the open road. He figured he had made better time than they could have. Eventually, they would have to pass him. So, he continued to wait.

When sufficient time had passed, he guessed they had either switched routes or stopped somewhere. He back-tracked along Highway 40 through Arizona, one of his least-favorite states. At night, Arizona looked like what people saw when they closed their eyes.

He stopped at each gas station along the highway. Questioned every convenience store clerk. "I got separated from my sister-in-law. Have you seen an older silver four-door Buick with California plates drive through? We were supposed to meet here."

Just before the Yucca exit, his pager beeped. He took the exit and pulled up to the self-serve pump at a gas station. He strolled over to the payphone and returned the call. "You paged?"

"We have a priority request from one of our customers. It just came in."

"I'm already on a delivery." Unprofessional. This disappointed him. He had thought he had trained his staff better. Then, it struck him. "Or is it the same customer?"

"It is."

Odd. Odd and unsettling. Working with Lockhardt had grown chaotic lately. "The same customer who requested a delivery to North Carolina and left me a mess to clean up? The same customer who apparently thinks we run a tracking operation and not a delivery service?"

"That's him. Do we need to re-educate the client on company policy?"

Good idea. And more in-line with his expectations of his employees. "Yes. And if—*when*—he calls back, refuse his order. Tell him I'll need to speak with him personally before we initiate any future transactions."

"Understood."

"Have you obligated us to fulfill this new delivery?"

A concerning pause followed. "I'm sorry. I was unaware of your position on this matter at the time I took the call."

"What's the order?"

"The customer requests an unrelated delivery to New York. It sounded urgent, so I charged him double the processing fee. He's pre-paid."

He checked his watch. "I'm about two hours out of Vegas. Have the tickets waiting at the counter. I'll call back for the details."

"Right away."

He replaced the receiver and went to fill up the car.

Had he bothered to ask the attendant if she saw the car he sought, she could have told him about a couple who had used the same payphone and filled the tank of a silver Olds with California plates just the other night. In fact, she could have told him the car was still parked in front of the shabby motel down the road. It had been there when she drove into work. She remembered because it was dirty, with litter scattered around by its trunk.

But he never asked. He paid for his gasoline and a pack of chewing gum, then drove off, heading to Vegas to catch his flight to New York.

CHAPTER 25

I VY SANK ONTO THE SOFA, stupefied. Slack-jawed, eyes fixed and faraway...and most noticeably, silent. Lance had never encountered a speechless Ivy Spencer. Still, he had warned her. At least she would not have to wonder anymore—though she would have one less topic over which to start a row.

"It's all right, sweetheart." He sat beside her, encircling her in a supportive embrace. "This doesn't change anything."

She neither moved nor spoke. The results of the DNA test slid from her hand onto the carpet.

Their entire relationship, Lance had led Ivy down an uncertain path to an even more uncertain destination. He had never even said he loved her, though he did. Emotional tirades notwithstanding, he went about his business, happy to have her beside him, offering no commitment, no hint whether he intended to make their relationship permanent. He had given her nothing.

"I'm not leaving you," he assured with a squeeze. He nudged her head down to rest on his shoulder.

She moved clear of the embrace. "There's something I have to tell you."

He scooted closer.

She backed farther away.

"Don't be like that. C'mere. Everything will be okay." He reached for her.

She pouted, peering up at him with downturned eyes. "You don't understand."

Maybe their differences were a bigger deal than he realized. Ivy was young and inexperienced. Largely unschooled. Naïve. Overbearing. Plus, she did not particularly fancy music. When they met, not only had she not recognized him, she had never heard of him. She knew of Mirage and had heard a couple of their songs, but she would not have been able to pick any one of its members out in a lineup.

None of this bothered Lance, though. If anything, it endeared her to him. It quashed the usual pressure to play the rock star role to a would-be love interest. Besides, they had more in common than one might think. They both liked sports, fast cars, and the occasional night at home with a bowl of buttery popcorn and a case of ale.

"You'll hate me," Ivy insisted. "I know you will."

"It doesn't matter to me. It's the past. We'd just started seeing each other."

"That's not it," she insisted, tears spilling down her cheeks.

Lance patted her knee, then went to track down a box of tissues. When he returned, Ivy was wiping her tears with the back of her hand, searching for her purse, which she had flung carelessly across the room upon her arrival in her haste to open the test results.

"What are you doing?" He went to her, hand outstretched, offering the tissue box.

She shouldered past him, located her bag, and headed for the door. "I'm going home."

"Don't go."

"I can't stay."

"Why not? I'm not upset. Why should you be?"

"I bloody told you. You won't understand."

He grabbed her hand and wrestled her back to the sofa. "Don't run away. We need to talk this out for once. I hate seeing you like this, sweetheart."

As usual, her mind was not easily changed. It took several minutes of drying tears and reassuring her he would not get mad. Finally, she confessed the reason for her anxiety and the story behind Colin's conception.

"I'd gone 'round to the Milk Bar with Rachel, you see..."

"I thought you and Rachel had a row and didn't speak anymore."

"You'll see."

He settled into the sofa, hooking a foot under his thigh.

Ivy sucked her bottom lip. "You were in Germany with your band. I was home with Mum and Dad, feeling bored and sad and missing you. Rachel thought a right knees-up would put me right. I didn't wanna go. I wanted to stay home in case you rang. But I guess I went anyway."

The subtle deflection of accountability amused him. When the corner of his mouth hitched up in response, she continued, less apprehensive. Her sad, doe-like eyes flickered with guilt and excitement. She touched his upper arm with both hands. "Oh, Lance, it's the mutt's! Have you ever been?"

"Once, I think. Before we met. Loud, if I remember. Posh."

"It *is*! Rachel knew this bloke who got us in. Anyway, we were drinking and dancing. I went for a fag and on the way back in, this bloke asked to buy me a pint."

Lance felt his cheeks warm. His jaw tightened. "You don't need to do this, love—"

"Oh, I didn't fancy him or anything. I mean, not at first. He was quite shy, actually. But he sat with us and kept buying more drinks. I don't remember how it came up, but he said *he'd* been in a band once, and that made me think of you. I told him my boyfriend was in a band and was on tour. We couldn't belt him up after that. On the pull, of course, but I guess I had a few too many and..."

"I get it, Ivy. You met, got rat arsed, and then ended up at his place for a bit of the old how's your father." He stood and stretched, realizing he had snapped at her and probably needed a break. "Fancy a drink?"

She nodded, quieted by his reaction.

Lance went to the kitchen and returned with two fizzy drinks, handing her one. Before engaging the pull tab, he decided he was not thirsty after all. He sat the unopened can on an end table.

"I'm sorry."

He touched her cheek. "I told you. It doesn't matter. I'm just glad you're safe. He could've been bloody Charles Manson."

She scrunched her mouth to one side. "He took me home."

Lance fought to remain impassive. Nonchalant. To hide the anger he had sworn did not exist. And he was not angry, really. At least not at her.

"You see," she said, fidgeting with her own unopened can, "at some point, I guess Rachel left. I wanted to go, but she'd left me there with this stranger. I had no way to get home, so he offered to drive me. I didn't have another choice, did I?"

"Is this why you and Rachel stopped talking?"

She lunged forward, hand on his forearm. "*Yes!* That's it exactly! Anyway, I snuck him out before my parents got up in the morning. I never saw him again. You came back. Things went back to normal."

"And you found out you were pregnant."

Tears welled in her eyes. She collapsed into his chest, sobbing. "I don't even remember his name! I'm a complete tart."

Her melodramatic self-loathing eased the sting of his wounded pride.

Despite himself, he chuckled. "You're not a tart. Not a complete one, anyway."

"Am too. I don't even deserve Colin, let alone you."

He lifted her chin, contemplating her blotchy swollen face. He had always been curious, but had never asked about the pregnancy. Maybe he should feel betrayed, but he did not. It was over. She had been faithful to him since. Why end the relationship for it?

Ivy let him comfort her, then stood up again and walked to the door. "Okay. You know now. I'm going."

He hopped up and followed behind. "So, you tell me you cheated on me and then you leave? That's not very nice, is it?"

She faced him, unamused. "I knew you wouldn't understand."

"Of course I understand!"

"Why are you laughing at me?" She rubbed the moisture from her eyes.

"Because you're barmy. I meant what I said, you daft cow. I don't care. I knew Colin didn't belong to me. I said it'd be okay."

"You'll use it as an excuse to go to America and have another go with your band."

"We all said no. Mirage is through. Besides, you said you wouldn't let me go, remember?"

He had talked with Samantha several times over the last couple of months. She confessed that her inability to arrange a reunion, even for one night, was a personal failure. It struck Lance as odd, given the band's history, that it mattered so much to her. Sam and Bobby had earned much of their experience untangling the various messes Mirage got themselves into—particularly Faith.

During their last European tour, they had played Amsterdam. After the show, Faith had gotten wasted and hit the city center's Red-Light District. She had harassed the tourists bustling about the streets of De Wallen, flashing her breasts, kissing everyone in sight—men and women—and snorting an obscene quantity of cocaine in addition to partaking in the local cannabis offerings. When authorities attempted to sort the situation, she slugged two of them before they could contain her.

Since then, they had matured. Getting the sack from LSI had sobered the lot of them. It had taught him not to get upset about things. Even the situation with little Colin did not ruffle his feathers. Much.

Ivy's guilt-fueled emotions slowly subsided. She stayed for dinner and a video, and even helped cook, which Lance appreciated.

As they cuddled together on the sofa later that evening, he was relieved to have finally dealt with the paternity issue. Not so much for his sake, but for Ivy's. Now, he could finalize some decisions he had made. He had wanted to take a more active role in Colin's life, but had hesitated, wondering if the real father would turn up to exercise his parental rights. Now, Lance was confident it would not happen.

"Ivy?"

"Shh," she scolded. She stuffed her mouth with a handful of popcorn. "This is the best part."

He waited until the movie ended, distracted by a flipping stomach and a constricting throat. Was he nervous? Impossible. He had not felt nervous since his first time on stage. Yet now, he struggled to remember what video they had picked out. What if she quizzed him later on the details?

His own father had never been engaged. He had grown up without much of a home at all. His mother worked three jobs keeping him and his brother in clothes and food. He grew up wanting more. He had worked hard for more. Now, he had it in spades.

He toyed with the idea of making a life with Ivy. It might be fun sharing a flat and watching Colin grow. Despite his career, Lance figured he could be a stable influence on the boy. His money would provide everything they needed, and he would never leave Colin the way Lance's father had left his mother.

But could he commit? He had never looked after anyone other than himself. In fact, he rarely did that. No one had ever relied on him.

"We need to talk about Colin," he said as they gathered up their popcorn bowl, soda cans, and napkins. "He needs a father."

"And you're volunteering?" Ivy walked to the kitchen, dismissing the statement out of hand.

"Yes."

She spun around. "Don't bloody do this."

"Just hear me out."

"You don't understand."

"*That* again?" He advanced, taking the empty soda cans from her and holding her hands. "You said that before and look what happened. It got sorted, didn't it?"

"There's more," she pouted sorrowfully.

"What could possibly be any worse?"

"It's not that it's worse. It's just...*more*."

He studied her. Something was definitely wrong. It dawned on him she had not yelled at him all day. "What else could there possibly be?"

She raised her chin at him. "First, let me ask you if you're sure—*really sure*—about becoming Colin's dad."

"I love him, Ivy. I love you both."

Her narrowed eyes widened. "You do?"

He nodded.

She flew into his arms. "You do?"

"I do. I always have. Ever since we met."

"That long?" She buried her head in his chest, smiling.

He stroked her spiked hair. "That long."

"Cheeky bastard," she whispered, play-slapping his arm. "And you really want to be Colin's dad?"

"Are you daft? I've said it a hundred times."

Ivy peered up at him. "I'm pregnant."

***

Bobby Lockhardt rarely traveled on public airlines. Even his first-class accommodations on his return flight from Missouri made a poor substitute for the personal Lockhardt jet. Nonetheless, he stepped off the 767 at La Guardia that morning in high spirits. He whistled his way to Baggage Claim, jiggling the change in his pocket. It was a good day. A beautiful day. Not only had he returned to New York after four weeks on the road, he had returned a success.

His driver parked curbside. As he exited the car and hustled for the sliding doors, Bobby waved him off, signaling he would get his own luggage.

When the baggage carousel spit out his two large, leather suitcases, he grabbed them and headed out into the frigid mid-February afternoon, eager to return to the office.

His dad had ducked out of their scouting trip early on. It was as if fate had intervened. Though initially unsure of himself, he soon acclimated to his new role.

The trip had given him perspective. He now understood what LSI meant to his father, and to himself. For the first time since receiving the news of his father's impending retirement, it sunk in. By this time next year, the company would be his, lock, stock, and barrel.

From there, the trip had adopted a deeper purpose. He found a rock'n'roll band in Salem, Oregon that was out of sight. It would fill the void left by Mirage. Combing the Pacific Northwest, he found solo acts and bands so plentiful, it was as if the heavens had parted to reveal an enormous sea of talent created expressly for LSI. Alternative rock was his favorite, though he knew Lockhardt Sound needed to broaden their list with hip-hop, reggae, and grunge. Time to bring the label into the future.

On the last leg of the trip, he stopped off in Branson, Missouri. There, playing in a coffeehouse for tips alone, Bobby discovered the most incredible female talent he had heard in years: Charlene Johnson.

Charlene Johnson. Okay. So, the name did not pack much of a punch, but those things were easily changed. *Charlene Johnson*—a golden-haired goddess with violet eyes and a voice to make angels weep. Even better, she wrote her own songs. Hers was a sultry yet innocent vibe. By some miracle, he was the first to stumble upon this untapped gold mine.

His driver loaded his luggage as Bobby climbed inside his limousine. He unbuttoned his suit jacket and loosened his tie, exhausted and content as he relaxed into his seat.

Yes indeed, Charlene Johnson. For three days now, her image had lingered in the forefront of his mind. Young. Probably no more than twenty-one, though he had been so mesmerized, he had neglected to ask. Her skin glowed like a full moon reflecting the sunlight. Charlene. The crest of LSI's new wave of hit makers. And he had found her.

"Where to?" his driver asked. "Home or straight to the office?"

"No rest for the weary, Jack."

The driver nodded, checked his mirrors, then pulled away from the curb. "The office it is. Welcome back, Mr. Lockhardt."

As the limo navigated congested traffic into Manhattan, Bobby indulged himself a moment to reflect on LSI's better days. He had not coveted a position as one of its central figures. His father had Ross and, later, Samantha spearheading the company's success. Bobby had been content at the heart of the operation: the publicity department.

Over time, he had learned the industry's ins and outs. What worked, what did not. What attracted promoters. What sold records. Bobby studied the trade and developed his own recipe for success. Only once, and briefly, had his career path veered off course.

"Traffic's not too bad," Jack said over his shoulder. "After I drop you off, I can take your bags on over to your place if you like."

"Sounds good, buddy. Thanks."

Bobby reached inside his suit jacket for his wallet. He retrieved a tattered, proof copy of an old publicity photo he had saved. So beautiful. So talented. Even Charlene Johnson could not match the fire Farin lit in a crowd. Despite her short career, she had become the single most successful female artist LSI ever had.

Farin. The last night they saw each other remained a blur. All he knew was that he had fallen in love with his best friend. He had stopped taking his Haldol—the drug that had ensured his sanity in exchange for his manhood—in the hope she might one day love him back.

"Any plans this weekend, sir?"

"Happily, not a-one." He tucked the picture back into his wallet and his wallet back into his suit pocket. He stared out the window as they motored past pedestrians bustling about the New York sidewalks. "I'd hoped to make it to the game tonight but I think I'll just stay in and relax."

"Passing up a Knicks game?"

Bobby laughed. "I forgot who I was talking to."

"It sure is a shame to waste box seats. They're playing Miami tonight."

His smile faded. "Miami, huh?"

"Yes, siree."

The limo pulled up to the curb outside the LSI building.

Jack hit the hazard lights, exited the vehicle, and jogged around to open Bobby's door. "I'll get that luggage to your place right away. Don't work too late."

Bobby stepped out and buttoned his jacket. He leaned back in to grab his briefcase, but Jack beat him to it. Bobby thanked him and headed for the lobby. Before reaching the entrance, he doubled back, just in time to see Jack pull away from the curb.

He waved his arms and whistled loudly through his teeth. "Jack!"

The vehicle stopped abruptly. Its reverse lights blinked on. Amidst a cacophony of horns blaring in protest, the limo backed up. Jack rolled down his window, stuck his arm out, and waved them on. He then rolled down the front passenger window and leaned across the seat. "Forget something?"

Bobby braced his knee against the door, balancing his briefcase on top. A quick search yielded the desired results. He snapped the case closed, straightened his jacket, and handed Jack an envelope.

"What's this?" When the man looked inside, his jaw dropped in amazement. "Are you kidding me?"

Bobby reached in and patted his shoulder. "You're right. It'd be a shame to waste box seats. Have a great time."

***

Ross was just heading into his office when Bobby stepped off the elevator. He acknowledged him with a passing chin lift but continued at pace. The day had dragged on. He was in no mood to socialize.

"Wait up!" Bobby called, jogging casually inside.

"Welcome back." His lack of enthusiasm was evident as he closed the door behind them, but no matter. He gestured toward a chair. "How was the trip?"

"Productive! I found some amazing talent."

"Wonderful. I'm sure A-n-R will be sweating bullets."

"Maybe they should. There's a lot of low-hanging fruit out there. But yeah, it's wonderful. Better than wonderful—you'll see. How are things around here? Dad seemed strange when he bailed on me back in Cali. Everything okay?"

Ross lowered himself into his desk chair. "You know your father. He's concerned about turning LSI around before November. Other than that, things are fine."

Bobby's features overflowed with a confidence that demanded Ross's attention. "I can handle LSI. I can handle my dad's reservations, too. For now...how's our little safety net?"

"We're leaving that in place until we've had a good four or five quarters in a row. And not just by cooking the books. Real ones."

"Right, good. Smart move—not that we'll need it. Not after this trip."

Ross had mixed feelings about Bobby's knowledge of Double Maguffin. Of course, it might not matter much longer. Their short-term solution to imminent bankruptcy sat mostly dormant, save the occasional stock buy when the market dictated. Jameson had recently directed Ross to liquidate it. Out of an abundance of caution, Ross had waited.

Bobby plucked a lint ball from his trousers. "We haven't discussed it before, but have you given any thought to Dad's retirement party?"

"Party? To be honest, it hasn't been on my radar."

"I want it to be special. The guest list should be an industry who's who. Dad's contemporaries should all be there to wish him well."

"Of course."

"And I want the LSI employees there as well. Think there's any chance we can surprise him?"

He drummed his fingers against his armrest, lips puckered, and gave the question due consideration. "It'll be a challenge, to say the least. Not much goes unnoticed with him."

Bobby stood to leave. "We'll figure something out. Something big. In the meantime, can you start working on the contracts for our new acts? We need them in studio asap."

Ross contemplated the animated figure of LSI's anointed king. Bobby stood proud and confident, determined to usher his kingdom into its next era of prosperity. Until this moment, Ross had not realized his own plans might alter the boy's course. Bobby's fervor nearly caused him to rethink his decision.

With an outstretched hand, he indicated Bobby's vacated chair. "We, uh...we should probably have a talk before I do that, son."

Bobby turned a sober eye his way. "Something's obviously eating you—something serious, I'd bet. I saw it when I got off the elevator. What's up?"

"It's about my position here at LSI."

Bobby sat back down, his concern dissolving into a hearty laugh. "Is that what this is? Are you afraid I won't want you here after Dad's gone? Because I can promise you—"

Ross raised two fingers. "That's not it at all. The problem's me."

"You?"

"I'll be leaving in November along with your father."

Bobby stared at him, blinking.

"I'm sixty-eight, son. Just as your dad's ready to retire, so am I."

Bobby threaded his fingers through his slicked-back hair. "I don't know what to say, Ross. Dad leaving is one thing, but you?"

"I thought you should know in advance so we can find you a replacement. Someone you can trust. We should start looking right away so I'll have ample time to get them up to speed."

Bobby rose and squared his shoulders. For a fleeting moment, Ross saw a younger Jameson Lockhardt before him, extending a cordial, if professionally distant, hand. Never before this moment had Ross realized how much Bobby resembled his father.

"You've always been there for Dad," Bobby said. "And for LSI—hell, for *me*. I respect your decision. We'll appreciate your input as we identify someone to take your place—not that anyone could."

Ross accepted the handshake with a curt nod, then watched Bobby leave, closing the door behind him. He had neglected to mention that, whoever they tapped to replace him, it had better happen fast.

He emailed Bobby several boilerplate contracts, hoping the lad would not request too many changes. For the final hour of his day, he returned calls.

At 4 PM, he realized he had not heard from his bride all day. He picked up his phone to call home, then remembered Josephine saying she had volunteered to help plan their church's Easter program and would not be home early enough to cook. They had made dinner reservations for the Chateau Hathorne, where they would meet at eight.

On a whim, Ross cleared his desk and powered down his computer. Eight o'clock was too long to wait. If he left now, he could make it home and shower before heading over to the Warwick establishment. He needed to spend every possible remaining moment with his bride before Jameson exacted his pound of flesh.

Before heading out, he jotted down some notes about the party Bobby had mentioned. No sense leaving any loose ends. It would be Jameson's last triumph to hand over the reins of the company to his only son. The boy deserved his support to ensure a memorable event.

Too bad I won't be there to see it myself.

***

Breaking into the Alexanders' Greenwood Lake home had been simple. Disappointingly so. He had taken his time, ensuring neither the target nor the spouse were home. In the end, his extreme caution was unnecessary. Their sophisticated alarm system, though connected and to all appearances in working order, had not been activated. He sprung the basement window and slipped inside, wiping it down and securing it behind him.

Careless.

Standing in the basement next to the water heater, across from a washer and dryer—all gas operated—he evaluated his options. Making a diesel explosion look like an accident required more effort, but had presented less of a hands-on strategy. He preferred the personal touch. His work had become so boring.

He stripped to his socks, tied his boot strings together and slung them over his shoulder, then slipped on a second pair of latex surgical gloves. Soundlessly, he crept up the basement stairs and into the kitchen. He searched the counters, cupboards, drawers, and pantry for anything the target might use for defense, tucking the information away in case things went awry.

A thorough search of the downstairs yielded nothing more threatening than kitchen knives, an ice pick, and a fireplace poker. Upstairs, he performed a similar sweep. In the master bedroom, inside the bedside table drawer next to a King James Bible, he found the gun. He admired the ungainly revolver, a nickel-plated Smith & Wesson .357 magnum long barrel, as he unloaded it. *Very nice*, he thought, stuffing the rounds into his pocket.

After a thirty-minute search revealed nothing of note, he crawled under the bed in the guest room to wait. Jet lagged from the recent uptick in travel, the soft carpet and quiet darkness lulled him to sleep.

Car tires crunching the gravel driveway forced his mind awake. Headlights flashed in the misty dusk, skimming the room's curtains like a fleeing specter. He would need to ensure the proper party had returned—alone. Killing the spouse would not only complicate matters, it would be messy. Besides, he had already given Lockhardt one freebie.

The garage door opened and closed, followed by the sound of footsteps ascending the stairs. Though hidden beneath the bed, he scooched farther from the door to ensure a triggered light switch would not expose him.

As the owner approached the master bedroom, he positively identified his mark. Strolling on elderly legs into the bathroom, the target engaged the shower.

He slipped out from under the bed and set his boots atop his clothes. On sock-clad feet, he crouched outside the bathroom door. He tried the knob. As predicted, the mark had neglected to lock the bathroom door.

In the end, the job turned out to be a snap—specifically, a snap of the neck. He left the water running and adjusted the corpse just so. It took him twenty minutes to leave the scene, ensuring everything was as he had found it and he had not left behind so much as a fingerprint or strand of his hair.

CHAPTER 26

WHEN FARIN BLINKED OPENED HER eyes, the absence of beeping machinery disoriented her. There was no faint humming of halogen lighting. No smell of pungent bleach. The bare walls, naked windows, and empty closet were familiar. The rest made no sense.

Then, she remembered. Again. She was safe.

Daylight streamed in through ocean-sprayed windows on the west side of the room. Had she the strength to stand, the Pacific Ocean waited for her like an old friend on the other side. If only she could move unassisted more than a few painful inches at a time. If only she could remember.

At one time, Jordan's belongings had occupied its enormous space. Now, only two plastic chairs and a lonely twin mattress next to the master bath filled the otherwise abandoned room. It made her feel tiny, insignificant.

Beside the bed she had convalesced in since her arrival three weeks ago stood an IV pole. Its pliable plastic tubing ran from the clear saline bag to the needle piercing her right forearm. Though Marci had explained, she did not remember arriving.

When the bedroom door opened, she tensed and jerked her head, still unsure why every unexpected sound or movement caused the automatic reaction. "Dr. Maxwell," she greeted weakly, her atrophied muscles relaxing as the physician approached her. "What time is it?"

"Just before eight." He dragged aside the plastic chair between them to kneel down on one knee. From his bag, he retrieved a stethoscope, which he swung around his neck. Mindful of the IV tubing, he hop-scooted forward, sliding his arm behind her to help her into a sitting position.

"Don't worry about a schedule," he said, his dark eyes staring into nothing as he positioned, then repositioned, his stethoscope onto several locations on her chest and back. "Right now, you need your rest. We've been working you pretty hard the last couple of days. Muscle spasms still giving you trouble?"

She nodded. "But I want to try and walk again today. I think I can do it."

Ethan took her wrist, felt along for, then pressed her radial artery, and stared at his watch. "All in good time. Let's not push it."

He lifted her chin and flashed his penlight into her eyes, then squeezed her fingernails and studied her nail bed to check her circulation. Finally, he eased her back down to palpate her abdomen for signs of tenderness or pain. Her intestines had remained empty so long, solid food challenged her system. When he felt her lower abdomen, she shut her eyes and grimaced.

"Still painful I see. I wish we could do some more thorough tests." He returned his stethoscope to his bag, then patted her hand.

"What's wrong with me?"

He sat down in the previously-relocated chair. "The good news is, the blood work I smuggled into our lab looked better than I'd expected, what with the long-term Thorazine use. Once you're a little stronger, I'll figure out a way to do more comprehensive tests. I'd like a CT and ultrasound. But enough of the physical. How are you doing otherwise? Have you remembered anything?"

"I'm trying, but..." She glanced over at the untenanted master bath. A point of reality. The bathroom existed. The bedroom existed. She knew this. Marci and Dr. Maxwell were real. The rest she refused to believe.

"We're about finished weaning you off the Thorazine."

"Will I get my memory back?"

Her mind would not allow her to accept Jordan's death, even though she had witnessed his murder just days ago. *No*—she corrected herself for the thousandth time—*three years*. More than three years had elapsed since that awful day. "I don't even remember leaving Bobby's house after..."

For days, Dr. Maxwell had given her just enough medication to prevent her from going into shock over the bloody scene she had witnessed. *Jordan, what will I do without you?*

"Memory loss is a funny thing, Farin. I've studied the chart notes Marci took, but still can't definitively determine when you started taking it. My guess would be roughly two years. That could result in memory loss. But coupled with the trauma of everything else, who knows? That may play an even more significant role. We'll have to wait and see." He rested a hand on her arm. She flinched at the gesture but did not jerk away at the contact like usual. "Should I get you something to calm your nerves?"

She declined the offer and struggled to sit up. He assisted, propping pillows behind her upper and lower back. "Is Marci here?"

"She's downstairs fixing your breakfast. Think you can eat a little for us today?"

"I don't know."

"We'll try some dry toast and weak tea. It'll help you get your strength back. Marci tells me you're fond of the ocean," he said, hitching a thumb over his shoulder toward the window. "Don't you want to take a look?"

She gazed at him with mournful eyes. "I'll try." She wanted to smile, if for no other reason in gratitude for all he was doing for her, but found her mind locked in other memories. Of laying in this room, in a king size bed. Jordan's arms encircling her as they listened to the roar of waves and watched the moonlight through beautifully-patterned curtains. Singing silly songs. Harmonizing. Telling bad jokes. Making love.

"Morning," Marci greeted as she entered the room with a tray of toast, pudding, and hot tea for two. She rested the tray next to Farin's bed, then bent to kiss her friend's cheek before sitting beside her on the floor. She looked at Ethan as she prepared the tea. "I didn't know if you wanted to join us. You'd said you'd eaten already."

Ethan grabbed his bag and headed for the door, chuckling softly. "I had a real breakfast this morning. As soon as Farin's up and around, we'll all have breakfast together somewhere. How does that sound?"

"Deal." Marci looked at her friend. "Doesn't that sound good, Farin? I bet you're dying for some bacon. You love bacon."

Farin lifted the corners of her mouth into an obligatory half-smile.

Ethan left the women alone to check his messages while they shared their mostly-dry but solid breakfast.

Farin rolled halfway onto her side, reaching out to touch Marci's stomach. "I can't believe you're pregnant."

"I was beginning to lose hope," Marci confided. "We tried for over a year." She bit into her toast. While wishing she could elaborate about her condition, she was concerned she might sound insensitive.

Ragged, uneven lesions appeared to have been carved into Farin's abdomen. They had startled Marci even more than the deep, jagged scars on her wrists, feet, knees, and ankles. She had not realized the extent of Farin's suffering when she lost Melody in France.

"I'm glad you're here," she said, her voice a whisper. "We were all so..."

Farin rested a weak hand on her arm.

She covered it with her own. "Anything yet? Any memory at all?"

With a slow shake of her head, Farin scrunched her mouth into a sad frown. "I've had this dream. It makes no sense. It's foggy and I'm driving. It feels like I'm driving forever."

Marci tilted her head. "Where to?"

"I dunno. I wanna say I was trying to find my dad."

"So, it was like..."

"No, not like the nightmares. It was more like a clue. I can't explain it. I was driving, and then I parked in some parking lot facing this gigantic pink bird. Next thing I can remember, I was walking a cement gangplank or something. I walked a long way, and then I was twirling in circles."

Marci narrowed her eyes. She strained to follow the recollection from one bizarre image to the next. Dr. Maxwell had warned that, until Farin regained her strength, they should not discuss what little they knew about the events surrounding her kidnapping. Farin still did not know Jameson had perpetrated this crime against her, or about her confinement in Dorothea Dix. Likewise, she did not remember talking to Chris at the motel in Yucca.

"Inside, the walls were water, or maybe it was a waterfall. Huge seashells and waterfalls, and then I was in a circus tent. That's all there was."

"I have no idea what any of that means."

Farin fell back onto her pillow and stared at the ceiling. "My gut tells me it means something."

"Circus tents? Waterfalls? Big birds and cement gang planks? Seashells? I don't know."

Farin reached for her tea with trembling hands. Marci placed her own hands over them, steadying them enough to take a sip.

"Dr. Maxwell says I'll be off the Thorazine tomorrow."

"That's good news. Progress."

"There's a chance I'll get my memory back, too. I need to fill these holes. And no matter what you two say, someone's going to help me start walking today."

Marci leaned in for a quick hug. "Stubborn as usual. You're getting better already."

***

For the seven hundredth time since 7:30 AM, exploding illumination blinded Julie Swanson Grant. With each "click" of Andy Pogue's Canon EOS-1N, Mylar umbrellas behind thousand-watt strobes bathed her skin, hair, and eyes in a pool of living light.

She had long since grown accustomed to the niggling ache of weary eyes following a shoot. Though she could barely make out the photographer through dazzled orbs, she took her cues as much from the distinctive high-pitched whine of the camera motor advancing the next frame as from Andy or the creative team's art director.

Ten shots per roll, dozens of rolls of high intensity color and black-and-white film captured nine wardrobe changes and fourteen products—an ambitious assignment, even by Dahrvey Cosmetic's standards. Including light tests and Polaroids, over three thousand flashes would blind and bedazzle the seasoned supermodel before the session concluded.

Click-flash! Whine. Click-flash! Whine.

Andy Pogue's studio nestled in a strip of multi-story buildings three blocks from Rodeo Drive. Inside the stucco structure sat an open space of alternating light and shadow. Its polished Brazilian cherry flooring gleamed under recessed ceiling lights, reflecting strategically displayed framed photos affixed to twenty-eight-foot walls like a living portfolio. Enormous, brightly lit murals painted on textured demising walls erected throughout the open floor plan separated the lobby from the studio's three sets, creating isolated, shimmering worlds amidst the cavernous studio.

Click-flash! Whine.

Julie enjoyed working with Andy. When Dahrvey had called to schedule the shoot for their upcoming fall line, she had immediately requested LA's most sought-after lensman. The intimate yet open-air vibe his studio exuded had salved her insecurities during their first gig together six years ago. Since that time, Andy had shot her for clients ranging from underwear to evening gowns. Today, he was the only tolerable element in her world.

Click-flash! Whine. "That's great, Jules! Gimme that pouty look again."

Gloria Monroe had dropped her off at five sharp, lingering inside long enough to discuss Dahrvey's expectations with the creative team over a shot of espresso. Julie had nibbled on sliced cantaloupe while waiting for the light tests.

Click-flash! Whine. "More eyes. That-a girl!"

She had stepped under the lights around seven thirty. Andy snapped Polaroids, the film spitting out like a spoiled child sticking out its tongue. *Click-flash! Buzz. Click-flash! Buzz.* The creative director had the crew make last-minute lighting adjustments. *Click-flash! Buzz. Click-flash!*

Buzz. Click-flash! Buzz. Click-flash! Buzz. Only then did Julie head to wardrobe and makeup, where she sat patiently before the glowing, globe-encased mirror while hair and makeup transformed her into a goddess.

Click-flash! Whine. Click-flash! Whine. Reload.

He handed the camera to his assistant, Dawn, who immediately switched it out for a loaded replacement. With swift, expert movements, she unloaded its contents, attached labels, and jotted careful notes before bagging the canned rolls of film.

Andy's voice barked authoritative yet kind direction as he focused his lens. "Okay, Jules. Black-n-white this time. I need some of that glamor stuff."

Click-flash! Whine.

The morning had passed in a flurry of changes: clothes, hairstyles, lipstick, foundation, eye shadow, mascara. From the sultry wet look of a mere towel, to more playful jeans and wispy ringlets, to consummate diva in high fashion attire and piles of perfectly pinned curls in a sophisticated updo, she wiggled, teased, and exhibited her million-dollar smile as Andy worked his magic. Dahrvey Cosmetics had paid a handsome price for her pretty face. The fall campaign they shot today would appear in the September 1995 issues of magazines like *Vogue, Cosmopolitan, Red Book, Allure, Glamour,* the *Canadian Chatelaine,* and *Harper's Bazaar.*

Click-flash! Whine.

Her looming thirty-fourth birthday agonized her. By industry standards, she was a fossil—yet the contracts kept coming in. For months, Gloria had turned down requests from companies clamoring for a piece of her hottest client. Thanks to her fresher-than-Isabella-Rossellini's face, Dahrvey now topped the cosmetics industry. Somehow, the subtle lines and imperfections had gone unnoticed...so far.

Click-flash! Whine. Click-flash! Whine. Click-flash! Whine. Click-flash! Whine. Click-flash! Whine. Click-flash! Whine.

Despite the maelstrom of her current circumstance, she smiled radiantly, the embodiment of energy and enthusiasm. She blithely tossed her hair, laughed, and batted false eyelashes for the camera. When Andy suggested Dawn turn on some music to set the tone, Julie gyrated her hips, swayed seductively, and raised her arms in the air as carefree as a teenager while she sang along to Sheryl Crow's "All I Wanna Do."

Click-flash! Whine. Click-flash! Whine. Reload.

But inwardly, she roiled.

Her mind pulsated with cached loathing. It had grown into a living force, ascending red, thick, and hot from the depths of her wounded psyche. Anger filled her insides as completely as flashing strobes bathed her outside.

Click-flash! Whine. Click-flash! Whine. Click-flash! Whine.

Since his heroic cross-country quest, Chris had made love to her exactly once: the night he and Sam's fiancé had settled Lady Lazarus and her pregnant nursemaid into their otherwise unoccupied Malibu beach house. In her frenzied desperation to affirm their intimacy, she had pleasured him in ways that could set a new standard for the art of passion. Even her world-renowned philandering husband seemed stunned as she swept over him in fluid movements, devouring every inch of his body.

Click-flash! Whine. "Stay with me, Jules!" *Click-flash! Whine.*

The next day, he had announced the next few weeks would be busy ones. *Aftermath*'s summer tour preparations were in full swing. He had to make up the commitments his handlers had pushed while he was away. And soon, he would need to get back into the studio to start recording his next album.

Click-flash! Whine. Click-flash! Whine.

It was all very convenient.

Click-flash! Whine. Click-flash! Whine. Click-flash! Whine. Reload.

"So, Jules." Andy slid half his posterior onto a bar stool while waiting for Dawn to reload the three cameras he had chosen for the shoot. "What about that Victoria's Secret gig coming up in June? You in on that? I've been trading voicemails with their agency for a week."

Julie gathered the folds of her dress and dropped down heavily on the hard wooden floor. "I'm booked through the end of the year." She deliberately dismissed the first thought that came to mind. "I've got a friend over there, though. I could give her a call if you want."

"That'd be great. I'd appreciate it," he said in earnest. "I'm thinking of expanding. Adding a few more employees. Competition's tough these days, you know?"

The corners of her red-tinted lips rose painfully into a passable smile. *Yes, I know all about competition.*

He hopped off the stool, thanked Dawn for the loaded camera, and waved Julie over. "Great! Let's continue, shall we?"

As the creative director cooed and vocalized his approval of each pose she struck, she studied her photographer between intermittent flashes of light. Andy had a nice face. An inconspicuously handsome type. Probably a few years older than she. Long, strong fingers and a marvelous physique. He wore his shoulder length brown hair fastened in a ponytail. Casual, trendy attire.

Click-flash! Whine. Click-flash! Whine.

Most photographers she had worked with were gay, but she had seen Andy with a handful of women over the years, if that meant anything. Julie wondered what he was like in bed. The notion played itself out in her mind as she moved to the music, the camera shutter, and encouraging calls from the creative team. Never had she strayed in her marriage. Not even in the privacy of her mind. She doubted Chris could say the same.

Click-flash! Whine. Click-flash! Whine.

"I'll give the agency a call when I get home," she promised, her eyes fierce and intent as she lowered herself onto the floor. She stretched her torso, then dipped her chin low and to the side.

Andy nodded from behind the lens. *Click-flash! Whine.* "Thanks. Don't lose your neck now. That's it. Oh yes, beautiful!" *Click-flash! Whine. Click-flash! Whine. Click-flash! Whine.* "Didn't you say Chris was coming by to get you this afternoon?"

Her eyes narrowed into a seductive arch as she rose from the floor to shift her pose, tossing her head into place as the lights popped and flickered. "Oh, Andy," she purred. "Why do you ask?"

Click-flash! Whine. "Please." He laughed off the innuendo, one eye peering through the lens, the other fused shut, as he snapped the last frame.

Click-flash! Whine. Without changing his stance, he brought a newly loaded camera to his eye and continued, his movements fluid and purposeful.

Click-flash! Whine. Click-flash! Whine.

Julie painted on her most dazzling smile. She cocked her head to the side. "You know you don't have to beg."

Click-flash! Whine.

"Give me a break." He laughed again, continuing without pause. "How long have we known each other? And how long have I known Chris? He'd kill me if I got anywhere near you. I don't have that kind of insurance, babe."

Click-flash! Whine. Click-flash! Whine.

"Are you going to tell me, Andy Pogue, that in all the time we've known each other, you've never even been...curious?" She shot him a playful pout as she twirled and then froze, her gown spiraling in wispy elegance around her hips, thighs, and legs.

Click-flash! Whine. Click-flash! Whine.

He lowered his camera, his handsome smile transforming into a sideways frown. A flash of discomfort skirted his features as he eyeballed the dozen or so other people loitering on the otherwise closed set. "You okay there, Jules?"

She exaggerated a coy shrug. "I was just playing, silly."

His eyes twinkled with amusement or relief—she could not tell which. He raised his camera into position. "Okay, gimme some cleavage." *Click-flash! Whine. Click-flash! Whine. Click-flash! Whine.* Reload.

When they broke for lunch, Julie pouted in her dressing room instead of partaking in the sandwiches and snacks ordered in from a local deli. In a few short months, her lovely, flat stomach would protrude from her svelte figure. No more swimsuit spreads, no more strapless evening gowns. No more work, period. The thought of her breasts swelling, then sagging, terrified her.

At least the universe had spared her the suffering of morning sickness. When Chris had relayed his account of Marci's ordeal during their trip, she barely contained a sadistic snicker. Better Marci than her.

She had tried and failed to change her mind about procreating. Since the day Chris had walked out to fetch his lost love, she detested everything about pregnancy—hers or anyone else's. And her promise to Cheryl to tell Chris the moment she saw him? That time had come and gone.

The afternoon dragged. The final set was scarves, sweaters, and hats in a spectrum of earthtones. As she melted underneath warm layers of clothing, she grew thirsty. The one physical sign of the unwelcome stowaway in her womb, besides the absence of her monthly cycle, was a baffling, unquenchable craving for ice-cold lemonade. For weeks, she had drunk gallons of the stuff. She had never particularly cared for the sour libation. Now, she could not get enough.

On the flight home from Miami, she had snapped at the flight attendant when he informed her they did not stock the beverage. Obviously, the little invader inside her had begun to exercise its will. She envisioned the parasite violently pounding and kicking the lining of her belly, yelling, "Get some more lemonade down here, *now!*"

Click-flash! Whine. Click-flash! Whine. Click-flash! Whine.

"What's wrong, Jules? Need a break?"

Andy's voice slit her thoughts. For a moment, her carefully constructed façade had slipped out of place. She needed to be more careful. "Yeah. I think I need five. Do you have any lemonade?"

He set the camera down as the creative director instructed the crew to take ten. "And all this time I thought you were a gin girl. No, no lemonade. I've got fresh lemons for tea. Want some tea and lemon? Will that do?"

She smiled congenially beneath a dead stare. "Maybe some water with lemon in it."

Andy called to his assistant. "Hey, Dawn? Can we get Julie some—"

Julie exited the set. "I—I can get it myself. It's too much trouble."

"I can't have you cutting and squeezing lemons in the break room, Jules. Forget about the liability of you accidentally losing a finger on Dahrvey's dime. The last thing I need is for you to squirt lemon juice in your eyes and get them all red."

She shot him a look of patient condescension as she tromped to the break room, shedding the coat she wore along the way. "Need me to sign a liability waiver? Honestly, Andy, it's just a few lemons. I'll be back in a sec."

Dawn sat cross-legged on the floor next to the tripod and labeled the last several rolls of film, then busied herself preparing for the final shots while Julie hovered in the kitchen, rolling, cutting, and squeezing lemons into a tall water glass. Not a drop on her outfit—or in her eyes. She rummaged through the cupboards for sugar, mixed the ingredients with a plastic spoon until it tasted passable, then added a handful of ice cubes from the freezer.

She glanced at the wall clock as she finished a full glass, then calculated the time as she prepped a second. Chris would be there any minute. This evoked mixed feelings.

On one hand, she was happy they would have some time together despite their schedules. On the other, she resented the fact his sole purpose for stopping by was to pick her up on his way to Malibu. Inexplicably, he had decided she should join him while he visited the invalid, the tragic fallen star of yesteryear, the helpless victim of some sadistic game Julie did not pretend to understand—the bitch.

She gulped the last of her lemonade substitute, then rinsed her glass in the sink. Out front, Chris's laughter echoed from the studio. Andy chatted him up, telling him how much he liked *Aftermath*. How, even as they spoke, it sat in his car CD player where it had stayed for weeks. They reminisced about the wrap party in St. John following the "Obsession" video and the photo session days afterward. Chris spoke enthusiastically about the subsequent vacation he and Julie had enjoyed and about the publicity photos Andy had shot for the album cover.

Memories skewered her. They had been happy in St. John. So happy, in fact, she had overlooked the fact that Chris had penned the song for Farin. She had played the dutiful, supportive wife—and it had been no act. Now, things were different.

It took every ounce of decorum she could muster to leave her empty glass in the sink. She wanted to hurl it at the far wall. To listen to it shatter, crash, and splinter. To behold something fragile broken and scattered all around her. She wanted to walk on the sharp tiny pieces in bare feet. To feel them rip and shred the bottom of her feet. Instead, she went to makeup for a touch-up before returning to the set. Dahrvey would not get less than the best Julie Swanson Grant could offer.

"There she is!" Chris beamed as she entered the room. He embraced her, brushing her cheek with his lips to avoid smearing Dahrvey lipstick all over her perfectly-powdered face. "Looks like leaf-raking season around here. How's the shoot coming along?"

Again, the corners of her mouth climbed upward, counterfeiting a happy face. "You know how well Andy and I work together." She winked at her photographer. "Speaking of which, I need to get back to it." She slipped out of his arms, gestured to a nearby chair upon which he could sit, then positioned herself under the lights to give the performance of her career.

Click-flash! Whine. Click-flash! Whine. Click-flash! Whine.

Chris stuffed his keys into his jeans pocket, then hopped up on a stool, settling in to study the dance of model and photographer. He loved watching her work, savored each choreographed movement of her body. She emitted strength and sensuality—two of his favorite qualities in a woman. And what a woman.

He stared with pride and admiration as she glided about the set. She flirted with the camera, using her scarf or hat or any other handy prop she could find to create an air of playful sexiness into the shots while ensuring maximum product exposure.

A warm and willing body next to his. An uncomplicated partner whose life goals mirrored his own. Personal and professional compatibility. These things mattered. She was right for him in every possible way.

Look at her, he thought as he watched, mesmerized. *She's stunning.*

Beneath the studio lights, her movements were fluid, like liquid fire—graceful, hot, and even a little dangerous. A mischievous glint in her eye as she all but climbed inside the camera lens. How oddly fortunate things had turned out. Somewhere along the way, he had realized he possessed nearly everything a man might dream of: fame, wealth, security, a perfect home, a loving wife...everything except children.

Perhaps Elliot's announcement that he and Marci were trying for a family had started him thinking. Or maybe it was that he had once believed he might be Melody's father. Whatever the case, he longed for a child. Julie had tentatively agreed, though they would wait another year. Two, tops. After all, no matter how striking or popular, modeling was a younger woman's business.

He could wait. For now. With Farin safe, secure, and on the mend, he would finally get the answers he craved. Soon, all would be well in the world.

Click-flash! Whine. Click-flash! Whine. Click-flash! Whine. Reload.

Andy exhausted the roll and handed over the spent camera. His assistant once again swapped it out for another, fully loaded replacement.

"It should only be another hour," Julie said, readying herself for the next set. She rattled her head, careful not to touch her hair after the stylist had restyled it into loose waves for the final wardrobe change. She shifted her weight from her right to left hip and stared directly into the camera.

Only an hours' reprieve. As far as she was concerned, the session could last the rest of the day and into the night. Though her feet ached and her eyes burned from hours of luminous abuse, she dreaded the thought of driving to Malibu. With any luck, the heavy afternoon traffic would frustrate him enough to turn back and try again another day, or week, or never.

Oh, who was she kidding?

Click-flash! Whine. Click-flash! Whine. Click-flash! Whine. Click-flash! Whine. Click-flash! Whine. Click-flash! Whine.

When Andy finished the next ten shots, Dawn reached out to exchange cameras but he held up his hand, mentally summarizing the day's progress. He conferred with the creative team, who nodded as he spoke, then turned back to face his subject. "You know, Jules, we have more than enough here. I hate to keep Chris waiting. You were magnificent as always.

Dahrvey will be pleased. Let's call it a wrap."

Julie's insides twisted. In that moment, she hated Andy Pogue. "Are you sure?"

He shook Chris's hand, told him it was nice seeing him again, then nodded her way. "I'm sure. Besides, Chris mentioned you two were taking a drive up the coast. You could probably use the rest after what we've put you through today. And hey—before you leave, why don't you grab something to snack on? There are still some sandwiches in the break room." He turned away before she could object and started shutting down the light panel while his assistant tidied up.

Julie stared sharp blades into his back. "No thanks. I couldn't eat a thing."

CHAPTER 27

SAMANTHA SHIFTED INTO PARK, KILLED the engine, and popped a Tums—as if it would do her an ounce of good. She checked the mirrors, then exited her BMW and circled it on foot, gauging its potential visibility from the road or beach. Ethan's car was nowhere in sight, probably in the garage. Once reasonably certain the vehicle would not be spotted, she opened the driver's rear door and extracted a large to-go bag from the Ivy.

She marched across the driveway, grinding her teeth with a determination that belied her nerves. It had taken her too long to visit, even if the additional comings and goings presented a risk, as Ethan had warned. She needed to see Farin face-to-face.

Holding her breath, she poised herself to ring the doorbell but stopped short. She set down the bulky lunch bag and extracted another Tums from her purse, then tucked it under her arm, clutched the to-go bag by its looped handles, and pressed the button. When she heard footsteps, she popped the second Tums into her mouth.

A churning stomach had plagued her since receiving the news of Farin's safe return. She knew Jameson to be a merciless, cruel foe...but *this*? The heart-wrenching image her fiancé had described had haunted Sam. Finally, she decided to seek out the girl. If nothing else, to ease her conscience. Ross had passed her the news of Farin's situation like a baton at a relay race. She should have acted sooner.

Ethan ushered her inside, quickly shutting the door behind her. She held up the bag as she scanned the empty living room. "I brought a late lunch...or an early dinner—whichever you prefer."

"Mmm...just what the doctor ordered." He kissed her. "How'd you know?"

"I always know," she teased with a seductive whisper.

He relieved her of the heavy bag and walked her to the kitchen to unpack the food. She tabled the enormity of the moment, moving through Jordan's empty home as if he had never occupied its space. She was not the sentimental type but, as Ethan placed the bag on the bare granite kitchen island, she felt a catch in her throat.

She unpacked the paper plates, napkins, and plastic utensils. "I, uh...didn't know what everyone wanted, so I got a few salad variations, the grilled veggies, some corn chowder, and a couple different entrees."

He sniffed the air as she arranged the food, potluck-style. "I'm starving, but I don't think I can eat all this. And Marci's iffy at best these days."

She shoved a fork and spoon into each of the containers. "Maybe Chris and Julie will eat. Or maybe you can stick the leftovers in the—" She flitted her wrist to point to the fridge. There was a vacant space where a refrigerator should be. Her hands fell to her sides. "Maybe not."

"No electricity. We can't take any chances. We've got a propane camp stove to cook, not that she's eating much yet."

"How is she?"

"Trying too hard. She wants to get up and do cartwheels."

"But that's good, right?"

He bobbed his head around a bared-teeth wince. "I just don't want her to have a setback."

Sam held his face with her hands. "Thank you for doing this. I realize nothing makes sense. I just want you to know..."

He drew her in, hushing her with a lingering kiss. "Marry me."

She wiggled the fingers of her left hand. "I'm wearing your ring, right?"

"I want to set a date."

"Okay," she said softly, resting her forehead against his chin. "Let's set a date."

There came a knock at the door. Ethan held a finger to Samantha's lips and motioned for her to stay put. He crept across the expansive dining room to the entranceway and checked the peephole. Marci appeared at the top of the stairs as Ethan turned around to call back to the kitchen, "It's Chris and Julie."

Though Julie had never seen Jordan's former home, she shuddered as she crossed the threshold. The house creaked and moaned with tales of sadder times. She scanned its space for some hint of life or legacy, but could not visualize what it might have looked like when a father and son existed within. It felt uncomfortably familiar. An image of her brother came to mind.

She took in the expansive sunken living room, the kitchen door beyond the dining room, and the pristine white carpet. No pictures hung on the walls, though slightly brighter paint swatches of various sizes were evidence of previous adornments. Chris, Marci, and Dr. Maxwell chatted as they disappeared through the swinging kitchen door. Their subdued voices echoed, bouncing off empty spaces into nothing. She followed behind, fuming at the close proximity of her husband to his true love.

Samantha extended a hand, then pulled her into an embrace. "Julie! It's been ages. How are you?"

Pregnant. She donned the smiling, congenial mask she had worn, and worn out, all day as she pulled back, clasping Samantha's forearms. "It's good to see you again."

They ate in the kitchen, either leaning against or sitting atop the counter. Chris grabbed a burger and fussed at Julie until she grudgingly chose the grilled veggies. Marci used a spoon and fork as tongs to fill half a paper plate with Cobb salad. Ethan went for the lime chicken and a helping of Caesar salad, leaving the mesquite salmon for his fiancé.

"How is she?" Chris asked around a mouthful of burger. "Better?"

"She ate this morning," Marci said. "Some tea and dry toast. She's kept it down, so I think we're making progress. Right, doc?"

"Every day." Ethan scanned the counter. "Did we get any drinks?"

Sam's eyes bulged apologetically. She covered her full mouth with the back of her free hand. "I forgot," she said, swallowing.

He tapped the side of a large Coleman cooler with his foot. "I can offer everyone water or iced tea."

Julie blew air through tightened lips but did not complain.

"Sorry," Samantha said, accepting a bottled water from her fiancé. "My mind...it's been so..."

Chris opted for iced tea. "We're all the same. It's a bloody disaster, isn't it?"

After distributing the bottled beverages, Ethan deftly hopped up and back onto the counter without spilling a morsel off his plate. Samantha cut eyes at him. "Show off."

Legs crossed, Marci scooched back into the corner counter near the sink. "At least she's back. If we hadn't found her when we did..."

Samantha nibbled her salmon, head low.

Julie pushed the veggies around her plate with her plastic fork.

"She's pretty much off the Thorazine," Ethan told them. "There are no signs of permanent impairment. A little bit of the ol' Thorazine shuffle there for a bit. Other than that, you'd never look at her and know."

"Except for the scars," Marci added matter-of-factly. She uncapped her water bottle and took a hearty gulp.

"Except for the scars." Ethan concurred. "And the weight."

Chris ran his tongue across his upper teeth. He frowned at the last of his burger. He had seen those scars. In fact, he had seen the wounds that made them. "It's a wonder she didn't bleed out that day, huh, Jules?"

Julie's lips parted, as if caught passing notes by a high school teacher. "Oh...yeah. Awful."

"She got them from the broken glass at Bobby's. My guess is, she crawled over it to get away. She's scarred on the balls of her hands, the top of her feet, her shins...knees. She was bleeding pretty bad when she showed up at our place."

A palpable silence engulfed the kitchen. One by one, they abandoned the remainder of their lunch and cleared their plates, utensils, napkins, and empty bottles or cans. Discussing the situation out loud somehow made it more real, and more dangerous. Unfortunately, until Farin filled in the gaps on what little they knew, no one could suggest a reasonable course of action.

"The next hurdle is getting her appetite back. I've been keeping her hydrated and fighting to stabilize her with IV supplements, but it's tricky. The chart notes don't say how long it's been since her system had real food. Marci's made a chart of her intake. It's a long battle. Tonight, we're adding chicken broth."

"How's her memory?" Chris asked, his back to the group. He stared out the kitchen window at foamy waves crashing against the shore, a hostage to the memories of his last visit to this place. Before today, he had not stepped foot in the house since right after Chase's memorial service. He had hired professionals to clean it up after having taken ownership. Now, he could not remember what he had planned to do with it. Perhaps it had been waiting for Farin all along.

Marci sealed their garbage in a plastic bag, then cleaned her hands with a baby wipe. "She's struggling. She wants to remember. There's this recurring dream she's had about circus tents and gang planks and giant birds. I can't make sense out of it."

He tucked and cocked his head.

She lifted her palms. "You know Farin's bizarre dreams. The good news is, the nightmares she had growing up seem to be gone."

"That poor girl," Sam said.

Marci clapped her hands together to address the room. "Okay. We can't go see her if we're feeling sorry for her. She's skittish."

"And a flight risk," Chris added with a smirk.

Julie scowled at her husband's back.

Marci pointed his way. "Exactly, although we do have the rare upper hand here because she can't walk independently yet."

"So, who's first?" Samantha smoothed down her skirt and checked her watch. "I have to jump on a call at five. Sorry, I can't reschedule."

Ethan slid his arm around her waist. He nodded in Marci's direction. "You're the cruise director here. What'll it be?"

Marci snorted out a soft titter.

Ethan squeezed Samantha's waist. "I keep telling her she's missed her calling. She'd make a terrific nurse."

"I'm sure she'll make a terrific mother, too." Chris winked her way.

Marci whirled around, mouth open and grinning. "You *knew*!"

"Of course I knew! Have you *met* my sister-in-law? Last I talked to Ben, Cheryl's been knitting since we left Florida."

Julie stood near yet apart from the group, eyeballing them sullenly as she picked at her cuticles.

A flash of understanding registered in Marci's eyes. Her features softened as she and Chris shared an unspoken thought. She laughed. "You weasel."

For the first time in six years, he knew she had not intended to insult him.

***

Farin lay staring at the ceiling when Marci returned. "I remember nothing. What if it never comes back?"

Marci performed a quick inspection of the IV bag level, tubing, and injection site. "Maybe you're trying too hard. Dr. Maxwell keeps telling you to relax."

She emitted a frustrated scoff. "My entire existence has been reduced to bedpans, buckets, dried toast, and weak tea. My best friend's now my physical therapist, my personal groomer, and a maid. No problem. I'll just relax."

Marci stared down at her. "Be patient. We'll try having you sit up independently again in the morning."

"Look at me go." She rolled her eyes. Quietly, she said, "I wanna walk on the beach. I wanna remember the last three years. I...I wanna say goodbye to my husband."

"You're better off than you were a month ago, so stop complaining. Anyway, you up for a visitor?"

"Wh—?"

"Samantha Drake's here. She'd like to see you."

Farin slid her hands across her abdomen. She could not recall the last time she had bathed. Her hair lay in long, dull strings about her face and shoulders. She wore nothing but a pale, yellow hospital gown, which Marci exchanged daily for a fresh replacement. Her body felt dense and numb, save the itchiness of her legs and underarms. Neither had been clean-shaven in who knew how long.

Marci had taken care of her from the time she had first opened her eyes. Grooming, oral care, muscle manipulation. She helped her eat what little food she managed. If it came back up, she held a bucket for her, keeping the hair out of her face. She did all this and more while struggling every moment with her own morning sickness.

With much effort, Farin dragged herself into a semi-sitting position. "Do you have a mirror?"

Marci propped pillows behind her. "You can't hold a teacup by yourself, let alone a mirror."

"I need to brush my hair."

"In a minute."

She cast forlorn eyes at the window. How she yearned to do more than listen to the sea outside.

Perceiving movement at the door, she looked back. "Samantha?"

"Hello, Farin." Samantha smiled warmly, shoulders slouched as she padded forward in a tentative creep, like an unannounced neighbor peeking in on a newborn just home from the hospital.

Farin studied her as she approached. Sam was as leggy and stunning as ever. The shock and pity mantling the woman's face humiliated Farin. She resented her frail state. Thin. Ghostly pale. No wonder Marci resisted getting her the mirror. She looked as if she had not seen the light of day in years. In fact, she had not.

She spared Samantha a strained smile. "How are you? I haven't seen you in..." Her voiced faded with the realization she could not finish her own sentence.

Samantha dragged one of the two plastic chairs next to the bed, sat down, and took her hand. "How're you feeling, sweetie?"

"I'm not sure." The kind gesture confused her. "I can't remember more than what I've been told."

She squeezed her hand. "I'm sorry about Jordan. I'd promised Ethan I wouldn't say anything to upset you, but I needed to offer my condolences."

Farin glanced back at the window. "Thank you."

"If you need anything…"

"Dr. Maxwell's your fiancé, right?"

"Yes."

She faced her. "Then, thank you again."

Samantha patted her hand, then rose to leave.

Farin watched her cross the room. She heard a muffled sniff as Sam exited without a backward glance.

Marci sidled up to her. She ran a brush through her greasy, impossible mane. "You okay?"

"I want to understand. I want to remember."

Marci fingered Farin's curls into a passable do, stood, then stretched her back and arms. "I'm gonna go get you some more tea. You've got a couple more visitors, if you're up for it."

"Who is it?"

Marci's right brow ticked upward.

Farin clutched her chest.

She nodded.

"You said it wasn't safe."

"Since when did that ever stop him?"

He had tried to stay away. Everyone had agreed it was for the best. For all they knew, Jameson had trailed him to Malibu. But Farin living beyond that night in Yucca had galvanized him. Her survival symbolized the first victory in his vow to make Lockhardt pay for what he had done to her.

Every day since their return, he had called Marci for an update on her condition—specifically, whether she had remembered anything. He needed to know what happened to Jordan. Farin alone had the answers.

Guilt over his past actions weighted him like Jacob Marley's chains. With Farin lucid now, maybe he would break free.

His stomach flipped as he entered the room. Through force of will, his mind ignored his racing heart. The look of her sitting up in bed, alert and smiling at him despite her circumstances. He ignored the instant longing he felt as their eyes met.

He sat in Sam's vacated seat. "How are you feeling?"

"Marci said you helped bring me here."

"Do you remember?"

"No."

"Dr. Maxwell says you've been as stubborn as ever." He reached out for her, as if it were natural to do so, but then quickly pulled away. "You want to get up and go clubbing or something."

Her laugh was small and strained, little more than a wisp of smoke. "I want to look out the window. I want to see the water."

He glanced up at the IV pole. "That's unlikely, isn't it?"

"I guess so."

"You'll get there."

"Marci said you released a solo album."

For several minutes, neither their past nor present mattered. None of the usual tension marred their conversation. Then and now melted into a void.

He looked the same as he had the last time she saw him on the beach the day before Jordan's death. He sat with her now as he had then. A bit run down, perhaps. A touch older. A slight bend to his nose. But despite those things, he also looked settled—content, even.

They discussed his post-Mirage comeback. She listened, rapt as he spoke of his upcoming tour and the popularity of *Aftermath*. He told her about his crazy publicity schedule, confessed his mixed feelings about touring alone, and assured her that her fans had remained loyal despite her absence.

The thought of her career hit her like a wrecking ball.

"It'll be fine," he comforted. "Everything gets better from here. Marci says she's been working to strengthen your muscles, and Dr. Maxwell says you'll be walking again soon."

She hung on his every word, concentrating on his eyes, his mouth, his familiar voice. Inside, she ached. She missed Jordan's smiling face and the contentment of his arms around her. How she longed to hear him laugh and sing again. Chris's voice had always sounded so similar, from inflection to timbre. The melodic burr of his British accent comforted her. It reminded her of whispered endearments and intimate conversations...

"...*Jordan, nooooo! Jordan p-p-p-p-lease!*"

Gruesome images flashed into her memory, paralyzing her with fear. She saw Jordan's body crumple in a heap to sprawl on a glass-covered floor.

She saw herself wading in pooled blood. Lacerating her knees, shins, and the tops of her feet. She saw herself on Chris's front porch, pounding on the door and ringing the doorbell.

Tears welled as she struggled to decipher Chris's words. They sounded garbled and far away.

He leaned down, eyes wide with concern. "Are you okay?"

She jerked back, recoiling from the images.

"Farin?"

Her heartrate and breathing increased as the scene played itself out on an endless loop. Though initially hazy, the images sharpened in focus. Soon, it resembled reality more than nightmare.

This is real. This is what happened.

Chris bolted up, sending the chair skidding backward onto the carpet as he raced for the door.

"Wait!" she pleaded.

He wavered. "Are you okay?"

She swallowed hard, battling to hold back tears and table the memory for a more private time. "I'm fine. Just a muscle spasm. They come and go."

He righted the chair, sat down, and fixed his eyes at her. "You're *sure*?"

"Positive."

He chuckled uneasily. "You scared me there."

The soft rap of knuckles against the bedroom door saved her from further interrogation. Julie opened the door and poked her head in, then stepped inside. "Am I interrupting?"

Chris waved her in. "Not at all. Come in and say hello," he said, then, to Farin. "Julie wanted to check up on you."

Farin deflated as Julie cross the room and sat down beside her husband. She remembered her in a white silk robe, hovering over her on the porch. She was talking on the phone. Farin remembered running, but could not for the life of her recall leaving.

Marci appeared with hot tea, towels, and Dr. Maxwell's leather bag. He followed behind carrying a large stock pot half-filled with piping hot water.

"Sorry, guys," he said. "I need to check Farin's vitals and then head over to the hospital."

Chris reached down and squeezed her hand before vacating his chair. "We'll talk again soon," he promised with an encouraging wink.

She nodded and looked at him, then Julie. "Thank you for coming."

Head high, Julie linked her arm in Chris's and walked toward the door a half-step ahead of him.

Ethan checked Farin's pulse and respiration while Marci prepared the tea and dipped a hand towel in the hot water. He palpated her stomach and listened to the sounds of digestion. "You should be fine for the night. Marci's staying with you, and I'll be back in the morning. Need anything before I go?"

Farin shook her head, thanked him, and looked at Marci. "Can you help me change?"

"Absolutely." Marci nodded towards Ethan. "We're good, doc, thanks. We'll see you in the morning."

He packed his stethoscope and left, but stopped before Marci shut the door behind him. With a grin, he back-stepped out of the room. "Any idea how long it'll be before you people start calling me by my given name? Sheesh!"

Marci untied, then gently tugged the gown's thin fabric at one shoulder. Farin grew frustrated as she strove to maneuver herself out of the garment. With this, her first collaborative attempt at changing clothes, her atrophied muscles protested as she moved her arms, legs, and torso to slip out of one gown and into the other.

The pain was excruciating. Her only distraction was her recovered memory, which had expanded to include additional information.

As the gown slid out from beneath her, she shuddered under the initial shock of cool air on exposed skin. She looked away, embarrassed at her naked body.

Marci adopted a brave, almost professional smile as she sponged her down. "Remember when we were twelve? I was so mad you got your period before me. But you? You were terrified. You ran away to your mom's place and hid in the treehouse until I came for you. Gosh, I don't even remember how long I looked before I realized where you'd be. I was afraid my parents would be mad because it was getting dark and I thought we'd miss dinner. Remember?"

Farin stared at the wall.

"Anyway, I had to go inside the house, get a bucket with hot water, and try to find a clean wash rag and towel. Beth begged you to let her climb up and help you, but she was drunk, and we both knew she'd kill herself if she tried. So, there we were, the two of us, shivering to death in our rickety old treehouse in the middle of January as you stripped down and had me help you clean up. You wouldn't put your underwear and pants back on because they got all stained, so I had to go back into the house and find you something to wear. I ended up grabbing a pair of your old sweats and your dad's tattered U-Dub T-shirt—the one you'd hid so your mom wouldn't throw it out. You'd thought you'd lost it when you moved in with me. The shirt was a man's large and the sweats were three sizes too small."

The corner of Farin's mouth flickered a brief smile. "I remember."

"Look at me."

Slowly, Farin turned her head.

"It's okay," Marci said. She rinsed the cloth, dried Farin off, and ran a stick of deodorant across her armpits. "We got through that day and we'll get through this. Don't get modest on me now."

"It's just..." She reached down and tried to grab the sheet, but found her stomach muscles too weak.

"Hush," Marci insisted.

Farin dropped her arms to her sides. "I remembered something."

Marci side-eyed her, hopeful but nonchalant. "Yeah?"

"Have you heard from Dale?"

"Eastland?"

Farin nodded.

"Not for a few weeks."

"But you've talked to him?"

"We talk before Christmas every year and usually get together for your birthday. Obviously, we missed this year."

"Has he said anything to you?"

"About what?"

"I sent him something. In the mail."

Marci wrinkled her forehead.

"Never mind."

"No, what did you remember?"

Farin shook her head. "Forget it. He must not have received it."

"Received what?"

"It doesn't matter now. You'd know if he had them."

"Had *what*, Farin? What aren't you telling me?"

"Could you call him and ask if he got anything in the mail from me?"

Marci's mouth twisted into a doubtful frown. "Sure. I'll just call him up and start asking strange questions. That shouldn't raise any suspicions."

As Marci gathered the folds of a fresh gown and prepared to dress her,

Farin dared to glance down at her bare body. She looked hideous and emaciated.

Her skin was white and dry, like dehydrated potato flakes. It sheathed her protruding ribs and hip bones as thinly as a layer of filo dough. Her breasts sagged slightly to either side.

Then, she noticed the jagged scars covering her lower abdomen.

Downstairs, Samantha attempted to have an uninterrupted conversation with Chris, but her cell phone rang repeatedly. The seventh time it went off, she powered it down, hoping whoever it was would give up before her conference call.

Phone off, she and Chris discussed his schedule as they prepared to leave. The tour would begin in June. She had coordinated with his manager and agent to rearrange his schedule once more in order to better accommodate the preparations. A tour band had already been assembled. Despite the temporary setback, they were on track.

"How long will they keep him from me?" Julie cuddled into his shoulder.

"Mid-September," Samantha told her. "It's a short tour—an exclusive to whet their appetites, if you will. Once his second album's out, fans will demand a world tour and he'll have enough material without having to lean too heavily on the old Mirage stuff. But I'm sure you two can arrange some time to spend together on the road. Knowing Gloria Monroe, she'll finagle a way to get you two in the same place at the same time. I seem to remember a little working vacation in St. John."

Chris put his arm around Julie. "Sam's right. Call Gloria. You don't want me alone and missing you for three solid months, do you? It's my first solo tour. Don't make me feel totally abandoned."

Julie giggled, lacing her fingers with his.

They headed out. Ethan brought up the rear, having double-checked the secured doors and clearing any visual evidence of recent activity inside the house, should someone come snooping around.

Chris opened the front door and stepped back, letting everyone pass. Before closing it behind them, they heard a bone-chilling, tortured scream coming from the direction of the master bedroom.

CHAPTER 28

THE FIRST UNITED METHODIST CHURCH in Greenwood Lake, New York drew more than two hundred mourners that cold, windy Friday in late February. Ross had postponed the service a few days so Josephine's friends could fly in from Palm Springs.

Her sister, Betty, had insisted on attending the funeral of her only sibling. Though still recovering, she hobbled through the sanctuary door with her head high despite quivering lips, eyes brimming with tears, and the cane she found herself dependent upon since her stroke.

Ross sat broken and disheveled upon the right front pew, the closest space to his bride's open casket. He stared at her as if in a trance. The condolences of mourners who approached him before taking their seats fell to background noise. He focused his attention on his Josephine, who lay still and cold and dressed in her favorite blue dress. Her lilting laughter echoed in his mind.

The mortuary beautician had done a wonderful job. A natural beauty, Josephine had worn little makeup even during the most spectacular of evenings attending industry galas or charity events. The image of her in repose could easily trick one into believing she was simply asleep, as if she would awaken any moment.

He emitted no sound of longing, despair, or heartbreak as he viewed his wife's body. He felt empty inside. Little remained. He had lost his own life—the only thing that mattered to him—a week ago when he came home and attempted to surprise Josephine by joining her in the shower before their dinner reservations.

The reverend took his place behind the lectern as the organist finished "Amazing Grace." He bowed his head to begin the service with a prayer for the deceased.

Ross lowered his head and fused his eyes shut. While praying with the reverend and the others, he prayed with his heart and mind that both God and Josephine would forgive him. He added his own prayer that God would bring swift justice to those responsible for the "accident" that ended the life of his mate.

While he did not know who had broken Josephine's neck, he knew in his gut who had solicited the deed. That same man and his son currently sat three pews behind him in this church, this holy space, endeavoring to conceal a remorseless sneer of victory.

Ross knew Jameson was an atheist. He also knew his attendance today was neither for appearance's sake nor to feign support for an old friend and colleague. The intention was to proclaim, in his own subtle way, that Josephine had paid the wages of Ross's sin.

To Jameson's credit, he had not smiled once at the belief that he had won yet another battle in his life's war against those who dared cross him. He had merely imposed his presence upon the only living soul who could understand how an impressively fit woman like Josephine Alexander could have taken a fatal slip in the shower at the relatively young age of sixty.

She had died thirteen days before their forty-first wedding anniversary.

"We come together today to mourn the passing of a fine woman and a loving wife," the reverend began when the prayer ended. In the distance, Ross heard scattered, muffled sniffs throughout the room. "Josephine Alexander loved the Lord, loved her husband, and loved her church. Over the last twenty-five years of her life, she was actively involved in the arts and in her community. She served on various boards and organized fundraisers for such worthy causes as child abuse prevention, animal rights, and countless church-sponsored missions and activities."

Ross felt a hand on his left wrist. Turning, he found Betty weeping silently beside him. He took her hand in his and gave a gentle squeeze, wanting to comfort her, wanting to apologize in some way for being the root cause for this gray morning.

Through sad, swollen eyes, he gazed back at the coffin and listened as the reverend continued cataloging his wife's accomplishments. She had indeed participated in many fine and worthy causes. But inside, Ross knew Josephine's greatest achievement in her too-short life had been enduring the tumult his long association with Jameson Lockhardt brought to their marriage.

She had never strayed from his side. She had invited Jameson into their home on many occasions and had played the perfect hostess despite the fact he made her feel uneasy. Josephine had neither understood nor encouraged Ross's friendship with Jameson. Still, though she did not attempt to hide her feelings, she never tried to sway Ross into abandoning

Lockhardt Sound or their friendship. Only once, during those particularly long nights more than five years ago, had she put her foot down: if Ross's schedule did not return to some semblance of normal, he would find trouble at home.

"The one great disappointment of Josephine's life was that she and her husband never managed to start a family of their own," the reverend continued. "Instead, she surrounded herself with dozens of friends and remained close to her family, of which now only her sister, Betty, and Betty's children and grandchildren, remain. Josephine acted as a loving aunt to her two nephews and to their children, as well as a surrogate mother or grandmother to countless children in her neighborhood, the church Sunday School, and the hospitals and orphanages where she volunteered her time."

Another hand fell on Ross's arm, this time to his right. He blinked in amazement when he saw Samantha beside him. He had not noticed her entrance and wondered how long ago she had arrived. They had not seen each other since their meeting in California. Somehow, he could not help but believe that day had sealed Josephine's fate.

He looked pleadingly at Sam...for what, he did not know. No matter how he tried to define his thoughts, he found nothing but agony.

Together, they had signed her death warrant. He read in Sam's eyes she felt it, too. She was no more fooled by the "accident" than he. He clasped her hand tightly and turned back to the beautiful, still form of his bride. Sam wept softly beside him as Betty rested her head on his left shoulder, sobbing uncontrollably.

"Josephine's husband, Ross, has prepared a few words for you today," the reverend told the congregation. He nodded his cue for Ross to rise and proceed to the pulpit. "Afterwards, if anyone here would like to come up and share some words or memories, please feel free to do so. Then we'll say a final prayer for our sister, Josephine, and conclude the service."

The organist played "How Great Thou Art" as the reverend took a seat away from the lectern and the congregation waited for Ross to make his way past the coffin and up three steps to deliver the words he had scribbled on a legal pad over the last few days.

When he rose from between Betty and Samantha, he faltered, then stumbled. In a flash, Bobby Lockhardt was at his side, a half-step ahead of Samantha. They each linked one of his arms to right him.

"I'm so sorry," Bobby whispered in his ear.

Ross nodded absently at Bobby, who stole a quick embrace from Samantha before returning to his seat.

He locked eyes with Samantha, again pleading for help he could not define. She nodded once for encouragement, then stepped back to her seat. As he passed the coffin, he paused, unable to take his eyes off his wife. He would never look upon her again after this day. Moments later, he became aware of warm tears spilling onto his suit jacket. For the life of him, he could not move.

Forty-one years of Josephine's laughter and smiles lighted upon him like a summer's breeze. He could not reconcile in his mind that he would never again see that smile of hers or feel her next to him, telling him how much she loved him. In four decades, Ross had rarely slept alone, especially in his own bed. Now, he would spend the rest of his miserable existence without her body beside his. His life mate, his love, his bride, gone.

Betty and Samantha stood in unison. They flanked his sides. Ross shook his head, signaling them to return to their seats. He cleared his throat into his fist and lifted his chin, then walked on shaky legs to stand before the crowd of family and friends. Positioning himself at the lectern, he straightened his jacket and looked out on the congregation. Something inside him warmed, granting him brief respite from the burden and grief.

Before him sat many of his wife's friends, associates, and neighbors. He recognized her bridge companions from Palm Springs, a few of the families of various patients she had lent her spark of laughter to while volunteering at the hospital, and friends she had made over a lifetime of kindness and charity. He saw their nephews seated toward the back of the church, struggling periodically with one or another of their younger, more active children.

Looking down, he regarded his handwritten notes with blurry eyes. He cleared his throat again, swiped away tears, then slid his reading glasses from his breast pocket. "Thank you, Reverend Daniel," he began, adjusting the spectacles on his face. "And thank you all for coming today to help me say goodbye to my...my...to my b-bride." As the words left his lips, the full weight of his grief crushed his heart.

Josephine, I'm so sorry.

More tears came as he peered out at the crowd. Was his role at this sorrowful service to give strength or hope or wisdom to those who came to mourn, or did they bear the burden of comforting him? As a man, it seemed unconscionable to weep like a baby in front of everyone he and Josephine had ever known. But standing there, he realized he did not understand the rules of the game.

He felt alone, and small, and very much like he would rather crawl into Josephine's coffin and let Reverend Daniel seal the lid. He wanted to be with his love. He had vowed to be with her, forever. Nothing in his life mattered without her. Nothing.

Facing the mourners with muddled eyes, his gaze settled upon the stoic form of Jameson Lockhardt. He sat there beside his son, silent and unmoved, staring at and through him. In that instant, something within Ross Alexander rose up and told him what he needed to do.

During his eulogy, he relayed touching stories of private moments they had shared. Memories he was grateful to have written down over the last few days. Every once in a while, a particularly moving account would bring the mourners to tears or laughter.

Yes, Josephine had lived a full life, though she had been taken too soon. He assured the reverend, the congregation, and even himself that he believed that God, in His wisdom, must have needed Josephine even more than they did, and that He had decided to bring her Home. Stepping down off the stage and returning to his seat, he realized he had meant those words—although it no longer mattered. In his moment of clarity, he realized his own remaining purpose in life.

He would not fail Josephine again.

"That was beautiful, Ross," Samantha whispered. She dabbed her eyes with her handkerchief and rested her head on his shoulder.

More in control now, he patted Samantha's stocking-sheathed knee.

Several of Josephine's closest friends, along with those she had served with kindness and friendship during her life, took turns recalling the various moments they had shared. When they finished, the reverend rose and returned to his lectern.

Beside Ross, Betty withdrew a second travel tissue package from her purse. Ross put his arm around her.

"I read now from the book of Ecclesiastes, chapter three, verses one through twenty," the reverend began. *"To every thing there is a season, and a time to every purpose under the heaven: A time to be born, and a time to die..."*

After Betty's stroke cut short their Palm Springs vacation, Ross had planned to surprise his bride with a trip to Monte Carlo for their upcoming anniversary. Josephine had loved the Mediterranean. They had vacationed there before, around the time they had learned of Ross's infertility.

With Jameson's retirement, and his own, mere months away, Ross was giddy with anticipation. Finally, a clean break from the Lockhardts! The idea of surprising Josephine for their anniversary had eased his fears over any possible retaliation Jameson might plan over Farin's escape.

"...A time to kill, and a time to heal; a time to break down, and a time to build up; A time to weep, and a time to laugh; a time to mourn, and a time to dance..."

Their tickets had arrived the afternoon he tendered his notice, the day Bobby had returned from his trip. Ross had intended to tell Jo at dinner that night over dinner.

The package from the travel agency remained unopened in his briefcase.

"...A time to rend, and a time to sew; a time to keep silence, and a time to speak..."

When Ross climbed the stairs that evening and heard the water going in the master bath, he had decided to join his bride under a relaxing, warm shower before heading off to dinner. He had stripped off his clothes and placed them on the bed alongside the beige pantsuit Josephine shed before stepping into the bathroom. Once inside, Ross had moved stealthily across the tile, then slid the shower door soundlessly across the metal runner.

Ice-cold water had sprayed his bare skin. Looking down, he found his bride lying crumpled in a heap in the tub.

"...A time to love, and a time to hate..."

When the service ended, the mourners filed slowly out of the church, climbed into their cars, and proceeded to the gravesite where Josephine Alexander's body would be committed to its final rest.

Betty wrapped her arms around Ross's neck. She held him for several moments, sobbing on his shoulder while he hushed and comforted her.

Betty had lost her husband some months back. Since then, she had leaned on Josephine to help her through the initial mourning period. Now, they would need to lean on each other. While Betty had children and grandchildren to help her grieve, he and Betty would share a common bond, for they both knew the pain of losing a spouse. Some things could not be explained to those without experience.

At last, Betty transferred her sorrowful embrace to one of her sons, who led her down the aisle and outside, leaving Samantha and Ross alone on the front pew as guests filed out of the sanctuary.

She offered her own comforting embrace, then sat straight, smoothing the skirt of her black linen suit. Her hazel eyes narrowed in concern as she rubbed his shoulder. "You had me worried there for a sec."

He glanced around them for any trace of the old man. "We need to talk—soon."

"I'm sorry I didn't pick up the phone earlier that day. I had no idea."

"I didn't know who else to call. No one else could possibly understand."

"It's unimaginable."

Bobby politely cleared his throat as he approached them. When they stood up, he shook Ross's hand, then Samantha's. "Sorry to interrupt. I've got a call I have to take so I can't stay. I just wanted to tell you again how sorry I am, Ross. If you need anything..."

"Thank you, son. I appreciate it."

The young man gave him a mournful nod, then shook his hand again. Before he left, he drew Samantha in for a hug. "It's good to see you, Sam, except under these circumstances. Let's talk soon. I'd like to keep in touch. You look great, by the way."

She thanked him, promised she would try to call before she returned to Los Angeles, then watched until she was sure he was out of ear shot.

As they sat back down, Ross asked, "How's Farin?"

The question stymied her. She looked quizzically at him. "Better every day. But please, Ross, let's not think about that today."

"Of course I'll think about it today. I'll think about it every day for the rest of my life. That's the real reason we're here, isn't it?"

Samantha let his words settle upon her. She marveled at his courage to speak the unutterable fact that had kept her up for two nights after hearing the news.

"I don't think Ethan really believed me until now."

"Believed what?"

"That Josephine's accident wasn't...well, really an accident."

"After all he's doing with Farin?"

"I know. He said I was being paranoid. But now."

"Now, what?"

"Now, he believes no one around Farin will ever be safe."

Ross stole a glance at his bride's coffin.

"He's finding a new place for Farin. I told him I didn't think he needed to do that, but he insists. And, this time, he's not telling anyone where they are."

"Has he mentioned if she'll suffer any long-term damage?"

"Farin Grant's grown into a strong woman. Stronger than I ever thought she'd be, for sure. She's sitting up on her own. She's started walking a bit. Ethan said she graduated from broth to oatmeal yesterday."

Two men in dark suits appeared from the side of the pulpit and approached the casket. They gestured toward Ross, wordlessly asking if he wanted them to wait. He shook his head sadly, then watched the still figure of his bride for the last time as they closed the lid. The men rolled the casket through a side door toward a waiting hearse.

"The poor girl," he said, his tone a combination of grief, remorse, and disbelief. "She's had to start over from scratch. When Jameson first did this, I didn't realize how bad things would get. I-I just didn't know. How could I keep silent all these years? I'm as guilty of the capture and detainment of that innocent woman as Jameson." Ross's body quavered as he considered the details of Farin's horrific situation.

If only Samantha knew the entire truth of the matter. It was so much worse than anyone might suspect. Farin, Bobby, Jordan, Jameson, Chris, Mirage—even Samantha's own career. Everyone had played their part, and it all led to this moment. Josephine was gone. Everyone in this game had paid a price. Everyone except Jameson.

Samantha rose, smoothing her skirt again in that idiosyncratic way of hers, and then stepped into the aisle. "We'll talk more later. We should get to the cemetery."

"Hello, Samantha," came a gruff, imposing English accent from behind her.

Ross stood, his expression blank as he looked at, then past, Sam to the figure standing behind.

Head high, she turned on her heel. "Jameson."

A span of five years wrinkled and disappeared before her. She checked herself, then rechecked, awaiting the familiar alarm to sound inside her, alerting her to the dragon's presence.

He nodded curtly. "I trust you've been well."

"Never happier," she said, haughty as she rolled a shoulder and sized him up. Still sharp. Vital. Older, perhaps. A tad slower in his movements. But those steely eyes of his still possessed the calculating glint of a true fire-breather. A man who watched. Everyone. At all times.

Sam wondered fleetingly what he saw when he looked at her. For the first time, she did not care.

He brushed her aside as if swatting flies. "If there's anything I can do," he said, shaking Ross's hand. "Take as much time as you need, of course."

Samantha linked her arm in Ross's and led him outside to his waiting limousine. She no longer felt the need to pretend she respected, or even feared, Jameson Lockhardt. Not anymore. Not ever again.

***

"Call him back."

"Shut-up."

"He's been leaving messages for a month and a half."

"Stay out of it, Billy."

"Give the guy a break!"

Alicia slammed her palms down atop her desk. She peered at her partner through dark-slitted eyes. "I'm not calling him back. Now get out of here so I can finish this report and go home. I've got a date tonight."

"A date, huh?" Bridgeman propped himself, half-sitting, upon her desk and shot her a dimpled grin. "That's great!"

"Don't you and Penny start calling wedding planners. I promised my aunt I'd take her to the movies."

"Oh."

"And no more talk about Macy, got it?"

He gave her a mock salute, then returned to his desk. "Whatever you say, Al, but I'm telling you—"

That her personal life had become fodder for office gossip bothered her. So much for the hard-earned acceptance, and respect, she had spent years cultivating. When she had entered the academy, male counterparts had teased her mercilessly about her gender, her height, her age, and her looks. Having that "if Gloria Estefan and Sophia Loren had a baby" thing going on did not help one bit—professionally *or* personally.

"Did we get the FSB report yet?" she snapped, abusing her keyboard as if practicing for a whack-a-mole tournament.

Bridgeman studied his computer screen. He maneuvered his mouse upon its rubber pad, periodically clicking its left-side button with his index finger. "I haven't seen it. These things take time."

"Time." She stabbed the back button repeatedly before continuing to slaughter her keyboard at seventy-five words per minute. "Good thing there's no statute of limitations on murder, eh? *Time.* Let's hope those samples you collected didn't degrade."

Being raised in a nearly all-male household had toughened her up. She had learned to give back more than her brothers dished out. In high school, she had nearly broken her brother Quito's arm when he stepped in to defend her honor against an upperclassman. Quito had been popular at the time, mostly by virtue of the fact that it was his third stint as a senior. When Alicia publicly bested him, it earned her a reputation as a badass who should not be challenged. Naturally, that led to near-constant challenges for the rest of her high school years. She probably would have been better off had she let Quito defend her.

"So, this 'date' with your aunt. Gonna wear green?"

Focused intently on the screen before her, the question did not register. She clamped down on the chewed-up pencil in her mouth, but not hard enough to make it splinter or snap. The unconscious habit, which she had picked up in college, tickled her partner—so much so, she had tried to break it.

He continued his interrogation. "I mean, you'd hate to have strange men coming up and pinching you all night."

She stopped typing, removed the pencil from her mouth, and squinted at him. "What?"

"Even if Miami doesn't have a particularly dense Irish population, St. Patrick's Day is a great excuse to go out and get drunk. Pinching girls who don't wear green? Call it a perk—or a conversation starter."

"Any man who pinches me had better have good insurance."

"And know a good wound care specialist."

She opened her mouth to speak, then replaced the pencil and clamped shut. Much of what she wanted to say was inappropriate for the station anyway—even in Spanish.

Bridgeman roared with laughter whenever she swore in Spanish. He loved it, begged her to teach him some choice phrases. Instead, she screamed her reply in the privacy of her thoughts.

Alicia longed for colleagues to see her as more than a face and curves. To that end, she had practiced strict discipline in her career, which spilled over into personal relationships. She could outrun, outmaneuver, and often outthink even the most decorated members of the force. If colleagues mentioned her at all, she wanted it to be in admiration of her accomplishments. Weak, emotional, females got nowhere in life.

Bridgeman stood and stretched, yawning so loudly, nearby desk jockeys glanced his way. "I need coffee. Want anything?"

She shook her head without glancing up. As he left for the break room, her phone rang. He paused and lifted his chin her way. She glanced at the caller ID, set her jaw askew, then returned her concentration to her work.

Bridgeman ambled off, half-whistling, half-singing, *"Chicago, Chicago, that toddlin' town..."*

Alicia peered at his retreating form, then glanced back to her phone.

She had not banked on softening to the hazy memory of an intimate evening, or wishing she could more clearly remember it. Miles had breached her tough exterior. A warm, satisfying ache had filled her for days after their encounter. Privately, she cherished that ache.

But Alicia dealt in facts. In her mind, she had cataloged every reason a relationship with Miles Macy would end in disaster.

First, the probability of seeing him again: doubtful at best. Long-distance romances failed. She had learned this the hard way with a soldier stationed in Orlando. They met one Saturday when he and some buddies drove to Miami on a weekend pass.

Bottom line: they dated; they fell in love. Or so she thought. When he got stationed overseas, she promised to wait. They corresponded. Three months later, he stopped writing. Two months after that, her letters came back unopened. No word. No explanation. The end. She had since blocked out further details—including his name. Never again would she date a man with a temporary address. Or if talking to him necessitated a long-distance charge on her phone bill.

Second, homicide detectives required sharp, keen minds. Overlooking vital details of an investigation while fretting over what to wear to dinner could kill a career. Odd hours. Bringing work home. If she hoped to land in a captain's chair one day, she could ill afford to get tangled up with a man.

Third, she would not sacrifice her privacy on the altar of personal intimacy. Few people made a home in her heart. Those who did were sacred. Her brothers, parents, and her favored aunt and namesake, they mattered. Like her partner, they stood ready to book the church. But unlike Bridgeman, they knew when to back off. Further, though unhappy about it, they accepted that her biological clock had been set on permanent snooze. She adored children but had no desire to be a mother. That was reason four.

With time, effort, and commitment, a suitable mate might overcome every one of those reasons. Number five, however, was a deal breaker.

Should she ever decide to pursue a deeper connection with the opposite sex, he would have to be someone within her faith and Castilian culture. This bridge between them could never be crossed. Her heritage meant everything to her. A night of sex—even the best sex she had ever experienced—would not sway her conviction.

So, who cared if something about him had set the windmills of her mind in motion?

"Psst!" came Bridgeman's unsubtle attempt at getting her attention.

She saved her final report, hit print, then turned to find him waving a sealed envelope her way. She squinted to make out the return address. "I thought you went for coffee."

"I stopped by FSB on the way back."

Her eyes widened. "We got it?"

He scanned the room for itching ears, then inclined his head at a vacant interrogation room. With a nod, she rose from her desk, shimmied the wrinkles from her slacks, then walked the opposite way so as not to attract attention—or start rumors. Minutes later, she doubled back and slipped inside the room.

"What does it say?" she asked, gnawing her thumbnail. "Anything we can go on?"

He sat in a small wooden chair, petting his bald chin as he consumed the report. Every so often, he would grunt or shake his head in disbelief.

"*What?*"

"Amazing."

She flounced atop the table occupying most the space in the room and crossed impatient arms. Bridgeman's expressions alternated between surprise and outright shock.

"Well, it's definitely a professional job," he said at last.

"Did they find the cause of the ruptured fuel tank?"

He nodded. "It was exactly what I thought. Looks like they used some sort of remote to ignite a combustible chemical mixture, which triggered the explosion—a magnesium job. Once that trigger lit the magnesium, it was over."

"Wouldn't they need oxygen to get the fire going?"

He unintentionally disregarded the question as he stared off into the middle distance and thought aloud. "So, a thermite-slash-magnesium mixture gets dropped into the tank with, say, a nine-volt rigged to a timer or remote-control device. Someone triggers the device."

"How close do you think they had to be to set off the trigger?" she pressed.

"The magnesium burns so hot, it sets off the thermite and soon, the fuel tank ruptures."

"But what about—"

"In seconds, black smoke fills the back of the limousine, then expands to the front."

"Billy."

"By that time, both occupants are dead due to blast injuries. The compression alone—"

"*Billy?*"

"The limo crashes into the K-rail—"

She shook his arm. "Hey, *Billy.*"

Bridgeman looked at her. "Yeah, Al?"

"We should probably discuss this somewhere with fewer ears."

"Good call." He stood and massaged the back of his neck. "I'd hate the guys to put us in a position to answer questions."

"We can go to my place," she suggested as they left the interrogation room.

He stopped and smiled. "You're inviting me over?"

Her eyes flashed out a warning.

"What about your date?"

"I'll call my aunt and reschedule. She'll understand. This is important."

"I'll call Penny and let her know I'll be late."

She checked her watch. "Let's meet at my place in an hour. Sound good?"

He gathered his paperwork. "I don't need to bring any tequila, do I?"

"Shut-up."

***

The killer sat in his rented Chevy Caprice, just off the Pacific Coast Highway, as the sun set. With the assistance of his Bushnells, he surveilled the property as he had done for several days. Two people—a man and a woman—occasionally entered or left the abandoned residence.

Identifying a predictable pattern of comings and goings was not as easy a task as he had hoped. Sitting in his vehicle for days on end left him vulnerable. Vulnerability left him edgy and angry. Someone might notice him—someone who might later identify him if he grew careless. Better to get in, get the job done, and get going. Thus far, he had witnessed little activity. It simply would not do. He and Lockhardt needed to talk.

They had argued these and other points weeks ago, when he had insisted on lying low for a couple months before heading back to finish the Grant job. No need to start pushing limits now. Besides, unless the old man had exaggerated his mark's weakened state, she was going nowhere soon. Why not let her gather some strength and a false sense of security? It would make the victory so much sweeter.

His association with Lockhardt had left him wealthy and exposed. As soon as he concluded this job, he needed to take some time off. Perhaps collect his payment and head for the blue lagoons of the Maldives while the dust settled. He made it his business to memorize the list of countries without extradition. Once he killed Farin Grant, he would spend a few months on some sun-drenched beach, swimming the blood off his hands.

He waited until dark before sneaking onto the property. Once upon a time, it had probably been a handsome place. He noted the remnants of a pleasant yard, imagining the view from inside must have been exquisite. However, the outside now lay in shambles. Weeds grew tall and thick about the grounds. This made getting around a hassle. Unless he exercised extreme caution, he might step on a dry twig or disturb a stray branch, alerting someone in the house to his presence.

In back, he found a drained, ill-repaired swimming pool. Beyond that, he spotted a sliding glass door, which he expertly avoided while searching for an alternate way inside.

As he explored every square inch of the outer structure and committed it to memory, he began to formulate his plan. Lockhardt had stated he not only wanted to get rid of his problem, he wanted to send a message to anyone who might have assisted her. This presented a challenge. Clearly, whomever Lockhardt intended to scare off already knew his intentions. They had even eluded him, up until his little side trip to New York.

He accessed the stairs at the end of the yard and descended to the beach, where he found a small room tucked back beneath the deck above him. The incautious owner had neglected to lock it, which made getting in a breeze. Inside, he found the solution he sought.

The walls of the long, narrow room sported bright spray paint with racial slurs, gang symbols, and several variations of, "I love you, Jordan!" along the back. A fuse box hung at the far end, its wires partially exposed and greatly damaged. If they stayed that way much longer, he would not have to do a thing. The problem would resolve itself.

Whoever owned the house had not cared enough to keep it free of the occasional vandal. This worked to his advantage. Given the disarray, he could easily accomplish his mission without attracting attention.

Judging by the setup, he would need to deal with not only his mark, but her caretakers as well. The man visited every day, though at inconsistent times. The woman, however, rarely left. When she did, she did not stay away long. The only other occupant he had glimpsed briefly the other evening.

He had staked out a place on the beach in hopes of identifying the subject of the man and woman's visit. The setting sun had become an obstacle, as it temporarily obstructed an otherwise perfect view inside the window. For several minutes, he saw nothing. In fact, he had prepared to leave. Then, he spied a redhead pacing slowly around an upstairs room, the flicker of candlelight illuminating little more than her face.

This was his target. And she would not die alone.

Of course, either way was fine with him. One, two, three—or even a hundred people. It made no difference. He would see to it they went out with a bang.

CHAPTER 29

TODD DALTON ENJOYED HIS PRIVACY. As such, the converted oast house he had purchased in Marden five years back had welcomed few visitors. He had taken his time remodeling the two-story, ivy-covered stone structure, gutting its interior, redesigning and expanding the floor plan, and reroofing the two large kilns on either side of the stowage with slate tiles topped with treated metal cowls. Acres of shade trees, pastoral gardens, and towering manicured hedges encased the grounds, consummating an environment designed for optimal creativity. The finished product was sturdy, visually breathtaking, and utterly soundproof.

Who cared if he had no one with whom to share it?

Initially, he had envisioned it an oasis of sorts, a picturesque haven from fans, a secluded refuge from big cities, demanding producers, and record company executives. Mirage's personal Valhalla. They could write and record their music without vying with other acts for expensive studio time or arranging for increased security. Now, it merely shut out the world. Until recently, only Faith had known his address.

A part of him dreaded Lance's impending visit. Though he had eventually apologized for his behavior the day he had agreed to meet for a drink at the Brenchley pub, the idea of seeing his longtime friend and former bandmate left him unsettled. He found himself wandering his estate, inspecting each detail of the place to ensure everything looked in place. Syringes, pipes, bongs, rubber tubing, and burnt, curved-handle spoons were locked safely away in a hidden wall safe. The last thing he needed was for Lance to report back to the others that he had fallen apart—even if he had.

At exactly 4 PM, his doorbell rang. The sound echoed through the massive, unadorned foyer and hall, sounding not unlike a death knell despite the occasional tapestry wall hangings that might otherwise absorb the sound. He bounded up from the double chaise lounge chair in his viewing room, grabbed the remote to kill the telly, and sprinted through the wide halls, rolling down his shirt sleeves, zipping his pants, and buttoning his shirt before he reached the front door.

"You're on time," he said, opening the door wide. "Fuck me."

Lance admired the exterior walls. "You said four."

"You've never been on time in your bloody life. Come on in."

Lance entered, whistling as he beheld their surroundings. "Are we still doing *this* well? I'd thought I'd noticed a decline in royalties of late."

"I invested my money." He shut the door. "It was the rest of you who went mad."

Lance chuckled and stuck out his hand. "It's good to see you, mate."

Todd rejected the gesture. He stood in place, staring at Lance's hand, then his face, as if desperately uncomfortable.

He turned and headed for another room. "Fancy a tour, then? Or can we get to it?"

The smile ran away from Lance's face. He followed Todd into a great room. The dark wood and furnishings seemed fitting.

"Fancy a drink or something?" Todd asked awkwardly.

Lance shook his head. "No thanks. I just came for a chat."

"The others know you're here? I figure Faith gave you my address."

"She did. That's all right, isn't it?"

"I suppose." He sat upon one of two large tufted leather sofas separated by an enormous sheepskin rug. He gestured for Lance to do the same. "It's not like Chris is about."

Lance draped his arm across the top of the sofa and crossed his legs. "Don't be that way."

He scoffed. "Right."

They sat in silence. Todd fidgeted with the fringe of a chenille throw while Lance absorbed his surroundings.

"Sure you don't want a drink?" he asked at last, scampering to his bare feet like an anxious child on a sugar high. "I'm having one."

"All right, sure. Whatever you're having."

For five minutes, Lance sat alone in the great room, wondering how to turn his visit from uncomfortable to productive. He had thought they cleared the air over the pub incident. The last time they had seen each other, Todd had acted strange. But not *this* strange. And not toward him.

Todd returned with a bottle and two glasses filled with ice. "Chivas." He sniffed twice as he poured the drinks, handed one to Lance, then toasted the air. "To happy bloody endings, eh?"

"You talked to Sam?" Lance asked tentatively, nursing his drink.

"If you're here to convince me to get back together, you can sod off, Lance. It's over."

"I'm not here to convince you of anything, mate. I just came to visit. Why are you so bothered? C'mon, then. Let's give it up. What's done is done."

Todd gulped his drink and poured another, which he promptly downed before pouring a third. "Then why are you here?"

"Because we've been friends since we were ten," Lance answered, clearly insulted.

Todd snorted, fixing a sightless gaze upon the opposite end of the room. "I thought so, too. But like you said, what's done is done, innit?"

Not one for prolonged drama, the comment evoked a patient chuckle. He sipped his Chivas to quiet what might have grown into all out laughter. For a few moments, silence once again filled the room. Finally, Lance asked, "Gonna show me the studio?"

"Nope. Nothin' to see."

"Oh, c'mon," Lance prodded. "Faith said you finished it. Let's have a look, then."

"She told you that, did she?"

"Yep. Said you put a fortune into it, too. I wanna see for myself."

"No," Todd repeated, pouring another drink.

"For old time's sake."

"Bugger off."

"Now that's your girlfriend talking, there."

"I don't have a girlfriend."

Lance slid forward on the sofa, a mischievous glint in his eye. "Don't be a wanker, now. You know you want to show me."

"Psh! Show you the door, maybe."

"What's it gonna hurt?"

"No."

It seemed like a harmless quarrel, at first. Perhaps even one of their old sparring games. Lance felt sure he had detected the beginning of a smile despite Todd's continued refusal.

Another drink disappeared, then Todd shouted, "Leave it be! Seriously!"

Lance studied his friend in silence for a long minute. Of all the casualties of the Mirage breakup, this was the hardest to confront. Their friendship had long pre-dated the group. And now, Todd regarded him as no more than a stranger. Some drummer from his old band.

He finished his drink and set the glass on an end table. His lips parted, then clamped shut as he nodded his defeat and stood up. "Want me to go?"

"I'm not even sure why you came in the first place."

"Right." Lance shook his head. "Why not just ring Chris and make it up, mate? You can't stay mad forever."

Todd locked his eyes on Lance as if setting a target.

"This is bloody ridiculous." He sat down again. "What happened to you?"

Todd peered down at the melting ice in his drink.

"It wasn't his fault," Lance pressed.

"Where the fuck were you?"

"No, Todd. Where the fuck were *you?* You think you're the only one who lost Mirage? You don't remember Faith nearly killing herself over it? But it's done, mate. If Faith can recover, why can't you?"

"Does Chris know you're here?"

Lance deflated. His shoulders slumped as his head dropped with an incredulous shake of his head.

"Well?"

"I haven't talked to him since the Grammys."

"Probably too busy with his new solo career," Todd spat ruefully.

"Is that what's got your knickers in a twist?"

"Sod off."

"Show me the studio. C'mon, then."

It took twenty minutes and three more drinks for Lance to convince Todd to show off his studio. At last, they made their way to the back of the house and down the stairs into what Lance assumed was a basement. An endless corridor and three doors later, they arrived at the engineering room.

When the lights came on, Lance could scarcely believe his eyes. State of the art equipment, mixing machines, dozens of mint condition instruments and four sound booths of varying sizes and purposes. It looked as impressive as any professional studio he had ever seen. And he had seen many.

"There," Todd said, his tone a mixture of rage and irrepressible pride. "You've seen it."

"B-*loody* hell, this is amazing! Faith never said you'd built it underground!"

"No one knows."

Lance stared in open-mouthed wonder, pointing toward the largest of the four rooms. "That's as big as Studio Two at Abbey Road!"

Todd crossed his arms, visually assessing his favorite room.

"Let's lay something down!" Lance blurted enthusiastically.

"Not a chance."

He drew forward as if pulled by an external force. "We *have* to! I can't just leave here today knowing we didn't make use of this magnificent beast."

Todd chuckled for the first time since Lance's arrival.

Lance slapped him with the back of his hand. "C'mon, then!"

Hesitant at first, Todd drifted toward the main room.

Lance followed behind like a starving stray dog hoping for table scraps. He bolted for the vintage 1960s Gretsch set up at the back of the room. "Ah, you know me too well!"

"Where are your sticks?" Todd challenged, getting into the spirit despite himself.

Lance patted his back pocket, disappointed when he realized he had neglected to grab them before he left his townhouse. He looked beside the drum set and found a pair. "These'll do."

Todd surveyed dozens of guitars before settling on one that matched his mood. He slid the strap over his head then disappeared long enough to switch on the equipment. "I can't believe we're doing this."

Few people knew Todd Dalton played guitar. And piano. And bass. And drums. Nobody at Lockhardt Sound knew. None of their fans knew. The members of Mirage knew but never pestered him about it. His role had consisted of looking and sounding good, which he did—always.

Drum solo after guitar rift, Todd Dalton and Lance Turner played all the old material—theirs and others'. They played the Beatles, the Stones, the Who, CSN, and Def Leppard. They covered Zeppelin and Jefferson Airplane. They played their favorite Mirage songs, laying down the guitar and drum tracks before overdubbing keyboards. They sang lead and doubled the backup. For a few indulgent hours, they found themselves again—and rediscovered their sound.

"I miss this," Lance said when they grudgingly shut down the equipment at three the next morning.

"It's all right," Todd admitted.

"You know, we could start our own band," Lance suggested. "Bugger the rest."

"And bugger Chris Grant."

Lance grinned. "Miss him that much, eh?"

Todd switched off the tapes and powered down the console. "Fuck off."

***

Chris navigated side streets through the congested stop-and-go, resigned to the inevitable hour or so drive between ABC Rehearsals studios and home. When Ben called for their now-daily chat to discuss Farin's progress, he depressed the thick rubber speakerphone button on his Motorola cell phone's handset and left it cradled securely in its case. "Perfect timing," he chirped. "You can keep me sane whilst I crawl home."

"Where are you?"

"Snaking along on Sunset. I met with my road band today for the first time. Rehearsed a bit. It's a nice setup we have. Good thing since it's basically my new home until the tour."

The familiarity of his older brother's calm chuckle inexplicably eased him. They had finally rebuilt their brotherly bond—or maybe they had developed one they had never before shared, even in childhood. Through all the tragedies and drama that had widened the gulf between them, Farin's reemergence in their lives had necessitated their solidarity as a family. He only wished their father had lived to see the day.

"You'll do well, I'm sure. *Aftermath*'s a solid piece, Chris. You couldn't have hoped for a better debut effort."

He thanked him as he downshifted to stop at the intersection of Sunset and Stone Canyon. "It's an adjustment not having Faith there fussing at everyone or Lance pulling pranks on the road crew."

"No mischief in the ranks, then?"

"Dunno. We just met today. Talented lot. We managed to snag a few of my session musicians, though. I'm sure things'll liven up once everyone's comfortable together."

"Sounds like things are getting back to normal. That's good. We need a little normal in our lives."

"I don't know what's normal about any of this, Ben. Farin's back, I'm touring alone. The man I trusted with my career for twenty years turns out to be a bloody lunatic. I can't think life's anywhere near normal. I'm not sure I'd recognize normal if it spit in my face."

"A few months on the road'll put you right. You always did better on tour than lying about at home. You get in trouble when you're not doing something. Always have."

He would have liked to have objected to the subtle accusations behind his brother's words, but could not honestly disagree. "Well, there'll be no trouble from me. Not anymore. Julie'll see to that, I'm sure."

The line quieted. Chris could only imagine the myriad thoughts filling Ben's head. He and Cheryl had no doubt discussed their concerns. No one had said it outright, but Chris knew. They had every right to worry, given his and Farin's past.

"I'm sure she will," Ben said, a hint of doubt to his tone.

"You understand that part of my life is over."

Ben's failure to agree—or respond—hurt more than it aggravated him.

"So, what then? Is there some pool developing on whether I'll be begging Farin to run off with me again? What's the over-under? Maybe I'll go in on it."

"It's not that," Ben attempted, then trailed off.

"She's our only shot at finding out what happened to Jordan."

"She's more than that. We both know it."

"Not to me."

"You don't mean that. And no one expects you to just forget."

He made a right onto Sepulveda. His jaw ground with weariness and annoyance at the turn of their conversation. "I'm not leaving my wife. I'm not pursuing an affair. I want—I *need*—to find out what happened to Jordan. Don't you want that, too?"

"Of course! We all do. But Chris, Farin's not going to stop being part of this family once it's all sorted. Besides Marci, we're all she has. You know that."

"And does that forever role in our family mean I'll have to spend the rest of my life convincing you and Cheryl I'm being a *good boy*?"

"No." Ben sighed heavily. "You're right. Let's drop it. When's the tour start?"

"June ninth. They expanded the LA gig from one to three nights."

"Good sign."

"It is, it is."

He veered off Sepulveda onto Bel Air Crest Road. The security guard at the entrance to the community acknowledged him with a nod as he slowed down and motored through the gate.

"Any news today?" Ben asked.

"I haven't heard anything."

"When did you last visit?"

"Not since that day Julie and I met Sam there."

"Have you talked to her?"

"Uh...no. No, I haven't."

"Maybe it's better that way."

"I talk to Marci almost every day, though. Like I said yesterday, it was slow going for a while but Farin's walking and eating now. Good signs. No ill effects from the drugs. There is one thing I didn't tell you, though."

"Nothing bad, I hope."

"They're moving her."

"Why? Something wrong with the beach house?"

"Nothing like that." Chris made a left on Stratford Circle. The tension of the long day, the monotonous drive, and the anxiety of the conversation crumbled as he neared home. "When Sam and I visited, we may have compromised her position. If anyone's following us..."

"Where are they taking her?"

"They're looking for a place. I get the feeling they've found somewhere safe, but Marci won't tell me where it is."

Ben chortled into the phone.

"What?"

"You and Marci. I never thought I'd see the day you two would speak civilly—and regularly."

"A lot's changed." The words tasted hollow and understated on his lips.

"We have Lockhardt to thank for that."

"Yeah." Chris clenched his jaw. "And if I have anything to say about it, I'll be thanking him personally—for everything."

He parked in the driveway and went inside. Struggling with the bulky cell phone case in one hand and the handset in the other, he dropped his keys on the glass table in the entryway before searching the downstairs for Julie.

"You've done well, Chris. You seem happier now that you're with Minor."

When he could not find her, he headed up one of the two staircases and poked his head into the master bedroom. He heard water running in the bathroom. "Minor's brilliant. And Sam's really blossomed with the change. I've never seen her so contented."

"I'm glad you're both out. Of course, selfishly, you know I wish you'd move back here."

Julie emerged from the bathroom. Her complexion looked as pale as her champagne-colored silk pajamas. She shuffled with great effort to the bed, then crawled between the covers and lay sideways.

Chris frowned. "Hang on." He went to her, lowering the base of the phone from his ear. "You okay?" He noted the paleness of her skin. Tiny beads of sweat dotted her brow.

She lay still, lips parted, eyes closed. She grunted a weak reply. "Fine."

"I'll ring you back," Chris told Ben. "Sorry. I think Julie's sick or something."

After promising Ben he would call him back to let him know what was going on, Chris stabbed the "end call" button on the cell, secured the handset into the case, and set it down beside the nightstand. He crawled up next to his wife and encircled her in his arms, feeling her forehead and the base of her neck for signs of fever. "You're not warm or anything. What's wrong, love? Something you ate?"

Julie moaned, then grunted again. "I'm fine, really."

"You sure? Can I get you anything? How about a cool rag?" He moved from the bed and disappeared into the bathroom.

The cool cotton sheets against her cheek felt welcoming, though insufficient. She had been so sure she would skip one of the worst in a long line of pregnancy horrors. Morning sickness was the last straw. She would not endure months of nausea on top of a bloating, swelling, expanding body. The thought of a fattening figure had probably made the morning sickness worse, for with every passing day, the reality came ever closer to home. Her home. Their home.

"Perhaps I should ring the doctor," Chris suggested upon his return. He placed the damp rag on her head, crawled into bed beside her, and tenderly stroked her hair.

"No," Julie pleaded, then grunted once more. Try as she might, she could not will herself into a sitting position. She could not muster the resolve to paint a pretty picture for anyone—not even her own husband. Weakly, she cursed the parasite invader who lay festering, aggrandizing in her womb, robbing her of her strength and threatening its stronghold over her career and marriage.

"When did it start? You seemed fine when I left this morning."

"Couple of hours," she groaned, her tone froggish.

"Maybe there's a bug going 'round."

She had no strength to reply.

By the time this creature came shrieking into her world, her career would fall into irreparable ruin. She had rallied longer than anyone would have expected, but giving birth would bring a swift and irreversible end to it all.

As for her marriage, she agonized daily over the certainty Chris would leave her once her looks faded. Farin would look better and better to him. How could Julie possibly compete with their undeniable mutual attraction and history? Even on a level playing field, the task seemed insurmountable. But fat and swollen? Chris would run screaming into Farin's arms for sure. Something had to give. Julie refused to just sit by and watch it happen.

"Don't you need to call Ben back?" Her voice sounded thick and strained. The nausea twisted her stomach into knots. She anticipated another trip to the bathroom soon. For much of the last two hours, she had inspected the inside of their toilet bowl.

I do hate you, she hissed at the creature inside her.

Chris whispered into her ear. "I'll ring him later. Right now, I'm concerned about you."

She managed a slight smile of appreciation. "How's the band? Will they do?"

He rubbed her back and shoulders. "They'll be fine, I'm sure. It won't be the same, you know. Rehearsals start in earnest Monday night. What do you say? Think you'll be up for it?"

"I'd love to."

He pulled back, eyes narrowed as he unfolded then refolded the wash rag and repositioned it on her brow. "No doctor? You sure?"

"Positive."

"You should drink something. You'll be dehydrated if you don't get some liquids in you. How about I pop downstairs and get you a nice tall glass of lemonade?"

Her face contorted hideously at the thought. The nausea built to nearly unbearable, then softened just enough to assure her she did not need to rush back into the bathroom—yet. "Oh Chris, anything but lemonade."

"How about some water?"

"I hate water."

"You have to drink something."

"I don't think I can keep anything down."

"What about some chicken noodle soup? The sodium in the broth may help with the nausea. That's what Mum always made us eat when we felt ropey."

She grunted again, exhaling a long breath through puckered lips, then gave him a weak nod. Her insides protested the thought of it, but maybe if she agreed, he would stop making suggestions involving food.

"Chicken noodle it is." He kissed her cheek and scooted off the bed.

Before he had descended the stairs, she was on her feet, racing back to the bathroom.

A quick search of the pantry yielded disappointing results. As it turned out, they had no chicken soup. Chris considered running to the store, but the sound of her heaving in their master bath told him he should stay. Browsing the canned food, he discovered some chicken broth and decided it would make a better alternative, since it had little substance to it.

He heated the broth in a sauce pan, ladled it into an oversize bowl, and arranged it on a tray with some saltine crackers for bulk. When he hauled the tray into the bedroom, Julie was still indisposed.

"All right, then?" he called out. "We're out of noodle soup, so I brought broth and crackers."

Through the closed bathroom door, he heard the heaving grow louder. He winced and rested the tray on the dresser, then doubled back for the bathroom to see if he could help. Halfway there, the phone rang.

"Answer the phone," she moaned as he turned the doorknob.

"You sure?"

"Chris!"

Marci's greeting was pleasant but strained.

"You okay?" he asked, his attention shifting from the tortured groans emanating from the bathroom.

"We're okay. How about you guys?"

"Julie's sick. You haven't heard of something going around, have you?"

A cynical scoff filled the line. "I hear little these days, I'm afraid. The only illness I know of is my own. I tell you what—I'll be so glad when my diet consists of real food in real portions. I'm starting to feel like a mouse. I hope Julie will be okay. Did you call the doctor? Want me to ask Ethan?"

"She says she'll be fine," he said and thanked her for her concern. "I'm sure she'll bounce back soon. How's El? I rang him the other day. He's quite excited about the baby."

"He's the happy daddy, all right. He's started remodeling one of the bedrooms for the nursery. You wouldn't believe his plans. I mean, geeze, I'm not due until October! I think he's started looking at colleges already! Art colleges, of course."

"Of course. What else?"

"You're right. That's Elliot"

"He seems okay with your being away so much. If Julie were pregnant, I'd never let her out of my sight. Then again, El's calmer than I am."

"He keeps himself busy. He just finished a score for TriStar, but he's still spending a lot of time out and about. And he's smiling a lot. I think he's up to something."

"I'm sure it's just the baby. Anyway, how's Farin? Anything new develop?"

Marci's tone audibly shifted. "Do you have a sec?"

"Of course. What's up?"

Silence filled the line. From his side of the wire, Chris heard a door close, then the shuffling of feet across whatever room she inhabited, wherever she was. The static of her phone cut in and out of range for several seconds. Finally, she whispered, "I think she knows something."

Finally. "What did she say?"

"Nothing."

He plopped down onto the foot of his bed.

"Don't ask me how, but I know something's going on. It started the day you visited."

"Did she ever say why she screamed?"

"Nope, not yet. But I saw something that day. Like some weird flicker of recognition. She remembers something. It's like a trigger went off in her head, but she won't discuss it. I don't know if it has to do with the kidnapping, or Jordan, or what. All I know is, ever since that day, her recovery's been amazing. She's walking, eating well. But I'm tellin' you, she's got this look on her face. This determination or whatever. She knows something, Chris. Also, just before she screamed that day, she asked me about Dale Eastland."

"Who's that?"

"A friend of hers from a long time ago. He used to be in a band with her. He catered Chase's memorial service. And he just opened that new restaurant in West Hollywood, Colline."

Chris narrowed his eyes, trying to recall, but came up blank.

"Anyway, Farin told me she sent him something right before she took off for Jordan's funeral. I called him to ask if he received anything, but he said he didn't. I tried to be as casual as possible, but he must've thought I was crazy."

"What did she send him?"

"She won't tell me."

Chris heard the toilet flush. Julie shuffled back to her place beneath the sheets of their bed. He reached out and rested a hand atop the one leg she left out from under the covers. "Tell me where you are," he said into the phone.

"What?"

"I mean it, Marci. Tell me where you are."

"We can't chance it, Chris."

"Have you moved? Are you still in Malibu? Where is she? I have to see her."

"Look, I don't pretend to know what's gone on with that psycho, Jameson, but you know he must be keeping tabs on you. That's why we decided to move her in the first place! Be patient. We're close. I can feel it. She'll talk soon. You'll see."

"So, you're still in Malibu?"

She did not answer.

"I need her to talk to me, Marci."

"What makes you think she'd tell you if she won't even tell her best friend?"

"Because it's *me*!" Chris instantly regretted barking into the phone. He shot his wife a side-glance. She remained motionless on her side, the damp cloth covering her eyelids and forehead. He stared sightlessly across the room. "I'm sorry. I didn't mean to—"

Marci's voice lowered. "It's okay. I'm frustrated, too. I want to understand what's happened. Not only to Farin, but to Jordan as well. You and Ben have to be half-crazy, certainly worse than me. But until Farin decides to tell us, there's nothing we can do. She insists she doesn't remember a thing."

Chris bit his cheek. "Yet she mentioned her friend."

"Exactly."

Tucked beneath the sheets, Julie heard every word. A different, though equally sickening, feeling in her middle slowly replaced the nausea resulting from her pregnancy. That sickness had a name: Farin Grant.

For months, Julie had endured the reality of Farin's return from Deadsville, knowing from the moment Chris had announced the awful truth their days as husband and wife were short. Now, he sat in their bedroom, begging Marci to give him Farin's whereabouts. He begged for his true love right in front of her. Apparently, it no longer mattered if she knew of his intended reunion.

She considered her options, as she had done nonstop since the news of her pregnancy. The birth of this child would symbolize the defeat of everything in her life. And what would she have to show for it, save a protruding lower belly, sagging breasts, and a crying, snot-nosed brat she could not support?

Single motherhood was a reality she could not accept. Weekend drop-offs at parks and fast-food restaurants. Battling over every last cent of child support the judge would order. The ungrateful urchin loving Farin more than her—just like its father.

Something had to give. There was no life for her outside the popping lights of the cameras, the exotic cities and countries she visited on her shoots, the constant pampering, the star-studded parties at swank locations all over the world, the throngs of admiring fans. Sure, the air travel would pretty much come to an end, but even flying was better than the alternative. The chains of motherhood? Filthy, disgusting diapers? Constant screaming? Stretch marks? Cleaning up after some wild and out-of-control demon spawn spewing pea soup from various bodily orifices on a daily basis? Intermittent sleep?

No.

She had never signed up for this sort of hellish existence. Perhaps if Chris intended to stay with her and they could all be a family, she might consider it. At least together they might come to some reasonable decision about an overseas boarding school. Something very, very far away. Or even a full-time nanny. But not alone.

In her mind, she calculated the numbers. Her first trimester had come and gone, according to her due date around the end of September. If she planned to make a move, she had better make it fast. Soon, her belly would begin its horrid expansion. In fact, she felt certain she had noticed a slight paunch just last week. Subtle, yet noticeable—at least to her. She had nearly canceled a shoot for a swimsuit spread that same day for fear those around her might remark on her weight gain.

All at once, panic beset her. Cheryl knew about the baby.

Julie cursed herself for confiding in her sister-in-law. What could she possibly say to Cheryl if she suddenly turned up not pregnant anymore? Claim a miscarriage? Perhaps fall during a shoot? Provoke a physical altercation with a local street bum? Ram her Mercedes into the side of a building? Surely, she could think of something. She had to—and soon.

Before she realized Chris had ended his call, she felt him crawl up and wrap his arms around her. For the first time in weeks, she smiled without having to force the corners of her mouth into an upward half-circle. Almost immediately, it disappeared and she bolted to the bathroom once more.

Upon her return, Chris told her that if she still felt ill in the morning, he would insist she contact the doctor.

She kissed his cheek and snuggled close against his chest, smiling sincerely once more. "You're right, honey. I'll call the doctor tomorrow. I'm sure he can fix me right up."

CHAPTER 30

Lockhardt Makes Sound Recovery

-- Chicago, IL, Chicago Chronicle (AP), Tuesday, April 4, 1995 by Miles Macy

On the heels of an unprecedented fourth quarter financial recovery, it looks as though Lockhardt Sound, Inc. has escaped certain corporate death—however temporarily.

Six months ago, analysts responded to a rapid decrease in record sales and liquidation of assets with the prediction that the once multi-million-dollar recording leviathan would eventually collapse. Rumors abounded, first of an inevitable Big Six buy-out and, later, certain bankruptcy. Such conflicting speculation caused LSI stock to artificially spike, then drop to an all-time low.

In a press conference Monday, Bobby Lockhardt announced plans to begin a massive publicity campaign for a new stable of singers recently signed to the LSI label. Unlike similar statements made by Lockhardt in the past couple of years, it appears there may indeed be some validity to these current proclamations.

"We already have several acts recording in LA, New York, and London," stated Lockhardt Jr., son and sole heir of music mogul Jameson Lockhardt, president of Lockhardt Sound, Inc. "With the ongoing advancements in recording technology, we're able to get a perfected product out to the public in a faster, more streamlined manner. Fans are in for a musical renaissance unlike anything they've ever seen."

When asked about previous statements touting a turnaround in profits, Lockhardt stated, "We've always had our fingers on the pulse of the industry. We're just picky about the artists we sign. Pundits and critics who wanted to believe we were losing ground have misinterpreted our high standards. The quality of work we'll release in the next few weeks will speak for itself."

Much controversy has surrounded LSI in recent years. Aside from their struggles resulting from the suspicious and untimely deaths of Jordan Grant and Farin St. John—two of the label's top producers—rumors that Lockhardt sabotaged its own success by opting not to renew rock legend Mirage permeated the industry for years after the group disbanded. Mirage's notorious lead guitarist Chris Grant's subsequent solo deal with Minor 6th Records, coupled with Country and Western phenom Megan Price following in time, added fuel to the fire. With their final money maker gone, it was anyone's guess how LSI would generate the income to keep its corporate lights on.

When asked to comment on the likelihood of an LSI comeback, industry pundits are taking a wait-

and-see attitude. "It's like the little boy who cried wolf," said one insider. "It's hard to argue with their past success. But they've been spinning the same story for years now, and we've witnessed nothing to support their claims."

No matter what side of the fence you sit on, one thing is clear: recent fourth-quarter results show marked improvement. Only time will tell if LSI can rebuild their position with solid bricks and mortar, or if it's just a bunch of smoke and mirrors.

***

The chauffeur opened and held the door of the white Mercedes limousine parked in front of the Met. "Where to, sir?"

"HPN," growled Jameson. He climbed inside and sank into the luxurious leather interior, unbuttoning his tuxedo jacket and tugging loose the knot in his bow tie.

Weary and frustrated, Jameson was unable to concentrate on tonight's performance of *Pelléas et Mélisande*. He rarely found the time to attend public performances anymore, but had indulged this evening in a futile attempt at distraction from another long, unproductive afternoon.

Patience was a virtue he did not possess of late. Three months. *Three months* had passed with little word from Moreau, as he now referred to his personal messenger of death. Though pulled off the search for Farin in order to handle the Josephine Alexander matter, Moreau should have finished by now, despite his insistence that he needed to lie low for a while.

Every day Farin continued to draw breath, the odds of her full recovery increased. She was a loose cannon in his otherwise orderly arsenal. He could not risk an intact memory. Wherever she convalesced, her recovery could destroy everything he had built—and rebuilt—over a lifetime.

The limousine arrived at the Westchester County Airport, where a small Cessna awaited his arrival. As soon as he boarded and strapped himself in for takeoff, the pilot taxied down the runway, lifted off, and began the short northeast commute. In less than ninety minutes, he would be home.

He could count on one hand the number of people in his everyday life who knew the address of his Gilded Age estate. He had kept his whereabouts hidden his entire life—at first as a matter of survival, later out of fear, and now? Well, just in case.

Neighbors rarely caught a glimpse of the aging recluse inhabiting the enormous mansion at the southernmost tip of the gated peninsula with its stone fence, thick iron gates, and towering privacy hedges. Not even Ross knew his exact location. Once outside their corporate offices, he vanished into the night, only to reappear in the early hours of the next morning via the executive elevator, unnoticed by a soul.

The crescent-shaped estate hugged the curved, rocky coastline. It sat on nine acres of the most valuable real estate in New England. Designed for dramatic ocean views, its mid-30s Louis XIV chateau architecture exuded a regal beauty while its sequestered location maximized privacy. Its heavy, gray stone exterior—more wall than window—matched the gated Ocean Avenue entrance.

Inside, a thoroughly vetted staff took painstaking care to ensure the upkeep of painted and papered walls, hand-carved moldings, brass and gold fixtures, the priceless Persian rugs covering hardwood floors, and marble bathrooms and fireplace surrounds. They maintained an inestimable assortment of rare and original artwork and kept a treasured collection of vases, busts, figurines, Spode china, and Sterling silver flatware gleaming and well-preserved.

They worked professionally and quietly—aware that a state-of-the-art surveillance system recorded their every move. Should any of his meticulously inventoried possessions become damaged, broken, or misplaced, the results would prove catastrophic for the offending party.

Outside, a team of gardeners pruned, cut, weeded, watered, and manicured the lavish grounds, keeping fountains pristine, exotic plants and trees healthy, and meandering stone pathways clean, repairing even the smallest damage from age or weather. Endless effort went into preserving the place within and without, despite the fact its owner rarely spent time at home and virtually never received a visitor.

The estate resembled a palace, a museum, or—as the help labeled it— a tomb.

To incentivize loyalty, employees received wages others in their field found unimaginable. Perfection and anonymity did not come cheap, but he gladly paid.

Strategically positioned external illumination pierced the dark, cloudless evening as a limousine similar to the one he had abandoned back in the city hummed up the roadway and looped around the circular drive. Jameson noted with displeasure someone had neglected to turn on the house lights.

Laziness, just plain laziness, he thought as he exited the vehicle. He would address the responsible party in the morning.

After depositing Jameson safely on the steps of his expansive cement porch, the driver returned to the car and drove off with instructions to return promptly at five the next morning—the same routine he followed daily.

He marched straight to his den, removed his jacket, and flung it over the back of an overstuffed accent chair near the wet bar, then turned to his desk and stabbed the speaker button on the phone. He checked his home then business voice mail. Finding no messages from Moreau or the phony Z-Master Imports, he pulled the end of his bow tie from around his neck with an angry yank and tossed it atop his jacket.

Had he lost his edge? A younger Jameson Lockhardt would strike fear into the heart of an associate who behaved with such disrespect. Then again, a younger Jameson Lockhardt would have handled the job himself. Success and wealth had made him too comfortable. He should have known better than to hire out the wet work.

He trudged to the bar and poured two fingers of Macallan into a Glencairn glass, tossed the brown liquid to the back of his throat, and swallowed with a mighty gulp, then poured another. His thoughts twisted in on one another as he paced the room. Simmering like thick stew over Moreau's lack of communication, he stopped and fixed his eyes upon the roaring fire a dutiful staff member had started in anticipation of his return. Its orange flames danced and kissed the otherwise dark room like a taunting lover. Flickering tongues of light cast sinister, ever-shifting shadows against the walls.

When he had emptied his second glass and poured a third, he eased himself behind his desk, reclining into the tufted leather chair. Nowhere on earth did he feel more comfortable than sitting alone in his den.

Bigger than his New York office, he rarely visited the other rooms in his home. Why bother? Everything he needed was here—the enormous hand-carved cherry desk with matching credenza and hutch, a sofa comfortable enough to sleep on, lounge chairs and tables at which he could read or take a meal, a television-stereo ensemble, a fireplace.

A large east-facing window hidden beneath lined tapestry curtains remained closed and locked except while cleaned. Built-in bookcases comprised two of the four walls, their shelves pregnant with first editions, decades' worth of trade magazines, and volumes of newspaper clippings involving LSI. Unbeknownst to anyone, he had also compiled copies of periodicals featuring his son's brilliant, if childlike, visage on the cover.

As the liquor numbed his senses, he found himself musing over

Bobby's future and that of his company. The more he thought, the angrier he grew. He had not fought poverty, lost his wife, and escaped certain incarceration only to be undone by an impulsive, reactionary, pitiable redhead who did not have the sense to quit while she was behind.

He should have killed her himself the moment they took her.

For the second time that week, he picked up his phone and dialed the international number. When the automated recording for Z-Master Imports prompted him to leave a message at the tone, he raged into the receiver, "I'm inquiring about my 'package!' Its 'delivery date' has been 'overdue' for some time now and I've made numerous unreturned calls to that effect! I demand to know the 'status' immediately! Have your 'delivery department' call me as soon as you receive this message—this is *not* a request. He knows how to reach me." He slammed the receiver into its cradle.

"Damn UPS," came a familiar, unexpected voice from behind him. "I have that problem sometimes, too. Why not just have Stacy run it down for ya?"

Jameson spun around. His son stood before him, clad in paisley pajamas and a matching robe. Obviously, he had not just arrived. "What are you doing here?"

"Gee, Dad, I didn't mean to shake you up." Bobby chuckled apologetically. He dropped down onto one of two gilded, upholstered armchairs facing the fire. "You okay? What's the package?"

He drained his glass, poured a fourth, then plunked down heavily behind his desk. "It's business. Never mind."

"Anything I should know about?"

"It'll be handled before you take over. Don't give it a thought."

Bobby crossed his legs, wiggling his toes to avoid losing one of his suede slippers. "I thought I'd crash here tonight. Hope you don't mind. You'd said you were gonna go to the Met so I figured you'd be home pretty late. How was the show?"

"Fine." He sipped his drink and huffed. "How was the meeting with that new girl? What's her name again? Sharon-something-or-other?"

"*Charlene*. Anyway, I took your advice on the name thing. You were right. Charlene Johnson sounded too plain."

"And what did you decide on?"

Bobby's face brightened. He uncrossed his legs, twisted around in the chair to face his father, and spread his fingers wide at either side of his face. "We decided on…you ready? *Joni Leighton*! Doesn't that sound great?"

Jameson was in no mood to discuss any business unrelated to the acquisition and disposal of one Farin Grant. As his son extolled the virtues of what instinct told Jameson was Bobby's newest crush, and detailed plans for the next jewel in LSI's crown, Jameson wondered where she hid, what she remembered, and when she would start talking.

According to Moreau's last report, he had tracked an older model Oldsmobile to a small town some miles from the Arizona/California border. From there, the trail had run cold. Moreau had discovered the abandoned vehicle at a motel, its trunk filled with enough medical refuse to alleviate any doubt Farin had occupied the car at some point.

The vehicle registration belonged to her best friend, Elliot Lawrence's wife. A simple inquiry led to an address in Laurel Canyon, California. For days, Moreau had staked out the house and its inhabitants but learned nothing that might reveal his former captive's current whereabouts.

Moreau had stalked Chris's activities as well but fared no better. This confused Jameson. Surely Chris had helped Marci take Farin from Dorothea Dix. Not only would the girl have never learned of Farin's predicament on her own, but she could not have managed the escape without assistance. Chris was the obvious co-conspirator and, given his obsession with the girl, it seemed odd he would stay away if he knew where she hid.

As Bobby's enthusiastic yammering continued, Jameson wondered how many secrets Ross had given away. Should he expect only the American police, or might Scotland Yard pop up as well?

Shortly after Josephine's death, Ross had requested a leave of absence, which Jameson had eagerly granted. Since finalizing his retirement date, Ross had worked with Bobby to ensure the boy's smooth transition into the role of company president. They had met with shareholders, reviewed contracts for under-producing bands, and scoured the books, which had slowly returned to the black. Little remained to prevent Ross from taking time off. In fact, Jameson welcomed his absence.

"You didn't hear a word I just said, did you?" Bobby's casual grin was a feeble attempt to mask the hurt of his father's inattention. His crystal eyes flickered with resentment; the left subtly spasmed. "Gee, Dad, where are you tonight?"

"Sorry." Jameson cleared his throat and straightened in his chair. "So, Joni Leighton. Not bad. How's the recording coming?"

Bobby stared at the fire, still excited about the girl but less enthusiastic about repeating his story. "Great material, top-notch musicians. Her publicity photos are handled. Everything's ahead of schedule. She's a dream. I haven't had this much fun working with someone since Farin." He winced in instant regret as the name escaped his lips.

Jameson rose from behind his desk and strode toward his son. "I thought we agreed not to mention her again."

Bobby stared mournfully at the floor. "We did. I'm...sorry."

"I'm only thinking of your well-being."

"I know."

On June eleventh, Bobby would celebrate his thirty-ninth birthday. Peers and associates labeled him a force to reckon with. Over his career, he had been named one of the most eligible bachelors in the world by several magazines. He possessed the kind of success upwardly mobile men envied. Yet his sole desire was his father's attention, approval, and love.

They had had little contact during his childhood but Bobby had worshipped the father who had eventually built an empire from nothing, even if it did keep him busy enough to miss birthdays and holidays. The Lockhardt name garnered respect. It was impressive—and intimidating.

Alone and awkward, he had never quite found his crowd. While he had all the advantages money could buy and the obsessive devotion of his doting mother—a byproduct, he had believed, of his parents' separation— his peers' reluctance to accept him into their fold hurt and confused him. In the end, he had attributed their scorn to jealousy and wore their rejection as a badge of honor.

Privately, he had known his mother had scared them off.

Only Bobby had witnessed his mother's delusions, the incoherence, the increasing fits of rage. With his father in England at first, and then on the other side of the country later, she had little trouble concealing her deteriorating mental state.

"Swear you won't tell anyone, baby," she would plead during her more lucid moments. "It's our secret. Mummy couldn't bear to lose you, too."

He had sworn. Every time.

As he grew, he struggled at home and school. Sure, he had the grades. The curriculum barely challenged him. But his love of music, sports, and drama did not bring him the kind of success he found academically.

Coaches cut him from rosters. Drama teachers relegated him to set design. When he tried out for band, learning to read music proved impossible. Magnified by his father's success, these particular failures broke him.

At fifteen, he started drinking.

He drank to numb his feelings of inadequacy, to forget his father's absenteeism, and to escape the mother who treated him like an infant during rare moments of coherency. Alcohol soothed the pain of rejection the few times he mustered the courage to ask a girl out on a date.

In the end, his path to self-destruction nearly killed him. Three days before the Stearns Warf fire of '73, he totaled his Porsche—a token present from the father he had rarely spent time with. The accident preceded an immediate and permanent change in his circumstances. He had been so wasted, he did not remember a thing.

"In any case, it sounds as if you have things under control. Which studio is she using?"

Painful recollections drove Bobby from his chair to the wet bar. He stared sullenly at the crystal bar set to his left, wishing he could imbibe a glass or two to banish the memories. "The Music Mill."

His dad's voice had originated from the seat beside the one he had just vacated, though he did not recall him sitting down next to him. "Are you all right, son?"

He flattened his lips. "I'm fine. Did you ever meet with any of the physicians the doc recommended? I'm almost out of my meds."

"I have, yes, and I've nearly made my final decision. I'll get you the name next week."

"Thanks. I'll set up an appointment right away." He scooted behind the bar and grabbed a club soda from the mini-fridge, then returned to his seat.

Together, they watched the fire's slow consumption of wooden logs. Bobby fixed his eyes on the pulsating orange glow of the hot black embers as they fell through the andiron and onto a pile of gray ash atop the hearthstone.

As fate would have it, his father had been in Los Angeles finalizing Mirage's contracts at the time of the accident. Earlier that same afternoon, he had come to rescue him.

The details were ill-remembered. Scared and alone, his mother had pushed him to his breaking point. When Bobby could take no more, he had fled the house. He awoke the next day to discover he had totaled his car, his mother had gone to a hospital, and he was moving to New York with his father. Once the decision was made, things moved quickly. They left two days later. Bobby had been given precious little time to even pack his things.

He finished high school in Rhode Island, plagued by the unremembered sequence of events and the abrupt change in his life. Once, he had overheard whispers from his father's study—something about someone dying in the accident. A man...last name O'Conner, if he recalled.

Horrified and consumed with guilt, he had questioned his father. In no uncertain terms, he had told Bobby to forget what he had heard and concentrate on finishing school. After all, he was a Lockhardt. He had a bright future in store.

The New England kids treated him no differently than his California classmates before them. They neither accepted nor included him. Soon, he stopped caring about school, his lack of friends—especially girlfriends—and even his mother.

He plummeted into a state of deep depression, which resulted in his father introducing him to the physician LSI kept on retainer. After gathering some routine background information, Dr. Childs researched his family history and scholastic records only to unearth the one piece of his social past that would permanently alter the course of his future.

According to Childs, Sarah Lockhardt had neglected to reveal what her beloved son never knew—presumably out of fear her own illness might be discovered. Bobby was aware there were stretches of time he could not recall, but he had attributed them to his drinking. He would have never guessed that during those moments he had exhibited frightening behavior. Armed with the shocking revelation, Childs echoed the diagnosis his mother had received some months earlier and started him on anti-psychotic medication.

"You have enough to get you through a couple of weeks, don't you?"

Bobby eyed his father as if from a great distance. "Enough what?"

"What is it you take—Haldol, isn't it?"

He nodded absently. "The drug of champions."

His father looked at him askance, then attended his drink. "Let me know if you get low. I'll arrange a temporary prescription to tide you over."

Bobby unscrewed the cap of his club soda, took a sip, then stared back at the fire. "Thanks, Dad. I sure will."

The diagnosis of schizophrenia had terrified him. Now, for all his efforts, the outside world would never see him as normal. Wishing to avoid embarrassment, his father kept the condition from the public. In the end, instead of gaining the love and closeness he had longed for as a boy, he bore the burden of single-handedly shaming the Lockhardt name.

As if to round out his ill-fate, he discovered Haldol rendered him impotent. He would never have a family. Practically speaking, he could never hope to have a girlfriend.

Then, he met Farin St. John.

Farin became Bobby's first real friend. She treated him like a normal person—a normal man. Troubled and secretive, she did not mind if he chose not to disclose his past. In fact, they had agreed early on that discussing their families was strictly verboten. It made them kindred spirits on some level.

Her whirlwind existence kept him reeling. Then, when news of her attempted suicide had reached him, something inside him erupted. It was then he realized he had fallen in love with his best and only friend.

At the time, he believed discontinuing his medication would give him the strength to tell her how he felt and give him the opportunity to follow through on those feelings. Her marriage had seemed destined for defeat and would always include the complication of Chris's pursuit. Bobby hoped Farin would find it in her heart to love him as he did her.

But before he built up the nerve to confess his most private feelings, he descended into the most prolonged psychotic episode he had ever experienced, according to his father. He woke up in Dorothea Dix Hospital days before Christmas and learned Farin had died in an automobile accident in Miami.

Crushed and confused, Bobby's torment was compounded by the news of Jordan's murder. At first, he feared he might have had something to do with it, but his father assured him he was already in North Carolina at the time of the murder. The investigation's subsequent pronouncement of a failed burglary relieved him, but he mourned Farin's death for months. In the end, his father insisted they never speak of her again.

"I have an early day tomorrow," Jameson told him. He stood, abandoning his empty glass on the side table between them. "You should get some sleep, son. You look tired."

Overcome with dismal memories, Bobby rose and studied his father. His thoughts raced by in a blur.

"What is it?" Jameson asked roughly.

Bobby searched his father's ice-blue eyes. At one time, he had been a handsome man. Women had flocked to him, though he appeared disinterested in female companionship. Bobby wondered if his father ever yearned for someone with whom he could share his life. Did he ever feel lonely? Tonight, Bobby felt very lonely.

"Have you been taking your medication?" Jameson asked, worry lines spreading across his aging face.

Bobby moved forward and wrapped his arms around him. "I love you, Dad." He pulled back before his father could react to the uncommon display of affection, then headed upstairs, adding over his shoulder, "Good night."

Jameson's brows furrowed as he watched his son vanish upstairs, unable to recall the last time they had embraced. He stood and listened as Bobby's footsteps reached the top of the stairs and receded down the long hall. At last, he heard the faint echo of Bobby's bedroom door close.

"Now wasn't that touching," came a voice from the direction of the fireplace.

The hair on the back of his neck rose as he spun around. He squinted into the darkness in the direction of the voice. His tired, aging eyes barely made out the shape of a man who seemed to materialize from mere shadows. The pulsing glow from the fireplace gave him a demonic, spectral appearance. There, but not there.

"Don't look too hard, Lockhardt," the man cautioned. "You don't really want to see my face, do you? I can't have people seeing my face."

Instinct told him to rush to his desk, grab his pistol from the left-hand drawer, and shoot blindly into the darkness. He gave the idea due consideration but ultimately abandoned such a ridiculous notion. Surely, the shadowy stranger could not only outpace him but was likely armed. "Moreau?"

The voice chuckled devilishly. "We're still calling me that?"

Jameson swallowed hard, deriding himself for uttering the moniker.

"I like it. A lot. Moreau it is."

The nasal quality of the man's voice grated on his nerves. He sounded young, cocky, and not overly masculine. The unmelodious pitch in his tone left him to guess Moreau chose visual anonymity for more than reasons of possible identification. Perhaps he was less intimidating in person—an unfortunate proposition for a contract killer.

Jameson deliberately slackened his facial muscles, his fleshy jowls pulling his timeworn skin taut until all expression vanished. It would take more than shadows and veiled threats to rattle him in his own home. Jameson had dealt with far more menacing characters than Moreau—or whoever he was—would ever know. And he had dealt with them decisively.

He squared his shoulders and strode to his minibar. "I was just about to have a nightcap. Care to join me?"

"Haven't you had enough for the night? Besides, I never drink on the job."

"I take it, then, you've come to discuss business."

"Indeed."

He filled a fresh glass and, at Moreau's insistence, took a seat at his desk at the far end of the room. Based on the direction of his voice, Jameson guessed he crouched somewhere right of the fireplace mantel. He wondered how the man had slipped into his home unnoticed—how he had found him in the first place. Was there a weak link in his personal staff as well? Could he trust no one?

"There seems to be a lack of understanding between us," Moreau began.

"And what misunderstanding might that be?" Jameson huffed brusquely. He reclined and rocked gently as he sipped his whiskey. The burning sensation inside his stomach comforted him.

"You seem to think I run a private investigation service."

"And you've broken into my home to tell me you've lost them?"

Moreau huffed impatiently. "Maybe it's a matter of explaining the terms. You corporate types like things laid out plainly, right? Okay, here goes. I *kill* people. *Locating* them requires an entirely different skill set—including patience, which has never really been my strong suit. And working with you, I've got a much shorter supply. You hired me to do a job, Lockhardt. The job I agreed to doesn't entail tracking the mark across country."

"I hired you to take care of a problem. Whatever taking care of the problem entails, *that's* what I hired you for."

"It's done."

Jameson stopped rocking, leaned forward, and peered into the shadows. "She's gone, then? What about the others?"

"Correction—*nearly* done. As I explained earlier, I needed to put some distance between myself and the scene of the impending crime."

"What does that mean? Is she dead or not?"

"Tell you what. You be sure to watch the network news tomorrow evening. You'll get a blast out of it, I promise. I can only guarantee the girl. There are others, but the doctor attending her and the best friend? I can't say. Nonetheless, I've finished the job you originally hired me for."

"So you've come here for payment?"

"Our payment arrangement's never been an issue. I just wanted to drop by personally and tell you two things. First, the job will be completed tomorrow. Second, if you ever contact me again, I will kill you. Do we understand each other?"

Jameson finished his drink and calmly set the glass on his blotter. He disliked the threat, but considered his options. "If you succeed with this, we'll never have to speak again. I believe that's in both our interests." He waited for the man's agreement. "Moreau?"

There came no response. A minute later, he dared to stand and search the den but found no one. Moreau had vanished as mysteriously as he had appeared.

CHAPTER 31

THE MOMENT MARCI LOOKED THROUGH the peep hole, she knew the day would not run as smoothly as she had hoped. Eyes shut, she rested her forehead against the door. Should she pray or curse?

"You shouldn't have come," she scolded in an urgent whisper, grabbing his arm and dragging him in. She peeked outside, surveying their surroundings like a gangster on the lam before shutting and securing the door behind them. His presence only marginally surprised her. The determination in his voice the last time they spoke had warned her he would come, no matter the consequence. "We're finally able to move her. If you start coming around, we'll have to find another place. What's wrong with you?"

He crossed the entryway and scanned the empty room. "I need to see her. You said she's doing better. I need to know what happened."

Marci raised her hands to her hips. "I'm not trying to be insensitive here, Chris, but we're trying to get her settled into the new place today."

"Where are you taking her?"

She spun on her heel, stomped toward the living room, then doubled back, pointing at him in frustration. "You come here knowing how dangerous it is—after we all agreed Lockhardt's probably having you followed—and you think I'll tell you where we're taking her? I may be crazy from pregnancy hormones, but I'm not *that* crazy."

"You said she remembered."

She shushed him, waving him into the kitchen to avoid their voices echoing upstairs. "I said I *think* she remembers."

He leaned back, gripping the counter with both hands. "The sooner she talks, the safer she'll be."

"I know that, you know that...but Farin?"

"She can't possibly think we'll let anyone hurt her. That *I*—"

"*You?*" She peered at him with challenging eyes.

"That's not what I meant."

She flexed the tension from her neck and scraped her top teeth against her bottom lip. Before she could find the words she searched for, he pushed off from the counter and headed for the swinging door. "What are you doing?"

"Is she awake?"

Marci caught his arm. "Don't. Ethan's on his way. We're finally getting her out. It won't be long now, I promise."

He stopped and studied her, then glanced sadly around the room. "You know, we all met in this house."

She deflated, her eyes misting at memories she had found herself confronting since their return from Raleigh. Good and bad—mostly bad. Jordan and Farin in accidentally similar clothes the day of the barbecue so long ago. Chase drowning in the pool later that day. The years she had wasted living here with Dan Albright and the pain of his emotional abuse. Her instant dislike of the man standing before her—the antihero in Farin's life story. That dislike had transformed into sympathy and even admiration as Marci witnessed his desperate struggle to right every wrong. "It was a long time ago."

"A lifetime."

She swallowed the lump in her throat. "Can I ask you something?"

He wove his head in a figure eight and shrugged.

"It'll only take a minute."

Chris followed her back to the counter, then helped her up to sit upon the butcher block island. She scooted backwards to its center and crossed her legs.

"Look," he said. "I know it's risky, but I couldn't let another day go by. And since I'm here now, she might as well talk to me. I'm not leaving until she does."

Marci fidgeted with her wedding ring, then her fingernails, noting offhandedly how strong they had become since starting her prenatal vitamins. "First off, I'm not questioning your motives. You've been great. Let's face it: if not for you, Farin would be dead now. We would've never known...well, we'd all still think...you know what I mean."

He squinted, nodding slowly to humor her more than anything else.

"You and Julie are happy, right?"

His eyes widened in understanding. "I'm here to find out who killed my brother and why Lockhardt had Farin locked in the basement of some nuthouse in North Carolina. Don't you want to know why she called that press conference the day of the funeral, or sent some package to that friend of hers and why he never got it?"

"Of course. It's just—"

"Well, so do I. I know what everyone's worried about. I get it from Ben about every time we talk. But hear me when I say, I don't want to complicate Farin's life—or my own."

"Good." Marci clasped her hand to her chest.

At least one of them had come to their senses.

For days, Marci had answered too many questions regarding Chris and Julie's marital situation. On one hand, it reeked of some convenient ploy to change the subject whenever Marci asked Farin about her memory. Each time, Farin had claimed not to remember, then drilled Marci with questions. Was Chris happy? Did he really love Julie? How were they as a couple? Just this morning, Marci had accused her of withholding information from the people who had risked their lives to bring her home.

On the other hand, Marci's gut told her the unsubtle interrogation might belie a desire to recapture something lost between her and Chris. Maybe Farin was having a harder time dealing with Jordan's death than anyone realized. Maybe she viewed Chris as a substitute, someone familiar to prevent her from being alone. While Marci would prefer to believe the former scenario, she suspected both were accurate.

At least Chris had his head on straight. Finally.

She slipped off the butcher block to grab a drink from the ice chest. She could hardly wait to relocate somewhere with electricity and running water. Helping Farin bathe and wash her hair without the creature comforts they took for granted was no picnic. "We've got water, Sprite, and a few Snapples. Take your pick."

"When can I see her?" he asked, this time more insistent.

She reached in and grabbed a Sprite and a water, tossing the latter to him before shutting the lid. "Before you go up, there's something you should know."

***

"Well, *hello* Alicia's answering machine! Long time no talk—or, uh, *hear*, since I do all the talking in this relationship. Anyway, you know the drill. Tell her I've called, ask her to call me back, and tell her I'll call again soon. Talk to you next time, answering machine. Bye!" Miles dropped the receiver onto its base and swiveled around to stare blankly out his office window at the surrounding buildings. He gnawed the nail of his left ring finger.

Lesser men would have given up by now. In fact, had Bridgeman not encouraged him to "hang in there," he might have done just that. When he had talked to his sister last week during a family dinner, she told him women loved being chased. If true, Alicia must be in Heaven. At least that would explain why she had not returned any of his calls.

"No luck?" Jeanne asked as she breezed in and immediately began tidying up his office. "I have to hand it to you, bossman. You're a trooper."

"Think she'll ever call me back?"

Jeanne gathered a stack of proofs off the floor, patted them into order, then stacked them on a shelf. "I think she'd be crazy not to."

He swiveled away from the window. "Do women like men to chase them?"

"Depends on the woman, I guess—well, and the man who's doing the chasing."

"Did Claude chase you?"

Her face clouded. She gave a quick head rattle and pinched her lips together. "I suppose. At first."

"Sorry." He rolled his chair back to his desk. "You okay?"

She planted her hands on her narrow hips and scanned the room. "I'm not the one we're worrying about right now, you are."

"Me?"

"Yes, you."

"I'm not worried."

"Well, you should be."

"You think so?"

With a beckoning flourish of her hand, she bustled toward him. "You look like a mess. Go to the men's room and freshen up."

"Freshen up?"

When he stood up and faced her, she fixed his collar and straightened his tie. "You're not taking this seriously. You know I hate it when you act like you don't care about your job."

He pondered her worried crystal orbs, chuckling despite himself. "I'm sorry, Jeanne, it's not funny."

She slapped him lightly on the shoulder, then continued straightening the office. "Every day, I have to remind you. I—"

"—need this job," he finished her sentence, bobbing his head side-to-side. "And every day, I remind you neither of us is going to lose our job."

She marched out to her desk, snatched up a piece of paper, then stomped back inside, waving it at him. "How many times has Frank Harper requested a formal meeting with you, hmm? In the entire time I've been here, the answer is a resounding *zero*. Oh, he comes by. He chitchats and asks how things are going, but he doesn't write a formal notice announcing he'll be here at one o'clock on the nose." She glanced at the wall clock. "You have exactly six minutes to get it together. He didn't sound happy."

Miles dropped back in his seat, resting his chin on his fist. "How can a memo *sound* like anything?"

She raised her arms, shaking her hands in the air.

"Look, if anyone should be angry, it's me. I'm the one whose piece was edited until it almost didn't look like what I'd written. From where I sit, he owes me an explanation."

"He's your boss, Miles. He doesn't owe you anything, especially when he told you ahead of time to tone it down."

"I *did* tone it down, trust me. I made it as positive as I could considering I don't believe a word out of that corporate spin house."

"Well, apparently you didn't tone it down enough. I told you Miami was a bad idea. I told you you'd get in trouble there."

Her comment pricked his lighthearted demeanor. His cocksure smile dimmed.

"That's what I thought." She folded her arms. "I talked to Harper's secretary, Leslie. My understanding is, he wants your head."

"My head?"

"Mm-hmm. She said that's what she heard." She tossed the memo onto his desk, turned on her heel, and walked to the door. "And you've only got three minutes left. Slick back your hair or something. I've gotta get to my lawyer's to sign the divorce papers, so I'm afraid I'll miss your drama, dealing with my own."

"Hey, Jeanne?"

She turned around, brows raised.

"Call me later if you need to talk. I'll meet you for a drink or something."

She grasped the door handle. "Call me if I need to come back and pack my things."

He shot her a brave smile and a thumbs-up. She winked and shut the door behind her. He watched her log off her computer, toss some files into her bottom drawer, and kick it shut. She snatched up her purse and walked off toward the elevator.

Exactly two minutes later, Miles saw Frank Harper headed for his office. With his vested, jacketless suit and stern demeanor, Miles decided he resembled Inspector Todd from the *Beverly Hills Cop* series—a comparison to which Harper had caught wind of but had not yet warmed.

As he approached, his dark, focused eyes, and controlled yet purposeful swagger told Miles two things. First, Jeanne was right. Second, any complaint the man intended to address had come from higher up.

Frank carried a manila folder in his hand. Not too thick, not too thin. Probably not Miles's personnel file, but he could not be sure. The *Chronicle* had never before expressed dissatisfaction with his work. In fact, they had always given him positive feedback. How that had changed, he could only guess. The whole scenario felt oddly familiar. This was how it had started at the *Post*—his boss marching into his office with a manila folder.

No sooner had Frank Harper crossed his office threshold than Miles heard the chirp of his phone. When Frank turned his back to close the office door, Miles glanced over at the display. His adrenaline surged when he saw the 305 area code. He fought the urge to pick up the receiver. When he looked back up, Frank waited expectantly before him.

Miles stood, a genial smile on his lips. He extended his hand. "Frank! How the hell are you?"

Frank ignored the enthusiasm. He dropped the folder on the desk, brought his shoulder forward, then eye-pointed to his backside. "Notice anything different about me, Macy?" he growled with an angry clip of his voice.

Miles stuck his lips out and narrowed his eyes, one brow arched as he held his boss's stare. He was not about to peek at his posterior—especially in an office with a glass wall. "Not sure what you're sayin' here, Frank. You, uh, look fine to me."

"Well, I'm *not* fine!" The man spun around, snatched up the folder, and dragged one of the two upholstered guest chairs forward to sit down. "I thought I made myself crystal last week. Thought you were a smart guy. Now, half my ass is gone! I left it up in Jack's office!"

He tucked his chin but held his tongue. Probably not the best time for a half-ass remark, especially one that might unintentionally poke fun at his boss's relations with his wife.

Frank slammed the folder on top of Miles's desk and opened it with an irritated flip. "You started here in January of ninety-three, as I recall."

The hair on Miles's neck stood at attention. Maybe Jeanne was right. He looked away to collect his thoughts, perhaps think of some clever way out of an uncomfortable situation. When he saw his desk phone's message light blinking, his eyes widened with renewed hope.

"So that's just over two years you've been with us," Frank continued.

He nodded, not quite following the logic.

Frank pulled a pair of black-rimmed reading glasses out of his shirt pocket and slid them into place. "A column a week for over twenty-eight months. Do you know how many of your pieces we've published since you've been here?"

Confused, he did not quite know how to respond. Something told him no matter what he said, he would get nailed. "Uh, no. Not offhand."

The man yanked off his glasses with a furious grunt and leveled his black eyes upon him. "One hundred and seventeen!"

His brows lifted up and down. He emitted an impressed whistle despite his better judgment. "Not bad. That doesn't even include my syndicated stuff."

Frank put the glasses back on and leafed through the folder. Miles recognized them as copies of each column he had written since moving to Chicago. He kept a similar folder at his house—obviously for different reasons.

From his write-up on Duran Duran's comeback with their "Ordinary World" release to his commentary on Whitney Houston's longest running #1 single, the cover of Dolly Parton's "I Will Always Love You," to his review of Woodstock '94, Frank Harper scanned them all.

When he got to Miles's December 16, 1993 column, he stopped and pulled it from the file. He lifted his head and peered down the bridge of his nose at the article. Mouth stretched downward, he appeared older than his fifty some-odd years. He tossed the paper across the desk for Miles to review. "You remember writing this?"

He reclined in his seat, hoping the relaxed body language would conceal his growing fear that he might have to call Jeanne about packing up her desk after all. "Sure, I remember! One of my better pieces, if I do say so myself."

"You think so, eh?"

"I do. It had humor, suspense..."

"And a thinly veiled threat against one of the world's most powerful entertainment icons."

Miles pulled his head back and frowned. "You think so, Frank? Gee, I guess I didn't think about it like that. But hell, it was so long ago, who can remember now?"

Frank snatched the paper back and returned it to the file, then stood and towered over the desk. "*I* remember! The entire editorial executive team remembers! And do you know why we remember, Macy?"

He shrugged and tilted his head. "Exceptional journalism?"

"No! Because thirty-seven percent of the columns you've turned in since that day have been about Jameson Lockhardt, Lockhardt Sound, or artists on their label! Those that don't have anything to do with your topic of choice still manage to include an honorable mention of some sort. Like that piece you did on Cobain's suicide? You just couldn't help yourself, could you? Had to mention Jordan Grant's murder."

"Okay, Frank. I see where you're going with this."

"I don't think you do. You're quickly becoming known around here as a one-trick pony, and it's got to stop!"

When scolding turned to lecture, Miles grew antsy. It did not particularly bother him to watch the gawkers outside his office staring out of the corners of their eyes as they passed. Even the yelling did not faze him—much. What caught and held his attention was the blinking red light on his phone. The sooner Frank Harper left, the sooner he could find out if that crimson beacon meant Alicia's machine had come through for him. And the sooner he exhibited the requisite amount of contrition, the sooner Frank would leave. If only he could feign regret he did not feel.

He leaned forward, hearing out his managing editor with few interruptions and no witty quips. To sell his manufactured remorse, he wiped the usual self-assured grin from his face and tried to look serious, complete with relaxed facial muscles, a slight squint around focused eyes brimming with regret, and an obligatory furrowing of the brow.

"Consider this a verbal warning," Harper barked as he collected the contents of the file then slammed it closed. "A verbal warning with a little increased scrutiny. Until further notice, I'll be approving every idea and every column you write. We'll revisit this issue in six months. Got it?"

Miles stood and pumped Harper's hand with a hearty grip. "Got it. You're right. I guess I lost my objectivity there for a while."

Harper stood straighter. He pushed his chest forward, hooking one of the belt loops of his pants with his index finger and hiking them up an inch. "Time to let go of what's gone, son. You don't need to go 'round chasing ghosts. Thought you came back to Chicago to leave that shit behind."

He nodded thoughtfully. "You're right. I see that now."

"I'm glad we understand each other." He turned and strode to the office door. When he flung it open, several eavesdroppers scattered in various directions. Harper eyeballed them with a mixture of suspicion and annoyance. "What the hell's so interesting?" He turned back and grabbed the handle to shut the door behind him. "And you might want to put a little extra thought into your future vacation destinations. Just a little advice."

Miles acknowledged with a curt nod. He remained still and standing as he watched Frank disappear down the hall, his self-important gait a clear sign of his satisfaction over putting Miles in his place. Several colleagues drifted past his office, gesturing with questioning hands. He pulled the corners of his mouth into a downward smirk and shook his head, assuring them he was fine.

When the hubbub died down, he took his seat, grabbed the phone receiver, and hit the button to connect him to voicemail. Only one message awaited him—a message from Miami.

"Hi, Miles, it's Sandra! Listen, I hadn't heard from you in a while so I thought I'd..."

***

Sometimes, Farin could not tell whether the sensations were real or imagined. The area surrounding the incision felt numb to the touch. It appeared to have healed well but every time she moved around, there came an internal tugging and a deep, dull pain where the scalpel had sliced muscles and severed nerve endings.

She often inspected the marks on her body. A dark, jagged line separated her belly from her pelvic region like an inexpertly drawn border on a map. It resembled a grimace, save the slight pooch of flesh that promised to invade its perimeter should she gain excess weight.

The accompanying stretch marks looked different from the rest of the scars on her body. They resembled thin, pale, waxy tiger stripes whereas the rest of the scars were thick and dark. Each time she examined her naked image in the bathroom's full-length mirror, she grew angrier.

Jameson had exacted his revenge like a master—much more precise than the crude slash Dr. Childs had left as a triumphant reminder she would never again bear children. Years ago in France, Dr. Lardan had said he doubted she would ever be able to have more children. Now, no question remained.

Memories of the forced hysterectomy had erupted the moment she had confronted the hideous scar. Disjointed and sketchy at first, she could not recall the reason for the physical mutilation of her body. It took days to stitch the timeline together, but now she knew.

She knew everything.

A quick succession of knocks sounded at the door as she combed through her damp curls. Marci peeked her head inside. "You decent?"

She waved her in. "I was just getting ready to come down. Is Ethan here already? I'm still in my nightclothes."

Marci entered the room, an unconvincing smile painted on her face as she closed the door behind her. "He didn't get home from the hospital until early this morning so he needed some sleep first. He'll be here soon." The smile faded. "But, uh…you do have a visitor."

A glimmer of hope fluttered across her doe eyes.

Marci's mouth twisted downward in disapproval. She raised a brow and nodded toward the large suitcase laying open on the floor. "Go ahead and change. I know you want to."

With halting, careful movements, Farin slid off the bed and dug through the clothes Marci had slowly siphoned off her wardrobe at home. She removed shirt after shirt from the case, holding each against her chest before discarding them. "I wish I could get outta here and do some shopping."

"I did the best I could," Marci told her, a tinge of hurt in her tone. "Just tell me what you want. Maybe I could get some catalogs or you could give me an idea of what you're looking for."

Realizing the callousness of the remark, she struggled to her feet and put a hand on Marci's shoulder. "I didn't mean it that way. Don't pay any attention to me. I'm thankful just to be able to get up and dress myself. Honestly, it's probably nerves."

"Why would you be nervous?"

She stooped down, wincing, to continue her search. "I dunno, only ten thousand reasons. Besides, the last time Chris saw me I looked terrible."

"You didn't ask if he was alone."

Her pace slowed. "Oh…Julie's here, too?"

"No, he came alone this time. But she's usually with him these days."

A breath of hope filled her lungs. She resumed rummaging through the pile, this time with more enthusiasm.

"You realize he's married, right? I know it's hard to hear this, but he loves her."

She dipped her head, pausing briefly, then continued searching the suitcase. Of course she knew. She knew all too well.

Marci knelt beside her. As Farin tossed aside each reject, Marci scooped up the discarded item, folded it, and replaced it in the suitcase. "What's going on with you?"

"What do you mean?"

"We've always read each other, but it feels like something's...well, *off*. I'm trying to understand. I wanna help, but sometimes I don't know what to say."

Farin lifted a shoulder.

"I-I can't imagine what you've gone through, or what it must be like to wake up and remember your yesterday was actually years ago. Or to have to regain the strength to move around. I'm just glad you're back." She wrapped an arm around her shoulder.

Farin returned the embrace, then faltered as she stood again to stare down into Marci's cornflower-blue eyes. She did not know how to respond. The cynical side of her wondered if it was another trick. Maybe if Marci waxed sympathetic long enough, it would make her slip up and reveal more than she intended. Well, no dice. "It's great Ethan's kept his old apartment, huh?"

Frustrated by the latest dodge in their conversation, Marci rose, braced her hands atop the back of her hips, and stretched. "He says it's safe, so that's good. Being so close to the hospital, he'll be able to check in on you more often—even during his shift if he has to. And he'll get you in for those scans once it's safe."

Farin grabbed a pair of jeans off the foot of the bed and painstakingly slipped them on under her nightshirt, stumbling back onto the mattress as her strength failed her. Marci stepped forward to assist, but she waved her off. "He said he'd almost decided to let the place go."

A wry grin taunted Marci's lips. "He teases Sam about keeping it just in case their relationship falls apart."

She picked up the wide-tooth comb off the bed and shuffled off toward the bathroom, calling over her shoulder, "I'll be down in a couple of minutes. Will you let him know?"

Marci opened her mouth to say something, then gave up. "Be careful with the stairs," she cautioned, kneading her temple as she left the room.

Farin stripped off her nightshirt. She tried to make Marci's bra fit, but ultimately abandoned the effort. Even at her bulkiest, she had never filled a D-cup. She would simply have to do without.

Another attempt at narrowing down an acceptable shirt proved unsuccessful. Topless, she returned to the bathroom and evaluated her appearance, examining her gums, teeth, tongue, and face in the mirror. Her pale skin bothered her. Until today, she had seen no reason to apply makeup.

With a twist and a flip, she banked her damp hair on top of her head and secured it with a large barrette. Jordan had always loved when she wore her hair up. He loved removing whatever clip she had used to fasten her curls and watching them cascade around her neck and shoulders.

She paused as she caught the image of sad eyes staring back at her.

In many ways, she blamed herself for Jordan's death even more than she blamed Bobby. Had she not spent her life grieving her father, they would have never been there that day. Jordan had begged her to cool down first, but she had not listened. She never listened.

All her life, the people who loved her had made allowances for her behavior, no matter how selfish or unfair. They had coddled her, worried more about the damage she might inflict upon herself than the damage she caused others. Everything she believed, everything she knew, intersected and came to a screeching halt that day in Coral Gables. If not for her, Jordan would still be alive.

No more of that, Farin Shae. You promised.

She turned away from the mirror to find the makeup bag Marci had brought at her request. She checked the medicine cabinet and two drawers before spotting the clear plastic pouch on the otherwise unoccupied bottom shelf.

When she released the cabinet door, it snapped shut with a loud bang. The noise startled her. She discharged a hitched breath, winced again at the painful tugging in her abdomen resulting from the start, glanced at her mirrored reflection to regain her center, then winnowed through the bag's blushes, eye shadows, and foundations.

Time, space, and reason had vanished into a milky haze when Bobby pulled that trigger. In an instant, Jordan was gone. She had fled the house with no thought as to whether Jameson would regain consciousness after being clouted on the head with the butt of the pistol that would kill Jordan moments later.

Her jaw fixed beneath narrowed eyes. She finished applying

foundation and a hint of blush. A wave of anger washed over her as she threw the two compacts back into the bag.

To her eternal regret, she had pleaded for Jameson's life that day—even after learning the truth about his multiple manipulations. She had resolved to confront Bobby with the pain she had endured over eighteen long years, pain she believed had impeded her ability to move on with her own life, and had vowed nothing Jameson said or did would stop her from avenging her family. He had promised she would regret it the rest of her life.

Jameson was right.

She unscrewed the top of a mascara tube, angrily pumped the applicator, then scraped the tip against the lip of the tube to eliminate excess globs. Her hands remained steady as she stroked her eyelashes with calm expertise despite recent practice.

The first year of her confinement, Jameson had kept her conscious, though he threatened the lives of those she loved should she try to escape. She had no idea where he had taken her. There were no windows, and the door remained locked. Those who checked in on her maintained their anonymity by wearing bulky nursing scrubs, skull caps, and surgical masks. During his infrequent visits, he taunted her over her miserable end and blamed her for his son's illness.

Eventually, she had come to grips with her past. Her self-destructive patterns had ushered her straight into the pitfalls of her successful life. The result? A fate worse than fame.

Over time, she stopped hating herself. Her list of regrets seemed endless, but no amount of mourning would resurrect Jordan or her parents. In the confines of her prison, she finally buried her sorrow. Her only lingering regret was that Jameson had survived that blow to his temple.

Marci had recently confided Jameson's intention to kill her once and for all. Little did he realize the Farin O'Conner he knew had already died. He had succeeded in a way he would have never suspected.

She double-checked her image, then returned to the bedroom to decide on a shirt. A pinch in her abdomen reminded her to move slowly. She willed the pain away and hunted through the clothes inside the suitcase, settling at last on a basil green dress shirt. Little things like choosing her own clothes again meant everything to her. She had worn nothing but threadbare hospital gowns for what felt like an eternity.

Tucking the front of the shirt into her jeans, she returned to the bathroom, using the mirror as a guide to pop the collar. She moved her neck and shoulders about as she creased the starched fabric slightly higher than its natural fold. Not bad for a dead woman.

She applied a finishing touch of lipstick, pursed her lips to evenly distribute the stain across her wide mouth, then took several squares of toilet tissue and blotted away the excess. Weeks of therapy, coupled with nutritional supplements and moderate exercise, had mostly reversed the effects of atrophied muscles and dry skin. Soon, she would be whole.

She tried not to worry about things she could not change, but wondered how Chris would respond to what she planned to tell him. From what little she had gleaned from Marci, he had suffered cruelly over Jordan's death. Did he blame her? Did he blame himself?

Did he still love her?

Months of grieving had prompted her to take an honest look at herself. Most of what she saw, she disliked. Those who had accused her of ruining Jordan's life were right. No matter how she justified her thoughts or feelings during their life together, she could not deny the truth.

They had never been well-suited for each other.

The realization had devastated her. Yes, they had loved each other, but Jordan deserved someone who would not complicate his life as she had. His love was steadfast, yet he had never possessed the requisite strength to deal with her emotional instability. Chris had been right the whole time. Jordan had endeavored to fix her. To solve her problems. But try as he did, he never succeeded—even though he gave his life to make it so. She prayed that somehow he could forgive her.

Another quick rap at the door sounded. Marci poked her head inside. "You okay? Chris can't stay long. He's got practice this afternoon."

Farin fussed with a few rebellious curls. "How do I look?"

Marci studied her top to bare toe. "Soon, you'll look better in my jeans than I do."

She peered down at her ensemble. "I feel good. It's a good day."

"You always did look good in green. Isn't that the shirt I—?"

"You bought it for me...oh gosh, probably..." She struggled to reset her thoughts, taking her lost time into account. "I'd say, ten years ago? You thought you bought us each one, and then we fought over it until I moved to Miami."

They laughed at the memory.

"You used to hide it from me in the laundry basket," Marci chided.

"I used to try and keep you from hiding it in your closet!"

"That's right." Marci laughed, then regarded her more seriously. "What else do you remember, Farin?"

Her smile dissolved. So much needed to be said to so many people. *Soon*, she vowed. She moved past Marci to the door. "Let's go. I don't want to keep Chris waiting."

CHAPTER 32

B RIDGEMAN SLOWLY REPLACED THE RECEIVER. His eyes darted across his desk as he considered his next move. Should he wait until the end of their shift to fill her in, or should he risk drawing unwanted attention by dragging her into an interrogation room? If something imminent was headed their way, it might be worth a few turned heads.

He stuffed the note he had scribbled into his trouser pocket. "Pst!" he called across his desk.

Alvarez lifted her head and scanned the room, unsure where the sound had come from. She removed the pencil from her mouth, then drummed the eraser end absently on her desk blotter.

Bridgeman lightly kicked the back of his desk. The noise caught her attention. She peered over at him. "What're you doing?"

He lifted his chin toward their usual meeting place, which had become so usual, they fooled no one in the department. She rattled her head, aiming a surreptitious thumb toward the hall. With a nod, he stood and left the room.

"What is it?" she asked, joining him, her accent no less prominent when she whispered.

He rested his flattened palm high against the wall, taking a casual stance, though visually sweeping the corridor. "I got a message from your buddy over in FSB."

"But we already got the report."

"I know. And apparently, someone else knows, too."

She stiffened. "What?"

Before he could elaborate, he spotted Captain Ward lumbering down the hall toward them. Bridgeman dropped his hand, pivoting himself against the wall to let the man pass.

"You headed out?" Captain Ward asked as he walked by.

Bridgeman nodded. "We're on our way to Golden Shores to check out that floater."

The captain gave them a thumb's up without looking back or breaking stride.

He leaned down and to the side, whispering to his partner against the back of his hand, "Let's talk on the way."

They left the station and climbed inside their unmarked vehicle. Alvarez remained unusually quiet as they pulled out and headed east.

"I got a message from him," Bridgeman explained as they motored north on I-95. "He didn't want me to call him back at work. He left another number and a time he'd be available. We'll have to stop on the way."

"Did he sound like there was a problem?"

He shook his head. "He sounded nervous."

"Think he got in trouble for breaking protocol?"

"Let's hope not. At some point, we'll need to bring the investigation out in the open, but we need to know what we're dealing with first. Stark couldn't have buried this on his own."

"Maybe Macy's onto something with those records, huh?"

He thought hard. "Whoever took the trouble to blow up that limousine obviously thought its occupant was a threat."

She stared out the window as they navigated around slower vehicles in their path. "Farin Grant made her label a helluva lot of money. I can't see a motive there. Why kill her? What did she know?"

"Probably who killed her husband. That murder scene links the son with both our vics. And then there's that press conference she'd asked Macy to set up. The son must be involved."

"But how? I rechecked the information we had on him. His physician gave a sworn statement that Junior was admitted to a North Carolina hospital the day *before* the murder."

"But why North Carolina?"

A cynical burst of laughter escaped her lips. "You're asking the wrong girl. Maybe too much money makes ya nuts. Either way, it's outside our jurisdiction."

Halfway to Golden Shores, they exited the freeway and pulled into a convenience store to use the payphone. Bridgeman retrieved the message from his pocket and dialed the number. He angled the receiver so they could both hear.

Alvarez began the moment the call connected. "What happened? Did someone figure out you were doing a little side job for us?"

The voice on the other end sounded shaken. "I'm not sure what's going on, but I'm not taking any chances. Usually, I'm able to fly under the radar on things like this. It's not like I make a habit of offering up such risky favors. You two owe me big on this one."

"What happened?" Bridgeman asked.

"After I sent you the report last month, I secured the specimens and took them to storage. Like I always do. Then, I filed a copy away in my private files in case you needed it later. To be honest, I didn't give it another thought. Then yesterday, it dawned on me something was wrong."

"What?" Alvarez pushed with her typical impatience.

Bridgeman gave her his "calm down already" look. She lifted her shoulders and made an innocent, open-palm gesture at the phone.

"You said you thought Stark botched the investigation, right?"

"Yeah."

"Well, I think you're right...and I think he had help. In fact, he had to have had help."

Bridgeman's eyes narrowed. "How do you know?"

"The fuel cell was clearly the source of the blast, just like you thought. But it was never taken off the vehicle and processed. I can't find any record of it being tested at all before I ran the specimen you collected. There's no way Fire Rescue's investigation would be so sloppy they'd miss the fact there was an incendiary used. Yet the 'official' record rules out the possibility altogether. It pushes this narrative about it being an accidental explosion secondary to impact due to human factors."

"In other words, blame the driver," Bridgeman said.

"Exactly. No definitive identification of the source of impact. And no mention that a vehicle with a diesel engine would've never exploded like that on its own. Either someone did some really shoddy work or they wanted to avoid further investigation. Any decent cop who got this report would have had questions. Not to mention insurance investigators. It's incomplete at best and falsified at worst. But these are just the lab results for the chintzy work done after supposedly ruling out foul play. I haven't seen any other reports."

"Neither have we," Alvarez blurted out.

"You haven't?"

"Some things appear to be misplaced," Bridgeman explained.

"After all that's happened in the last twenty-four hours, I'm not surprised. Unfortunately, there's more."

Bridgeman sucked his teeth. "Yeah?"

"Before I ran the tests, I'd pulled up the report from nineteen ninety-one to see what they'd already done. I didn't look too closely. Just the summary. But when I realized the whole fuel cell problem yesterday, I tried to log back in to take a second look...and my access was denied. It said I needed *higher level logical access.*"

"What's *higher level logical access* mean?" she asked.

"It means someone's taken an interest in your case."

Bridgeman and Alvarez locked eyes.

"I logged off and back on three times but it gave me the same error each time. I was able to get into everything else as usual, but not that file. That's when I realized something was up. So, I checked the hard copy records we used up until the computer migration and found the paper record."

Alvarez kicked at the pavement with the toe of her high-gloss Oxfords. "What did it say?"

"The 'official' report wasn't the original. A big red mark crossed out the 'second draft' designation at the top of the page. We're supposed to keep all drafts of a report, but this original isn't there."

Bridgeman listened intently, trying to piece the puzzle together. The more intricate the details, the more he cozied up to Macy's theory. It would take awfully deep pockets to pull off such a bold cover-up. "Whoever paid Stark off must have spread the wealth around."

Alvarez asked, "Did you get the name of the person who filed the report?"

"I did. Her name was Eunice Perez."

"She still with FSB?"

He paused. "She died in ninety-two. Suicide. Police found her in her garage with the car running. She'd taken some pills first, then let the CO_2 do the rest."

"So, we can't question her."

"Afraid not."

"Can we get a copy of that document for our files?" Alvarez asked.

"Sure thing," he said. "As soon as I get in tomorrow, I'll grab it. Need copies of the Coral Gables scene as well? I checked my access on a hunch and got the same error. Whoever took an interest in your car bomb must think the cases are connected by more than just a name."

They drove the rest of the way to Golden Shores in silence. For the next several hours, they processed the scene. Almost certainly an accidental drowning, though they would need to wait for official confirmation from the Dade County Medical Examiner's office.

According to several reluctant neighbors' statements, the victim was the rich wife of an often-absent husband. Bored, lonely, and usually chemically impaired, she may have decided to go for a swim before going to bed. Based on the body's presentation, they estimated she had died sometime the night before. Had her best friend not come over to check on her after being stood up for their scheduled lunch date, she might have been there a whole lot longer.

To be thorough, they left a unit in place for the evening. They would return tomorrow after the morning briefing to wrap up the scene. With no signs of struggle in the house or injury to the body, almost all drownings ended up getting ruled an accidental death.

They stopped for a bite before driving back, eating in contemplative silence when their sandwiches arrived. The unsettling news they had received from Alvarez's friend in FSB had sent Bridgeman's head into overdrive. He worried not so much that they were out of their depth, but that they had broken protocol on what might turn out to be one hell of a complicated case involving several jurisdictions.

"Why would they change his security access but only on these two cases?" Alvarez asked as they neared the station.

Bridgeman squeezed the steering wheel. "They didn't change his security clearance. They reclassified the documents. I think I know what happened, and I think I need to make a call."

***

Chris paced the empty living room while he waited. It had never occurred to him that meeting with Farin might result in more harm than good, but as Marci's words of caution swam through his mind, he wondered.

Could it be true?

He had ached to hear the three words Farin never uttered. Now, he hoped Marci had misinterpreted her inquiries. So much time had passed, so many damaging things said and done between them. He could never go back, no matter his feelings.

For weeks now, Ben had questioned his intentions. Even Julie had acted concerned despite her outward support. What was he supposed to tell them? Yes, he had loved Farin—beyond reason, beyond his own sanity, and at one point, beyond the grave. But he had grown to love Julie. Differently, but with every ounce of commitment he had never received from Farin.

None of it mattered anymore. Their shared bond had begun and would end with Jordan. Any moment now, Farin would emerge and they could make things right.

He checked his watch. One o'clock. Even without traffic, it would take him over an hour to get to the studio. He hoped he would not have to cancel.

Preparations for the *Aftermath* tour were coming together, though prior tours with Mirage often filled his thoughts. He had told no one how much going solo frightened him. Mirage had been as much a part of him as his arms or legs. Yes, he had found success as a solo act. But he often wished they could resolve the issues between them and try again with Minor 6th.

Faith would be the one to convince. If she agreed to come out of retirement, the others would follow—even Elliot, despite his stated contentment with his life in the Hills. Faith had always possessed a certain influence over the rest of them.

Maybe he would call her.

"You're here." Farin hobbled unsteadily downstairs, her hands clinging to the railing for support while taking one full step at a time.

He met her at the bottom step, impressed at her vast improvement, yet saddened by the residual effects of her ordeal.

Ignoring the offer of assistance by way of his outstretched hand, she wrapped herself up in his arms. "Thank you for coming. I've been wanting to talk to you."

Eyes shut, he held her tight. She smelled of lavender lotion and citrus conditioner. Moreover, she resembled the incomparable beauty he had met in this very house. The woman whose image he had once vowed to keep with him forever. Lingering wordlessly in the embrace, the enormity of the moment overcame him.

At last, he pulled away. He could not—would not—have these feelings. "How are you?"

He helped her sit down on the carpet as Marci disappeared into the kitchen.

Farin gave him that wide smile he remembered, but had too rarely seen. Still, he noted her red-rimmed eyes. "Better every day. Ethan's been great. And Marci...well, you know Marci." She reached for his hand. "It's good to see you."

He repositioned himself on the floor, leaning back onto his fists. "We'd heard you'd improved but, wow. You look fantastic. Julie sends her love. She would've been here, but she's been a bit under the weather. We didn't want her getting you ill."

Her smile dimmed. "I wanted to talk to you privately, anyway."

He nodded. "There's much to discuss."

Marci returned with bottled drinks, which she silently distributed. Every now and then, she cut eyes at one or the other of them, warning or encouraging them to remember the reality of the situation.

Chris accepted his second unopened water and set it beside him. He asked Farin, "You finally look outside that window?"

With a girlish titter, she tucked a fallen strand of hair behind her ear. "I watch the sunset every night."

The warmth of her smile set the rhythm of his heart. If he did not get down to business, he would lose his resolve. It made sense, he told himself. It was natural to still harbor feelings over their past.

He rubbed his neck. "Bear with me. This isn't going to be easy to say."

Again, she reached for him, this time with trembling hands.

He hastened to his feet, positioning himself at his familiar perch against the fireplace mantel. Every detail of the home flooded his memory, from the white wraparound sectional to framed pictures of Chase covering the walls. He had spent many a post-tour afternoon seated near the hearth, playing Old Maid with his young nephew. His brothers had converged here the day of Chase's memorial, puzzled over Lockhardt's bizarre reaction to meeting Farin—and Chris had defended the man.

Since taking ownership of the property, he had done whatever necessary to avoid having to walk these floors again. His management made sure the property taxes and dues were up to date. If any complaints came in about the neglected landscaping, they had someone come around to give it a once over.

He had ignored it until it had fallen into disrepair, not unlike he had done with his relationship with its previous owner. The difference was, this time he realized his error before it was too late.

Maybe when he finished the tour, he would fix it up. He and Julie could move out of Bel Air. Make the beach their home. Later, when she was ready, they would have kids. He would make right decisions for their lives and stop being selfish. And Farin would help him with the first step.

Head low, he fixed his eyes on his wedding ring. "I need to ask you something."

Farin looked at Marci, who had taken a seat on the stairs. "I think we need a minute."

Marci opened her mouth as if to protest, but then left the room.

Farin watched the kitchen door swing shut.

When they were alone, Chris continued. "I know you keep saying your memory hasn't recovered, but we have reason to believe it has. So, I came here to ask you myself. What happened that day? Who killed my brother?"

The subtle deflation of her body told him it was not the question she had anticipated.

She began pulling at the white, loomed carpet fibers. "I wish I could tell you but—"

"Don't." He stepped forward, hand open and up. "Don't say you can't remember. You can't fool me. You never could."

She lifted her gaze to his.

"*Who*?" He knelt beside her. "I know you don't want to discuss it. And I hate asking questions you can't bear to answer, but we need to know. Did you see the person? Can you describe him?"

Her lips pinched together in a sneer.

"It's okay," he said, drawing her into a comforting embrace. "You won't go through this alone."

Her body stiffened in his arms.

He pulled back in bewilderment.

"I can't."

"No one's gonna hurt you, Farin. Not Lockhardt, not anyone."

"I'm fine. I just can't talk about it."

"But you have to. Why on Earth—"

"Not yet." She accepted his assistance to stand, then paced slowly about the room, rubbing at her hairline with the tips of her fingers. "I know you and Ben and everyone else want to know what happened. All I can say is, when the time's right, I'll know. You need to trust me."

"You're not making any sense. If you're afraid—"

"Afraid?" Her pacing came to an immediate stop. She faced him, her dark eyes bitter and beautiful.

He dropped heavily onto the floor, stunned. All this time, he had assumed she was too afraid to talk. But as she shuffled toward the staircase, he saw no trace of fear. Determination and resolve had replaced the once-delicate creature he had rescued so many times and in so many ways.

She leaned against the banister. "I need time. Not because I'm this fragile porcelain doll anymore, but because I need to handle things the right way. We all know Jameson wants me dead. I can't go to the police. If they knew I'm alive, they'd want to question me. I don't have answers for them...not yet."

"Every minute you stay quiet, everyone's in danger. We need it out in the open so we can finish this thing, whatever it is. You know that, right?"

"I know better than anyone," she snapped. "I lived it."

"Then why won't you tell us?"

Her dispassionate stare went right through him.

"Bloody hell, Farin. Don't do this."

"I'll handle it."

"We're talking about Jordan's *murder* here!"

His rage did not move her.

"Did Lockhardt kill him? Is that why he took you?"

"I know it's hard to hear I won't fill in the blanks. I loved him, too."

Frustration mounted until it stuck in his throat. With an incredulous shake of his head, he rose to his feet. "Tell me this isn't about us."

"What?"

His eyes bored into hers, a chaotic jumble of pain and remorse. He thought of the cemetery. The motel. The endless pleading with God for one more chance to see her. Even if only to apologize. "I'm sorry."

"Sorry?"

"I tried to apologize. B-before."

She moved to him. This time, he did not increase the distance between them.

"I—I was wrong about us. About everything."

"Chris, you—"

He raised his hands between them. "Let me finish. What I did all those years. Chasing you. It was wrong. It was...cruel. I can't apologize to Jordan, but I can apologize to you. I'm sorry, Farin. But please, don't punish me now. Not this way. Help me make this right. For all of us."

Her breathing quickened. "You don't understand."

"Then *help* me."

"You weren't wrong, Chris. *I* was."

"Then we were both wrong. Jordan didn't deserve what we did to him."

She studied him with misty eyes. "You've changed."

"Yes."

"Well, so have I."

"You know I'm right."

"I know one thing," she said. "I know if Jordan and I had belonged together, I wouldn't have been able to cheat on him. And no, there's no excuse for what I did. You and I, we were out of control. Now, here we are—both 'changed.'"

He slid his hands into his back pockets.

"I'm not saying I didn't love Jordan. I did. Yet all I did was hurt him. And you knew why better than I did. I was just too stubborn to admit it to myself. I wanted to make him happy, but I couldn't. He deserved better than me. Most of the time we were together, I thought about you."

His voice fell to a whisper as he searched her eyes. "Don't tell me this."

She cupped his stubbled cheeks, drawing him in for a kiss.

He removed her hands from his face, placing them at her sides.

"I love you," she said.

Her declaration was the most tragic confession he had ever heard. For years, he had longed for her to say those words. Now, he hated himself for hearing them. Worse, she meant it.

"Tell me that means something to you."

His voice cracked, barely more than a tortured whisper. "Farin, I'm married."

"You told me you didn't love her."

He recalled their final moments together on the beach in Key Biscayne. "I...I shouldn't have said that to you."

Her dark eyes pierced his. "But you meant it."

As they stared at one another in a familiar contest of will, every cell in Chris's body ached. His head pounded. His muscles tensed. His mind was foggy. He had no more fight in him. Everything she said was true. And not one word of it mattered, now.

"We've both said a lot of hurtful things, Farin. That's what we do best, right? I don't want to hurt you anymore, but I'm married. I love Julie. I've put the rest behind me."

"Behind you? What does that even mean?"

He shook his head, unable to think of one thing to say.

Farin looked away at last. "So, Marci was right," she spat bitterly. "It was all a game."

"You don't believe that."

"Don't I?"

He reached for her.

She elbowed him back. "Don't you *dare* pity me."

"What was I supposed to do? You were *dead*."

"Did you lie when you said you loved me?"

"Did you lie when you said you don't remember who killed Jordan?"

Her eyes narrowed to rageful slits. Arms stiff at her sides, her hands balled into angry fists. "You want the truth? The *real* truth?"

"Tell me."

"Fine. Here's the truth: I remember. *Everything.* I remember watching my husband die." She lifted her arms to display her scars. "I remember crawling across shattered glass, shredding the palms of my hands and my knees. I remember running for my life. I remember running to *you*."

He winced at the memory.

"I remember thinking I was gonna die, too, so I ran. I ran like I always ran. For two days, I hid in a hotel, trying to think of a way to save myself. And *you*...you knew I was there but didn't come! You'd chased me to Europe. You'd chased me until Jordan found out about us. But you didn't come when I was six minutes away and needed you!"

He swallowed what felt like a balloon in his throat.

She swiped beneath her damp lashes. "But hey...thanks for the flowers."

"Farin, I'm so sorry."

"And in the end, it didn't matter how much I ran, did it? He caught me anyway."

"But I did come for you, as soon as I knew."

"Yeah. Better late than never, huh?

Chris stared into the empty living room. Everywhere he looked, he saw his brother. "I can't do anything about my many failures, Farin. But I can make Lockhardt pay for what he's done. Did he kill Jordan?"

Her features turned blank and unyielding.

"Marci said you'd sent something to a friend of yours. What was it?"

"It doesn't matter. He never got it."

Her stubbornness grated on him. He wanted to shake her. Worse, he wanted to kiss her. The sooner he left, the better. As it was, he would have to cancel the day's rehearsal. LA traffic was unforgiving at the best of times. The merry-go-round he had boarded with Farin showed no sign of stopping.

Her voice softened. "Did you ever love me?"

He struggled for words. Words to explain. Words that would not betray his wife. "I could never make you understand."

She raised her hands, then dropped them to her sides. "I'd think it'd be worth a try. I mean, if it was all bullshit, we managed to screw up a lot of people's lives."

It occurred to Chris that the past had a funny way of changing a person's perception. Farin's death had left him to romanticize their time together. Until today, he had forgotten how difficult she could be. "You know how I felt."

"How you felt while you knew you couldn't have me?"

"Let's not do this."

"Maybe I could forgive myself if I thought it was more than a fling."

"A *fling*?"

"You heard me."

His patience emptied like water down an unstopped drain. He wagged his finger, blinking away the fog from his brain. "Hold on. You say you remember everything? Then you remember constantly rejecting me."

The arrow hit its mark. She stepped back, plunging her hands into her jeans pockets.

"You pushed me away for years, then wonder why I moved on?"

"You chased me for years and then just give up?"

"You *died*!"

"I'm back! I'm right here!"

Years of grief and resentment settled upon him until he found himself stomping the living room, arms flailing as he ranted. "You want to hear I missed you? I did! You want to hear I loved you? I did! But don't you think I had to find a way through it? Julie's *good* to me. She loves me, and I've grown to love her. If it's not the same thing we shared, so what? It's bloody well *solid*, isn't it? I'm sorry if that hurts you, Farin, but we both know it's the right thing."

His mind raced ahead of his pacing feet as he prepared for the next round. This was the part he did not miss—the yelling, the fighting, the pain of her rejection. Only now he had to reject her, which he decided felt infinitely worse. He told himself her anger was less about him and more about their situation. Whatever had happened, she was too scared to talk.

When his vexation finally subsided, he realized the room had gone quiet. Somewhere in his rage, she had turned away, burying her head in her hands. The muffled sound of her tears tore at him like claws scraping an unhealed wound.

He reached out, but did not touch her. "Please don't—"

"You're right," she cried. "I'm sorry. You had to move on. What else was there for you? I shouldn't have said those horrible things."

His brain demanded he stay put even as he inched closer. "I loved you more than my own life, Farin."

Then, they were in each other's arms.

The feel of her body against his, her arms wrapped around him, her hands gripping his hair weakened him. Then and now melted into a single moment. Yet as they embraced, he knew it would be for the last time.

"Thank you for saving me," she said.

He squeezed her tighter. "We have to work together to fix this. We owe it to Jordan, don't we? Let me help you."

Gently, she shoved him back. The crying had stopped. She stood before him, composed.

"I've never been a very trustworthy person," she said, dabbing spent tears with the sleeve of her blouse. "But I need you to trust me now. I know what to do. I won't let another person I love get hurt."

He searched her eyes, caged by their beauty. A montage of every tender moment they had ever shared flickered through his mind. "You win. You usually did."

"I'll be careful. I promise."

"I can't tell you how sorry I am."

She smiled softly. "I'm happy for you. I won't mention it again." She walked toward the kitchen and called Marci.

"You two okay?" Marci edged into the living room, glancing back and forth between them. "Nothing broken?"

"There's nothing here to break." Farin flourished a hand his way. "It's about two. Chris is gonna be late if he doesn't leave soon."

Marci checked her watch. "And Ethan should be here any minute. I'm gonna run upstairs and get the suitcase. Everything else packed up?"

She nodded. "I think so. The makeup bag's still out. I'll be up in a sec."

Chris waited until Marci disappeared down the hall, then went to Farin. He took her hands in his. "I should get going."

"Of course," she said, her tone politely distant. She backed off and headed for the stairs. "You take care. Send my love to Ben and Cheryl when you talk to them. Tell them I'll call as soon as it's safe, and that I love them."

"Farin, wait." He stalked after her, brushing her arm. "You okay?"

She patted his shoulder. "I'm not that woman anymore, Chris."

"We'll see each other soon," he promised. "Think about it. I want to help."

Farin nodded. "Go. You don't wanna be late."

He watched her climb the stairs with careful, challenging steps, using the handrail to steady and absorb some of her weight. When she reached the top, she disappeared down the hall without a backward glance.

***

At exactly 6 PM, Jameson switched on the new television he had had installed into his office media center earlier that day. His fingers employed the remote, navigating through countless channels until settling on one of the three major networks' evening broadcasts.

He contemplated his victory as anchors reported various stories. The House of Representatives had voted on corporate and individual tax cuts. They gave an update on last week's murder of Tejano singer Selena.

Soon, all would be well.

After the first break, he endured an update on Franklin Delano Floyd, who had allegedly kidnapped an Oklahoma boy from his school several months before and now accused the FBI of wrongfully claiming the boy was dead.

Jameson waited impatiently, unable to sit. He poured himself a drink, then ambled to the window and watched as the skyline faded to black beneath a breathtaking sunset. Soon, artificial light would illuminate the dark buildings.

As the sun faded to twilight, he smiled. When dawn broke the next morning, his life would be decidedly different. No more worrying he would lose his company, or his freedom. He had finally won.

He lifted his glass to his reflected image, twisting his lips into an evil snarl. "To me."

Nearly half an hour crawled by with no hint of the breaking news Moreau had promised. Another drink as the weather report came and went. In sports, the Knicks would play the Bucks tonight in Milwaukee. The Yankees' spring training was in full force. Nothing for him there.

At 6:30 PM, his anxiety kicked in. Perhaps something had gone wrong. He considered calling Moreau despite the warning to lose his number.

For fifteen minutes, he paced. A dozen scenarios plagued his thoughts, all of them unpleasant. If Moreau had botched the job, he would need to start from scratch. Consumed with dread, he nearly missed the announcement.

"...this just in."

Jameson spun around. He fixed his eyes on the television.

"At approximately two o'clock this afternoon, an explosion took place in an abandoned home in Malibu, California. We take you there live via our local ABC affiliate, where reporter..."

His eyes fixated on the chaotic scene behind the Docker-clad reporter. Thick, dark smoke billowed skyward in a toxic cloud as firemen aimed large spun polyester nylon hoses at the burning heap, spraying arches of water into the blaze.

"Fire crews started arriving shortly after dispatch received the call just over an hour and a half ago. As you can see behind me..."

Slowly, Jameson's lips curled into an eerie half-circle.

The anchor inquired if anyone had been in the house prior to the explosion.

"We haven't heard anything yet about possible inhabitants. According to neighbors, the house has been unoccupied now for several years. Once the home of pop star Jordan Grant, the house reportedly belongs to his brother, former Mirage guitarist, Chris Grant. The word from local police is that they've been unsuccessful locating him so far..."

Jameson watched the inferno with half-demented zeal as angry flames thwarted the firefighters' attempts to contain the blaze.

"...We're getting reports now that nearby homes have suffered minor damage, mostly broken windows. A local resident was said to have been out walking his dog on the beach at the time of the explosion, apparently just yards away. He's been transported to a local hospital for treatment of minor cuts, burns, and smoke inhalation. Unfortunately, the dog is still missing."

Realizing some time would pass before he received confirmation that at least one body had been found inside the house, Jameson switched off the set.

His mind flipped through what little facts had been relayed like a secretary searching a Rolodex. According to Moreau, a Dr. Ethan Maxwell—Samantha Drake's fiancé—had visited regularly, obviously to nurse Farin back to health. No point questioning both their involvement now. Perhaps the doctor was in the house at the time of the explosion. Jameson certainly hoped so.

The only other near-constant presence Moreau had witnessed was

Marci Lawrence. Although not overly familiar with the girl, what poetic justice if the two died together. No more evidence of the wasted life of Farin O'Conner. All the doors would close on that rather unfortunate chapter in Jameson's life.

But the reporter had mentioned another name, which intrigued Jameson to no end. Chris. As the current property owner, it made sense they would contact him. However, they had had no luck "so far," Jameson quoted aloud.

Was it possible?

A rush of elation he had not experienced in decades washed over him like a wave at high tide. In fact, he could not recall ever feeling more satisfied than he did at this very moment. A lifetime of machinations had finally given him a desired end.

Beth O'Conner. Gone.

Farin Grant. Gone.

All his secrets. Safe.

Every burden Jameson had carried for the last two decades had burned to cinder and soot—never to be identified. It was finished.

"Goodbye, Farin." He lifted his glass and toasted the air with a victorious sneer. "Say hello to your mother for me."

THE END

Afterward

Dorothea Dix Hospital in Raleigh, North Carolina is used fictitiously in *A Fate Worse Than Fame*. As I constructed the storyline, I envisioned a large mental institution as the backdrop of the most sinister plot twist in the book.

My then-editor was a native North Carolinian, so when I explained the picture I'd had in my head, he immediately suggested Dorothea Dix. He said the way I described what I was after was eerily similar to the campus.

We traveled there some time later to begin the research leg of *Fate's* journey. Lo and behold, he was right.

While visiting the campus, we had the great honor of working with Faye McArthur, Director of the Community Relations Department at the time. Mrs. McArthur was both knowledgeable and gracious with her time and resources.

During my first two visits to the Dorothea Dix campus, the Royster Building looked exactly as described in *Fate*, though it was later restored and utilized as office space. I like my introduction to the building better than its updated state, to be honest.

When I first saw the Royster, it was marvelously damaged and worn—exactly as I'd pictured in my mind's eye. It was broken and caved in, and doubtless held many stories. Faye McArthur allowed us temporary and supervised access to the inside of the building (yes, we wore our hard hats!). Walking the halls, I saw with great clarity what I'd only ever imagined. That exquisite, tragic building would ultimately serve as the location for one of the most heinous and life-changing events of my most troubled character's life.

And how fitting it was that a woman suffering from chronic grief syndrome should find her freedom from those dark chains alone, without professional assistance, in such a place.

The chapel standing to the left of the Royster Building was an unexpected gift. A thrill of disbelief mixed with a sense of destiny overcame me as I entered and saw the open Bible sitting on the podium at the far end of the aisle in front of the altar. Curiosity gave way to speechlessness when I read the passage to which it had been left open.

That very same passage is listed as the Epigraph in this work. How could I use anything else?

Before leaving that first day, I purchased a tree from the Women's Auxiliary. Faye promised to have it planted in front of the Royster Building. In subsequent visits over the years, I watched it grow. At its base, there was a marble plaque that read: "In Honor of Farin Shae O'Conner."

I'd love to suggest you visit if you're ever in the area. However, the last I heard, the property in its entirety was being transformed into a park. It saddens me to think of the buildings—particularly my personally beloved Royster Building—being laid waste, even for a park. There was history there. Stories. Memories (however good or bad).

I don't know what became of the tree planted for Farin. Maybe they kept it, along with the hundreds of others planted in memoriam within the sprawling acreage while they were fashioning this park. I don't know. But I will admit I traveled across the country to take my marble memorial stone before they had the chance to unearth it in the name of progress. It's heavy and awkward, but it's mine. I will treasure it always.

Originally, I had promised the Dorothea Dix folks to put a little blurb in the back of the book to summarize the history of the campus and its founder. Even though it no longer exists, I feel compelled to give a final nod to the incredible woman who built a legacy no bulldozer could tear down.

Dorothea Dix was a champion of the mentally impaired. She spent her entire—and single—life working to further the knowledge and better the treatment of those whom society had long ago washed their hands. In her time, Ms. Dix founded some 32 mental institutions, 15 schools for the feeble minded, a school for the blind, and training schools for nurses. She was involved in the establishment of libraries in institutions such as hospitals and prisons. A pioneer. A doer. A strong woman who made a difference in the lives she touched...and well beyond.

(H.O. 2/5/2023)

About the Author

Heather O'Brien lives in Nevada with her husband. She enjoys music, travel, cooking, documentaries, and research.

To learn more, or to read an excerpt from book three in the Music is Murder saga, *Ballad of Someday*, visit: www.booksbyheather.com.

Iconic Moments in Music History

The 1800s:

February 19, 1877 — Thomas Edison invents first recorded sound

November 8, 1887 — Emile Berliner invents Gramophone

1887 — Columbia Records founded.
It remains the oldest surviving brand name in recorded sound.

The 1940s:

July 1940 —1st Pop Music Concert

September 10, 1940 — South Hallsville School bombing

October 1, 1943 — Birth of Vinyl Records

October 12, 1944 — The Columbus Day Riot

The 1950s:

1951 — Alan Freed popularizes term "Rock'n'Roll."

March 21, 1952 —1st Rock'n'Roll Concert

October 7, 1952 — American Bandstand airs

July 9, 1955 — "Rock Around the Clock" hits Billboard Charts

November 21, 1955 — Sam Phillips sells Elvis to RCA

February 3, 1959 — The Day the Music Died

May 4, 1959 — 1st Annual Grammy Awards

The 1960s:

April 4, 1960 — Motown Records is founded.

Iconic Moments in Music History (cont.)

The 1960s (cont.):

April 25, 1960 — Payola Investigations

November 1961 — Phil Spector's "Wall of Sound"

October 24, 1962 — James Brown at the Apollo Theater

August 30, 1963 — Introduction of the Cassette Tape

January 1, 1964 — Top of the Pops first airs

February 9, 1964 — The Beatles on Ed Sullivan

July 20, 1965 — Dylan Goes electric

September 15, 1965 — 8-Tracks introduced

June 16, 1967 — Monterey Pop Festival

August 27, 1967 — Beatles manager, Brian Epstein, found dead

August 15-17, 1969 — Woodstock

December 6, 1969 — Altamont

The 1970s:

October 4, 1970 — Janis Joplin joins the "27 Club"

November 8, 1971 — Stairway to Heaven is released

April 7, 1973 — Mirage plays the Speakeasy Club

December 10, 1973 — Hilly Kristal opens CBGB

December 19, 1975 — Stax Records closes

October 20, 1977 — Lynyrd Skynyrd plane crash

April 22, 1978 — Bob Marley's One Love Peace Concert

July 12, 1979 — The Day Disco Died

Iconic Moments in Music History (cont.)

The 1980s:

August 1, 1981 — Video Killed the Radio Star

1982 — Hair bands

October 1, 1982 — first CD is released

March 25, 1983. — Michael Jackson moonwalks on VH1 Music Awards

March 5, 1984 — Jordan Grant signs with Lockhardt Sound, Inc.

January 28, 1985 — We Are the World is recorded

July 13, 1985 — Live Aid concert

1987 — record labels consolidate to the "Big Six"

June 9, 1988 — Jordan Grant meets Farin O'Conner at Le Dome

August 6, 1988 — *Yo!* MTV Raps first airs

March 3, 1989. — "Like a Payer" video is released

July 21, 1989 — Milli Vanilli

August 29, 1989. — "Down Deep in Love" hits #1

The 1990s:

March 20, 1990 — Gloria Estefan bus crash

May 6, 1991 — Pro Tools released

November 24, 1991 — Freddie Mercury dies

November 30, 1991 — Mirage's farewell concert

January 26, 1994 — Chris Grant signs with Minor 6th Records

April 5, 1994 — Kurt Cobain dies

Iconic Moments in Music History (cont.)

The 1990s (cont.):

circa July 1995 — Suzanne Vega's "Tom's Diner"
used to test MP3 technology

November 14, 1995 — Jameson Lockhardt's retirement roast

March 9, 1997 — Hip-Hop rivalries

1998 — Graveyard Summer's debut album

December 10, 1998 — Big 6 record labels consolidate to Big 5

January 25, 1999 — Eminem's "My name is…"

June 1, 1999 — Napster

The 2000s:

June 11, 2002 — American Idol airs

April 28, 2003 — iTunes

January 6, 2004. — GarageBand released

August 5, 2004 — Big 5 record labels consolidate to Big 4

July 23-24, 2005 — the return of Lollapalooza

February 8, 2009 — Death Cab for Cutie's Grammy protest of Auto-Tune

The 2010s:

August 2, 2010 — "Jaded" released on Minor 6th Records

July 23, 2011 — Amy Winehouse dies

September 21, 2012 — Big 4 record labels consolidate to Big 3